The Secret Life Of Alfred Nightingale

Rebecca Stonehill

PUBLISHED BY:

Sunbird Press

ISBN: 978-1-9998601-0-3
eBook ISBN: 978-1-9998601-1-0

Also by Rebecca Stonehill

The Poet's Wife
The Girl and the Sunbird

For my mother Elizabeth,
who bought me my first backpack,
and lit the kindling of my passion for seeing the world.

'The only thing I know is this:
I am full of wounds and
still standing on my feet.'

Nikos Kazantzakis

'Welcome to Matala.
Today is Life.
Tomorrow Never Comes.'

George Germanakis

1941

I am beginning to think that yes, just perhaps, I have a chance to keep moving, breathing, living. For so long I believed all of that would be forever beyond my reach after what happened to my friend. But, watching her graceful figure moving out of the shallows and over the sand, the smile on my face is as wide as the skies and as real as her presence. She turns around. Waves at me, strands of dark hair blowing over her eyes. I raise a hand to wave back, and that is when I hear it.

PART ONE

Chapter One
Twickenham, 1967

When I open my cupboard doors on Saturday morning, it's immediately clear that all my trousers have disappeared.

'Bloody hell Ma, not again,' I mutter.

I rifle through t-shirts and underwear, pulling out pairs of folded and ironed socks and push splayed fingers through the shirts that hang neatly, accusingly, on their hangers. I blink into the dark of the wardrobe and catch sight of myself in the small mirror, running a hand through my hair. Dark woody brown and long around the ears, far longer than what my father considers respectable. Just yesterday he told me that if I didn't get my hair cut, he'd pin me into a chair and cut it himself. Treating me, as always, like I'm seven, not bloody well seventeen.

I frown at the poster of The Who and give the wardrobe door a great kick. I can smell toast and bacon, crisp and sweet and my stomach flips, almost battering my resolve. But no, I clench my jaw, I know this trick, I *know* what this is all about.

Pulling on a pair of underpants and a vest and shirt over

my head, I march downstairs where I find Ma at the stove in her pleated apron, breaking eggs into the frying pan, her hair in curlers. She always keeps her hair in curlers for Friday night *and* the whole of Saturday, the only day of the week she never leaves the house.

Swivelling on her slippered feet, she smiles brightly.

'Morning, Jimmy!'

'Ma,' I say firmly. 'What have you done with all my trousers?'

She turns back to the stove, but I can see the slight tension in her shoulders.

'Trousers, dear?'

'Trousers, Ma,' I say slowly. 'Where are they?'

She leans over to the windowsill and switches on the radio, the staid voice of a BBC reporter booming out.

'…we can expect the temperature to reach a pleasant seventy degrees today, if not a little more. Perhaps summer has finally…'

I flip the dial off.

'Ma!' I say sharply. 'Will you stop playing games and talk to me!'

She turns to face me. I can make out a faint smudge of yesterday's mascara under one eye and wisps of her dyed brown hair escaping from her curlers and I suddenly feel deeply irritated by her.

'What was it you wanted to talk about?'

'You know very well what. It's Saturday. I need to put some trousers on and go out, but you've hidden them again.'

'They're all in the wash, dear,' she says blankly.

I throw my hands up in the air in exasperation as I turn from Ma and sink into a chair at the table.

'Won't you have some bacon?'

'*Why*, Ma? Why are you trying to stop me going out again?'

She purses her lips as she marches over to the sideboard and starts slicing through the loaf of bread with a knife, thick slices crumbling as she attacks it.

'You know your father doesn't like you going to that island.'

'I forgot,' I mutter, 'Father doesn't like it when I actually *enjoy* myself. Anyway, who says I'm going to the island?'

Ma turns, breadknife in hand and points it at me.

'Well, aren't you? Tell me you're not, then.'

'I'm eighteen, Ma, I'm an adult now.'

'Seventeen.'

'Practically eighteen. And it's not what you think it is, it's just a bit of music and dancing. All very...quiet really.'

She snorts as she finishes cutting the bread and thrusts it into the toaster.

'Actually, I will have some of that bacon, it smells damn good.'

'Language,' Ma retorts, but her features soften as she fetches a plate and cutlery.

'Honestly, Ma,' I continue, 'you should come with me some time, so you can see for yourself that it's all very tame.'

I have absolutely no intention of my mother coming to the island with me; I know very well that all her worst fears would be founded, but I'm also aware that my invitation may make my jaunts over there seem more innocent. Ma sighs deeply as she sits at the table opposite me and watches me eat.

'Your father will be furious if he knows you've gone,' she says wearily.

'I know,' I reply. 'God Ma, this bacon is amazing. The thing is…' I pause as I chew. Ma gets up to butter the toast. 'The thing is, that hiding my trousers isn't going to stop me going. You know that really.'

'But why? Why do you want to make your father so upset and angry?'

'I don't want to make him angry, I'm just living my life. I need to be my own person – '

'When you leave school, *then* you can be your own person.'

'You know that won't make a blind bit of difference. You know that Father will still be on at me the whole time, to do this and be that and join the family business. I'm not the same as him; I'm not *him*. He's completely forgotten what it's like to be young – '

'Just do your A levels, love.' Ma reaches over the table and pats my hand. 'I'm sure your father will take the pressure off a little after that.'

'Now *that*,' I point my fork at her, 'is a lie and we both know it.'

I finish eating and walk to the back door where I pull on my boots.

'You're not going out like that – '

'I told you, I have to.'

'But – '

'Super bacon Ma, thanks ever so much.' I lean over, peck her on the cheek then snatch my sunglasses up from the table and with that, I slip out of the back door and break into a trot.

Ignoring the stares of Twickenham's Saturday morning shoppers, I run down the high street in my underpants, shirt and sunglasses, veering off the main road after several minutes into a quiet, residential street lined with semi-detached houses; garden gnomes and window boxes in their front gardens. Stopping outside the last one tucked neatly away at the end of the road, I pick up a pebble and throw it up at the top window. For a while, there's no response so I take a few more small stones and try again. Eventually, the curtains open and Charles sticks his head groggily out of the window, blond hair sticking up.

'What time is it?'

'Time you got up, tosspot. And chuck us some trousers, would you?'

He reaches for his spectacles and then raises an eyebrow. 'Mater been in the wardrobe again?'

'Just give me some.'

'What's it worth?'

'I'll buy you a Watney's Ale tonight.'

He stretches his long, pale limbs lazily. 'Fair enough. Hang on a tic.'

Moments later, he reappears at the window and throws down a pair of black trousers. I pull them on, wincing.

'God, they're a bit tight, aren't they? Skinny runt.'

'Don't worry darling, you look ravishing. Give me five minutes and I'll be down. Are we going to L'Auberge?'

I nod and grin, then I sit on the pavement to wait for Charles. Holidays! Six whole weeks of living and dreaming of music, girls and Eel Pie. The parents have long since given up on holidaying over the summer months, thank God. The last time was when the three of us drove to Dover in Father's Morris and took the ferry over to France. There, we rented a caravan in some flat, desolate seaside town near Calais. It rained the entire week and my only clear recollection is of shivering in the caravan in shorts and cold, damp socks whilst eating soggy baguettes. I need to be precisely nowhere during these six whole weeks of summer holidays and there's nothing I need to do except plan my next jaunt to the island.

At half past seven, Charles and I make our way back over Richmond Bridge and along the towpath that tightly hugs the Thames, spilling with wild garlic. A Mini zooms by with 'Just Married' emblazoned on the back in crazy foam and tin cans tied with string clanking along behind it. My head is throbbing from all the coffee I've drunk at L'Auberge. Alright, so the honest truth is I can't stand the stuff. But I'm sure I must look rather debonair sitting at one of the inky-dark tables with my shades on, sipping strong black coffee and chain-smoking. But I'm all out of cash now. During term time, I sometimes help the old man out, sticking envelopes down at his accountancy firm to earn some pocket money. But what little I've earned has been long spent, so Charles has been supplying me with cigarettes and coffee all day. It's a still, balmy evening; the last of the sun's rays have left but the warmth of the day is lingering and a few pleasure boats are winding their way along the silver thread of river.

'I'm off to Felixstowe at the end of the summer,' Charles says, jingling the coins in his pocket.

'Christ, *again*?' I turn to look at him in surprise. 'How can you stand it? All that cosy family holiday crap with the parents and sisters?'

Charles shrugs. 'I'd rather not go and just be here with you and go to Eel Pie. But it's really not *that* bad. I take my guitar with me and have lots of time to fiddle on that. Besides, the sea brings out my poetic side and I always come back with lots of new songs and poems.'

I hoot, increasing our pace as we round the corner of the towpath, and clap him on the back. '*So* romantic, my friend!'

Really, it's a mystery sometimes that Charles and I are friends at all. If someone had told me, when he first joined Twickenham High School for Boys about four years ago, that we'd be best mates one day, I'd have laughed in their face. On the surface, Charles and I are pretty dissimilar. For a start, Charles is just so up his own arse sometimes with his intellect. He adores Latin and Greek and reads Descartes, Kant and Plato for fun, for fuck's sake. But alright, I can't deny it – he *can* play a mean blues on the guitar, something that's always been beyond me. Plus, as the months had passed at school, I found that this boy who'd been placed next to me in class had a sly sense of humour and razor-sharp tongue that could, when in the right kind of mood, cut the teachers down in an instant and rile them beyond belief. Especially that twat Bally – *sorry*, Brigadier Johnson - our headmaster, who also teaches us history. My father was a pupil there in the school's more illustrious days and he's of the opinion that once an academic institution has reached a certain standard of success, it's impossible for this to be overturned. He thinks the headmaster's a 'fine chap.' Ha! If he knew the half of it! My father could not be more out of touch, and the truth of it is that Bally's worn out and washed up and a heavy cloak of pipe smoke and gloom surrounds him like a bad smell.

'We're a good pair, you and I,' Charles once said to me. 'Oh yes?' I'd asked. 'How so?' 'Well, what with your looks and my brains, I'd say between us we're fairly irresistible.' We'd fallen about laughing at the time, but he had a good point.

Shame that neither of us were blessed with *both* but you can't have it all, I suppose. Anyway, Charles doesn't seem too interested in girls yet, which is a complete mystery to me. With all those sisters at home, perhaps he's rather sick of females. He does always say how much he adores the peace in my house, though clearly he's never been there when Father's been having one of his usual rants at me. I suspect Charles has kissed one or two girls at the dances with the Girls' High School, but give him a choice between spending an afternoon with girls or books, I suspect he'd opt for the latter.

I glance over at his skinny frame beneath his army surplus jacket and his bespectacled face framed by that ridiculous thatch of scruffy blond hair and feel a surge of affection for him. I instinctively reach out and punch him lightly on the shoulder.

He clutches a hand there in mock pain. 'Excited, are we Jimmy boy?'

'You can say that again. But *Lord,* these trousers are tight.'

'Perhaps you need to slim down.'

I snort. 'I'm in perfect shape, thank you very much. Perhaps *you* need to gain a little muscle weight, *Charlie*-boy.'

'Wait!' Charles suddenly flings an arm out, hitting me across the chest as he stops me in my tracks.

'What?'

'That! Can you hear it?'

I scrunch up my nose and shake my head.

'It's Trad Jazz - listen!'

As soon as he says those words, there it is, the distant strains of trumpet, trombone and clarinet floating over the closely packed rooftops.

Charles closes his eyes. '*Magic*, that is.'

'Yes,' I agree, 'magic indeed. But come on!' I tug his sleeve. 'Let's get there.'

He grins at me as we leave the music behind us and quicken our pace, hurrying along the path that smells of lingering cigarette smoke and cow parsley.

And then, there it is, like a mirage rising from the Thames in the dusky half-light: a small island covered in a green tangle of wild foliage with the hotel sitting in the middle in all its crumbling splendour, the Eel Pie Hotel. When we near the footbridge that leads over the island, Charles and I sit on a bench and share an Embassy Filter.

'How much money we got left?'

'*We*?' snorts Charles. 'Don't you mean me? You don't have a shilling.'

I take a long drag and hand the cigarette to Charles. 'Alright then, *you*, rich boy.'

Charles fishes around in his pocket and counts eightpence out on his hand. 'This is all I have. It's got to last us all evening.'

I grimace. 'That's only just enough to get us both over the bridge.'

'But if I use it all for the bridge, we won't have enough for a drink, you tit. Anyway, you promised *you* were buying the drinks this evening.'

'I know.' I run a hand through my hair. 'I'll do some work for the old man soon. I *promise*. But in the meantime, you're the one with the cash.'

Charles hands the cigarette back to me and stares ahead at the bridge, forehead knotting and his blond eyelashes catching the evening light.

'I've got another idea. Why don't I go over the bridge and you swim and then we'll have enough for a pint of Watney's Red Barrel to share.'

'Swim? Oh, not again. *Fuck.*' I sink my head into my hands.

Charles pushes my arm with his elbow. 'Don't worry, it's a warm enough evening. You'll be dry in no time once you're out. Besides, I've got the tickets in my pockets. Wouldn't want those to get wet.'

I groan. 'Bad reasoning, Adams. But looks like I've no other choice.' I stand up and walk over to the river's edge. 'Which way is the current going?'

'Come on, Jimmy boy, that's an ankle-biters' swimming pool. Any old prick could swim that.'

'Sure you don't want to do the honours?'

'Perfectly sure.'

I shake my head and, without giving it a great deal of further thought, pull at my boots, strip my socks and trousers off and tug the shirt over my head.

'Here goes, then.' I stuff the clothes and my Eelpiland passport into Charles' outstretched arms. 'See you on the other side.' And with that, I dive gracefully into the water and make my way across the swell of the river. I heave myself out on to the riverbank, panting. The current was way stronger than the last time I swam across. I lie back in the long grass in front of the hotel and close my eyes, allowing the final gentle rays of the day to warm my skin. Moments later, a shadow blots my eyelids and I open my eyes, shielding my hand against the sun.

'Took your time, didn't you?' Charles throws my clothes down and sits beside me.

'Shut it,' I retort and dry my dripping hair with my jersey. 'Shit, that water was colder than I remember it. Can I wear your jacket just to warm up?'

'Pussy,' he retorts, removing the coat and throwing it to me.

'*You* swim next time.' I gratefully wrap myself up in the warm coat.

Charles jangles the coins in his pocket. 'Who holds the purse strings, *mon ami*?'

Ignoring him, I lie back down again as he empties his pocket and counts out his money.

'Right, we only have enough money now for one drink to share and…' he peers into his cigarette packet, 'three cigarettes to last us all evening.' Charles shakes his head..

'So two for me, one for you,' I murmur as I break off a stalk of grass and put it between my teeth.

'Ha, funny man.'

At that moment, we both hear laughter behind us and turn at the same time to see two girls sitting in the far corner of the garden, beneath a greengage tree, their legs beneath short dresses stretched out in front of them. They look in our direction, smothering giggles, and then cover their mouths with their hands.

An opportunity not to be missed! I jump up, pulling on my trousers and removing the coat now I'm feeling warmer. Before Charles has a chance to cotton on to what I'm doing, I grab the packet of cigarettes and pad over to the girls. I can hear Charles protesting behind me but, ignoring him, run a hand through my hair and approach them. Closer up, I can see how heavily made up they are, probably far too young to be here, younger than us even. Their eyes are crusted with thick, black mascara and lined underneath with kohl, and their mouths are slashed with white shimmer. But beneath all their make-up they are pretty and soft and plump. I try to stop myself from staring at their firm breasts that press against their jersey dresses.

'Evening ladies,' I say. 'Fancy a smoke?' I hold out the packet to them and they giggle again.

'Don't mind if I do,' the blonde girl says as she reaches out for the packet.

Her friend, following suit, smiles and takes one. I take the third cigarette and place it in my mouth and then, remembering something, turn round.

'Hey Charles! You got the matches?'

Charles pretends to ignore me, grabbing at a handful of grass.

'Charles!'

Begrudgingly, Charles stands and, with a grimace on his face, walks towards us.

'Matches please, my friend, for these young ladies here.'

Without saying a word, Charles lights a match and leans in towards the girls. Then, in one swift motion, he removes the cigarette from between my lips, replaces it in his own mouth and turns the still-lit flame to the tip.

'I'm Maggie,' the girl with the short dark bob says, holding her hand out. We both shake it.

'And I'm Lorna,' the blonde girl says, tugging at the hem of her dress.

'Lorna?' I ask.

'Yes. My parents named me after Lorna Doone.'

I swat a fly away from my ear. 'Uh-huh. Who's that then?'

'Don't mind my friend,' drawls Charles. 'He's not terribly cultured.'

The girls giggle again before Lorna takes a long drag from the cigarette and promptly begins coughing. 'Lors, bit strong, aren't they?'

'What are they?' asks Maggie, turning the end of the cigarette around and staring at it suspiciously.

'Embassy Filters,' I reply as I lean, one hand against the tree, as nonchalantly as I can. 'They're all the rage.'

Maggie pats Lorna on the back and then looks up at us through her layers of mascara. 'Anyway, you haven't told us your names.'

'Ah. I'm Jimmy and this is Charles. It's a pleasure to meet you,' and I give them my best never-fail smile. Appraising the girls now, I like Lorna's hair and the way it hangs in thick lengths over her shoulders; it looks like vanilla ice cream and contrasts perfectly with her chocolate-brown eyes. But Maggie, I can see quite clearly now, has indisputably larger breasts and a cheekier look about her.

'So, have you heard the Yardbirds play before?' Charles asks.

Maggie and Lorna shake their heads.

'Actually, we've never been to the island before.' Maggie says. 'Our parents aren't dreadfully keen we're here at all.'

'Pah!' I say, so loudly that they all stare at me. Regaining my composure, I dig my heels into the ground and puff my chest out a little.

'Well,' Charles says. 'You're in for a treat if you've never heard the Yardbirds before. Speaking of which,' – he grinds his cigarette out on the ground – 'I think we ought to be getting in. You coming, Jim?'

'I suppose I ought to be getting some clothes on,' I grin at Maggie, trying hard to keep my eyes from her breasts. 'We'll see you in there, ladies?' I take both their hands and plant a kiss on them. Charles sighs loudly and rolls his eyes whilst the girls giggle and nod.

Chapter Two

The Eel Pie Club, or Eelpiland as we affectionately call it, is a building of faded opulence, with a network of undergrowth and trees winding thin branches and roots around it, laying claim to it. It doesn't matter a hoot that the floorboards are rotting, the paint is peeling, the plasterwork is crumbling, the arched windows looking out onto the Thames have lost most of their glass and the mural behind the stage depicting a frenzied scene of music and drums is fading. This is a place that Charles and I feel more ourselves than anywhere else. Of course, there's L'Auberge, a place to smoke and talk and pretend to drink coffee. But that is a place for the daytime. There is nowhere else that comes close to Eelpiland.

We've been coming here since we were fifteen, having managed to cadge an Eelpiland membership card off an older boy at school who arranged it for us at a cost. The card states that we are eighteen years of age but it's clear, looking around the joint, that not that many people who come are much beyond that age. The card is our passport to Eelpiland and gives us '*assistance he/she might require in his/her lawful business of jiving and generally Cutting a Rug.*' To say that it's my most treasured possession would be a vast understatement.

Music usually just plays at the weekend. On the occasional weeknight, if we have enough money for the bridge fare, we go along to the club to join in with the anti-apartheid and nuclear disarmament meetings. I usually spend these evenings at the jukebox, occasionally re-joining the discussion with a serious face and raised eyebrows, but on the whole, I find the political conversations a little tedious and can't understand what Charles and everyone else are getting so worked up about. Charles says I *should* engage; that this is life and the issues affect all of us. Perhaps he's right, and it would peeve the crap out of my father if he knew I was involved in CND conversations, so that almost makes it worth it. The truth it though, music and dancing and girls are languages I understand far better.

A man with a beard and a frilly white shirt beneath a duffel coat prints a rubber stamp on to our wrists, then we saunter in. It's packed inside the club, a hot tangle of limbs. The Yardbirds haven't started their performance yet but music is blaring out from the jukebox, an energetic jive that seems a little old-fashioned but it's going down a storm. My feet start tapping and, before I know it, Charles and I are amongst the crowd on the sprung maple dance floor that swells up and down like a wave as we let our bodies take over.

After several minutes, I stop dancing and lean against an arch to watch everyone and everything. The window in front of me has lost a great deal of its glass and the evening light, fading fast, is spooling in and lighting up dancing dust motes in the dull glow of the room. I cross my arms, letting it all wash over me, feeling a great flood of love for the place. Almost simultaneously, I feel a heady surge of hatred for my father. He does nothing but criticise Eelpi and, but he knows nothing about it. Everything he's heard, everything he's read about the island he's just swallowed unquestioningly. But when has he ever taken me aside and asked for the truth; asked what it's really like here? Never, because he doesn't want to know. He'd rather believe the Mirror's view that the island is lawless; a promiscuous den of iniquity. Frankly, I wish my time spent here *was* full of sex but sadly, it isn't. And I certainly don't know anybody personally who has managed to get *that* lucky on the island.

What's wrong with my bloody father anyway? Why is he so repressed and unfeeling and uptight? What Ma sees in him, or has ever seen in him, I can't fathom. My fingers have balled into tight fists and the nails of my fingertips are squeezing hard into my palms. With great effort, I release them and stare down at my hands in the dusty, dimming light. Little half-moon bluish ridges have appeared in both hands and I glare at them. I hate him, I hate him, I hate him. He's a bloody monster. Unfeeling, no emotions, not a tiny bit of love or empathy or any of the things that are good in this world. Why, for Christ's sake, do I have to get stuck with a fucking father like *him*? At the end of term, I'd won the Art Prize. And how had he responded? With a grunt and a *Maybe if you apply yourself, you can get the mathematics award next term.* For fuck's sake. Ma had caught up with me afterwards, out by the school gate. *We're proud of you, Jimmy,* she'd said. *Both of us.* I'd grimaced at her, then stuffed my hands in my pockets, walked faster.

I take a deep breath and lean into the arch to steady myself. I can always feel it coming on, this burning anger. It comes out of nowhere sometimes and I don't know what the hell to do with it. I'd like to kick someone so hard that I want to feel as much pain as the person I'm kicking or put my fist through a window and listen to the icy tinkle of breaking glass. But I can't do that here. For a start, most of the windows are missing their glass and secondly, I'd get kicked off the island.

But then, the inevitable accompanies the anger, the twin feeling that always follows the rage with equal intensity: a bottomless sadness that punches all the air from me, making me feel hollow and alone, squeezing against my chest like a leaden weight. I close my eyes, trying desperately to remember a time when my father was different. But no, nothing comes. Only the criticism, the disapproval, the disappointment.

People jostle and elbow their way past me and my eyes flicker open as I stand and stare at the dying embers of sunlight streaming in through the smashed windows and a memory comes back to me in a flash, one so buried and hidden, that it almost winds me. I'm a young boy, I don't yet realise what a prick my father is and still try to do small things to please him. It's cold and frosty, a fire spitting in the hearth. Ma asks me to take Father his cup of tea and biscuit in the living room. It's the first time and I'm almost cross-eyed with concentration as I keep my eyes on the steaming cup and saucer grasped in my hands. I feel proud to be doing this; it's such a simple little thing, and yet to me it's not little at all.

Ma understands; she gives me an encouraging smile and holds the kitchen door open. On I walk, tongue lolling out to one side of my mouth and eyebrows knitted. I'm about to place the cup and saucer down on the small side table beside the armchair when I'm distracted...a dog barks somewhere outside, loud and angry. I turn towards the sound but somehow lose my balance and trip. The tea comes cascading down, narrowly missing my father as the teacup smashes and splinters on the wooden floor.

He looks up from his paper, face darkening. He pulls out his pipe and glares at me.

'Clumsy child!' he yells. 'What do you think you're doing?'

What did I think I was doing? I was trying to be helpful. I remember bunching my small fists up, furious with him for talking to me like that. And then promptly bursting into tears and running from the room.

'Hello, Jimmy.' I hear a voice beside me and blink.

'Oh, Lorna, hullo!'

'It's Maggie.'

'Yes. Maggie.' I stand upright.

'You alright?'

'Yes, why?'

'You...' She reaches the fingertips of one hand out towards me and then, thinking better of it, pulls them back to her side.

I can feel wetness on my cheeks and roughly brush it away with my sleeve. 'Smoke getting in my eyes.' I clear my throat. 'Where's Lorna?'

'She's over there, dancing. We've seen some of our friends. Where's Charles?'

'Dancing too.' I grin at her.

'Shall we get a drink?'

'I...I don't have any money left, I'm afraid.'

'Don't worry, I do.' And with that, she catches my hand

in hers and pulls me towards the bar. Her hand is warm and firm and I smile to myself, staring once more at Maggie's breasts, all thoughts of my father thankfully banished.

I drape an arm around Maggie's shoulders and she doesn't remove it – a good sign - certain that at any minute I can ask her outside for some fresh air. I'm biding my time; I know, from past experience, that if I ask too early, I'm more or less screwed. The Yardbirds have been fantastic and the four of us have jumped up and down, the floorboards bouncing and helping us go higher, whilst all around us, kids piggyback one another to get a better view. Charles and I shared a bottle of Red Barrel and then Maggie bought us all another couple of rounds. Now I'm feeling ever so slightly drunk, that warm, pleasant feeling with the edges blurred.

'You know what, Jimmy?' Maggie's shouting over the din.

'What?' I shout back as I squeeze her shoulder.

'I'm poached in here, completely poached. Can we go outside?'

Victory! An assertive girl, I like that. Without saying another word, I take her by the hand and pull her through the crowd, stepping on people's toes and ignoring their cries as I push them aside. I need to get her outside as quick as I can, before she changes her mind. She shouts something after me but I press on, reaching the door and pushing it open.

Once we're outside, she shakes her hand free from mine.

'Water!' she says. 'I'd like a glass.'

It takes a little time to register what she's asking as it's hard not to concentrate on just one thing, and Charles's sodding too-tight trousers aren't helping.

'Water!' Maggie says again, putting her face closer to mine and raising an eyebrow.

'Water. Yes.' I point down to the Thames. 'Plenty of water over there.'

Maggie takes a step back and, hands on hips, narrows her eyes. They really are very pretty eyes. Even in the dim light, I can make out their unusual shade of dark blue, almost navy. I've never seen a girl with navy blue eyes before. But she isn't looking impressed.

'Right, Mags, you stay here.' I take her by the elbow and steer her away from the entrance of the club, over to a patch of grass not far from where I first saw her. 'Don't move, right? Back in a tic.'

She nods, the hint of a smile forming on her lips again.

Hurriedly, I push the door open so fast it almost whacks me back in the face.

'Steady on, laddy. What's the rush?' A voice emerges from the darkness and I turn to see the faint outline of black-rimmed glasses and a shaggy beard over the top of an ironic smile.

'Water,' I say, pointing to the bar. 'Water!' I push my way back through the crowd, stepping on the same people's feet until I've safely reached the bar. Charles and Lorna are standing there with a couple of other girls.

'What have you done with my friend?' Lorna instantly asks, eyeing me suspiciously.

'I've done nothing with her,' I reply defensively. 'She's over-heated and needs some water and I'm getting her some.'

Charles smirks and pats me on the shoulder.

'My friend Jim. Always the gentleman.'

I shoot him a look and lean through the two of them to call to the bartender.

'A large glass of water over here, quick as you can.'

The bartender studiously ignores me. After a couple more attempts, I sigh loudly and push myself up so that my waist is leaning over the bar and I can have a good look around. I spy a jug of water filled with ice but can't see a glass and tut loudly. Charles only has a small amount of beer left so I grab the glass from him, drain it and then slosh some water into it.

'You complete prick!' Charles cries.

'Thanks, darling,' I reply, patting his cheek before making my way back outside. I'm relieved to see that Maggie is still sitting on the grass, her long legs spread out in front of her beneath her black jersey-dress. She smiles when she sees me.

'Thanks,' she says when I hand her the glass.

'So,' I say as I sit down close beside her, and then can think of nothing more to say.

'So,' Maggie says and smiles shyly at me.

The conversation is not forthcoming and so Maggie takes a large gulp of her drink. She suddenly begins to cough violently, one hand over her mouth as she pushes the glass into my hand.

'God!' she squeaks. 'What are you trying to do to me? Get me completely legless?'

'What?' I say. I frown and pat her back. 'What's the problem?'

'That!' she shrieks, pointing to the glass. 'That is. Taste it! Go on, taste it!'

I gingerly take a sip and wince. It isn't water at all, it's gin and tonic, though possibly more gin than tonic. 'Christ, I'm sorry, Mags. The Eel Pie Hotel must have gin coming out of its taps instead of water.' I look at her and she bursts out laughing. And *relax*. Disaster averted. I like this girl.

'Well, in that case,' Maggie says, 'I ought to drink a little more.'

I hand her the glass back and she takes several dainty sips, staring steadily at me over the top of the glass. Once finished, Maggie physically relaxes and leans back on her elbows, staring out at the Thames and the blinking lights of Twickenham on the other side.

'I love it here,' she says softly. 'It's magical, isn't it? Eel Pie Island. Even the name sounds enchanted.'

She's right, but I'm not all that interested in talking about the obvious qualities of the island. Now that Maggie is leaning back, I can see the curve of her generous breasts pressed against her dress and cannot tear my eyes from them.

'Don't you think?' Maggie asks.

'M-hmm.' I turn so I'm facing her and roll over to the side, propping myself up on one elbow and cupping my chin in my palm as I pull a floppy lock of hair over one eye.

'I don't know what all the fuss is about over this place. Did you read the article about the club in the Mirror a few weeks ago? Well, the Bishop of Twickenham responded and even *he* said this was a good place for young people to come. I think that's what appeased my parents a bit. I'm here thanks to the Bishop of Twickenham of all people.'

I'm only half listening to her. I edge ever so slightly closer.

'Maggie.'

She turns to face me and her dark bob swings as she moves.

'Yes?'

Her lips are slightly parted and between the pale shimmer they have been painted, I can see neat white teeth, surprisingly small.

'You're ever so pretty.'

She turns away from me and starts inspecting her nails, pushing the cuticles down. Her hair swings back, covering her face from me. I reach out and tuck it behind her ear.

'You are, you know. But I suppose everybody tells you that.'

Maggie casts a shy look at me. 'Not especially.'

'Well. I think you are.'

Silence. I wish Maggie would say something, or do something. I can hear the dull throb of music coming from inside the club and the rustle of wind in the leaves overhead. I frown, wishing I could make this part easier, a little less awkward. Lord knows I've had enough practice at it but, nevertheless, I still find the very point of contact excruciating. Biting my lip, I move closer still and then throw myself at her mouth, pinning her against me, one arm flung around her waist. Maggie lets out a small noise. I hear it escaping from her but, undeterred and encouraged by its immediate cessation and my awareness of her relaxing against me, I guide her down to the ground so that her head rests against the grass. I haven't yet mastered what I ought to do with my tongue; it feels like a frustrating obstacle and inconvenience whilst kissing. I would like to neatly tuck it away at the back of my mouth but, that being impossible, instead experiment with keeping it at one side or the other. Maggie appears unsure about this; clasping both hands on either of my shoulders, she pushes gently, but I'm unclear what to read from this. Perhaps it's an increase in excitement? That must be it. Encouraged that things are going well, I think it about time to up the stakes. Flexing my free hand (the other being pinned uncomfortably beneath Maggie's shoulders), I maneuver my fingers to the bottom of Maggie's blouse. But then I remember with frustration that she's wearing a dress. This is going to be a far harder task. I keep kissing her, pleased that she seems to be enjoying it so much and at the same time, move my hand stealthily downwards so that it rests on the hem of her dress. This is made a little easier by the fact that Maggie's knees are bent and I slowly move my hand up the inside of her dress, brushing against her warm bare thighs, intent only on the higher destination of breasts.

Maggie suddenly lets out a loud squeal and pushes with her all her might against me with her hands. Shocked, I fall backwards on to the grass.

'What are you *doing*?' she yells at me, her face a picture of crumpled fury.

'What d'you mean? I'm…I was just – '

'Just *what?*' Maggie's face is flushed red and mascara's smudged beneath one eye.

What have I done wrong? I'm sure I read all the signals right and she was enjoying it.

'Sorry,' I mutter. 'I thought you were…you were…you know, digging it.'

'*Digging it*?' she shrieks. 'Well, kissing is one thing, but what you were trying to do is quite another!'

It suddenly occurs to me that Maggie thought I was trying to get at another place when really, it was all quite innocent and all I wanted was her breasts.

'No, you don't understand,' I say, frowning.

'I understand all right.' Maggie is smoothing her dress back over her legs and then begins to pull out blades of grass from her hair. Then, right at that moment, we both see a man approaching us from the entrance of the club. It's the older man I spotted earlier with the beard and glasses.

'Oh, fan-bloody-tastic,' I mutter.

'Everything alright, love?' the man asks, his bearded face peering down at Maggie and taking in the smudged mascara.

Maggie sits upright and blinks.

'What have you been up to, my boy?' he persists. 'You been giving this young lady trouble? Because if you have, I shall throw you off this island as fast as you can say tin whistle. You hear me?'

I know who he is, this is Arthur who runs the club and the weeknight discussions. He owns the license for the place. Some people, Charles included, revere him like some kind of Demi-God but, frankly, I think he's a bit up himself.

Maggie has composed herself and is sitting upright, her lips pursed. 'It's alright, thank you. I'm fine,' she says tightly.

'You sure, love?' He takes off his glasses and wipes them with a handkerchief, then looks at her again closely. Maggie nods and Arthur puts his hands on his hips. '*Any* more trouble from you, young man and I'll take your Eel Pie passport away, you hear me?'

I nod sheepishly.

'I said, you hear me?'

'Yes sir, I hear you.'

'Good.' Arthur grunts and taps the side of his nose. 'I'll be watching you, laddie.' He stalks off back to the club and I turn to Maggie.

'Oh Mags, thank you. And listen – '

She has already begun to stand up. 'No, I shan't listen to you, thank you very much.' She smoothes down her hair and glares at me. 'And you keep your hands off me from now on. I'm leaving.'

'But Maggie – '

'I don't want to hear it.' And with that, she marches back into the club. Moments later, I watch as Maggie troops outside with Lorna and a couple of other girls. All four of them fix me with a fierce glare as they pass, before walking over the bridge. I blow out a hot burst of air. Girls! Law unto themselves. I yank at blades of grass and tear the petals off a couple of daisies, my fingers twitching. God, I need a cigarette. Just as I'm considering going back inside to find Charles, he walks out of the door with a couple of other boys. He saunters over to me, a look of amusement on his face and a cigarette dangling from his mouth.

'Now then, Jim, what did you do to that poor girl?'

'What are you talking about?' I snap defensively. 'I didn't do anything to her.'

'Well, she left pretty damn quickly. Shame. I was enjoying talking to her friend. Come on,' Charles punches me lightly on the shoulder. 'What did you do?'

I remove the cigarette from Charles's mouth and take a drag from it before handing it back. I feel much better now. 'I didn't do a thing. Strange girl, she was. We were just having a bit of a kiss and a cuddle and she suddenly got scared.' I shrug. 'She definitely liked me though. I'm sure I'll see her again.'

Charles laughs lightly.

'Yes, my friend. She looked head over heels with you as

she ran over that bridge, as fast as she could possibly get away from you. Never mind, old boy. There's always next time.'

I scowl at him, eager to change the subject. I nod over to the door. 'Who are they?'

Charles looks round and his face lights up.

'Oh, I was chatting with them inside the club. Art students. They're great. Hey, John, Doug, over here!'

They walk over and Charles introduces us. They're a few years older and have long hair that reaches to their shoulders and that look of studious nonchalance. How the hell do they do that? I need to take some mental notes. One of them is wearing beige, crushed velvet, bell-bottoms. By rights, he should be looking a wanker but somehow, they just compliment the hair and the overall look. They nod in my direction and sit down on the grass beside us. Bell-bottoms-bloke, Doug, immediately fishes about in his pocket and rolls a joint.

'You better watch it,' I say, peering over the tops of their heads. 'Old Arthur's on the warpath.'

John laughs. 'Relax, man. Arthur doesn't care.'

'I wouldn't be so sure about that,' I mutter.

'You want a toke?' Doug says to Charles, handing him the reefer.

Charles looks a bit nervous but takes a quick drag. John laughs.

'Come on, man. Let yourself inhale some of it. Doesn't work otherwise.'

'Someone told me you shouldn't mix alcohol and marijuana,' Charles says in a small voice that makes me wince. Fuck's sake, he sounds like such a schoolboy.

John leans back and stares up into the dark sky, peppered

with stars. He's dressed from head to toe in black and looks the epitome of cool. Maybe I need to try wearing all black next time I'm on the island. 'Uh huh. Who told you that?'

Charles frowns.

'Can't remember.' He takes another drag, this time allowing the smoke to go in deeper and then blows it out noisily.

'That's the way.'

I'm pulling off daisy heads, still feeling pissed off about Maggie, when Doug nods in my direction. I reach out and take it, inhaling deeply. I've only smoked once before and it wasn't a particularly good experience. A couple of boys from school got hold of it from somewhere, claiming it was from a reputable source and had come all the way from Afghanistan. I wasn't convinced. It left the most horrible, acrid aftertaste in my mouth and a grinding headache. But this, I know, as I exhale slowly, is good quality. It feels lighter but stronger. I close my eyes, enjoying every minute of the experience.

'That's good stuff,' I say eventually.

'The best,' John says, nodding his head slowly.

Doug puts on his shades and leans back, resting his head against his arms.

'You know, my friend came back with this from Matala; a bloke sold it to him there who had brought a big wad from somewhere on the Ganges.'

Charles is now visibly relaxing as he reaches out for more.

'Yep, it's good stuff.'

John chuckles and hands him the joint. I feel more alive than ever; it's as though I can feel the trajectory of my blood channeling its way through my veins and each tiny hair on my body standing up to attention. Shit, if only I had enough money to buy this kind of thing on a regular basis. School would be more bearable; the music would be even more wonderful and perhaps I could even tolerate my father more.

'Where's Matala?' I murmur, eyes heavy, as I turn towards Doug. Just over the top of his head, I see a blur of people making their way slowly, reluctantly, back over the bridge to Twickenham.

'Hmm?'

'Matala. You said your friend got this from Matala.'

Doug lifts himself up slightly and looks me intently in the eye.

'Matala. It's on a Greek Island somewhere. Can't remember which one. There's a community of people living in caves – '

'*Caves*?'

'Yep, caves.'

'You mean Greek people, living in caves?'

'*No* man,' Doug says patiently as he takes another drag of the spliff. He pauses and flicks his fingers through his hair with his spare hand. 'I mean people from all round the world, they've gone to colonise the caves. Travellers, you know. It sounds far-out. Dancing, naked swimming, orgies, wine coming out of your ears – '

I sit upright. 'Orgies you say?'

Charles gives a loud guffaw. 'Calm down, Jimmy boy.'

'Shit, man' John rejoins, 'we don't know how much of this stuff is true. But that's the picture our friends painted. Whatever is there, it sounds pretty damn good. It's an ancient village in a bay with prehistoric caves that the travellers are living in. We're planning on heading there sometime soon. Too good to miss, we reckon.'

'When?' I lean forwards. Everything suddenly looks brighter, Doug's bell-bottoms transforming from beige to lurid yellow and the water of the nearby Thames sparkling with an almost amethyst sheen.

'Huh?' reply John and Doug in unison, both pretty stoned.

'When are you going there?'

John laughs. 'Whenever we feel like it. Sometime this summer.'

I don't know what it is - whether it's the marijuana tingling my nerve endings, but there's something in my body that is physically responding to this information about Matala.

'Christ, I wish I could go there. I'd give *anything* to go there.'

'What's stopping you?' Doug asks lifting his shades a fraction to reveal lazy, bloodshot eyes staring out from underneath them.

'That small issue called money,' I reply tersely, picking at the grass blades next to me.

'What do you need money for, man?' Doug asks.

'Well, I'd have to travel down there by bus, or train or something like that – '

'Don't be a dickhead. Have you never heard of hitchhiking?'

Hitchhiking. Yes, I have heard of hitchhiking but I know precisely nothing about it. As though reading my mind, John shakes his head in bewilderment.

'There's nothing to it. You just stick a thumb out, wait five minutes for someone to stop, then jump in and go.'

'Five minutes?'

'Shit man, five minutes, ten minutes, whatever. Then you get in, tell them where you're heading and if they're not going the same way you want to go, they'll just drop you at a point where you can get a new lift. It's exhilarating. It's freedom.'

Doug, looking suddenly very bored with this conversation, leans back and puts his black shades on. I nod and glance at Charles who is staring down at the river. I'm not convinced he's listening to any of this.

'Anyway,' Doug says, heaving himself up with great effort. 'John, we need to be heading.' John stands and sticks a hand out to Doug.

'Wait, wait a tic.' I jump up, blood rushing to my head. 'When did you say you were going there?'

John shrugs. 'Maybe this summer. Nothing's planned, it's just a place we'd like to go to.'

I nod vigorously. 'Yup, it sounds amazing. Amazing. Doesn't it, Charles?' I elbow him.

'Mm-hmm.' With great effort, he pulls his gaze away from the Thames and stares at me. Christ, he's stoned.

'Can I...could I take your number, and then if you go, Charles and I could hitchhike down with you?'

Charles lets out a derisive snort. 'You're on your own, Jimmy boy.'

I push his leg briskly with my foot. 'Shut it.' I turn back to Doug and John. 'Well?'

John shrugs again. In fact, he looks like he spends an awful lot of time shrugging.

'Sure. I don't have a pencil though. Or paper for that matter.'

'Pencil, pencil…' I feel in my pockets unsuccessfully. 'Damn. Look, just tell me the number, I'll remember it.'

'You will not,' says Charles, who is now sitting cross-legged and rubbing a hand roughly across his face.

'I will. And if I don't, *you* will.'

'It's easy enough to remember. TWI 7893. Got it?' John and Doug start to walk away, barely looking back.

'Got it!' I yell after them. 'I'll call you soon. Ok?' But they aren't listening.

I sit down beside Charles with a thump and start to count letters up on my fingers until I reach the corresponding numbers.

'G-H-I-C. I think I'll be more likely to remember the number if I put it to a phrase. What has a good ring that starts with those letters?'

'GHIC?'

'Yes.' I raise my eyebrows expectantly.

'Greece Here I Come?'

'Ha!' I say loudly, clapping Charles on the back. 'That's bloody brilliant. Greece Here I Come. I like it. So, you coming with me?'

Charles frowns. 'Oh, don't be a tosspot. You're not serious, surely.'

'Fuck, yes. I'm serious. Didn't you hear them, Charles? It sounds like some kind of paradise.'

Charles pushes his glasses up onto the bridge of his nose and raises an eyebrow. 'Paradise, ha! You are a hopeless dreamer, mon ami. Not my scene, Jimmy boy.'

'How can you possibly know it's not your scene if you've never been there?'

Charles shakes his head. 'Alright, fair point. I shouldn't

judge it before I've been there. But listen, even if we *did* think seriously about going, why don't we wait till next summer? After our A Levels?'

I shuffle on my knees round to the front of Charles and grasp him by both shoulders.

'We can't wait till next summer. It might not *be* there by next summer.'

'You tit, they're ancient caves, of *course* they'll be there next summer.'

'I'm not talking about the caves, Charles. I'm talking about the people, the vibe, the parties. Everybody may have moved on to the next place. We have to seize the day!'

'You'll have to seize the day without me, my friend.'

I let out a frustrated sigh and slump back beside him. I can smell something cooking and my stomach growls. Perhaps it's one of those late-night chippies back on the mainland. 'You still haven't given me a single good reason,' I grumble.

'I don't need to give you a good reason, I'm just not that interested.'

'But it will be like *this* place. Good music. Good people. But instead of being kicked off when the music finishes, it will be for twenty-four hours. Can you imagine that?'

At that, Charles is quiet for a while, thoughtfully staring at the river. Then moments later, he pulls himself to his feet and starts to walk towards the bridge.

'Sorry, not interested.'

I get up and begin trotting behind him. 'We'll be back by the start of next term.'

'Nope.'

'At least tell me you'll think about it.'

'No.'

'What the hell else do you have to do the entire summer?'

Charles remains resolutely silent as we make our way unsteadily over the bridge back to the mainland, the music and marijuana coiling round our nerve endings.

Chapter Three

I'm woken by the sound of church bells. I've got a raging headache and can just make out heavy sheets of rain teeming down the window through my half-closed eyelids. Despite being in bed all this time, I've had a terrible night's sleep. I had to listen to Father through the wall, groaning and moaning so loudly in the night that I felt physically ill. I was forced to stuff two pillows over my head to get anywhere close to muffling some of the sound out, the revolting vision of my father smothering Ma, lingering for far longer than I'd have wished. I pull the blanket over my head so that only a tuft of hair pokes out over the top. So damned inconsiderate, those church bells. What about us poor people who want to sleep in on a Sunday?

I hear a soft knocking on the door and hope that, if I ignore it, it'll stop. But the tapping continues and, giving no response, I hear the creak of my door handle and the soft padding of slippered feet across the wooden floor. I try to push away the noises from last night, shuddering beneath the blanket as I do so.

Ma sits on the side of the bed and places a hand on my covered heap.

'Jimmy,' she whispers. 'Jimmy love what do you want for breakfast?'

'Not hungry, Ma,' I croak.

'It's half past ten, love. You need to get up.'

'Why?'

She tugs at the blanket ruched around my head, drawing it down. I recoil from the light and yank it back up.

'Jim, your father's in a terrible mood today.'

From the dark warmth beneath my blanket, I grimace. For a few blissful hours, I'd forgotten Father's inevitable wrath. I squeeze my eyes shut, willing Ma to leave so that I can go back to sleep.

'Listen, I've an idea. Why don't you do a couple of weeks' work for your dad, earn yourself some pocket money and then the three of us could go away for a long weekend together. Would you like that, hmm? We could go to Calais again.'

I snort and then grumble 'Can't you let me sleep, Ma? I'm so tired.'

'That's because you're out till all hours.' I can hear the edge of irritation in her voice now. 'Even though you know your father doesn't like it.'

Right, *now* I'm getting pissed off. No point in trying to get more sleep, is there? I fling the blanket back down over my head.

'And what about you?'

'What about me?'

'Do you not like it either?'

Ma sighs. 'You know I don't.'

I rub my eyes. 'I don't believe you. I think you just say that because Father doesn't like me going to the island. I don't believe you really mind.'

'Don't be silly. Now listen, will you please come down and have some breakfast?'

'Do I have to?' My head is beating like a skiffle drum.

'Yes. And for heaven's sake, don't antagonise your father.'

Ma leaves and I let out a groan as I press my fingers to my forehead. Ten minutes later, I sidle into the kitchen. Ma is spreading Robertson's Jam on toast and Father's head is bent low over yesterday's Mail, strands of his thinning hair falling over his nose. He has his pipe in his mouth and coils of grey smoke dance in the sun motes round the kitchen. If he's heard me come in, he makes no indication of it and I quietly pull a chair out at the opposite side of the table and sit down.

A Whiter Shade of Pale is softly playing on the radio, cheering me up momentarily. I clasp my hands in front of me and twist them nervously and then, in a sudden mood of defiance, unclasp them and frown. *Damn* him for making me feel like a naughty little schoolboy. I've done nothing wrong. Nothing whatsoever.

Father keeps turning the pages of his newspaper, slowly and methodically, occasionally pausing to read a few lines of an article before continuing. The kitchen smells of pipe smoke and burnt toast and my stomach recoils in horror whilst also giving out a sudden yowl of hunger. I haven't had a thing to eat since lunchtime at L'Auberge yesterday. Ma brings me a slice of toast spread thickly with jam just how I like it. I grin up at her and her mouth twitches upwards. As I take a large bite, Father looks unsmilingly up from his paper. I continue chewing and, when I've finished my mouthful, smile at him lopsidedly.

'Can I look at the paper, Pops?'

'Don't you Pops me,' he growls. 'Why did you go to that place last night?'

'Who said I went there last night?' I reply feebly. 'I was – '

'No game playing!'

Father clenches his fist and bangs it down on the table. Ma, who's washing up at the sink, jumps at the sudden sound and lets out a small, surprised gasp.

'I expressly asked you not to go there, yet you chose to ignore that. Why is that, James?'

I stare down at the thick red globs on my toast, my appetite waning. I take a deep breath.

'Father. Will you let me explain something to you, please? I want to tell you about what it's like there. What it's really like. It's not what you think, you see – '

'Don't you tell me what I think. I want to know why you choose, again and again, to disobey me?'

Ma walks over to the table, frying pan in hand as small soapy suds drips on to the floor.

'Why don't we hear him out, love? Just hear what he has to – '

'Nancy!' Father snaps. 'This is between James and myself.'

I stare at Ma, willing her to stand up to him. There is a pause, a tableau of frozen silence and tension around the kitchen table. Then Ma blinks and it's broken. She looks down at the soapsuds that have dripped on to the tiles.

'Oh, *look* what I've done,' she says, talking to the floor. 'How terribly careless I am.'

I turn back to Father.

'The problem is that you want to know why I'm

disobeying you. But you won't allow me to give you the answer, because you won't let me tell you about this club I love going to. Listen, young people are *helped* there – '

'But you admit it then!' Father removes the pipe from his mouth and points it accusingly at me. 'You admit that you went to that island last night?'

I cross my arms and glare at him. How I loathe him, his sanctimoniousness and narrow-mindedness. I give a little shudder and pull my jersey sleeves over my hands. 'Yes, I admit it, but – '

'You see, Nancy? You see what our son has been up to?'

Ma stands at the sink, her back to the two of us with her shoulders tensed up around her ears. She turns her face so that she stands in profile towards us, mouth pinched and forehead betraying the tangle of a frown. But she says nothing.

'Whenever I go, I'm with Charles,' I say quietly. I doubt this will appease him, but I know that he approves of him as he's bright and a dab hand at being polite to parents.

'Hmm,' Father grunts as he attacks his bacon. 'He's a sensible boy. You could learn a thing or two from him.'

'But Father,' I say, resentment bubbling inside me, 'Charles loves going to the island too, not just for the music but for the meetings so he can discuss things like nuclear disarmament and anti-apartheid and – '

'Well, I take back what I said about him, then. The pair of you have your heads stuffed with straw.'

He turns the bottle of brown sauce upside down and gives it a violent thwhack so that a large pool of liquid brown covers his sausage. I stare down at my half-eaten piece of toast, appetite vanished.

'I'm not particularly hungry,' I say as I stand up. 'I'm going to have a bath.'

'Sit,' responds Father as he chews. He waves his knife downwards. I frown in his direction.

'Why?'

'Lord, has there ever been a more defiant boy?' Father says, speaking to no one in particular. 'I say black, you say white! I say sun, you say rain.'

What a ridiculous analogy. I sink back into the chair and slump low. I pull my hair over one eye and glare up at him through it. Father continues chewing his sausage and then dabs at his mouth with a napkin. He pushes his plate away, taking up his pipe again.

'I mean, what is going on in this country right now? Would you believe – would you *believe* this, Nancy…' He turns to Ma, his fork jabbing in her direction, 'that there was a Legalise Pot rally yesterday in London? Some Yankee poet, Allen Ginsborough or some such name –

'Allen Ginsberg,' I cut in. Charles's favourite poet.

'Ginsborough, Ginsberg.' Father waves his fork in the air. 'Apparently the police asked him to stop playing his harmonium. Well, he stopped alright but then he handed the policeman a flower. A flower, I ask you! The nerve of the man. And *then*…'

Father's getting warmed up now. I fold my arms. 'And *then*, as if this isn't enough absurdity for one day, the BBC newsreader gave a ridiculous Indian Namaste sign into the camera before he signed off!'

Both Ma and I let out a stifled chuckle.

'I see, you think that's funny, do you?'

I frown and swallow my grin, glaring at him. Humourless bastard.

Father clatters down his cutlery on to his plate and surveys me. 'Why can't you spend your time at a youth club?'

'A youth club,' I repeat.

'Yes. The Twickenham Youth Club for example. Or there's always the Young Conservatives. Or the Young Farmers.'

Ma makes a noise in her throat as though she's clearing it and loudly pulls open a kitchen cupboard door, pulling out a tin of Fray Bentos.

'Steak and kidney pie alright for you both for lunch?' She fixes us with a stare over her shoulder.

'Capital,' Father replies before looking back at me. 'Well?'

'Well, what?' I mumble.

'What's wrong with the youth club? You think you're too good for it?'

'I didn't say that. Father, you don't listen to me. The youth club just doesn't…it doesn't interest me. It's…' I sigh deeply. 'It's out of touch, alright?'

Father shakes his head and pushes his chair back. 'Well, since you've eschewed the youth club and you're clearly finding it difficult to fill your summer holidays with useful activities, I'd like you to come and do some work for me.'

Oh, great. Bloody great.

'You'll earn yourself a little pocket money that you can spend on…' he waves his pipe in the air, searching for something, '…records and what-not. But *not* shenaniganing on that island, mind. D'you hear me?'

I begin to tap my foot against the table leg, arms crossed over myself.

'Any more bread, Nancy?'

'Only a Wonderloaf, love. That alright?' Ma replies.

'Fine, fine.'

Ma reaches into the bread bin and takes out the package of bread wrapped in paper, carefully removing a slice and popping it into the toaster.

Christ, I can think of nothing worse than spending the summer working for the old man. I watch as the contents of his pipe are emptied and Father opens a small tin and re-fills it. Revolting, smelly things, pipes. Why can't he just smoke cigarettes like normal people?

'Well?' Father presses as he lights a match.

'Well, what? Well, will I work for you, or well, will I spend the money I earn on going to the island?'

Father shakes his head as Ma hovers over me, clearing the plates away. She shoots a look at me, raising an eyebrow.

'Fine,' I grumble, looking straight at Ma.

'Fine, what? Fine that you'll work for me or fine that you won't spend the money on going to that place?' I hear what sounds like a chuckle escaping from Father and I turn to glare at him. 'Two can play at that game, sonny Jim.'

My head is pounding more than ever. I want nothing more than to be released from this odious conversation. I drop my elbows on to the table, massaging my temples.

'Yes, yes. Fine. Whatever you say,' I mutter.

'Marvellous.' Father looks immensely pleased with himself and even Ma's mouth twitches upwards. Traitor. 'Let's start tomorrow, shall we? Out of bed at 6.30, at work by 8 and I'll give you one hour's lunch break if you work through till five. Agreed?'

I sigh deeply and stand up. 'I'm going to have my bath.'

The office is nestled down a quiet side road off Twickenham Green. I've been there a few times before but I don't go if it can be avoided. This time I see it'll be impossible to escape the redbrick building with its pathetic potted pansies lining the gravel path.

Father tells me to make sure I look presentable and I scowl into my wardrobe, trying to find something smart that won't make me look like the biggest wanker ever. I settle on a brown shirt and a pair of black trousers and, before I leave my room, I stand in front of the mirror to tussle up my hair and put my shades on. As I leave the house, Ma slips a couple of marshmallows in striped silver and red paper into my pocket and winks at me. Alright, so I loved them when I was a kid, but if she thinks this is going to improve my mood, she's wrong.

Father is in annoyingly good spirits, whistling as we walk down Twickenham High Street. If he can be so bloody cheerful about going to work, why is it that he can't be a little more enthusiastic about listening to me speak? Unlike the previous day, the sun is shining but, regardless, Father carries his long umbrella with the wooden handle. He swings it out in front of him as he strides, tapping it down beside him with a thud.

'I'll introduce you to everyone in the office first,' he's saying. 'I know you've met some of them before, but it's been a little while. And then I'll get you settled at a desk.'

I'm only half listening. We've just walked past Rendezvous Records and I pause outside. The shop isn't open yet but even through the closed doors, I can smell dust and coffee and the promise of music. For a moment, I press my nose against the glass as I try to make out the window display from the gloomy interior. There's a record player, a haphazard pile of records and a –

'James!' Father's voice cuts through my thoughts. 'Keep up!'

I pull myself away from the window. Part of me – well, most of me - is utterly furious with my father for making me work for him. But alright, I can't help also thinking about the golden promise of money at the end of the week. Money for cigarettes, money for beer. And money to get me onto Eelpiland so I don't keep having to swim to the damn place.

In the office, I'm introduced to a succession of nameless, faceless people, made drab and grey by their surroundings. Finally, I'm taken to a corner desk and Father rummages around in a drawer and pulls out a mountain of paper.

'Now,' he says as he licks his forefinger and leafs through the pile. 'What I want you to do is go through this lot. These are all the details of people who have applied for mortgages in the past six months. I need you to get all their personal details – name, address, telephone number, company and write the information in here.'

He thumps a large, hard-backed book onto the table and hands me a fountain pen. 'Does that sound like something you can do?'

I can detect a faint note of sarcasm and I glare at him, aware that in the past twenty-four hours my face has been almost permanently set in a scowl. But I don't care, particularly if I'm wearing my sunglasses.

'And these,' Father continues, as with one smooth swipe he removes the shades, 'you *won't* be needing in here.'

I consider standing up right now and leaving. I can't deal with this and I certainly don't need to be patronised. But then, there it is again, the image of a packet of Embassy Filters, with one cigarette artfully pulled up above the rest, ready and waiting to be placed in my mouth. This sudden longing pulls me back to the present moment and I even manage to force a smile on to my lips.

'No problem.'

'Super, super,' Father says, taking the lid off the fountain pen. You can break for lunch at one. Half an hour should do – '

'You said an hour, remember?'

'Did I?' Father looks at me absently over the top of his spectacles and then shrugs. 'Fine. Take an hour. There's a sandwich shop around the corner.' He counts a couple of coins into my hand. 'You can go and eat it on Twickenham Green. No point going home.'

I nod and stare at the fountain pen between my fingers and then at the pile of papers on the desk. Oh God, this is too much like…*school.*

At the end of the day, Father counts two shillings and sixpence into my hands. Bloody slave labour.

'Good job,' he says, smiling at me more warmly than I've ever seen. I don't smile back. To say I feel depressed is an understatement. Just one day of filling in personal details into a large black book and it's like my soul has been ripped from my body and wrung dry.

I telephone Charles in the evening.

'Hard luck, old chap,' Charles commiserates, his words conferring sympathy, but I can hear the smirk in his voice.

'I can't go back for another day, I just can't.'

'Think of the money.'

'I've almost spent it all on cigarettes.'

'Well…' Charles breathes down the line heavily, 'think of being able to smoke them all.'

'I've *already* smoked them all.'

There was a pause. 'Look, why don't we meet at Rendezvous Records tomorrow during your lunch break? Surely that will kill the monotony of it a little?'

I brighten at this thought. An entire working day with nothing to break it up is dire, but half a working day with an entertaining interlude will certainly help move the hours on a little.

I slam the office door shut and sprint as fast as my legs will carry me on to Twickenham High Street. I push past shoppers and one old lady with her shopping trolley who glares and calls after me;

'Watch where you're going, would you?'

I glance back over my shoulder.

'Sorry!'

Reaching Rendezvous Records, I stand for a moment with my hand against the warm handle, head leaning against the door. Then I push it open and walk in. It's hot, dark and smoky inside and it takes a little while for my eyes to become accustomed to the gloom after the bright glare of the street. Charles is in the corner, scrutinising a box of records through his dark-rimmed glasses, one side of his shirt hanging out over his trousers. I stare at my friend and breathe a sigh of relief.

'Christ, it's good to see you,' I say as I walk towards him.

'God, you *must* be desperate,' Charles replies, grinning toothily.

'Found anything good?'

'Look at this beauty.' Charles reverently pulls out a Jefferson Airplane record and holds it at arm's length. 'Surrealistic Pillow. Hmm,' he raises an eyebrow. 'Good name. Let's listen to it.'

We hand the record over to Len at the counter who always lets us hang around for as long as we like. He raises his suede-jacketed shoulders an inch and lets them fall. 'Which track?'

Charles turned the record over and scans down with his finger.

'Ha. Track three. My best friend.' He turns to me and grins, digging me in the ribs. We squeeze ourselves into the tiny booth and put the headphones on. Charles pulls a packet of cigarettes from his pocket, places two in his mouth and lights them both before handing one to me. We nod our heads to the music, occasionally catching each other's eye and bursting out laughing.

'I follow your dreams, do you know what I mean?' Charles croons. *'Oh, you're my best friend.'*

I return to work in far better spirits, humming the Jefferson Airplane song. But the minute I step inside the door, Father looms up in front of me.

'What time do you call this?'

'I don't know. I don't have a watch.'

'You've been gone an hour and a half.'

I sigh impatiently. 'Look, I don't have a watch, I just told you that, Father.'

He walks past me and stands at the doorway to my office, then nods his head briskly. 'In here. Please.'

I grimace and walk slowly into the office. Father shuts the door behind him then turns round.

'Please don't call me Father in front of other people here.'

I look at him blankly. 'Why not? Everybody knows you're my father.'

'That's not the point.' He walks round the desk and sits down. 'It's unprofessional.'

I cross my arms and lean back against the door. 'Right.'

'Right. Well…' Suddenly Father looks flustered and begins to move paper around on his desk. 'Let's get back to work, shall we?'

I continue to lean against the door, surveying him through narrowed eyes.

'You do realise, *Father*, that as long as you insist on treating me like a child, the longer I shall keep acting like one?'

It's as though he hasn't heard me. He's looking at me, or rather through me, but his deep-set, blue-grey eyes have a distracted look about them as he continues, with his hands, to shuffle the paperwork on his desk.

'Work,' he says absently, pointing to the door.

I continue to stand there a few moments longer, idly wondering if we have ever had a two-way conversation. I can't recall one, so I suppose it's unlikely. Sighing deeply, I turn, walk through the door and head back to my desk.

Chapter Four

'I've made your favourite, Jimmy. Vesta beef curry.'

I'm sitting at the kitchen table, legs pulled up so I'm cross-legged. I've got one hand in my pocket where I can feel the rough edges of the opened pack of cigarettes. I wonder what Ma would say if I lit up in the kitchen.

'Brown sauce, tomato sauce or mustard?'

I wonder if she really would be beside herself with rage, or not mind all that much. After all, she sometimes smokes at home.

'Jimmy, love? You alright?'

I swivel round in my chair and stare at her moodily.

'Mmm.'

Ma opens the cupboard door, extracting all the sauces and walks over to the table and lays them down. She ruffles my hair.

'You've not been yourself these past few days. Is it the work with Dad? It can't be that bad, surely.'

I look up at her with pleading eyes. 'Ma, it's *dire*.'

'Dad says you've been doing ever such a good job.'

I grunt. 'A five year old could do what I'm doing.'

Ma smoothes her hands over her apron and brushes a curl

of dark hair away from her eyes, ringed with grey eyeliner. She's pretty, my mum. Not beautiful in an Audrey Hepburn kind of way but curvy and attractive. I know that for her age, she looks good. I've inherited her thick, dark hair and blue eyes and for the umpteenth time, I feel thankful I got her genes rather than Father's. Standing behind me, she plants a kiss on the top of my head and walks back to the cooker where she eases open a tin of peas and begins to hum.

The front door bangs and both of us turn our heads at the same time. I look back and stare morosely at the sauces in front of me as I hear Father hanging his coat and hat up.

'Hello, love!' Ma calls out amidst the sizzle of frying beef.

Father walks in and rubs his hands. 'That smells capital.' He pecks Ma on the cheek and hands her a brown paper bag. 'I popped into the bakery on the way home and bought these for our dessert.'

'What are they?' Ma smiles.

'Well, open it and see.'

I don't turn, but I can hear the rustle of the bag as Ma opens it. 'Oooh, iced buns!' She exclaims. 'What's the occasion?'

'We're celebrating. Because I thought it was about time that we took a holiday. The three of us.'

My shoulders stiffen.

'Do you hear that, Jimmy? A holiday!' Ma says as she walks to the sideboard and takes out one of the best plates with gilded flowers around the edge. Carefully, she eases the iced buns on to them.

Father pulls up his shirtsleeves and comes and sits down at the table. 'James here has been working hard, haven't you lad? And besides, it's been a very long time since we went away.' He reaches behind him where his pipe and tobacco sit beside the iced buns and places them on the table.

'Don't start smoking now, dear. We're about to eat.'

'Ah,' Father chuckles and puts them back. 'I've been told, then.'

I can't quite decide whether he is more detestable in jovial or bad mood. Ma hums as she spoons two large heaps of Vesta curry on to two plates and a smaller amount on her own before piling up fluffy white mash beside it and heated peas from the pan.

'Have some of mine, Ma,' I say. 'You've given me way too much.'

'I won't, thank you Jimmy.' She pats her waist. 'This is plenty for me.' She places the plates on the table and walks round to the other side, pulling out a chair. 'Where were you thinking to go, love?'

'Do you remember that splendid place we went to near Calais? How about going there again? The forecast is looking good for the next few weeks. We could do some walking and fishing. Get some lovely French food and fresh air into us. It'll do us all some good.'

Two pink spots appear on Ma's cheeks and she flushes with pleasure. 'That sounds just marvelous.' She looked at me, and smiles. 'Doesn't it, Jimmy?'

I stare at her imploringly and then turn my eyes back towards my plate of food.

'Doesn't it?' she says again and I can feel a pressure against my foot beneath the table.

'Yes,' I manage to mumble.

'Good,' says Father. 'Then it's all settled. I shall make some phone calls in the morning and book something up for a couple of weeks' time. Shall we get a caravan like last time?'

'Yes, let's,' says Ma, passing the brown sauce over.

'Capital,' he says as he gives the bottle a hard wallop. 'Just capital.'

After forcing down the iced bun, which now sits solid as a rock in my stomach, I escape at the earliest opportunity up to my bedroom. Closing the door, I hurl myself down on the bed and lie with my face in the pillow. Going on holiday. With my parents. To a caravan near Calais. For an entire week. As the facts begin to slowly sink in, I feel like weeping. As if my summer holidays haven't got off to a bad enough start already, and now this?

'Fuck,' I say out loud. 'Fuck, fuck, fuck.'

I pummel the pillow with my fist and move my head back and forth. Rolling on to my back, I stare up at the ceiling and the large poster I've tacked on to it of Bob Dylan with his guitar. I stay there for a while, hearing the sound of my parents' laughter floating up the stairs, drumming my fingers on my chest. And then, a thought flashes into my head, or rather a word, quick as lightning, and then it's gone again.

I sit bolt upright and swing my legs over the bed. Padding over to the desk where I do my homework, I push up the wooden lid and rummage around inside. Finding a book and pulling it out, I hurriedly turn to the index and bring it close to my nose. Frowning, I fling the book to the floor, walk across the room and open the door quietly, pausing at the top of the stairs to ensure Ma and Father are still talking downstairs. I creep into their bedroom, the evening sunlight spilling in through the open window. In the corner of the room is father's bookcase, a heavy, dark wood antique filled with immaculately dusted books. I crouch down and scan through them, running my finger along the spines. British Birds...Military History...Garden Shrubs...Aha! World Atlas. Carefully, I ease the vast, heavy book from the shelf and sit with it resting against my legs. I turn it over and open it from the back, scrutinising the index. Matala. There it is! Page fifty-seven, C7. Flicking impatiently back to the atlas's interior, I start whispering *Matala, Matala, Matala* under my breath until it sounds like a mantra. I look closely at the map and there it is, Matala, nestled on the southern coast of Crete, jutting out into the Libyan Sea.

I am grinning stupidly down at the map, but at that moment I hear Father's voice nearing and realise that he must have left the kitchen. I close the atlas and jam it back into the bookshelf before scurrying out of the bedroom. As I approach the door, I meet Father at the top of the stairs. We stare at one another.

'What were you doing in our room?'

'I...it was stuffy in there so I opened the window. See?' I can feel a smile spreading across my face and point to the opened window, the breeze pushing the lace curtain back.

Father eyes me suspiciously. 'Hmm,' he grunts as he walks past me.

Twenty minutes later, when Father is watching Coronation Street, his feet up on a footstool, I tiptoe downstairs to the kitchen where Ma is still tidying up.

'Ma,' I say quietly. 'I'm just popping round to see Charles.'

'Really?' She turns to look at me affectionately. 'Why do you have to go now?'

'I won't be long, Ma.' I peck her on the cheek and hurry

out of the back door before we can get into more of a discussion about it. I light a cigarette outside and, unsteadily holding the bike with one hand, wheel it through the back gate on to the road. Once there, I pedal frantically, swerving out into the middle of the road so that I'm almost run over by a Morris Traveller, until I reach Twickenham High Street. Two minutes later and I've reached a red phone box. I jump off my bike, lean it against the side and pull the door open. I feel in my pockets and pull out a few coins then lean my head against the black chrome receiver and close my eyes. 'Greece Here I Come' I whisper. 'Greece Here I Come. 7813.'

Opening my eyes, I slot a coin into the machine and dial the number. A woman's voice answers the phone.

'Twickenham 7813?'

Instinctively, I stop slouching against the side of the telephone box and stand ramrod straight. 'Oh. Hello. Could I speak to John please?'

'John? Who's calling?'

'It's…er, it's Jim.' I twiddle with the cord. 'Please can you tell him that we met at…' But she's already gone, and I can hear the woman calling John's name in the background.

'Yep?'

'John. Hi, this is Jim. We met at Eelpiland.'

There is a long pause and I think I hear a yawn stretching down the line. 'Hello?'

'Yep, yep. I'm here. I'm just trying to remember – '

'Last Saturday, you remember?' I twist the cord nervously in my hand. 'You shared a joint with me and my friend, Charles.'

Another pause and then, 'Oh, yeah, yeah, I got you, man. What's up?'

'Well.' I take a deep breath. 'You know you were talking about that place, Matala, about how you might go there. So, are you still going to go? You know, hitchhike?'

'To Matala?'

'Yes, to Matala. Crete.'

'Oh man,' John sighs. 'I'd love to, but I've got no money.'

'But you said – '

'Forget about what I said. I was pretty stoned that night.'

I rest my head against the back of the phone box. 'Right. So you don't think you'll be heading there this summer?'

'No. Maybe next summer, but maybe not. I don't know, man, I don't – '

I hear a small bleep-bleep and realise that my money is running low. I fish about in my pocket for another coin. 'John. Wait a minute, I think my money –' And then the low, dialing tone cuts in. Slamming the receiver back down, I kick out at nothing in particular and push the door open.

The lights of the high street have come on and I can smell fish and frying chips. Without giving it too much thought, I jump on my bike and pedal as fast as I can round to Charles's house. His father opens the door. He's bald and stocky with a cobweb of thin red veins running across his cheeks and a perpetual expression of bewilderment.

'Ah, James,' he says, raising his eyebrows.

'Evening, Mr. Adams. Is Charles in?'

'Yes, he's here.'

'Would you mind if I came in, just to talk to him quickly?'

'We shall be having our supper shortly but certainly, come in for a few moments.'

I walk in, closing the door behind me. Charles is sitting cross-legged in an armchair, his glasses slightly crooked and his nose in a book. Despite the warmth of the air outside, it feels cold inside and smells of something old and dead whilst at the same time there's a scent of cloying sweetness. Something like tinned sponge pudding and custard. I shudder and at the same time, Charles looks up in surprise.

'Jim! What are you doing here?'

I glance at Mr Adams from the corner of my eye before looking back at Charles and grinning. 'Oh, just thought I'd pop round and…and…'

Charles raises an eyebrow, understanding that this isn't just a social call. 'Come and help me fix my bike, would you?'

'Supper in five minutes, Charles.' His Father sits down and picks up his newspaper. Charles nods and we walk towards the back door.

'What's that funny smell in there?' I hiss.

'What smell?' Charles looks over his shoulder.

'That…I don't know what it is. Something smells rank.'

Charles pushes the back door open and walks outside, then pulls himself up to sit on the wall. 'It's probably old books, dear boy. Or just books. Something you know very little about. Anyway. To what do I owe this pleasure?'

I shrug and fish in my pockets for my cigarettes. 'Just wanted to say hello.'

Charles leans down from the wall and removes the cigarette from my mouth. 'Not here, *mon ami*. My mother will smell it and have a hissy fit.'

I glower at him and push the cigarette back into my packet.

'Anyway,' Charles says as he kicks one leg against the wall. 'Out with it.'

'With what?'

'What you wanted to talk to me about.'

'Isn't a friend just allowed to come round and say hello?'

Charles gives me a withering look. 'You have approximately one minute, my friend, until you're booted out.'

'Right.' I knot my eyebrows and turn so that I am squarely facing him. 'The thing is, see –' I spread my hands out in front of me. 'You remember that place, Matala?'

Charles narrows his eyes. 'Oh *Christ*, not this again.'

'Wait. Hear me out, would you?'

I push a leaf around the backyard with my foot. 'Well, I've decided I'm going.'

'You're going?'

'I'm going. And I'm going to ask you one more time to come with me.'

Charles rolls his eyes and stretches his arms above his head lazily. 'I've already told you, Jim. I'm not going. And I don't believe you are either.'

I stop pushing the leaf and glare up at Charles, jutting out my bottom lip. 'Why won't you come? What have you got to do the entire summer?'

'I'm going on holiday with my family, remember?'

'Yes, but that's not till right at the end of the holidays. The last week, you told me.'

Charles sighs. 'Did you call those blokes…what were their names – '

'John and Doug. Yes, I did phone John.'

'And?'

'They're not going anymore.'

'Ha!' Charles jumps off the wall. 'And neither am I. You're on your own, Jimmy boy.'

I start to feel my resolve slipping. I've never been further from home than Calais and the thought of hitchhiking all the way to Greece on my own suddenly feels daunting. Insurmountably so. I try another tack.

'Listen, Charles. We only need go for a week, then we can come home again.'

Charles bursts out laughing. 'You are a tosspot, Jim. It will take at least that to even get there. The *very* least.'

'Alright, alright, two weeks. Come on Charles, I don't want to do this on my own. It'll be an adventure. It'll be amazing.'

'What, hanging out in some commune with a load of overgrown beardies eating grapes and beans? No ta.'

At that minute, Charles's mother pokes her head around the back door. 'Charles, supper's – ' All of a sudden, she spots me. 'Oh, hello James dear…I didn't realise you were here. Would you like to stay for supper with us?'

'Hello Mrs. Adams. No thanks, I've eaten already. I'm just leaving.'

She smiles and nods at me before vanishing back round the door. Charles starts making his way inside. He turns and looks at me.

'So when are you planning to depart on this adventure of yours?'

I shrug sulkily. 'Dunno. Soon, though. I can't take this job for much longer.'

'Ah,' Charles nods his head knowingly. 'That's what all of this is about Escaping from something rather than going *to* something.'

'No,' I snap. 'That's not it. It's not *just* it, anyway. The way they were describing that place…it sounded magical. Aren't you even a little bit curious?'

'Curiosity killed the cat, my friend.'

I exhale loudly, my shoulders drooping. 'Just tell me you'll think about it. Promise me that.'

He opens his mouth to say something and I hold a hand up to silence him. 'I said, just *think* about it. Surely that's not asking too much.'

Charles laughs as he grabs my arm. 'Sure, sure, I'll think about it,' and he pushes me through the door.

By Tuesday afternoon, I've had enough. I've been working for Father for seven days and I can't take it a moment longer. I cycle home, fling down my bicycle and push against the back door. It's locked. Ma must be out. I turn and walk to the small garden gnome with the secret compartment in its arm where the spare key is kept. I fish it out, scowling at the gnome's inane grin and kick it over so that it lies forlornly on one side.

There's a box of Viota Cake Mix poised on the kitchen work surface, presumably for Ma to make for a teatime treat. I suddenly feel a profound irritation. I don't *want* her cakes, I want her *support*; for her to stand up to Father and to back me up more. I sigh. I know that's just not the way she does things. And actually, they are bloody good, her cakes.

I bound up the stairs three at a time and open my bedroom door. My desk has been tidied immaculately with my pens and pencils evenly spaced and perfectly arranged. I walk over to my bookshelf and pull out a heavy Latin grammar book. I open it up to reveal the hollowed-out section that I made when I was younger to conceal banned sweets and chewing gum. These days, I keep the little cash I have in it. I empty all the money on to the floor, adding the coins that I earned today. I kneel beside it, my hair falling over my eyes as I begin counting it out. It doesn't take long, for there isn't much, but once I've finished, I sit down heavily with my back against the bed and stare ahead of me.

The coins feel clammy in my hand I jump to my feet, dropping the money so that it spills all over the floor. Rushing over to the record player, I rifle through my collection and pull out last year's Simon & Garfunkel album. I place it on the turntable and drop the pin gently and a soft sound comes out. Turning up the volume to its highest level, I fling open the window, stretch my arms above my head and grin. To the sounds of *Leaves that are green*, I hurriedly pull my chair out from under my desk and place it beneath the wardrobe. Standing on it, I yank open the top cupboard, rummage around and pull out a small khaki backpack. I used to take it on scout camping trips when I was a child; it's been years since I've laid eyes on it and there is a film of dust covering the badges. I brush it off and cough and then throw it down onto the floor.

I'm not altogether sure what to pack, so just throw in some underwear, a pair of socks, one pair of shorts, one pair of trousers, a jumper, two t-shirts and a bar of soap as an afterthought. Then I fling the backpack on to my bed and hurry downstairs, eager to make use of the telephone whilst my parents are still out. I realise that my fingers are trembling as I dial the number, praying that Charles answers it and not his parents. I breathe a sigh of relief as I hear my friend's voice at the end of the line.

'Charles, it's me.'

'Bon soir, *mon ami.*'

'Shut up and listen. I'm going, tomorrow morning.'

'Where might you be going?'

'Matala. Crete. I'm going. I'm packed. This is your final chance. Will you come with me?'

'For fuck's sake, Jim. *Still?* You're still persisting with this?'

'No, *you* listen, for fuck's sake. I just wanted to phone and tell you, so that if you don't come, you're not wondering where the hell I've got to.'

There was a pause and then Charles says, 'What do the folks say?'

'I haven't told them yet. I'm – '

At that moment, I hear the key in the front door and the sound of Ma's heels in the hallway.

'Ma's home,' I hiss down the line. 'If you're coming, meet me at 6am at the station tomorrow.' And with that, I slam the receiver down.

I'm jittery all through supper, which we eat in front of the television watching *World in Action.* I barely touch my bangers and mash and keep tapping against the side of the chair with my foot until Father tells me to 'pack it in.' I'm filled with a nervous energy, both buoyed by my decision to go, but also nervous at the reaction I know it'll provoke in my parents. Ma's had her hair done today. Her gentle curls bob neatly above her shoulders and she's painted her lips pale pink, and keeps dabbing them with the end of her napkin.

Once the programme has finished and we have also sat through *Police 5,* Father switches off the television. Ma jumps up, carrying the dishes through to the kitchen and once she's back, Father beams at her.

'Well,' he says, grinning broadly. 'I've some good news.'

Ma leans against the sideboard, moving around the neatly stacked pile of her beloved McCalls magazines that she treats herself to every now and again. She looks so excited, so hopeful, and I feel a pang of guilt.

'The holiday is booked!' Father says, beaming at Ma and then at me. 'One week, Picardie Campsite, Calais. What do you think? It's about time we all had a holiday.'

Ma smiles, her white teeth flashing. 'Well, that's wonderful news, dear. Isn't it wonderful, Jimmy?'

I feel sick. I stare at Ma's discarded dinner napkin, which lies on the coffee table, smudged with pink lipstick. I consider whether I should just go and not bother telling them. At least then I'd have no need for this conversation. But no, I must tell them, I can't just disappear. I owe it to Ma, at least. I take a deep breath.

'I need to tell you something.'

Clearly, the way I say those words sound sufficiently serious to make both my parents look at me expectantly. Ma's fingers leave the cover of her magazines and she stands up straight. I'm aware that what I'm about to say will hurt her, and I feel bad about that. But I'm seventeen, I'm an adult, and I need my parents to know that they can't control my life. I feel certain that Ma will ultimately understand that.

'I...I...' I take another deep breath, my courage failing me, and then immediately feel furious with myself. 'I'm sorry, but I'm not coming,' I blurt out.

The silence that fills the room is deep and hollow and painful and my eyes flicker between both of them, waiting for a reaction. I'm aware of all the small sounds I can hear around me; the trilling song of a bird on the window ledge outside, a scooter whizzing past, the distant occasional drip drop of the leaky tap from the outside lavatory. And then Father does something that I'm not expecting at all: he laughs. Ma looks at him nervously and I frown. Why the hell is he laughing?

'You're not coming,' he repeats, his mouth curved into a wide, disconcerting smile. 'You have something better to do.'

I wedge my hands beneath me and sit on them, leaning forwards to try and gauge how Father is framing those words, because it doesn't really sound like a question. When he doesn't say anything else, I take a deep breath.

'No. Not better. It's just somewhere I want to go to. Only for a week or so…' I trail off as I stare into Father's expressionless face. 'Charles might come too,' I add hopefully.

'James.' Father's voice is quiet and even and it's unnerving me. I'd prefer it if he just ranted a bit and we had an argument of some sort and then got all this out of the way. 'Do you have any idea, any idea at all, how selfish you are?'

I raise an eyebrow.

'Your mother hasn't had a holiday in years. We've already talked about this. We are going on holiday to Calais next week and you are coming. This conversation is closed.'

With that, Father stands up and walks into the kitchen.

I follow him, Ma behind me. He has already sat down at the table and picked up *The Daily Mail.* He brings it in front of his face and opens it out into a double spread so that I can only see a tuft of grey hair sticking up over the top of it. I sit in the seat opposite and place my hands squarely on the table in front of me. I glance at Ma, standing in the doorway, who has a strange, contorted expression on her face. She looks back at me and, almost imperceptibly, moves her head from one side to the other.

I suddenly feel exhausted; exhausted by the constant battling with Father and with the fact that I'm having to deal with this kind of shit when I'm seventeen. The thought occurs to me that, if I give in and just go to Calais with my parents to sit on a cold, windy beach and play gin rummy in a caravan every night, would Father like me more? Would we get on any better; have the kind of father-son relationship that other people have?

As I sit at the table opposite him, I turn these thoughts around in my head. I try, I really *try* to envisage myself as the compliant son. But it doesn't work; the conclusion I keep coming back to is that, no matter what I do for Father, it'll never be good enough. No, I think. No, no, *no.*

'No,' I say out loud. 'This conversation isn't closed.'

Father keeps the newspaper up and a ripple of irritation surges through me.

'Father,' I say sharply.

He slams the newspaper shut and bangs it onto the table. His face is red and blotchy and his lips are pursed together.

'Father,' I say again, this time in a quieter voice. 'You never listen to me. You never talk to me. Not properly, not as an equal.'

'I am your father. I am *not* your equal.'

My hands curl into small, tight fists. 'That's what I mean. There you go again. I try to talk to you, to tell you what I'm feeling, what I want. But you don't listen to me. You don't care. I'm seventeen, this is meant to be a time for enjoying myself, for – '

'Who said this should be a time for enjoying yourself?' he counters sharply.

'*Love*,' Ma lays a hand over Father's, but he shakes it off.

'This is a time for studying, for passing exams and going to college and then getting a job. You have all these opportunities, James, and you squander them!' His voice is progressively getting louder and I can see a thin purple vein pulsating in his temple. 'When I was your age – '

I push my chair back violently so that it scrapes across the linoleum floor. 'But I'm not you!' I cry. 'I am *not* you. I'm me! If you treated me differently, if you respected me, even a little, I may feel inclined to come on your *stupid* holiday with you – '

'Right, that's it.' Father stands up, ramming his chair under the table. 'I want you to go to your room and have a good, long think about everything you have said to your mother and me today.'

'I'm not a child!' I hear my voice, high and shrill like a small girl's, but I don't care. 'And I'm not talking to mother, I'm talking to *you*!'

Father's bottom lip is quivering with rage. 'I…am going out.'

I dart round the table and stand with my back against the door. I have to finish what I've begun. 'Not until you hear what I have to say.'

Ma continues sitting at the table and she turns, giving me a pleading look. Father makes towards the door and then stops, his hands planted on either side of his waist, his face a contorted tangle of ugly frowns and lines. He doesn't say anything, so I continue.

'I know you don't support me in this decision, but I'm an adult. I am going to go on holiday without you.'

'Holiday,' Father sneers and his arms come up, crossing over themselves. 'And where precisely do you intend to take this holiday of yours?'

'Crete,' I reply. 'I'm going to Crete.

There is a long pause. Then eventually Father repeats the word. 'Crete,' he says slowly.

'Yes. It's a Greek Island.'

'I know where it is, for *Christ's* sake!' he spits out. I'm shocked to see that Father is visibly shaking. His long hairs that cover the balding pate have worked their way free and slowly, Father smooths them back over and turns so that he is facing away from me, arms still crossed.

Ma takes the opportunity to stand up from her chair and move over to me. She grasps me around my wrists and stares hard at me, her lovely cornflower eyes wide and pleading.

'You,' Father says quietly, with his back still turned to us, 'are not going to Crete.'

I gently remove myself from Ma's clasp and walk towards Father's back.

'I am,' I say. 'I *am* going to Crete. I'm going tomorrow.'

Father swings around, his nostrils flaring and his fists clenched.

'Don't you dare defy me!' he shouts.

'I don't want to defy you!' I shout back as I square up to

him. 'I want you to support me! But you won't, so I'm going. I'm just going!'

'You're not bloody going anywhere. You hear me? You are the most disrespectful, the most selfish, rudest boy anybody has had the misfortune to be a father to! I…' He is quivering with rage, his face a strange purplish colour. 'I can't talk to you anymore. Get out of my way.'

My body is heavy and leaden and I would like to sit down and for Ma to put the kettle on and make us all a cup of PG Tips and for this conversation never to have begun. I realise that tears are forming in the corner of both eyes and angrily, I wipe them away.

'I'm going to Crete tomorrow, and you can't stop me.'

I think I hear it more than feel it, the swipe of a hand through the air and the clap of contact against my cheek. I'm not sure which part of his hand Father uses but I know that he has used a great deal of force, more force than I knew he possessed. For several moments, I feel nothing, but then a sharp sting flares up and I instinctively bring my hand up to my face. I hear Ma screaming, though I can't make out her high-pitched words, and the next thing I know she is running, standing between us. She's crying, a thin trail of black mascara smudged down her cheeks.

'Stop it!' she screams. 'Both of you, stop it! Haven't you hurt each other enough?'

I become aware of two things: firstly, it's the only time I remember seeing Ma cry. Secondly, I don't remember Father having ever touched me before this. Except…I blink twice, and there it is, the faintest cloud of a memory; not so much a picture of anything but the feel of the rough underside of father's chin and the smoothness of my bare legs against his cotton shirt. I can't remember ever sitting on father's shoulders but there it is, the imprint of a memory fading as quickly as it emerged. And now, making contact with him again after all these years, I feel obscurely elated. I keep my hand against my cheek, trying to remember the precise feel of Father's hand against my skin.

We stand there for some time, the three of us, not knowing where or how to move forward from this point; me with my hand against my cheek, Ma crying her silent, black-streaked tears and Father reeling in shock, holding his breath as he stares at me.

My other hand is tightly clenched, my finger nails, which need trimming, digging painfully into my palm. I would like to kill him at this moment, this man who fathered me. How *could* such a man father me? He is a monster, nothing more than an unfeeling, emotionally stunted monster. I am shaking, the anger building up from the pit of my stomach and threatening to burst out of me like a fire-spewing volcano. I don't know what to do with this fury, red-hot and violent. But I don't need to consider it for much longer, for moments later the anger recedes, hurling itself, spent, upon rocks like a waterfall at the base of a cliff. It is replaced with something quieter, an emotion far harder to understand; it is a slow, aching grief that almost cripples me in its intensity.

A grief for what? For whom? I don't know, but it's so powerful it feels as though all the light has been banished in me for evermore; sunlight blotted out by black clouds threatening rain and thunder.

What the hell is *wrong* with me? I'm going to cry, I can feel it coming, and this sadness that is welling up inside me is quite unlike anything I know what to do with. It goes far beyond the sorrow I feel at father's hatred of me; it's something deeper, but exists in a silent, closed place I can't get at. I need to leave this room now, before I break down in front of him. No doubt that would be satisfying, for him to watch me sob like a small child.

One hand drops from my cheek to my side, the other fist unclenches and I move towards the door that leads out of the kitchen.

Tripping up the stairs, three at a time, tears flow freely from my eyes. But it is not until I am safely in my bedroom, door closed behind me, that I let the caldera of grief erupt. Snot streams from my nose and mingles with the saltwater of my tears as I try desperately to regulate my breathing. At this moment, I hate them both. Even Ma: my good, beautiful Ma who has never been anything but kind and loving to me. But more than the hatred, the sadness has seeped into my bones and there is only one thing for it.

Wiping my nose with my sleeve, I pull my backpack on to my bed and rummage briefly through it, checking that my passport and everything else I'll need is there. I remember when we got my passport done when we went to Calais. Father told me to comb my hair for the photograph and look serious. But just to annoy him, I ruffled it up and grinned into the camera. I truly cannot remember a time when the two of us haven't been fighting one another.

I lie on my back and stare up at the dusky eyes and mournful face of Bob Dylan, wondering what *his* father was like, and if he ever hit him. The sadness has passed and I feel far calmer now, but I have no strength or will to move, even to get under the covers. At about ten o'clock, I hear Father going to bed and shortly after, I make out Ma's lighter footsteps on the stairs. I don't hate her anymore – of course, I never really did. I only wish she would stand up for me against that tyrant. How the two of them could *ever* have got together is simply beyond me. She walks towards their bedroom and then, pausing, comes back to my door and stands outside it for a few moments. Eventually, I hear a gentle tapping against the door and the handle being pushed down.

Ma has washed away the black streaks of mascara from her cheeks but she looks drained and her eyes are hollow. She doesn't say anything, just lays her hand on my ankle and slowly rubs up and down it.

'I'm sorry, Ma,' I say.

She pauses and glances up. The moon looks almost full outside and throws silvery light through the window so that the irises of her eyes seem brighter than ever.

'Sorry for what you said, or sorry for what happened?' she whispers.

'Sorry you had to see that,' I reply. 'It wasn't fair on you. I think it was building for a while, though.'

Ma smiles ruefully and draws her hands back into her lap where she starts to fiddle with her cuticles. 'How is your cheek?' she asks, without looking at me.

'I can't feel it,' I reply as it suddenly stings, as though it knows we are talking about it.

'I'm sorry your father hit you.'

I let out a small laugh. 'God Ma, you don't need to be sorry. It wasn't you.'

'Jimmy…' she says as she looks towards me again, her lips slightly parted. 'You didn't mean what you said, did you?'

'About what?

'About going to Crete? Were you just trying to vex your father?'

I sigh and push one arm back, settling my head into the crook of my elbow.

'No, Ma. I'm sorry, but I did mean it. I'm not going for long; it's just a little holiday.'

Ma closes her mouth and narrows her eyes.

'Don't go Jimmy. For me, don't go. If you do, I can't bear to think about how furious your father will be. I just can't bear it.'

I prop myself up on my elbows and look at Ma, sitting hunched on the side of my bed. Her shoulders are tense and her dark curls fall forwards on to the collar of her blouse.

'He…' I pause. It's the first time I've thought of this. 'He won't…*hurt* you, will he Ma?'

'What?' Her head jerks upwards. 'What do you mean?'

'You know, he won't…hit you or anything, will he?'

She laughs tightly, mirthlessly. 'My God, *no*. Your dad has never laid a finger on me in my life.'

I purse my lips. 'You promise?'

'I promise you, Jimmy.'

We are silent for a few moments as we listen to Father shuffling around next door in the bathroom.

'Why does he hate me so much, Ma?'

'What?' She stares at me, her eyes widening. 'Daddy hate you?' I haven't heard her call him that for years, and hearing it now I wince with discomfort. 'He doesn't hate you, of *course* he doesn't. You two needn't be at loggerheads all the time. Perhaps you're too similar – '

'We're *not*,' I say sharply. 'We're *not* similar. Please don't say that.'

Ma doesn't say anything, but reaches a hand out and gently strokes along the burning ring on my cheek.

'He shouldn't have hit you,' she whispers after a long while. 'Please don't go.'

She stares at me with pained eyes, and I take her hand from my cheek, bring it to my mouth and kiss it. I then curl in towards her, hugging tightly around her waist as I used to when I was a little boy as her fingers weave their way into my hair.

Chapter Five

I set the alarm clock for 5.30am, but when I hear the muffled bleeping sound from under my pillow, it steals into my dreams as the strains of a jazz band from Eelpiland. But after several moments, I stir, stretching out on the bed and burying my head into the pillow for another moment before fully comprehending that this is the morning of my departure.

It's still pitch black outside and I'm knackered. I was woken up twice in the night with father's yelling. Jesus, poor Ma, what the hell is he *doing* to her all these nights I hear him cry out? I never hear her voice, only his and it makes me feel sick to my core. This has been the backdrop to my nights for as long as I can remember – sometimes I don't hear him for weeks on end, but other times it seems like every night, the juddering shout of release that comes from the other side of my bedroom wall.

I shudder and fumble my way out of bed. I slept with my clothes on so I don't need to worry about getting dressed. Picking up my khaki backpack, I sling it over my shoulder. I slip my feet into my scuffed Chelsea boots and then, thinking better of it, kick them off and look for my sandals under the bed. Slowly and quietly, I open the door and creep out. I know that there is a single stair that creaks and, flattening myself against the wall, skip two steps and make it to the bottom barely making a sound.

The key for the back door is normally in the lock but it's vanished. I grope around the kitchen, looking in pots and on shelves but I can't find it. I tiptoe through the hall to the front door but once again, the key is not in its usual place in the basket. I frown and bite my bottom lip. Father must have hidden all the keys. For *fuck's* sake. I begin to make my way slowly up the stairs again, avoiding the creak, then back into my bedroom where I close the door behind me.

I walk over to the window and pull the sill up which makes a loud clattering noise. I wince and freeze, standing still in anticipation of the sound having woken my parents. But there is nothing and I peer through the window, over the roof and down to the pavement below. I am about to hitch my first leg over, when I suddenly think of something and come back. I open my desk, find a textbook and tear a piece of paper from it. Grabbing a pencil, I scribble on the note

Sorry Ma, love you. I'll write.

Then I hurry over to my bed, plant the paper in it and tug the sheets and blanket back over. I return to the window and, just before climbing out on to the roof and beginning my descent, pull the packet of cigarettes from my pocket. There is just one left and I light it, leave the empty packet on my desk and then carefully make my way down the drainpipe.

It's a chilly, drizzly morning and I wish I'd bought a warmer coat with me, but no matter. No chance I'm going back now. Reaching Twickenham station, there are a few people milling around, hunched in raincoats and hats, nobody making eye contact with one another. I move from one foot to the other, rubbing my hands to keep warm. I need another cigarette. I've got enough money to buy some but nowhere is open this early in the morning and I really need to be careful to make the money last all the way to Greece. I'm going to hitchhike the whole way down but still, I'll need to buy food.

I know Charles isn't coming and this makes me feel annoyed, sad and intensely nervous all at the same time. He's my best friend; *I* would have gone along with an idea of his and I just don't understand why he isn't prepared to forsake a couple of weeks of his summer holiday to do this with me. It's not as though he has anything better planned, plus he doesn't have a wanker of a father to make it difficult for him. I have no real idea how to hitchhike. Alright, fine, you just stick your thumb out and hope somebody will stop but then, once driving with them, is it the done thing to offer cigarettes or conversation? Do people *want* you to talk to them or don't they really care? Is it rude to just sleep?

I glance at my watch. It's five minutes past six. Ok, I'll wait five more minutes and then walk down London Road until I reach Chertsey Road, a main thoroughfare where I'll put my thumb out and...well, wait. But how I wish I didn't have to be waiting alone.

I can hear the early commuter trains pulling in and out and, when it reaches ten past six, I sigh, pull on my backpack and begin walking.

'Not going without me, I hope, tosspot.'

I spin round and there is Charles. Never, *ever* have I been so happy to see him, every single bit of him from head to foot, from the blond tufts of hair sticking up on his head down to his too-short trousers and mismatched socks. I almost fling my arms around him but restrain myself.

'Oh, yeah,' I say coolly. 'I knew you'd come.'

'*Well,*' Charles drawls as we begin to walk, side by side. 'I could hardly let a moron like you hitchhike on your own all the way to Greece. You'd probably end up in Spain by mistake.'

'Shut it, you tit,' I say as the corners of my mouth twitch uncontrollably upwards.

Travelling southwards, backpacks comfortably resting between our shoulder blades as though they have always been there, the days become warmer and the light more intense. After taking the ferry from Dover to Ostend, we hitch through Belgium and Germany and onto Yugoslavia, Charles insisting on calling it Yugoland.

He has thought of absolutely everything, this friend of mine, which is surprising considering how quickly he must have made his decision to come. Squirrelled away in the top compartment of his backpack is a strip of material that can be rolled and tied up. It consists of sections and contains cutlery and a tin opener. He also has with him – naturally – a tin mug and a water flask, neither of which occurred to me to bring. Plus there's the string bag that holds biscuits or tomatoes or some bread to snack on. *Christ,* have I come travelling with the most organised man on the planet? I can't deny it though, the further we travel, the more the string bag seems like a good idea so that my food doesn't get squashed amongst my clothes. As soon as I get the chance, I manage to buy one cheaply for myself.

For two boys from Twickenham who have only been out of the country a couple of times between them, it's impossible to know quite whether all this is what I was expecting or not. We see a lot of motorways; long stretches of road ploughing through interminable fields. But then we also drive through medieval German towns and impossibly beautiful countryside that is intriguingly foreign and most *definitely* not England. In Belgrade, we spend a night at the Youth Hostel, packed to the rafters with scruffy travellers like ourselves and a fair number of pretty girls which helps me to ignore the gripes of hunger from my stomach.

I'm hot, tired, bloody starving and deliriously happy. Why have I never thought to hitchhike before? What have I been *doing* with myself all these years? I love it all, every minute of it, even the strange-smelling food that looks and tastes nothing like Ma's. By the time we are nearing Greece, quite incredibly we haven't paid a penny for our transportation so far!

What this has meant is that we've had to endure countless journeys rammed up against sides of trucks with people who won't stop talking, or won't stop asking questions, even when I've been desperate to sleep. I even feel relieved on one overnight journey in northern Greece at sharing space at the back of a truck with several sheep! It smells bloody awful, but at least I can cease the relentless trickle of conversation that it seems hitchhikers are expected to impart. As my eyes pull slowly shut, the last thing I remember is a view of beautiful, craggy mountains and a sheep's arse pressed up against my shoulder.

Strange thing about this journey though, is that we're woken by the husband and wife team up front and taken to a local *taverna*, a squat, white building surrounded by vineyards, for dinner. As plump black chickens peck around our feet, we're served up with something insanely tasty called *souvlaki,* thin bread wrapped around meat, tomatoes, onions and parsley.

Charles and I are all ready to pay for it - it's our sole meal of the day - but then, to our utter surprise, our drivers insist on treating us! The mama keeps patting my cheek with her great big hand that smells of sheep's wool and chuckling away about god only knows what. Not that I mind; if we get a meal paid for, she can pat all she likes.

The further we travel, the more the villages, towns and cities become a blur of colours, sounds and smells as I remain fixed on our end destination. And yes I can't deny it, the name Matala has taken on epic, utopian proportions with each uncomfortable ride we've taken. Charles has behaved like a walking travel guidebook, pointing out each landmark we've passed complete with a potted history and cultural side note. How the bloody hell he knows all this stuff is anyone's guess. He's particularly excitable whenever we pass a Roman ruin, chattering non-stop about temples and architectural significance.

In Athens, we stumble across a strangely named little hole in the wall place called Niko's International Jetset Milkshop in the old area of Plaka where we eat one of the most delicious things imaginable that tastes even *better* than *souvlaki.* It's called *rizogalo,* a creamy rice pudding with cinnamon sprinkled on top. It's so damn tasty that Charles and I empty all our coins out on to the rickety wooden table in front of us, before throwing caution to the wind and treating ourselves to another.

The very friendly owner of Niko's tells us we are welcome to leave our backpacks in the basement whilst we explore. I'm just keen to get to Matala, but for the first time since we left Twickenham I'm not starving. Plus the narrow streets and red, sloping roofs of the houses are quite pretty so I agree to spending the night in a cheap hostel once we've had our walk. But no sooner have we begun than Charles ducks into the first grubby old bookshop he finds. I sigh deeply and follow him into the murky gloom, where he's quickly managed to find a paragraph about Matala in a pamphlet about ancient sites on Crete and reads out loud.

'Amazing!' he says, leaning back against a bookshelf, a cigarette dangling from his bottom lip. 'Listen to this... *When the god Zeus, disguised as a bull, arrives at the ancient harbour of Matala, he immediately kidnaps Europa, the Phoenician princess who goes on to give birth to the future rulers of Crete. It is also believed that...*'

'*Charles*,' I sigh, 'enough of your ancient history lessons. I feel like I'm back at school. Besides,' I add, hanging around by the door, eager to leave, 'you're in danger of sounding like a walking encyclopedia.'

Charles grins at me. 'Compliment taken. *Efharisto*.'

Then he wants – of course, to visit the Acropolis but at this, I put my foot down. '*Fuck's* sake, Charles, we're not doing the cultural tourist sights of Europe, you know. We're going to the caves.'

'Yes,' he replies dryly, 'so you keep reminding me at every opportunity. But why not enjoy the sights en route? When's the next time we'll be here?'

'I don't know, that's my point entirely. That's why we need to get there as quickly as we can.'

'What's the rush, my friend?' Charles takes off his spectacles and cleans the thick lenses on the back of his shirt. Then he looks up at me and smirks. 'Sorry, I forgot. The summer is marching and you still haven't got laid.'

I lean back against the wall, my backpack supporting me and close my eyes to the warmth of the sunshine. 'Yeah. Right. That's all it's about. Getting laid. Anyway, I've certainly got further than you have.'

'That's what you think.'

I open one eye against the glare of the sun to gauge my friend's expression but Charles's face is an impenetrable mask of nonchalance. I know I don't need to worry about competition from him on that front. Yes, Charles may have been first in line when God was handing out the brains but physically – I view him lazily through one open eye - with his thick spectacles and ill-fitting, old-fashioned clothes, we're *leagues* apart.

During the journey, Charles and I don't talk much about our parents. I once mention that my old man had been none too pleased about my decision to go to Crete, turning my face away from him as I speak. Charles, on the other hand, says that his parents didn't mind too much, as long as he promised to take extra care, as Greece has recently undergone a military coup and is now under a dictatorship. They told him that we should keep our heads down and not get into trouble.

'Of course we won't get into any trouble,' I scoff.

Charles raises an eyebrow.

'According to the military government, it's probably

illegal even staying in caves. The *junta* sounds pretty repressive.'

I burst out laughing. 'Don't be ridiculous. It's a free world, Charles.'

He just shrugs and looks away. 'Not as free as you might think. Anyway, we'll soon find out what the situation is there, won't we? As long as I'm back for the last week of the summer, I don't mind *what* we do.'

I feel a stab of envy. Alright, so my friend's sitting room may smell like ancient, rotting books but how is it that Charles's family are so…well, *straight forward* whereas I have to deal with a bullying, out-of–touch father and a repressed mother? Every time the image of my parents comes to the forefront of my mind, I push it away, lingering only for a couple of seconds on the pain I know Ma will be feeling at my absence. It's in Athens that this thought of Ma eventually pushes me to write to her – *and* Father.

I buy a dusty postcard with a picture of the Acropolis and two people, in oddly heavy suits, staring up at it in the glaring sunshine. I borrow Charles's stubby pencil and scribble on the back:

Hi Ma, Hi Father.
Charles and I have made it to Athens.
About to leave for Piraeus where we'll take a boat over to Crete.
Weather is hot.
Love Jim.

I chew on the end of the pencil, then scribble out Jim and write James. That's what Father always calls me; maybe he'll be less annoyed with me if I use the name I was christened with. The two of us wander around looking for a post office but, having no luck, decide to head to the port and look again there. I wedge the postcard into a flap of my backpack. The realisation that we will be in Matala the very next day hits me afresh and I feel insanely, deliriously happy. The fierce midday sun beats down on my head and as we stand on the roadside, waiting for a lift, I lift my face to the sun and close my eyes, smiling into the heat. *This*, I think, is life.

Charles is tugging at my arm.

'Come on,' he calls. 'Someone's stopping.'

I slowly open my eyes, savouring the moment, and as I jump into the back of a pick-up truck, the postcard dislodges and floats away.

'Hey! Your postcard,' shouts Charles, pointing towards it. But it's already gone, the dust churning up in the widening road behind us.

'Fuck it,' I shrug. 'I'll write another one when we get there.'

The ferry crossing from the mainland to Iraklion is half empty. From what I can make out, Charles and I are the only non-Greeks on the boat and, as I lean out over the ferry railing, the warm wind blowing in my hair, I can hear the click of ceramic beads on a long piece of string being turned over and over by an elderly man sitting behind us. I'm mildly concerned that the money Charles and I have between us is rapidly decreasing and the ferry crossing cost more than we hoped. Perhaps we can get a job in Crete for a couple of days, picking grapes or something like that.

Once in Iraklion, we find a lift without too much difficulty, in the direction of a village called Mires, in a beat-up old pickup. Our driver, a tiny, wiry man with dark, burnished skin and startling green eyes, speaks surprisingly good English. After regaling us with tales of an English girlfriend he once had, he wants to know where we're heading. When Charles tells him it's Matala, he turns and stares at us so disapprovingly, and for so long, that he starts making me nervous. Particularly as he's meant to be looking at the road. He starts muttering in Greek and pulls in just outside Mires, rather than driving us all the way in.

'What's he saying, Charles?' I whisper.

He shrugs. 'Not the foggiest.'

We climb out of the pickup, shouting our thanks after the hastily retreating driver as we are left in a thick cloud of scorched roadside dust.

'Did I say something wrong?' Charles asks as he looks at me.

He fishes about in his pocket and lights a cigarette for us to share.

'Who knows?' I say, 'but it seems not everybody approves of Matala. Even better!'

We snort with laughter, then begin walking the few hundred yards into Mires. From the village centre, we manage to find another lift heading south in a small truck with a burly man without a word of English. I let Charles do the talking. I learnt, fairly early on in our hitchhiking journey, that whilst I may have the charm, my friend undeniably has a greater flair for foreign languages. Coming into Matala, whilst I am jolted about next to the thickset driver with the bushiest moustache

I've ever seen, idly trying to count up in my head how many lifts we've hitched since leaving Twickenham, Charles is thumbing through a Greek phrase book. As he peers shortsightedly at it, continually pushing up his spectacles that appear to have a loosened screw, he speaks a few words then looks up, grinning triumphantly. The truck-driver roars with laughter and plays with the ends of his moustache before thumping Charles on the knee.

'What did you say?' I ask.

'I told him that Crete is very beautiful.'

I grunt and push myself up in the seat as I stare out at the rugged landscape. Beautiful? That's not the word I'd use to describe it. The hills are rocky and barren with barely a tree in sight and the earth looks parched, everything baked dry by the relentless sun. It could do with a bit of English rain here. Not that I mind the heat. I stretch out lazily and look at an old man with a straw hat we pass on the track, shepherding several goats. He is dressed in a manner I have never seen in my life, with a dirty white shirt over baggy, black trousers and leather riding boots, replete with sleeveless jacket, embroidered elaborately with flowers and leaves. He looks like an eccentric combination of wild-west cowboy and medieval peasant. Our eyes lock and I think he's waving, but then I realise that he is just shielding his eyes from the sun as we pass by.

The sky is a fiercer blue than I've ever seen in my life. There's the occasional puff of white cloud but this aside, all I can see is an unbroken band of sky. As the truck moves over the bumpy track I'm pushed up against the driver. I recoil from the pungent smell of body odour, as it suddenly judders to a halt.

I peer over the dashboard. It looks like the track has come to an end. The driver motions for us to get out and we follow him. We are in a tiny little square of sorts, flanked by a few houses. A tiny chapel rests above them and there is an ancient-looking column lying at the side of the dusty road that a squealing pig is tethered to with rope. The driver points and our gaze follows his outstretched hand.

There, in front of us, is the most perfect horse-shoe bay fringed by the calm ocean on one side and pale yellow sandstone cliffs on the other. The three of us stand there for some time, just staring at it, until the driver breaks the silence by saying something in Greek.

'Oh!' Charles says, fishing about once more for his phrase book.

I slam it shut. 'For Christ's sake, put it away. Let's just say thank you and go.'

Charles shoots me a look and pumps the driver's hand vigorously up and down. '*Efharisto, efharisto.*'

The driver grins and put his hand out. Charles' face falls a little, before he reaches into the top of his rucksack and pulls out half a packet of cigarettes. The driver seems happy with this, nodding at us one last time and making his way back to the truck.

'What are you *doing*?' I say, aghast, once the driver has closed the door. 'I can't believe you've given him our last smokes!'

'Jim,' Charles says patiently, as though talking to a small child, 'you do realise that man brought us out of his way? He was very kind to us, and he didn't need to be.'

'How do you know that?'

Charles pauses. 'Because I managed to decipher it from

my phrase book when he picked us up. Look – '

'I don't want to look, I believe you, mister Greek scholar.' I roll my eyes.

'Anyway, I'm sure there must be somewhere round here that we can buy some more…' His words trail off as he scans the horizon at all sides. Then he turns to me and smiles broadly and as he does so, I notice that his face looks a little different. His skin is warmer and he has a few freckles along the bridge of his nose.

'You've caught some freckles.'

'So have you,' Charles points to my arm.

'These aren't freckles, my friend. This is a deep, dark tan.' I stretch my arm out to admire the colour my skin is turning.

Charles chuckles. 'Yeah. Right,' he says as he turns back to face the caves and the sea where we can see a few fishing boats bobbing up and down on the swell of the waves. 'We've made it to Matala.' We walk together to where the track turns into a path, lined with cacti.

'Yes,' I say. 'We've made it to Matala!' I feel giddy with excitement but then consider the fact it's early evening and we've not eaten anything since breakfast. 'I'm famished,' I say.

'Me too,' says Charles, and we begin to make our way towards the caves.

Chapter Six

The sun has just begun to dip below the horizon but the air is still warm with a gentle breeze that buffets up from the sea. As the cliff face becomes clearer, we see caves stencilled into the walls. Small figures are moving around on the paths in front of them, and lower down on the beach. We stop walking at the same time and just stand there and stare, taking in the scene.

'Christ,' I breathe, 'would you look at that?'

'It's fantastic,' says Charles. 'I've never seen anything like it. I feel like I've been transported back thousands of years.'

'I hope there's a spare cave for us.' I turn to look at Charles who is staring at the caves and the bay with an expression of both amazement and excitement on his face.

'Only one way to find out.'

We both begin to move again, the warm wind at out backs. We instinctively reach down and pull off our shoes, letting our feet sink into the sand, still warm from the day's sun. Approaching the caves, we can see that there are several tiers and we make out more people milling around outside them, many of which have long lengths of material hung up to act as makeshift doors. Clothes are draped over string to dry in the sun and watermelon rinds are strewn on the beach. The scent of cooking wafts down and my stomach flips again with hunger. Anything would taste good right now. If anybody has spotted us, they certainly aren't paying us any attention and as we approach the bottom tier of cave dwellings, I shift my weight from one foot to the other.

'So, what do we do? Just poke our heads round and ask where to go?'

'Let's ask somebody,' Charles suggests and he points up a level to where we can see a small group of people sitting outside a cave.

We make our way slowly along the slippery, sandstone path and zigzag back on ourselves to where a group of four people are sitting. There is a primus stove in front of them with food bubbling in a pan and I realise that this is where the smell is coming from.

They all look up at us solemnly, eyes glowing out of their suntanned faces.

Three of them are boys, all bare-chested and wearing either frayed jeans or shorts. The girl is wearing an over-size shirt rolled up to the sleeves, her long dark hair loose over her shoulders.

They are all just staring at us, no hint of friendliness in their faces, which confuses me. Why aren't they saying anything? It's not as though I was expecting a welcome committee to be lining up to greet us, but at least a smile or two.

'Just arrived?' the girl eventually asks.

'Yes,' I say. 'We got the ferry over from Pireaus today.'

She nods and there is a long pause. 'Well...you want a room with a bath?'

At that, all of them burst out into hysterical laughter as though the funniest joke has just been told. Charles and I glance at one another and join in nervously, waiting for their laughter to subside. Now they know we've just arrived and the tension appears to have broken, they might offer us some of their food but another boy continues stirring the pot and no further words are offered.

Eventually, Charles asks 'So, do any of you know where the free caves are?'

The girl looks up at us with blue eyes. 'I think there may be one up at the top level.'

I wonder where they're from; judging by the accent, certainly not England.

'No,' says another boy. 'You mean the one Trixie and Jurg were in? That went two days ago.'

'No,' says the girl, shaking her head. 'I think not.' They begin to talk animatedly in their own language. Aha! German.

'So the answer is,' the first boy says, looking at us through his thick blond fringe, 'that we are not sure. There should be plenty. You can go see. Go look for yourself.'

Charles nods and begins to move away; I linger for a moment longer, staring at their pot longingly. Surely they will offer us just a small bite to eat? Realising that no offer is forthcoming though, I reluctantly nod at them and follow behind Charles.

We scrabble up, skirting the edge of the cave dwellings. I feel out of breath and tired. This walk, bloody difficult and steep, combined with my hunger, is making me feel irritable.

'I'm starving,' I grumble, pushing against my backpack that is slipping down over my shoulder. Charles doesn't say anything, just continues walking along the path, picking his way over rocks and round scrubby bushes. I stop and crane my head upwards. From what I can see, we're almost at the top level.

'At least we'll get a good view from up here,' Charles calls back.

'Well, that's if there *is* even a cave for us,' I mutter.

'Faith, *mon ami,* have faith,' Charles laughs.

'Yes, yes,' I retort. 'I'll have some faith as soon as I've got some food – '

My words trail off as we come to a sudden halt. We are about to walk up to the top level when we both see, at the same moment, a girl with her back to us, standing to the side of a cave entrance, hanging up a wet dress on a washing line. She is wearing a white bikini and her skin is tanned as dark as the Cretan earth. A rope of damp, dark blonde hair hangs down her back and droplets of water glisten against her skin. She hasn't heard us, but when she has finished hanging the dress up, she turns round and is about to walk back into the cave when she sees us standing there. She doesn't say anything, but brings one hand to her hip as she surveys us.

She is, most definitely, the loveliest creature I've ever laid eyes upon. I didn't know, until this point, that any human being could *be* that perfect, so whole. I want to tell her that; to let her know that she is more beautiful than any other woman on earth and that she deserves everything she has ever wished for. But I just stand there, gaping at her.

Charles eventually breaks the silence.

'Hullo. I'm Charles.'

He moves over towards her and offers his hand, which she shakes. I hurry over and follow suit. Up close, she is even more astonishing. She wears a piece of string around her neck which has been threaded with tiny white shells and coloured beads, hanging loosely against her slender neck. Her eyes are not quite brown, not quite green, with flecks of gold in them.

'Well, hello,' the girl says, a trace of amusement in her eyes. 'I'm Chenoa.'

'Chenoa?'

'Yep. Chenoa' she repeats.

I pull my backpack down from my shoulder and run a hand through my hair. 'So…' I say, 'we've just arrived and we're looking for a spare cave. To sleep in.'

At that moment, somebody appears from the cave's interior, stretching and squinting as he emerges into the daylight. In stark contrast to Chenoa, he is dressed in dark trousers, a shirt and a cardigan. He has curly brown hair and his jawline is framed with a thick, unkempt beard. 'I thought I heard voices,' he says. He comes towards us and shakes our hands, which I accept tersely, irritated that Chenoa is sharing her cave with a man.

'Hey,' he says in a friendly voice. 'I'm Ray. You're newbies, right?'

We nod.

'We were just asking Chenoa about any spare caves that we could stay in. You don't know of any, do you?'

'Sure,' Ray says as he sits down on the rock in front of his cave and begins to pull on a pair of socks. 'There are a few.' He jerks his thumb upwards. 'Definitely one up at the top level. Not a fun climb up, particularly after a heavy night,' he laughs. 'But you get a great view from up there at least.'

'Brilliant, thanks,' says Charles, smiling broadly. 'We'll go and have a look.'

'Sure,' Ray says and grins back.

'Come on, Jim,' Charles says as he starts to walk back towards the path.

I linger, my eyes narrowing as I take in the vision of Chenoa once more framed against the black mouth of the cave, her skin glowing in the evening light.

'*Jim*,' Charles says again.

The spell broken, I mumble something and reluctantly turn away. As we begin to walk up the path, Ray calls to us.

'Hey, everyone's doing a big cook-up on the beach tonight. Come along. Meet some people.'

'We haven't got any food to contribute,' Charles calls down.

Ray stands up and stretches lazily. 'Don't worry about that. You can contribute another night. This is Matala, man.'

'Ok,' Charles calls. 'We'll see you later.'

I look back over my shoulder. I feel sure that, even with that brief exchange, something passed between Chenoa and me. I will her to look at me, but after wringing out her damp hair onto the warm rocks, she walks into the cave.

'For Christ's sake,' says Charles a few moments later, 'would you put your tongue away?'

'Did you see her, Charles? Did you?' I scramble up the rocks, optimism renewed.

'Are we talking about Chenoa? Because yes, as a matter of fact I did see her.'

'Charles, have you ever, in your *life*, seen such an image of perfection? Tell me the truth.'

'Oh *Christ*, Jim. Please, for twenty minutes, will you stop thinking about your dick and help me find this cave? It can't be this one, there are towels outside it. Oh no, hang on a minute, there's an even higher level…'

But I'm only half listening. I'm thinking about Chenoa's brown green eyes and glistening skin and golden hair. Never in my life have I felt such an instant attraction to a girl.

'Here it is!' Charles cries triumphantly. 'An empty cave. Our cave!'

There is a stick poking out from the ground outside the entrance and Charles pulls out a large checked handkerchief from his pocket and ties it to the stick. It flaps lethargically in the breeze. A few large stones half-block the entrance and we haul them away and peer into the dark, musty interior.

'It's pitch black in there!' I say. 'How are we meant to see anything?'

'Hang on,' Charles says. 'Let your eyes adjust.'

We stand there a few moments longer, then both of us step gingerly forwards as we begin to make out scratchings on the wall made by previous cave dwellers and dried, hanging flowers next to the stone tombs.

'Oh shit,' I shiver, 'it's creepy in here. I'm not sure I want to sleep in one of those.'

'This is incredible,' Charles says. 'Do you realise how old all this is? These are proper ancient tombs. They must be hundreds and hundreds of years old.'

I kick at a stone on the floor of the cave and put my backpack down. 'Seriously, Charles. I'm not sure about this. Maybe I'll sleep on the beach.' I raise both my hands up to feel the roof of the cave. 'You can't even stand up properly in here.'

'It doesn't matter. You don't need to stand up to sleep, do you?' Charles opens up his bag and pulls out a white sheet that he lays in one of the stone tombs. 'You did bring a sleeping sheet, didn't you Jim?'

'A sleeping sheet,' I repeat blankly. I was hardly in a position, given the difficulty of my departure, to worry about things like sleeping sheets. 'It's too hot for sheets.'

Charles shrugs as he pulls some candles from the top of his backpack whilst I edge gingerly towards the tomb closest to the cave entrance. I stretch a hand out and feel the hardness of it, wishing that there was a mattress there. How can I sleep in a lowered stone tomb? I shiver again and my stomach growls in protest at the lack of food it's received today, but then I think again of Chenoa and find myself smiling.

'Do you think Ray is Chenoa's boyfriend?'

Charles ignores the question and lets out a little yelp. In the corner of the cave he has found a book lying face down, the spine creased and well-thumbed pages turned down at the corner in many places.

'Wow, it's *The Agony and the Ecstasy*. This is meant to be amazing. What luck.'

'What is it?' I ask.

'Michaelangelo and the Renaissance.'

'Hmmm. Sounds fascinating.'

'Yup,' Charles says. 'You can read it after me.'

'Thanks ever so. Perhaps I can use it as a pillow. So, what do you think? That Ray is Chenoa's boyfriend? Funny name that, Chenoa.'

Charles pulls out the last few items in his bag, neatly folded socks and pants falling on to the cave floor.

'Christ alive,' I say. 'Did your Ma iron all your things and then pack for you?'

Charles raises an eyebrow. 'Nope, I did it all myself. And yes, I imagine Ray and Chenoa are an item. They're sharing a cave, aren't they?'

'Yes,' I reply testily, 'but just because they're sharing a cave, doesn't mean they're a couple.'

'Uh-huh. Jim, may I give you some advice?'

'Advice on girls from Cassanova himself?'

'Advice from somebody whose life direction isn't entirely guided from his nether regions and can therefore see a little more clearly. You're not going to win any hearts by panting over someone. Play it a little cool. Get to know someone first.'

'Thank you for those wise words, Charles. I forgot what a sage you can be.' I pull out my money from my bag. 'Do you think our stuff is safe in the cave?'

'What,' scoffs Charles, 'all the riches we possess? It'll be fine. Everyone's in the same boat here, aren't they.'

'Yeah, but what about this cash?' I place it back into the bag and put it at the head of the bed.

'It'll be fine. This is Matala, man.' Charles impersonates Ray's twang and we both laugh.

'Right,' I say. 'Let's head down to the beach. God, I can't remember the last time I've been this hungry.'

On the sand, near the foot of the caves, somebody has started a small fire. From the tiny village – well, you can hardly even call it a village, it's just a scattering of low, white-washed buildings – some gaslights shine against the darkening sky on the other side of the bay. I can see the Germans and a few other people but no sign of Chenoa or Ray yet. One girl has a fish on the end of a long stick and she's holding it over the fire, turning it occasionally. Beside the fire, a pan bubbles on a primus stove and a boy sits beside it, shelling beans before dropping them in. I peer into the stove; all I can see are tomatoes and the beans but it smells like heaven itself.

'Smells good,' I say.

'Tastes even better,' the boy at the stove says. 'And we have fish tonight, so it's a feast fit for a king. You two English?'

Charles and I nod. 'Me too. Robert.' He holds out a hand and we shake it.

'You been here a long time?' Charles asks as we sit down in the sand.

'Too long,' Robert says, 'but as you'll learn, Matala is a hard place to leave. How long are you two planning on sticking around?'

'Just a week,' Charles says, 'then we have to get back.'

Robert laughs uproariously as though Charles has just told the most hilarious joke. 'A week! I'd like to see you try to leave after just one week.'

I grin. 'That's what I've tried to tell him. It's not going to happen.'

'What do you have to get back for, anyway?'

A levels, I think. Family holidays, Charles is probably thinking, but neither of us says anything and just shrug and smile. A few more introductions are made and I dig my hand into the sand and pull it up, letting fine golden grains run through my fingers.

Before I know it, a bowl is pushed into my hands. I look

for a utensil, but realising none exists, dip my fingers into the bowl and pull out the beans and tomatoes. I want to eat slowly, to make the food last, particularly as the portion isn't large, but it's impossible and I spoon the beans into my mouth with thumb and forefinger as though my life depends on it. Never in my life has food tasted so good. Charles has started to chat to other people around us but my attention remains steadfastly on the bowl.

As the warmth and energy of the food begin to seep into me, I feel myself physically relaxing. The moon is up, half full, and I look up at the cliff face of caves, illuminated by the moon's glow. A bottle of wine is being passed around, people taking long, deep swigs from it. Someone has started to play the guitar. I'm smiling; those boys on Eelpiland were right, this place is a utopia. Perhaps I'll stay forever. Who says I need to go back for my final year of school? What place do A Levels have in today's society anyway? As though Charles has been infiltrating my thoughts, I hear him mentioning the word 'utopia' to a small group of people beside him. I tune into the conversation.

'It comes from Greek roots and means 'no place,' Charles is saying. 'But Sir Thomas More coined the word utopia.'

'Who's Thomas More?' asks one person.

'Thomas More? Oh, he was a fifteenth century philosopher. But he wrote a book called 'Utopia' which outlined the ideal island nation.'

'That's what it is here!' another person says with long hair covering his eyes that he keeps pushing back.

'Yes. But ultimately, his perfect society can't be realised.'

'Sure it can,' the first person says.

'It can't,' Charles says, 'because…'

I tune out again. Charles, the ultimate fount of all knowledge, information and wisdom. I notice, with a twinge of something close to irritation, that more people have drifted towards him and are listening intently to him expounding on Utopian societies. But this thought evaporates as quickly as it arrived when I notice Ray and Chenoa picking their way across the beach.

Chenoa is wearing a long yellow dress, offsetting the colour of her skin and she has tied her hair into two long plaits that hang loosely over the dark shawl around her shoulders. She's at the far end of the group and hasn't seen us, but I can't take my eyes off her. Is this how it is, to fall in love? I've often wondered how it would feel, the moment of falling in love, and whether it would be clear right away.

Whilst Charles continues hypothesising, I ponder how and when I can remove myself and make my way over to her. Perhaps Charles had a point earlier; that I shouldn't come on too strong. I know I have a way with girls but even so, because I really like this one, I should play my moves very carefully. I just watch her, barely blinking. Ray produces a spoon from somewhere and then he passes a bowl of food to Chenoa. I can't hear from where I'm sitting what she's saying, or what is being said to her, but at one point she throws back her head and laughs with wild abandon, her white teeth gleaming in the moonlight and her shiny blonde plaits slipping like silk over her shoulders.

Once it looks as though the food has been finished, people get up and drift around, some of them moving nearer to the fire, others sitting closer to the guitar and a few more moving down to the edge of the sea to dip their toes in. Ray has stood up and moved away a little from Chenoa as the guitar is handed to him. This is my opportunity. Jumping to my feet, I skirt the edge of the group and make my way to where Chenoa is sitting. I run a hand through my hair and sit down beside her.

'Hi,' I say.

Chenoa looks up at me and brings her shawl back around her shoulders. She smiles.

'Hey. Charles.'

'Jim.'

'Jim. That's it. Enjoying your first evening in Matala?'

'It's incredible.' I pause. 'Just like Thomas More's utopia.'

Chenoa's shawl has slipped again, revealing one smooth shoulder. I want more than anything to lean over and kiss it.

'Who's Thomas More?'

'Oh, a Latin philosopher.' I shrug, keen to steer the conversation to something else. 'Where are you from in America?'

'I'm not from America.' Chenoa's amber eyes narrow and she cocks her head on one side, surveying me.

'You're not?' I say, caught off-guard.

'Nope,' she replies, not offering a further explanation. My mind races as rapidly as it can to geography lessons at school and the world map. Well, if she isn't from America, then surely it has to be...

'Canada!' I say triumphantly.

She raises an eyebrow and then looks away, feeling for her cigarettes in the sand beside her.

'Smoke?' she says.

I nod and she takes one from the packet and hands it to me.

'I don't have any matches,' Chenoa says.

'Wait a minute,' I reply as I pad down to the fire and stretch my arm holding the cigarette out towards it. I can feel Chenoa's eyes on me and I smile to myself. Once lit, I walk back and sit down. I hold the lit cigarette out towards her and Chenoa reaches forwards, bringing the tip of her cigarette to mine. As she inhales, she looks upwards and our eyes meet. I want to hold this moment, but she pulls away, leaning back on her elbows.

'So your name,' I say. 'It's Canadian?'

'It's native Indian. My grandparents were from the Iroquois tribe.'

I nod knowingly. That would explain the dark skin. I wish that she would ask me a question, but Chenoa seems quite content leaning back and smoking her cigarette.

'Have you been here a long time?' I ask before inhaling deeply on the cigarette which, even to me, is strong.

'A month or so,' she replies.

'Did you come with Ray?' I ask, trying to make my voice sound as neutral as possible. A flicker of amusement crosses her face.

'What you want to know is whether Ray is my boyfriend.'

'That's not what I asked – '

'But that's what you want to know, right?'

I look away and tap my cigarette on the sand so that small pieces of ash dislodge and roll over the ground towards the fire. I can feel Chenoa's eyes on me.

'How old are you?' she asks. I look back up, startled by her question. She has a challenging smile on her lips and I sense that a great deal is riding on my answer to this question. I take another drag on the cigarette and hold her gaze.

'Twenty,' I reply. 'You?'

Chenoa grinds her cigarette out in the sand. 'Twenty-one. But it's my birthday next week.'

'It's my birthday next week as well; actually, in two days!' I gush, and immediately regret it.

'So you'll be twenty-one?'

I nod. 'Yes.'

I dig my feet deep into the sand, still warm from the day. I glance at Chenoa who is smiling at me in a strange way. At the same time, we hear vigorous blues chords coming from the guitar and look round.

'That your friend?' Chenoa asks.

'Yes.'

'He's good.'

'Uh-huh.' Whilst she isn't looking in my direction, I use the opportunity to edge a fraction closer to her. I notice that she's wearing an anklet made out of tiny shells and there is a small scar running across her big toe.

'So. You didn't answer my question. About Ray.'

Chenoa pulls one of her plaits over her shoulder and fiddles with the end of it as she looks thoughtfully at me.

'He's not my boyfriend. I don't do boyfriends.'

'You've never had a boyfriend?' I ask blankly.

Chenoa's forehead puckers into a slight frown as she grinds her half-finished cigarette into the sand.

'I'm not into…' she pauses, waving her hand through the air, 'committing myself to one person. And neither is Ray.'

This time it's my turn to frown. Is she saying then that they *are* a couple, just not an exclusive couple?

'Right,' I say. 'I see what you mean.'

'You do?'

I shrug. If it means that she's a free agent, I don't really care whether she and Ray are officially together. 'I suppose so.'

Chenoa smiles at me then; a warm, open smile in which I read encouragement and possibility and I feel giddy with excitement. We are silent for a few minutes, listening to Charles playing the guitar on the other side of the fire. He has begun to sing too; it's the song of the moment, Bob Dylan's *Blowin' in the Wind*, and I muse that I've heard Charles play the guitar a great deal but rarely sing. Something else he's irritatingly good at. But then I look back at Chenoa who has leant her head back into the sand, a small smile on her lips, and I know that I have her attention, so nothing else at this moment really matters.

I consider that I actually have a chance with this girl. I can't quite believe it, but I do. I know it. There is nowhere else on the planet, nowhere at all, that I would rather be at this moment. I'd kill for a little more wine and I think about my lack of cigarettes and money in general.

'Is there anywhere near here I can do some work? You know, earn a bit of money.'

Chenoa takes a while to answer; her eyes are closed and I wonder for a moment if she has gone to sleep.

'Sure. A group of guys go a few times a week to pick tomatoes. You could go with them. Or there's always the olive cannery in Timbaki where you can earn a bit more. But it's quite a hike over there. No money?'

I shake my head.

'Me neither.'

'So how do you buy food? Drink? Cigarettes?'

Chenoa props herself up on her elbows and pulls the band out of the bottom of one of her plaits.

'Ray still has some he saved up from back home. But otherwise...' Her voice trails off and she pulls out her other plait and brings her fingers up through the crinkled golden waves. 'We forage a little, or rely on Mother Nature.' She points her chin towards the sea. 'Or other people's generosity, of course. Did you see Mama's Bakery?'

I shake my head.

'It's up that way.' Chenoa points to an indiscernible speck in the distance. 'Mama is an angel. I've lost count of the number of times she's let me have something and just written it down in a book when I don't have any money.'

'She can't be running a very profitable business,' I say, grinning.

Chenoa stretches her arms above her head and stifles a yawn. 'Yeah, well you know what they say. What goes around, comes around.'

I don't want Chenoa to be tired. I want to sit up with her all night long and talk and hear the lyrical music of her voice and watch the graceful movements of her beautiful limbs. I try to think of a way I can trap her.

'How long do you think you'll stay here?' I blurt out.

Chenoa doesn't answer for a while and I wonder if she's heard me. I'm about to repeat the question when she begins to murmur from the sand. 'Your friend. Charles, isn't it? He's good.'

I feel the same stab of irritation re-surface. Can't Charles just stop playing the damn guitar for a minute?

'So what do you think? About how long you'll stay here?'

'No fixed destination,' she says lightly. 'No plans. And in the meantime, I'm having fun hanging out here. This is where it's at. I mean, look at this place.'

I dutifully survey my surroundings. The crescent bay, the gentle dip of muted moonlight playing on the waves, the bleached-white sand. The greys and browns of Twickenham feel a million miles away, as does my father, thank God. Chenoa begins to softly sing along to the tune Charles is playing at the far end of the gathering and I know I'm losing her again and blurt out the first thing that comes to my mind.

'What do your parents think about you being here?'

Chenoa opens her eyes slightly, two green almond-shaped slits framed in her heart-shaped face. 'My folks? They didn't care much for my decision to travel. But I'm an adult. And they're a different generation. They're the guilt generation.'

'Guilt generation?'

'Yeah.' Chenoa sounds more awake now and she pushes herself up slightly on her elbows. 'Yeah, they had to go through all that shit in the war. And we don't have to deal with that. We have all these freedoms and liberties our parents never had, but they can't deal with that. They want to keep us close. Watch our every move. Make us suffer somehow, just because they had to suffer.'

I chew the inside of my mouth and look around to see if the bottle of wine is still doing the rounds. 'I know what you mean,' I say.

'You do?' She's sat fully upright and is staring at me intently. At the same time, without even taking her eyes from mine, she gives a little wave to the side of her and, like magic, a cigarette materializes between her fingers. Mesmerized, I watch as her mouth makes a perfect oval shape and she inhales deeply after the cigarette is placed between her lips.

'Of course. My old man gave me hell for coming here.'

Chenoa's head moves to one side as she contemplates this. 'And what did he do during the war?'

I blink, my body tensing. 'Dunno.'

She raises an eyebrow, smoke flaring through her nostrils like a golden dragon.

'What I mean is that he's never told me a thing. I bet he's never even told my mother.'

'Oh, c'mon.'

'I'm serious. I've never known anyone so repressed. And even if he weren't, he has his head shoved so far up his own arse that he doesn't relate to anyone around him. He's an idiot.'

Chenoa laughs, a light jingle of delicate bells and I laugh along with her but as I do so, grains of discomfort shift within me. I think of my father's nocturnal shoutings and his face of bitter fury when I told him I was coming to Crete; the sting of his hand against my cheek. Not *now*, I think angrily, don't start thinking of him, for Christ's sake.

Chenoa lies back down in the sand and pushes her hair out beneath her to both sides so that it frames her head like a halo. As she does so, she pushes her fingers out towards me, cigarette wedged between her thumb and finger. I take it from her, noticing the thick silver ring around her thumb and letting my fingers linger on hers for as long as she lets me.

I take my chances and lie down in the sand beside her,

thinking about Charles's words that I should play it a little cool and so make sure there are a couple of inches of sand between us. I wonder if this is the happiest I've ever been in my life. Away from my parents, free to do whatever the hell I want without people telling me I can or I can't and lying next to the most beautiful girl on the planet on a white, sandy beach.

Chenoa wants me to kiss her, I'm sure of it. As I lie there, my head reeling from the smoke and the music and...just *being* here, I try to gather my wits to think about the best way I can approach it. I really can't afford to mess it up with her as I sense that she's not the kind of girl to stick around if that happens. But at the same time, I don't want to miss my chance. I glance down and see that her arm is a mere inch from the fingers of my right hand. I could stroke gently up and down the inside of her wrist, I think hazily. That, surely, will turn her on. But just as I am about to do so, Chenoa sits bolt upright.

'Jim!' she exclaims. I frown and unsteadily heave myself up on my elbows. 'Jim!' she says again. 'Let's swim!'

'You want to...' I mumble, but before I know it, she has jumped up from the sand. I realise that I've been so engrossed in this conversation that I've failed to notice that many people have left the group and run into the waves. Some are in their underwear whilst others are clearly naked. I laugh out loud as my eyes scan around for Chenoa. She is standing a couple of yards away and I catch sight of her at the very moment that she lifts her dress over her head and drops it on the sand beside her, a pool of yellow against white. My mouth drops open as I watch one dark, slender leg push the dress away. She is wearing pants and a bra but

I watch as Chenoa hooks her fingers behind the clasp against her back and with one swift motion, the bra falls to the sand. Without even looking back, Chenoa strides towards the water, her hair floating behind her.

I gulp. I have to go. Right this minute, before somebody else jumps into the sea with her. Fumbling with the buttons on my trousers, I push them down hurriedly, accidentally pulling down my boxer shorts at the same time. I pull them back up and then, thinking better of it, push them off again, tripping as I remove them.

'Fuck it,' I mutter, pulling my t-shirt off from over my head as I tear down towards the waves.

The water is deliciously warm. It is nothing like swimming in the sea in Calais or in the Thames. At first I can't see Chenoa as there are several other people nearby in the water, splashing about. I spot her hair first which gleams in the moonlight and I swim up to her, just as a surprisingly large wave catches me unawares and crashes over my head. I swallow some water and cough, rubbing the salt from my eyes at the same time. When I bring my hands down, Chenoa is a yard in front of me, bobbing up and down in the water like a celestial, unearthly mermaid. Her hair fans out on the surface of the water and once I've caught my breath, I can just make out the curve of her breasts, the swell of the waves occasionally revealing the top of her nipples. I feel myself go hard and am relieved Chenoa can't see this.

She's smiling at me, but it isn't a smile I can easily read, or one that is inviting me to make my move. Dammit, I'm normally so good with girls but what is it about Chenoa that is so elusive? True, she's a little older than me but that only adds to her allure. I move closer but she begins to laugh, her teeth flashing and her hair streaming out around her. I frown and take another step towards her, intending to grasp her around the waist but before I know it, she has vanished beneath the water, her legs kicking out last above the surface of the water before two graceful feet are also submerged.

Caught unawares, I thrash about in the waves, waiting for her to come up. But I suddenly feel two strong hands grasping both my ankles and pushing them apart. I can feel her, beneath me, swimming between my legs and, as she does so, her hair, a whisper of seaweed, tickles against my inner thighs. Stop right there, I pray, but no sooner have I felt this sensation than it vanishes along with Chenoa. I turn about in the water, this way and that, straining my eyes against the dark night sky and the string of lights in the village at the far side of the bay. I can hear laughter and the chords of a guitar still, the gentle murmur of waves moving into the shore. But I'm interested in none of this. She's playing with me. She wants me to follow her. But where in God's name is she? I stay in the same spot for a while, hoping that she will materialise from amongst the few dark shapes that remain in the water

I swim closer to the shore and that is when, to my surprise, I catch sight of her, yellow dress damp and clinging to her skin as she wrings out her wet hair. She is standing with Ray, joking and laughing in a way that certainly wouldn't suggest she'd just swum between my legs and sent me into an agony of longing. I suddenly feel a dull throb at my temples and think that I need to go to bed, if you can possibly call that cold, hard tomb a bed. But there is no chance I can sleep in this state. As I edge out of the water, I feel far more sober and self-conscious of my nudity than when I went in, but I'm relieved that nobody, not even Chenoa, seems to be looking in my direction.

An old record player has materialized from somewhere, cranking out Greek music that a few stragglers are dancing drunkenly to beneath the stars. Perhaps Chenoa will want to dance? Pulling on my boxer shorts, I scan the diminished gathering for Charles, but there is no sign of him. As I'm putting my t-shirt back on, I notice that Chenoa and Ray have started to move away from the group and are heading in the direction of the caves. I hang back for a couple of minutes, dressing myself, and move towards them, away from the music that floats across the sand as I follow the two sets of footprints: one large and the other small but firm. I plant my feet into Chenoa's prints as I re-live that sensation again and again, the delicate brushing of hair against my inner thigh. Christ, this girl is playing hard to get.

I don't want Ray to see I am following them, so when they begin their ascent up to the caves, I hang back again. As soon as they turn a corner, I hurry after them, my trousers bunched up in my hands as my legs are too wet still to bother putting them on. Just before Chenoa and Ray reach their cave, in desperation I pick up a small pebble from the track and throw it gently at Chenoa's back. She spins round, eyes narrowed and then relaxes when she sees it's me. Chenoa gives me a questioning look as I place a finger against my lips. She turns back to Ray, who is about to walk into the cave.

'I'll come in a minute, I'm just going to hang up my wet clothes,' she says and I stare at the outline of her lovely body in the dim light, the dress hugging each and every contour.

Once Ray is inside, Chenoa walks back down the track towards me.

'Jim. Hey. Your cave is that way.' She jerks her thumb upwards.

'I know,' I reply. 'I know it's that way.' I feel numb with longing and with nausea and wish I could think of something clever to say. But no words come, and so I step towards her and with one swift motion place my hands on either side of her face and kiss her, pushing my body against hers. But she clasps my hands and pushes me gently away.

'Whoa, boy!' she says. And she begins to laugh again, that same beautiful, mocking laugh.

'What are you...I thought you...' I stammer.

Chenoa doesn't say anything, but continues to laugh.

'Why are you laughing at me?' I ask in a small, petulant voice that I immediately regret.

She waves a hand through the air dismissively. 'I'm not laughing *at* you. I'm just laughing.'

'Yeah, I can see that. Why?'

'Because...' Chenoa trails off and places one hand on her curved hip as she surveys me, face suddenly more serious. 'Because...you're funny.'

I run my fingers through my hair and frown again. 'Funny.'

'Yes. Funny.'

I try to think of something I can say in return to this, but before I know it, Chenoa has taken a step towards me and is kissing me lightly on the lips. Despite my surprise, I lean in towards her, trying once more to draw her into me but again, she stops. She places both her hands on my chest and pushes me away.

'Chenoa – '

She places one finger against my lips and narrows her eyes

that glimmer like a cat's in the dark.

'See you tomorrow,' she whispers, and before I have a chance to say another word, she slips into her cave.

As I run up the path towards the upper level caves, I feel charged with energy. She likes me. She definitely likes me. She kissed me. She and Ray aren't an exclusive couple, whatever the hell that really means. I actually have a chance with this sea-nymph.

It's pitch black up here and, stubbing my toe on a rock, I curse out loud. How in God's name am I meant to be able to find my bed – my tomb – when there is no light to be found? I suddenly remember that I should have a box of matches in my back trouser pocket. Groping in the darkness, I am relieved to discover they haven't fallen out and as I strike one, a thin yellow flare illuminates the dim mouth of the cave. Gingerly, I step forwards and make out Charles's feet at the end of one of the tombs. I'm about to say something when I hear a loud snore echo round the cave. His mouth is wide open and his glasses are perched crookedly on his face. Across his chest lies *The Agony and the Ecstasy* and I see he's covered by a thin sheet.

The match burns down to the end, reaching my fingertips and I drop it, cursing. I light another one and hold it in the direction of the other tomb. I grab my sleeping bag from the floor and roll it out on the bed, slowly swinging my legs over. Christ, it's uncomfortable. I lie back, arms crossed over my chest and then, dissatisfied, turn over, my nose pressing against the rocky side. This is surely the most uncomfortable sleeping arrangement imaginable. The thought of these being tombs, most probably with fragments of ancient human bones scattered around makes me shiver, despite the stuffiness of the cave. But even so, the grin won't leave my face. As sleep tugs at me, all I can think is Chenoa, Chenoa, the beautiful Chenoa.

Chapter Seven

When I wake up, I'm sweating. I am still fully clothed and half of my sleeping bag lies across me. My head pounds. My back hurts (I really must look for some straw or leaves or something to soften the tomb). My breath stinks and my mouth is dry; I open and close my mouth a few times, wishing I had some water. Which makes me wonder, where *do* you get water around here? I heave myself upright and glance over at Charles's bed. Empty. Trust Charles to be up early. He's probably doing some archaeological excavation or testing his Greek out on the locals.

I make my way uneasily to the cave opening and the fierce heat and sunlight crashes down on me, making me wince and take a step back into the cool darkness. I'm wearing boxers and a t-shirt and, whilst idly wondering where my trousers are, the previous night comes back to me. Chenoa. She kissed me. I shake my head in amazement but a crack of pain splices through it and I groan. I really, really need water. Right, I think. First, water. Next, something to eat and then I'll look for Chenoa.

I turn back into the darkness of the cave's interior and open my backpack to look for some shorts. I pull out a pair that I cut off from some jeans last summer that are definitely on the tight side for me. But no matter. Possibly even better. Pulling my sweaty t-shirt off, I drop it on the floor and step back outside. This time, I stand in the full sunlight and allow myself to become accustomed to the temperature and brightness. The sun is already high and, as the warmth begins to tingle against my chest, I stretch upwards, eyes closed and fingertips reaching high. God, that warmth feels good. I smile into the sky.

Opening my eyes, I see several people down on the beach, either lying out on the sand or swimming in the sea. From somewhere, I can hear the bray of a donkey and the sounds of laughter. Matala. There is nowhere else I'd rather be. Just as I am about to begin the descent towards the beach, I hear a noise and am greeted by Charles rounding the corner from the steep slope.

'Jim!' Charles cries. 'You finally decided to get up!'

'What do you mean, *finally*?' I counter testily. 'What time is it, anyway?'

'About midday. It's sizzling down there, I need some shade. I'm coming up to read in the cave.'

'You mean you got some sleep in your tomb?'

'Of course. Surprisingly comfortable, I thought.'

I grunt, then notice that Charles is holding a bottle of water. 'Oh, thank God!' I say, prizing it out of his grasp and downing the entire bottle in one.

'Well, that's charming that is,' Charles says. 'I just went and filled that.'

'Sorry, I was parched. Where did you fill it?'

Charles motions me forward. As we stand on the rocky outcrop, he points towards the tiny village.

'See that narrow track there....no, not that way. Go left, over there. Well, keep following the trail and there's a small shack there. See it? That's Mama's. Brilliant woman. Hilarious. All wild hair and barely a word of English. She's selling everything over there. From what I could make out, she was saying that the travellers are the best thing that's ever happened to her. Anyway, the single tap I have seen is near that. Oh...' He digs into his pocket and pulls out a packet of cigarettes that he throws to me. 'I bought some cigs too. You can buy the next pack.'

Charles blows his fringe up from his bottom lip. 'God, it's hot. I need to get my hat on.'

'Isn't it great?' I say.

'I hope you've got suntan cream on,' Charles continues, walking towards the shade of the cave.

'*I hope you've got suntan cream on*,' I mimic. 'Christ, you sound like my Ma.' I turn my face up towards the sun and close my eyes. 'I don't need cream, ta.'

'Yes you do.'

'Don't be ridiculous. It depends on your skin tone. My skin's far more olive than yours.'

'Right,' Charles says as he walks into the cave to fish around for his hat. 'Whatever you say.'

I saunter over to the mouth of the cave, and lean against the side, pensively blowing out a smoke ring.

'You seen Chenoa this morning?' I try to ask with as much nonchalance as I can muster.

Charles emerges triumphant from the cave with a beige, wide-brimmed hat on his head.

'God, you look a prick.'

'*Enchanté*,' Charles grins. 'What did you say earlier?'

'I said, have you seen Chenoa this morning?'

Charles raises an eyebrow. 'The gilded mermaid? No, I haven't. You still haven't managed to put your tongue away, have you?'

'Well.' I crouch down and sit cross-legged in the sunshine. 'It just so happens that she's definitely into me.'

'Oh yeah?'

'Yeah. We had a bit of a…a bit of a …' I shrug and run my fingers through my hair. 'Well, a bit of a *thing* last night, if you really want to know.'

Charles applies more suntan cream to his arms and laughs.

'Congratulations, Jim. Your charms must be paying off.'

I glare at him. *Christ*, it's hot. The temperature must be well over 100.

'Yes,' I reply. 'Must be. Any girls you like the look of here?'

'Jim,' Charles says slowly as he smears cream over his nose and rubs it in. 'I do realise this is almost impossible for you to comprehend. But I'm not here for the girls. I mean, great, if I meet one I like. But I'm not looking. I'm here to enjoy myself and to have a unique experience.'

I narrow my eyes against the sun's glare and ponder for a moment, before shrugging.

'Yup. You're right. Impossible to comprehend. Anyway, I think I'll go for a swim. That water looks damn inviting. Care to join?'

'No, thanks. Too hot for me in the middle of the day.'

I roll my eyes and reach for my towel that is hanging over the string outside the cave.

I spend the afternoon lying on my back in the sea, letting the strong sun beat down upon my chest, looking up every now and again to cast my eyes around the beach for Chenoa, but no sign. When I tire of the sea, I return to the cave to find Charles sitting in the shade, reading his book and eating some olives and slices of watermelon he's managed to get from God only knows where. He gives me a few slices that I devour – it's not enough, but thankfully the heat is making me far less hungry than normal.

By the time we reach evening, tanned and relaxed, I think to myself that I could *definitely* get used to this life. The only slight issue is money, which I don't have enough of. I head to the beach as the sun is setting, leaving Charles deeply involved in his book. As I sit on the sand, a long-haired man with a ring in his nose who I recognize from the evening before comes and sits beside me.

'Man,' he laughs. 'You're looking raw!'

'Raw?' I ask.

'Red raw,' he replies. 'You just come from England, right? You need to go easy with those rays.' The man pokes one finger into my forearm that is suddenly looking a little less tanned and a little more sunburned, and as he brings his finger away, a white circle forms on the skin where the finger had been.

'Ouch!' I say.

The man laughs again. 'Exactly. I'm Ardhendu by the way' and he reaches out his hand which I shake tersely.

'Ardhendu,' I repeat blankly.

'Yeah. It's my Hindu name. It means half-moon. My

guru Sri Ravi Satnam gave it to me a few months back in Benares. So, every half moon is when my aura is aligned with the moon and I have the most energy. The rest of the time, I just need to preserve it.'

I nod uncertainly. 'And what's your real name?'

Ardhendu shakes his head. 'Don't use it anymore.'

I feel a kernel of irritation in the pit of my stomach.

'Yes. Clearly. But what is it?'

Ardhendu shifts and laughs. 'Relax, man. It's Terrence, if you really want to know.'

'Ok, Terrence.' I dig my fingers into the sand and look up at Ardhendu's face that now has the makings of a frown etched across it.

'Hey, man. I just said, I don't use it anymore.'

'Uh-huh.' I'm losing interest in the conversation and look around behind Ardhendu to see if there is any sign of Chenoa yet.

'You're with that Charles dude, right?' Ardhendu presses on.

'Mm-hmm.'

'He plays one mean guitar,' Ardhendu says, admiration gleaming in his dark brown eyes. 'You play?'

I shift and pat my shorts pockets to see if I have brought the cigarettes down with me, grimacing when I find none.

'Yeah,' I lie. 'A little.' And then thinking better of it, in case I should be asked to play later, hastily add 'Well, maybe not as well as Charles. He's the musician, I'm the – '

'Sun-burned one?'

Ardhendu must have seen the look on my face because he lets out a peal of hysterical laughter as he claps me on the back, which feels horribly painful and well, raw.

'You should have just seen yourself. What a picture! I'm only messing with you, man.'

Right, I've had enough of this person now with his long, lank hair and ridiculous nose ornament. I crane my neck over Ardhendu's head and, to my relief, spot Charles picking his way over to the beach. Before he's approached us, Ardhendu's clearly had enough of me as well and, mumbling something about seeing me later, he stands and lopes off.

Charles is wearing a crumpled pale blue linen shirt and jeans and he is barefoot. His blond hair is damp and frames his face rather than sticking up like it normally does. He looks and smells fresh and clean and I stare at him in surprise.

'Don't tell me. You found an ancient Greek bathtub.'

He grins at me.

'Nope. Even better. I was lent a bucket and went to the pump. Same place where I got water. I took my soap along and had a grand wash. You might want to try it yourself tomorrow unless you don't mind…' Charles breaks off and makes a flapping motion beneath his nose with his hand, '…y'know. Stinking. For your birthday.'

'Ha. Funny,' I respond, still feeling irritated by the earlier conversation.

Charles sits beside me and pulls the new packet of cigarettes out of his pocket, offering one to me.

'Eighteen, Jimmy boy. How would you like to celebrate?'

I feel my mood lifting. I light the cigarette and inhale deeply as I stare out at the sea, purple shades of darkening light dancing on the waves.

'Dunno really. Hadn't thought about it. Being here is enough, you know.'

Charles taps ash from his cigarette on to the sand and watches it being slowly blown away. He points to the far end of the horseshoe bay where, on a rocky outcrop, sits a small building. As though by magic, the string of fairy lights that decorate the exterior suddenly comes on against the mauve sky.

'What is that place?' I ask.

'That,' replies Charles, pointing his cigarette in the direction of the fairy lights, 'is Matala's sole café, so I've been told. When people don't hang out here on the beach, that's the place to go.'

'The *only* place to go,' I add and we both laugh.

'Apparently the ouzo and raki are dirt cheap and there's dancing on the tables.'

I grin. 'Sounds like just the place to spend a birthday.'

'Particularly an eighteenth birthday.

I take another drag and blow out a perfect smoke ring. 'Speaking of which, you haven't…y'know, told anyone how old we are, have you?'

Charles raises an eyebrow. 'No. But who cares? Why does it matter?'

'Oh. Well,' I lean back on my elbows, feigning nonchalance. 'It doesn't matter, really. I just think I may have mentioned to a certain person I was a few years older, that's all.'

'Let me guess. The gilded mermaid,' Charles sniggers.

'Would you stop calling her that?' I snap, and then sigh before my face softens. 'She seems to have vanished today, anyway.'

'Don't worry, Jimmy boy. I'm sure she'll reappear. And *yes*,' he says slowly, kicking my foot in the sand. 'Your secret's safe with me. Although some women like younger men, y'know.'

'And in your vast well of expertise, which experience in particular are you drawing upon?'

Charles chuckles good-naturedly and ignores the question. 'We could ask all the people from here if they want to come over with us tomorrow evening to help you celebrate your eighteenth, sorry your *twenty-first* birthday.'

'Good idea. But whatever you do…' I lower my voice, 'don't invite that Ardhendu idiot.'

Charles instinctively looks around until he locates him, sitting a few yards away.

'Why not? I chatted to him a bit last night. Seems like an interesting bloke.'

'Interesting?' I scoff. 'First-class navel-gazing prick if you ask me. *My name's Ardhendu,*' I mimic, '*my guru in Benares gave me the name*. What a knob.'

'Jim,' Charles says, face suddenly serious. 'Don't be so judgmental. He's a good person.'

'Yeah, thanks for that. But I'm allowed to take a dislike to somebody if I feel like it, aren't I.'

Charles shrugs and takes a drag on his cigarette. 'Hardly seems worth it here. Everybody seems to just get on with everybody.'

'We've been here a *day*, Charles. Just a day. How can you possibly know that? How can you possibly know what little grudges and tensions are brewing between people?'

Charles eyes me in surprise, his blue eyes wide.

'Bloody hell! Listen to you. You definitely need some of that raki. What say we go and buy a bottle for tonight from Mama's Bakery?'

I shift in the sand. 'Well. The thing is, I'm pretty low on cash already. And if we're going to buy some alcohol, I'd rather save my money for tomorrow.'

Charles rolls his eyes as he stands up.

'You can owe me, Jim. For fuck's sake, don't worry about it.'

He reaches a hand down to help me and I realise at that moment that never in my life have I seen Charles so relaxed. As I get to my feet, I realise something else: that, happy as I am to be here with the wonderful promise of romance with Chenoa, I'm not feeling particularly relaxed. It isn't something I can put my finger on, or care to put my finger on for that matter. But it throbs like a dull, hazy undercurrent of unease beneath my skin.

We've been in Matala for such a short time, but it's impossible not to notice the way Charles feels at home immediately; how people like him and he likes them. I'm not used to being relegated to the position of being 'Charles's friend.' Back in Twickenham, it was always the other way round. I'm the joker, the good-looking one, the boy that all the girls like and who starts all the trends. Charles is the good-natured brainbox, dependable but ever so slightly boring. But for the first time ever, I ask myself if it really is like that or if this is the label I've attached to us both for all these years, because this is the way I've wanted to see it. And now here, in Matala, far from those familiar tags of school and home, where people are seeing us both for the first time, well, something just feels not quite how it ought to be.

Mama is so short that I almost don't spot her. A boy and a girl from the caves are in the dimly lit shop buying what looks like yoghurt. They stand in front of the counter, spooning it into their mouths hungrily. A few drachma lie scattered over the counter, which Mama seems in no hurry to take. The boy reaches for a small tub of honey and drizzles it into the yoghurt with a teaspoon. Mama stands, all four feet or so of her, behind the counter, dressed head to toe in black. A steady stream of Greek interspersed with the odd word of English flows from her small, bird-like mouth which is crowded full of teeth, several of them visibly chipped. Her hair, coarse as sheep's wool, is set in a hive of tight, white curls on her head.

When Mama spots Charles, she lets out a loud hoot and flings her arms in the air, screeching something incomprehensible. I can't help but laugh and the other two customers at the bar turn round in interest, a white snail's trail of yoghurt above the girl's top lip.. Charles says something in Greek and yoghurt girl raises her eyebrows and nods in surprised approval.

'What did you say?' I hiss.

'I said that I loved her shop. At least…' Charles pauses. 'I think that's what I said.' He shrugs. 'No matter. Mama, *aftós eínai o fílos mou.*' He grabs me by the elbow, pulling me towards the counter.

'*Jeem! Jeem!*' Mama says as she reaches forwards and pats my cheek like an indulgent grandmother. I feel myself blushing.

'*Polý ómorfo agóri,*' she says before removing the empty yoghurt glasses and putting them in a sink at the back.

I raise an eyebrow at Charles.

'She says you're very handsome.' Charles says, before reaching out and shaking hands with the two cave dwellers.

They are called Susanne and Wolfgang and have travelled overland from Munich. They have been here two months.

'Mama is a guardian angel,' Wolfgang comments, slotting the scattered drachma into a small tin. 'She never charges what she should, if at all. If not for Mama, I think us cave-dwellers would starve. One time when Susanne was feeling really ill, she even brought some medicine over to the cave for her.'

'No idea what it was,' Susanne adds, 'something with herbs in it. But I was well again very soon.'

'What other food does she do here?' I ask, my stomach growling again. It feels as though it's done nothing but rumble since arriving in Matala. Does nobody here ever eat properly?

'Bread. Sometimes sandwiches and fruit. Feta cheese,' Susanne says in her thick German accent.

She has a thick golden brown plait hanging over one shoulder, large hazel eyes and graceful limbs. Both of them wear what look like Wolfgang's shirts, Wolfgang with a pair of cut-offs beneath and Susanne, wearing it more as a dress which looks, I think, very odd indeed. *Never trust a kraut,* comes the voice of my father in my head, loud and clear. I frown and push the voice aside, resolving to be more friendly than ever towards these two.

'So tomorrow it's my birthday,' I say, grinning at them. 'And we're asking everyone along to the café in the evening. Will you come?'

'Of course! Have you tried the rice pudding there yet? It's the best on the whole island, probably the best in the world,' Susanne says enthusiastically.

'Rice pudding, is that *rizogalo?*' I ask.

'That's it,' says Wolfgang. 'They sprinkle a little nutmeg over it here. Tastes even better when you're stoned.'

'Bring everyone along you know,' adds Charles, 'to help Jim celebrate.'

'Happy Birthday for tomorrow. Good timing you made, to have your birthday here in Matala.' Wolfgang says and he pumps my hand up and down in a friendly manner.

I smile back at him and feel my earlier misgivings about Ardhendu receding. These two seem like decent people, and perhaps I've even read Ardhendu wrong. Even though he does look indisputably stupid with that ring through his nose.

'Let's hope the police don't come and break up your party,' Wolfgang adds.

'*Police?*' I laugh. 'Why on earth would they do that? Shouldn't they be worrying about criminals rather than breaking up innocent parties?'

Wolfgang shrugs. 'Of course they should. But there is not much criminality on Crete. And in the absence of that, well…don't forget the military *Junta* has a strong presence everywhere, on the islands as well as the mainland. If they think we are stepping out of line, there can be trouble.'

'What kind of trouble?' Charles asks.

'Once they came in the night, shining torches on our faces while we were sleeping.'

'You have to be joking!' I say.

'No joke,' Susanne shakes her head. 'They even took a Danish boy off to jail from one of the caves and he never came back again.'

'But *why*?'

'Must have found something they didn't like. Just be careful where you put your things. This is all we are saying. They are no joke, this police.'

I raise an eyebrow and shake my head. I don't want to think about police or dictatorships or my father or any of these unpleasant thoughts. It's my birthday tomorrow! After buying a cheap bottle of wine and bidding Mama farewell, the four of us walk back together towards the beach which is all but empty save for a few people munching on watermelon. I feel another stab of disappointment that I haven't seen Chenoa all day long but console myself with the fact that she will hopefully reappear the following day. Now that would be the best birthday present ever.

We walk back to the beach with Susanne and Wolfgang. Their cave is on the lowest corner of the cliff face by the sea and they invite Charles and me in to have a look around. Hanging on a pole outside the cave, like a votive flag, is a long string with some beads and shells attached to it. I pick them up for a closer look, but find myself dropping the string in horror seconds later, for what I am holding actually looks like old human teeth threaded on to the string along with small bits of shell.

'Jesus!'

Wolfgang laughs and walks over, patting me on the back. God, I wish people would stop doing that, it's agony.

'Yes, my friend,' he says. 'Human teeth. This has been passed on from one cave inhabitant to the next. The story goes they were dug up from inside the cave originally. Pretty old, I think. Anyway, we leave it here outside The Pit, to bring us luck.'

'The Pit?' Charles asks, coming over to study the teeth.

'Yes, most caves have a name. Yours too. You don't know it yet?'

I edge away from the pole to the cave door, which, unlike ours, is covered with bamboo bound together on rope that swings back and forth on its hinges.

'But why is this one called The Pit?'

'Can't you guess?' Wolfgang asks, his brown eyes shining with humour. 'We might not get the long walk to climb up to the top caves, but the bad thing we get here is…well, you can smell it, no?'

Up until now, I haven't been able to smell anything. But as soon as Wolfgang mentions it, I find myself instinctively crinkling up my nose and the faint pungency of an unpleasant scent filling my nostrils.

'God, what is that?' I ask, my hand instinctively clamping over my nose.

Susanne begins to laugh, swinging her thick plait over her shoulder. 'People have to shit somewhere, don't they?'

'Don't tell me they…' I motion towards the cave.

'No!' Susanne cries. 'Of course not. Not there. Round the back.'

'You two haven't shitted yet since you been here?' Wolfgang asks, grinning. It occurs to me that no, I haven't. And actually, it has been a few days. Surely not good news at all.

'The smell doesn't bother you?' Charles asks.

'This was the only cave free when we arrived.' Wolfgang replies as he sits down on a stool and starts to prepare his hash pipe. 'We wanted to move, but by the time one was free…well, we just get used to it.'

'Yeah,' Charles rejoins. 'You really can't smell it that much.'

'You bloody well can,' I say, keen to move away from there as quickly as possible.

'Only because they mentioned it,' Charles says. 'I don't think you'd have noticed otherwise.'

I raise an eyebrow and am about to suggest that we head up to our cave when Susanne asks if we'd like to look inside. Charles enthusiastically nods his assent whilst Wolfgang pulls the bamboo door back. We all stoop as we enter and I blink several times, trying to get accustomed to the dimness. It smells of incense and a pungent marijuana so strong that even without inhaling its musky scent, it makes me feel light-headed. Before noticing anything else, I see the blue curl of smoke rising from Wolfgang's hash pipe.

'Jesus Christ,' I say, 'what *is* that stuff you're smoking?'

Wolfgang laughs and turns round, his white teeth gleaming in the darkness. 'This, my friend! It is the best marijuana you are likely to find on all planet Earth. It is Green Afghan.'

'From Afghanistan?' I ask, regretting it immediately.

'From Afghanistan, of course,' Wolfgang replies.

'Have you been there?' Charles asks.

'No. But Susanne and I are on our way there. We are travelling overland to Afghanistan. Please – '

Wolfgang motions to a small wooden table in the corner of the cave with one leg shorter than the others, making the surface slope. There are no chairs, but around the table are brightly coloured mats with tassels on the floor and I sit down, leaning my back against the cave wall. I take in the small, cracked glass on the table that sits at a precarious angle, holding a bunch of wildflowers. Now that my eyes have grown accustomed to the light, I can see that the cave walls have been painted from top to bottom in a pale blue colour and there are even some shelves made from driftwood and nailed to the walls, holding an assortment of books and candles. Suspended from the ceiling is a huge, rusted anchor from which socks, shirts and dresses are hooked up and various photographs are stuck up all over the cave. Painted on the wall, I make out the words;

'I hope for nothing. I fear nothing. I am free!'

'Nice,' I comment. 'Did you think of that?'

Wolfgang chuckles. 'Not me. They are the words of Nikos Kazantzakis.'

'Who's that?' Charles asks, to my great surprise. He always knows everything about everyone.

'Cretan poet and writer,' Wolfgang replies.

Charles nods and I see him mentally scribbling down the name. He is about to open his mouth when I hurriedly say something, eager to avoid a discussion about Cretan poetry.

'It's like a proper home in here,' I say. 'Doesn't look like you're leaving for Afghanistan any time soon.'

Susanne comes and sits on a rug beside us at the table and laughs. 'The truth is we only wanted to come to Matala for two weeks. Maybe three. But we love it here. It isn't easy to leave.'

Wolfgang hands the hash pipe to Charles. 'Our mother is waiting for us. She is worried about us.'

'You two are brother and sister?' I ask in surprise.

'You thought we were a couple,' Susanne says matter-of-factly. 'Yes, many people do. I think not too many brothers and sisters travel together. Wolfgang and I are twins.'

I study the pair of them, and now that she has said it, I can see a resemblance in their hazel eyes and thick blond hair.

'Our father was killed in the war when we were still very small. We are all our mother has,' Susanne continues.

I shift on the mat. The truth is I've never met any German people before and if I'm being honest with myself, have never really wanted to. The war was a long time ago and I know next to nothing about it. But even so, I've always imagined that German people would be...well, not like these two. Not so very normal. And here is Susanne, sitting and talking about her father being killed. And very possibly by an Englishman. I glance over at Charles, whose eyes have instantly glazed over from the effect of the hash pipe as he unsteadily hands it over the table to me.

'I'm sorry,' I mumble to Susanne as I take the pipe, an intricately carved wooden contraption, which looks almost as ancient as the cave we are sitting in.

'Do not be sorry,' says Wolfgang cheerfully. 'We are in Matala. The centre of the universe. This is a place to not be sad. To forget about tomorrow and only live for today.'

'Here here,' Charles says, bending his nose down to smell the bunch of wildflowers on the table.

I inhale too deeply from the pipe and instantly feel my senses tingling and numbing. I lean back, close my eyes and smile. *This is a place not to be sad. To forget about tomorrow and only live for today.* This place is unique. This place is freedom. And this place has the best Green Afghan on all planet earth.

Chapter Eight

I wake the following morning at dawn, to a bevy of flies buzzing noisily around my head. It is the morning of my eighteenth birthday. I grunt and shift uncomfortably in my hard stone tomb and turn on to my side. Fuck, I will *never* get used to this. Charles is asleep, his mouth wide open as he lies, still as a corpse and oblivious to the discomfort. I would never admit such a thing in a million years; I don't miss a single other thing about home but *Christ* do I miss my bed. Oh well, I think groggily, as I heave myself out of the tomb and stumble slowly outside.

The sun has only just risen and the pale light gleams on the surface of the sea; still and flat as glass. I stretch and go to sit on a ledge looking out over the bay. Dotted along the beach, I spot a few sleeping bags. At first, I think that people have left them there overnight, but seeing a couple of them moving slightly, realise that some people must have decided to sleep there. Not a bad idea. Perhaps I'll take my own sleeping bag down to the beach tonight after going out. Also, that would mean that I wouldn't have to lug myself all the way to the top of the cliff after a long evening.

God, it's amazing here. It's pure freedom, it's beautiful

and it's unlike anything I've ever known. The thought of having to return to finish my final year at school so soon makes me feel physically ill and I hurriedly push it from my mind and concentrate on the view. In the distance, a solitary figure is picking their way along a rough track towards the tiny white chapel in the middle of the village. What must the locals think of us, I wonder. Well, I know what Mama down at the bakery thinks. Probably the best thing that's ever happened to her, us cave dwellers. But everybody else? The few villagers, the shepherds? Who knows? And actually, I muse as I stand up to stretch again in the pale warmth of the sunlight, who cares?

At that moment, I feel something brush against one of my feet. Thinking nothing of it, I shift a little on the ledge. But then I feel it again, this time a scurrying sensation and the hot patter of tiny feet. Looking down, I see a small, orange-brown creature with a long, curved tail bending back over its head and crab-like pincers, which it pulls itself along with, over my foot. I let out a piercing scream and fall backwards, kicking out at the creature as I do so and cursing.

Seconds later, Charles comes running out of the cave, bleary-eyed and just wearing a pair of boxer shorts. 'What the hell is the matter?'

'What the fuck is that?' I cry, pointing down to a rock where the creature now stands, stock still, surveying me.

Charles comes closer and peers down. 'That's a scorpion, you tosser -'

'A fucking *scorpion*?'

Charles squats down on his haunches to inspect it. 'Oh, *pl*-ease. Don't tell me you were making that racket about a tiny little scorpion.'

I edge backwards. 'A tiny little scorpion? A tiny little fucking scorpion? Their bites can kill, can't they?'

Charles finds a leaf and pushes gently at the creature so that it scurries off beneath a rock. 'Come now. I think we're over-dramatising a little. A big boy like you, scared of a little scorpion like that?'

He chuckles and shakes his head as I glare at him. Moments later, we hear footsteps and Chenoa rounds the corner. I feel myself reddening.

'Mornin', boys,' she says, surveying us with one hand on her hip. 'Everything alright up here? Only Ray and I heard quite a commotion, and I said I'd come and see if everything was ok.'

I gulp as I stare at her. In the soft early morning light, she is lovelier than ever. She looks sleepy, one side of her head in a plait with some string tied round the end and the other side loose. She is wearing a bikini, not the white one I saw her in the day we arrived but a brown one with large red polka dots on it. For a minute, I'm so lost in admiration of this vision that has appeared before me, framed by the yellow glow of sandstone, that I can't say anything.

'We're fine,' Charles says eventually.

'Fine,' I echo. 'All good, ta.'

'Ta?' Chenoa asks.

'Oh. Ta. It's...erm, well, it's English slang. It means thanks.'

'Uh huh.' She bobs her head up and down and raises an eyebrow inquisitively.

'There was a bloody enormous scorpion that just ran over my foot. Scared the living daylights out of me.'

'Yeah, the scorps,' Chenoa replies nonchalantly.

There's something about the way Chenoa speaks, I think, that makes me feel as though she's bored with the conversation before it has even really begun.

'They're everywhere. We got an infestation once in our cave. Most people get that at one point or another.'

'Really,' I say, eyeing the ground around me.

'Yeah. That's why you gotta keep a broom handy. Just in case you want to push a few over the rocks or knock one over the head. Mama will sell you one for twenty-five drachma. Anyways – ' Chenoa trails off. 'Glad everything's ok.'

She turns round and starts moving away.

'Oh…' she turns back. 'A few people left yesterday from a cave lower down. Cave Number One it's called. You may want a bigger space?' She shrugs. 'Anyways… '

Chenoa turns and begins to move away and I step forwards, panicking.

'Wait, wait…' I run my fingers through my hair. 'What are you doing today?'

'Ray and I are picking tomatoes again. We did it all day yesterday and we're doin' it again today. Pay is pretty bad, but it's somethin' at least.'

'Oh,' I say. 'Well, maybe Charles and I can come along too. We could do with some – '

'No,' cuts in Charles. 'No way. Not today, on your birthday. I've got other plans.'

I shoot him a look. 'You have?'

'Yes. We're going exploring.'

'Well,' says Chenoa as she walks down a level so that only her neck and head are visible. 'Happy exploring.'

'We're going to the café tonight, though,' I call. 'You'll come, won't you? You and…Ray.' There is a moment's pause.

'Sure,' she says and then, just as she disappears from view, she turns her head back, her eyes sleepy but mirthful. 'Hey. Happy birthday.'

I smile, my insides lurching.

As soon as Chenoa is out of earshot, I jab Charles in the arm.

'Why did you say that? We could have done some tomato picking. God knows I need some money.'

'Yes, yes,' Charles says, patting me on the shoulder in return. 'All in good time. Fact is, I really *do* have a plan for today. It'll be great, honestly.'

'Exploring,' I say dubiously.

'Yes. We can't come to Matala and all we see are the caves. We'll go to Mama's, buy some bread and olives and things, go for a walk then come back here for a rest before we go out this evening.'

'How very organised.'

'Well, one of us needs to be organised Jimmy boy. Otherwise all you'll end up doing is lazing in the sun, getting sunburnt and drooling over a certain girl.'

'Yeah, thanks for that,' I counter, but then, looking out across the bay, I concede that it isn't a bad idea; it will pass the time before the evening. 'Where we going?'

'Just leave that to me.'

'Fine. But can we go and see if that lower cave really is free? I hate this one.'

'*Hate*? Bit of a strong word, isn't it?'

'You can't bloody stand up in it. I've lost count of the number of times I've banged my head. And besides...' I cautiously eye the ground around me. 'It's infested with scorpions.'

Charles laughs heartily. 'I'm easy...but why not? We could go and investigate.'

Sure enough, *Cave Number One* looks as though it must have been vacated just the previous day. It's not at all far from sea level, I think gleefully, as I will be able to almost roll out of bed into the sea in the mornings. Empty packets of cigarettes lie in one corner and someone, oddly, has even left a sleeping bag there and what looks like a cooker in the middle, fashioned from an olive oil canister.

It is, concedes Charles, far bigger and more luxurious than our last cave, consisting of three different areas. One of these is almost like a living room replete with a couple of chairs and wooden table and a fantastic view of the ocean through the yawning opening. A screen in the doorway constructed of pink and red rags hangs from bamboo poles and a faded National Bank of Greece calendar from the year before is nailed to the wall. There is another sleeping cave with tombs with a curtain separating it from this one and a central, adjoining level that looks as though it's been used as a kitchen with olive stones and onion skins on the floor.

As I stretch upwards, nowhere near banging my head, I grin widely. This is more like it! I feel as though I have moved into the Ritz, on my birthday no less!

After pulling our backpacks down to our new home, we get ready for our walk. I watch in astonishment as Charles literally lathers himself from head to foot in suntan cream, covering even the areas that would never, ever see sunlight. He offers some to me but, shaking my head, I agree to wear a t-shirt over my shorts that will cover my painful red patches on my chest and back.

'Hat?' Charles asks cheerfully, pulling his own wide-brimmed one down over his face.

'Nope,' I respond, lighting my first cigarette of the day as we begin our descent towards Mama's bakery. 'Anyway, I didn't bring one.'

'That's alright. I've got another.'

'Why the hell did you bring two?'

'Because I knew that you wouldn't bother.'

I shake my head and ignore him. After filling up a bottle of water from the communal tap and buying some feta cheese, bread and a couple of slices of watermelon from Mama's (also discovering that the place doubles as a post office when we see some cave dwellers collecting letters), Charles leads the way to the far end of the caves and scrambles over some precipitous rocks as the sun rises higher in the sky, a clear, strong globe the colour of harvested corn. Charles is like a tour guide, or a geology guide more to the point, stopping every few moments to make an exclamation about a dull rock or hazard a guess at its age. He really is a ridiculous brainbox, I think affectionately.

As Charles rounds the bed, he lets out a triumphant 'Aha!' that startles me, making me lose my footing on the rocks.

'What is it?' I call.

'The Roman ruins. They *are* here. Somebody mentioned them on the beach the other night, but I just wanted to see them for myself.'

There is very little part of me that is interested in Roman ruins and Charles knows it. But I'm in a good mood: the sun is beating down on me, I've turned eighteen, I am carrying bread, cheese and watermelon in my bag and, more importantly than any of this, the most glorious creature on the planet will be at the café tonight. Humouring my friend, I stand looking down on the rocks, panting.

'So, what is this place, oh Roman history teacher?'

'Baths. Ancient Roman baths, I'm sure of it,' he replies as he takes off his glasses and wipes them on his shirt. 'Look,' he points downwards. 'You can still see the steps leading into them.'

Charles eagerly moves forwards and I follow, the two of us picking our way down sunken, crumbling steps, molded into the ancient rock around us. Tiny shells are fossilized into the baths and Charles bends down to study them with a look of intense concentration. How can a person be so interested in things from such a long time ago that have no significance whatsoever to our lives? In a way I envy him his easy ability to derive so much enjoyment from the landscape, the geology and history of our surroundings. But at the same time, I feel happy that I can simply enjoy the here and now; enjoy Matala for what it is, not what it was.

Whilst Charles continues to move around the ruins slowly, studying every little detail, I wander away from him and climb into one of the ruined baths. I lie back, the uneven gritty surface chafing against the sunburn on my back but, once I have found a comfortable position, surrender myself and close my eyes tightly against the glare of the sun.

Why would anyone choose to live in cold, miserable England when they could live on Crete? Alright, England has Eel Pie Island, but that really, I ponder, is its saving grace. Just that tiny little island on the Thames. Without that...well, life would just be dire and would consist pretty much of school, stifled meals with Ma and father, and what else? Nothing, that's what. That's why, right at this moment, as I recline in the ancient Roman bathtub, I think for the first time that perhaps I might not go home. At least, not at the end of the summer. Why do I need A Levels anyway? The world is changing and my parents are just too repressed to see it. A Levels don't *mean* anything anymore. But this? Matala? This is life! A glorious, colourful tapestry of experiences are unfolding around me and I intend to make the most of every moment here. To hell with my parents. Well, perhaps not to hell with Ma, I think a little remorsefully. She's alright. Too much a slave to my father, but I can't deny she means well. To hell with my father though; he doesn't give a shit about me anyway. The strength of this last thought causes me to open one eye and peer at the rugged peaks of the coastline ahead of me.

'Charles?' I call out as I heave myself upright. I look around the ruins and eventually locate Charles on his hands and knees, peering up at something on the underside of a bathtub. He looks so funny that I laugh out loud. 'Charles!' I call again.

'Yes?' comes the muffled reply.

'Is it lunchtime yet? I'm starving!'

The evening can't come soon enough. I even make an effort to have the first proper wash I've given myself since being here, walking down to the communal tap with a jug I borrow from Wolfgang and Susanne and a bar of soap and giving myself a good scrub. Sloshing the water over my dark hair, I let out a little yelp, but once I've got used to the temperature, it feels refreshing. The intense heat of the day has passed and, as the sun begins its descent over the sea, the early evening light transforms to burnished gold. I admire the darkening skin on my arms and wish I had a mirror to see what my face looks like. But no matter, I know I must look pretty good.

Satisfied that I've given myself a good enough clean, I walk back up to the cave barefoot, with just my boxer shorts on, towel slung around my neck. What to wear? I empty the clean remains of my clothes from my rucksack on to the dusty floor of the cave and bend down. Ah. There is only one remaining clean t-shirt left and a rather grimy looking pair of jeans. I'd much prefer to wear my white shirt, which would offset my suntan, but picking it up and giving it a quick sniff beneath the armpits, I hurriedly drop it again. Oh well. The remaining t-shirt and grubby jeans it will have to be.

I give a cursory thought to clothes washing – I'm all out of underwear now. Where *do* people wash their clothes here? Perhaps tomorrow I'll have to take a bar of soap and go and wash them under the tap. What a drag. But then – tomorrow is tomorrow. And today is today, and what a day it is. My eighteenth birthday, and the promise of alcohol, cigarettes, music and a particular girl hang sweetly in the air.

The sun has not long set and it feels too early to be heading to the café. But both Charles and I are ready. We have already sat on the ledge outside our cave smoking for at least half an hour and we're keen to go. We decide to walk slowly over the beach towards the café, that lies on the other side of the bay. Our old camaraderie has come back over the course of the day and any unease that I felt earlier has completely vanished. Charles is wearing his dark-rimmed spectacles and, as always, his blond hair is sticking up at odd angles on his head. Despite the warmth of the evening, he has pulled a thick brown jersey on over his shorts and I glance down at his skinny knees and ankles wedged into a pair of leather sandals he bought in Heraklion from a man with no teeth.

'This place is going to be hard to leave, isn't it?' he comments as we pick our way over the sand.

I can't help laughing. 'Listen to you. The amount of persuasion it took to get you to come here, and now you're the original Matala fan.'

Charles scratches his head and laughs. 'Yeah. You're right. I didn't know how amazing it could really be here.'

'Well,' I say, bringing my cigarettes out from my pocket. 'Who says we have to leave?'

Charles gives a little snigger then frowns, squinting at me sideways. 'I'm going back to do my A Levels, Jimmy boy. Don't know about you.'

I grimace and pull an imaginary trigger at the side of my head.

'*Errrr.* A Levels. Christ, what is the big deal? Do you really, honestly believe that our lives will be so much better just because we take those bloody exams?'

'Jim.'

Charles stops walking and turns towards me. The sun is shining directly into his face and I notice at that moment that my friend's eyes are actually more green than blue. How can I have known him all these years and not noticed that?

'Jim,' Charles says again. 'It's not easy getting a job out there – '

'Oh Jesus, you sound just like my father. Don't start. *Please.*'

Charles shrugs and turns away as we begin walking again. 'All I'm saying is that Matala's not going anywhere. We can come back next summer, and the summer after.'

'You think I'll be able to come again once I've gone back home? My father would sooner string me up by my balls or lock me in the basement before he allows me out of the house after the exit I made. No,' I say resolutely, as we approach the café. 'I've made it here this time. So I plan to make the most of it. And A Levels? Well, my final word on them is that they're the last fucking thing I plan to think about tonight on my birthday.' I clap Charles on the back as we walk up the wooden steps into the café.

By the time Chenoa appears, around eight thirty in the evening, I've already drunk most of a bottle of *retsina* and I feel amazing. As I tuck into the simple tomato spaghetti that everybody at the café has ordered, I can feel my cheeks glowing. It took *forever* for the food to arrive and now it's here it tastes like the best meal in the whole world. Somebody has hauled over a record player from their cave and Hey Joe by Jimi Hendrix is playing. I look around the group of people that have congregated to help me celebrate my birthday and muse that, apart from Wolfgang and Susanne, I can't remember any of their names. But it doesn't matter, I feel a deep affection for everybody tonight.

These are people like me, who think to hell with what society *expects* us to do and say and how it *expects* us to act. We are a new generation and we do things our way. And this is where it begins, in Matala. The birthplace of ancient civilization and the centre of our worlds. I grin as I hungrily prod and spin my fork into the spaghetti, olive oil dripping from it liberally on to the plate. It's funny, I think, how we managed to find this Cretan utopia from a chance conversation on Eel Pie Island. But then again, clearly it was just meant to be. *No*, I think, as I reach over Charles for a serviette, there's no such thing as chance. I am *meant* to be here, Charles is *meant* to be here.

As I drain the last drop of my *retsina*, I spy Chenoa over the top of my glass. She has, of course, come with Ray and I think I see her dropping his hand as they walk into the café. I wait for her to make eye contact with me and I watch her as she walks over to the record player, pauses to change the record over to The Byrds, and then approaches the bar where she makes a joke with the swarthy Cretan standing behind it, flicking back her blonde hair as she does so and idly looks around. She glances over to where I'm sitting and, expecting her to react, I raise a hand in the air. But, as though her eyes are just passing over a group of complete strangers, she continues to look around, her gaze lazy.

God, why does she *do* that? I feel irritated and embarrassed at the same time as I hurriedly bring my hand down. The café is starting to fill up, partly with cave dwellers I recognize – oh *great*, there's that annoying nose ring bloke with the funny name that I can't even remember – and others whom I haven't seen before. As I lean back in my seat, surveying everyone, I ponder what a raggle taggle bunch we all are. Scruffy and in need of a good soak in a bathtub, but despite all that, somehow exceptionally beautiful. I reach up and run my fingers over my four day old stubble. How long would it take me to grow a beard, one as impressive as the one I'm studying right now, its owner a man who looks to be in his late twenties. I recognise him from the caves but have never spoken to him.

There are cigarettes being passed round and my glass is being re-filled by a noisy red-headed American called Edgar who is sitting beside me. Edgar has been waxing lyrical for the past half hour about CND, the Cold War and dodging the Vietnam draft. I have only been paying a small amount of attention, although Charles, of course, has begun to debate animatedly with him. *Charles*, I think, as I sigh out loud, my brain-box, smart-arsed best friend.

I peer over the top of my empty wine glass. Now that Chenoa is here, I'm completely tuned into her presence, her every move. She is sitting up at a high, rickety bar stool and is drinking wine, every so often reaching down to extract an olive from a small bowl and popping it into her mouth. There's something maddening about this girl - I want to shake her and tell her to pay attention, to look at me properly, to look at *anything* properly. It's as though everything is too much effort for her. And yet, at the same time, she somehow seems to fit into Matala's cave life better than anyone, almost melting into her surroundings. The original cave girl. But for all her nonchalance, it only makes me want her more.

I sit, trying hard not to look at her as I carry on steadily drinking and listening to the record jumping, a pack of mangy dogs howling along with it. Occasionally, people come in, clap me on the back, and wish me a happy birthday and I grin inanely at them, accepting their offers of further drinks or cigarettes. Finally, after what feels like an aching eternity, I notice Chenoa climbing down from the bar stool and making her way over towards my end of the table. My head is swimming in a heady haze of wine and cigarettes but I pull myself up slightly and try to pick up the thread of conversation washing over me.

'But Charles,' Edgar is saying, leaning over the table, 'America's exploiting the raw materials of third world countries. All of us are, whether we like it or not.'

'Which...raw materials?' I cut in, focusing as I push my elbows down on the table.

Edgar turns to me in surprise. 'Which ones, buddy? You name 'em, we're exploiting them. Oil, water, rubber, wood, there's even a – '

'Hey,' I hear over the din. I turn my head at the same moment that Chenoa lazily extracts her cigarette from between her oval-shaped mouth and blows a trickle of smoke over my head. I smile, feeling my knees begin to jiggle up and down beneath the table.

'Hey. Got a spare cigarette?'

She pauses, eyes narrowing, before shrugging.

'Sure.'

Chenoa extracts one from the packet, lights it for me in her own mouth then hands it over. I try to keep eye contact with her.

'So,' she continues. 'Havin' a good birthday?'

'Just being here, in Matala, how can it not be the best birthday?' I reply, swiveling the chair round so that I'm facing her.

Realising that he's lost me, Edgar picks up the thread of conversation again with Charles.

Chenoa smiles at me, arching an eyebrow, her amber green eyes flashing in the light of the naked bulb she stands beneath.

'True.'

'Do you want to sit down?'

'No,' she says, adding the word 'ta' as an afterthought, making me laugh.

But once it's faded, I search around desperately for some words, more tongue-tied than I've ever felt in my life, clearly not helped by the alcohol.

'How,' I blurt out finally, 'how was the grape picking today?'

'Tomatoes,' Chenoa says, taking another drag from her cigarette. 'Hot.'

She is leaning against the wall, curtains of blonde hair falling over her shoulders, one knee lifted seductively up with the sole of her sandaled foot resting on the wall behind her. She blows the smoke straight at me this time, holding my gaze and I feel that excitement shift once again inside me that she likes me, that I actually have a chance. Emboldened by the wine, I pull the chair in a little closer and place one hand on her raised knee.

'Chenoa -'

No sooner have I said her name than I feel something else shifting inside me. This is not excitement, I know that for certain. This is something else. Something that I have been waiting to come for the past four days and why the *fuck* does it have to come now of all moments? *Christ alive.*

I whip my hand away from Chenoa's knee, lean in close to her ear and whisper 'Don't go anywhere. I'll be right back.'

She gazes at me, amused, as I roughly barge past the people sitting at the table, pushing their chairs in as I go, past the record player and yapping dogs till I'm at the door of the café. I hear Charles yelling after me, asking where I'm going, but I know I can't stop. Not even for a single moment. *Shit, shit*, why now? I tumble down the wooden stairs and curse under my breath, running fast, as fast as I can go when this pain is spreading across my rectum from holding it in and I'm even drunker than I realised. Just look for Wolfgang and Susanne's cave, I keep telling myself as I half run, half trip over the beach, trying desperately to keep my mind off it.

God, I need a torch. I can see fuck all here. Trying to pull myself together, I concentrate on the directions to the lowest, corner cave and feel my way along its wall, round to the back. Aha! Here's the path. The stench hits me instantly, but this time I feel relieved, because at least I know I'm in the right place. Blocking my nostrils with one hand so that I am only breathing through my mouth, I hurriedly pull down my trousers with my spare hand and crouch down. In sheer, blissful relief, I empty my bowels. Toilet Roll. *Jesus.* Of course, I didn't think of that. God, why can things never be simple? Most of the cave dwellers are at the café and I didn't spot anybody else on the beach on my way down. But, remembering Chenoa back at the café, my hand resting on her flirtatiously raised knee, I begin cursing again. Fuck it, I'll take my chances.

I drop my fingers from around my nose and with both hands, whip my trousers and boxer shorts off so that I am naked from the waist down. Stuffing the garments into the crook of my arm, I move awkwardly, hobbling almost as I pass Wolfgang and Susanne's cave once more and make my way on to the beach. I drop my clothes and rush into the shallow waters of the sea. Looking all around me and confident that nobody is there, I begin to clean myself.

Coming out of the sea, my first thought is *towel.* I don't have anything to dry myself with. Oh *God,* could this evening throw up any more complications for me? I'm dripping wet from the waist down, but putting my jeans on now, they'll only stick to me and leave soggy patches for everyone to see back at the café. Suddenly, I have a brainwave. Knowing that time is of the essence, I begin to vigorously dry my nether regions and legs with my boxer shorts. It works perfectly. Not knowing what to do with the soggy boxers, and not really caring, I fling them on to the sand, pull my jeans back on and start to tear back up the beach towards the fairy lights gently moving in the breeze. Half way along the beach though, I realise that I desperately need water, so cut back on myself, running the long route on to the top village path. There, I locate the single tap and turn it on its rusty hinges. I stick my head beneath the liberal flow, turning my mouth up and drinking until my stomach will take no more. In the process, water splashes all over my hair and on to my jeans. I grimace, muttering expletives under my breath as I shake my hair backwards and forwards, droplets of water flying. Enough. I need to get back.

Approaching the café, I hope that Chenoa will still be standing there, in the exact same position, with her blue blouse showing off her cleavage and her silky blonde hair loose around her shoulders, cigarette in hand and the sole of one foot resting against the wall. Just thinking about her makes me go hard and I take the stairs in threes. The door bangs as I go in and a loud cheer erupts from the revelers and even louder howls from the dogs. I smile awkwardly and immediately search the corner of the room for Chenoa. She's still sitting there but is engaged in conversation with Charles and Edgar and doesn't even look up. I see her throwing back her head and hooting with laughter, her eyes shining as she claps her hands together.

Well, that's just bloody marvellous. I was only gone for five minutes (ten, maybe) and I come back and she's talking to other people. No matter, I'll reclaim her. She kissed me. She likes me. And she certainly isn't interested in flame-haired, red-nosed Edgar with his Cold War theories or bespectacled, brainbox Charles.

The water from the village tap has helped to sober me up a little and I edge my way through the café a little more steadily than my earlier exit. I realise, now that I've had some air, just how drunk everybody is. As I approach the far end of the table, I see that Charles has extracted a pack of cards from somewhere and is mid-way through showing Edgar and Chenoa a card trick. Hang on a minute, this is *my* card trick. *I* taught him this one. Without giving it a second thought, I wedge myself between Edgar and Chenoa and sit down, taking the cards from Charles's hands and extracting a cigarette from his open packet.

Charles raises an eyebrow at me.

'Where did you get to? We thought you'd been swallowed by the Matala Monster.'

'You're so funny,' I reply, removing the cigarette from Charles's hand and lighting my own from the tip before returning it. 'Mind if I continue with this trick?'

Charles leans back in the chair and crosses his arms.

'Be my guest, birthday boy.'

I have no idea where Charles has got to in the trick and don't want to ask and so I jumble the cards up and start again, relieved when nobody counters my sabotaging. I haven't yet looked at Chenoa, but feeling her there, her shoulder pressed up against mine, is enough. She hasn't vanished. She is still real. I lay two cards out on the table face up, one red and one black, and launch into an explanation, no matter that Chenoa and Edgar have probably already been told, when I feel something on my right leg, a pressure. Chenoa's soft fingers are gently kneading my thigh like dough.

I stop speaking instantly, my mouth hanging slightly slack as the realisation kicks in. Charles, opposite, raises an eyebrow at me and leans forwards over the table. 'Yes? You were in the middle of explaining what I'd already explained?'

The pressure on my thigh strengthens and I gulp. I shake my head a little from side to side, my mouth opening and closing uselessly like a goldfish before I manage to pull myself together.

'Did you say you'd already done this trick?'

Charles smiles ironically at me. 'Yes, but you're the man of the day, Jimmy Boy. It's not every day you turn – '

'Oh yes, I remember what I do now.' Panicked, I cut Charles off. I don't want Chenoa to discover my age now, not when things are panning out as they are. She moves her fingers in small circular motions on my thigh. *Christ*, they are climbing higher and higher until –

'Yes!' I say, almost yelling. Edgar starts to laugh loudly, slapping the table.

'What's up with you, buddy?'

I continue to stare at Charles over the table, questioningly.

'What I was saying…' I mumble, 'was that yes, I remember what to do now. I haven't done this trick in ages.'

With this outburst, Chenoa gives my thigh a little squeeze and removes her hand, which I find a relief and a disappointment in equal measure. I manage – *just* - to make it through the card trick, but keep thinking of Chenoa beside me, her warm, beautiful body and dexterous fingers, wondering what else she might be able to do with those hands.

The trick finished, I lean back in my chair, feeling suddenly very drunk again. I take in my surroundings: Beautiful people. Warm night. I realise that the song that is playing keeps getting to a certain point and then stops and goes back again. It is playing the same three seconds of the track again and again but, looking around, I see that nobody else has noticed, even though a few people appear to be singing along to the words. Bloody hell, they must be even drunker than me.

The night rolls on along with the endless swell of waves from the ocean and I wonder how I can possibly get Chenoa outside without everyone seeing. But then, who cares if people do see? She is still sitting beside me and hasn't tried planting her hand on my thigh again but I turn to her, staring at her smooth brown shoulder that her pale blue shirt has slipped from, revealing a rather murky-coloured bra strap. I lean in close to her and murmur in her ear.

'Do you feel like going outside?'

Chenoa turns to me, her feline eyes twinkling in amusement.

'What for?' she drawls, her voice heavy and challenging.

I shift a little on my seat. She is playing with me, I'm drunk but not too drunk to not realise that much. But what I can't work out is how she wants me to play it. Does she just want me to grab her and kiss her hard or is she waiting to make her own move? Thinking about it too much is making my brain hurt and I frown and stare at her, trying to give her my best seductive look that I know has worked for other girls.

'For some air,' I reply. 'Or something like that.'

'M-hmm,' she murmurs.

She reaches into the packet of cigarettes on the table, slowly pulls one out and lights it. Right, so is that m-hmm yes or m-hmm no? Either way, that's it, I cannot take this a moment longer. Grasping her by the hand, I clumsily stand up from the table, pushing my seat roughly back and half pulling, half dragging Chenoa up with me. She lightly unclasps herself from my grasp and walks ahead of me, moving towards the door without looking back and leaving a thin trail of smoke in her wake.

I hurry after her and as the door bangs behind me, I catch her cigarette-free hand up in mine and pull her away from the café so that we are out of view. Once away from the twinkling lights of the café, I hurriedly encircle her slim waist and pull her into me, pressing my mouth against hers. It tastes of smoke and olives and something sweet, I can't tell what. It tastes delicious. She drops her cigarette in the sand and both her hands come up behind my head, roughly running her fingers through my hair as she kisses me back.

I know nobody will be watching us but even so, I want more privacy than this. I stare at her hard and suddenly, as though she knows what I'm thinking and what I want, she is the one leading me. Pulling me by the hand, laughing as she does so.

'Where are we going?' I ask as she leads me over the sand, that now feels like the longest desert in the world.

Chenoa doesn't say anything, she only continues pulling me on. All I can hear is the music of her laughter and the murmur of the waves. I can feel the softness of her hand pulling mine and the smooth dampness of the sand on my feet – where are my shoes? Finally, eventually, we cross the bay and find ourselves at the foot of the caves. Here, she drops my hand, turns around and kisses me again. I try to pull her to me but she pushes me away, turning once more towards the path. I follow the flash of an ankle or a flick of golden hair as she moves effortlessly, despite the darkness of the night and steepness of the route.

I'm panting from the exertion, my head beginning to spin in an alcohol-induced whirlwind. I stop for a moment, bending over and clutching my ankles as I take painful, rasping breaths of air. I've smoked too many cigarettes today and my chest is hurting. Glancing up, Chenoa has vanished round the bend up to the next level and I straighten up and push forwards.

She's standing in front of her cave. The doorway has a cloth hanging in front of it and a bunch of wildflowers spilling out of a cut-off plastic bottle, suspended from the entrance with string. I can see now that she's slightly out of breath. Not as much as I am, certainly, but enough to not be able to talk for some moments. But, I now know with confidence, she isn't interested in talking. I stand with my hands on my hips, trying to regulate my breathing and Chenoa laughs again, a flash of white gleaming in her mouth.

As I walk towards her, she starts to speak.

'So, Jim. How old are you really turning today?'

I stop in my tracks. The bastard Charles must have said something.

'I already told you the other night,' I reply. 'I'm turning – '

'Yeah,' she says, before blowing up from her bottom lip to cool down her face, pink and glistening from exertion. 'I know what you told me. But I'm just interested in knowing your real age. That's all.'

I move towards her and, my hand trembling, run a finger down a flushed cheek.

'Does it matter?'

Chenoa smiles, her head on one side.

'It must matter to you if you feel you need to lie about it.'

My fingers continue to travel down her cheek, past her chin until my whole hand rests on her collarbone. I've never really paid much attention to this bone before, not on anyone else, even a girl, and certainly not on myself. But staring at the angles on Chenoa's collarbone, bathed in moonlight, I think at that moment that it is the most beautiful thing I have ever seen. As I rest my hand there, I draw my other arm around her waist and pull her into me, pressing my lips on hers. But again, she stops me, tilting my chin up with one hand so that she is looking me straight in the eye.

'Have you ever been with a girl before, Jim?'

Christ. What's the right answer? My immediate reaction is that I should lie. I don't, of course, want to seem inexperienced and put her off. And after all, I have done a good many things with girls before. Ok, so I haven't been all the way but that doesn't mean I haven't *been* with a girl. It just means I haven't had sex before. But then, Chenoa staring at me like this, her eyes narrow and shrewd, I know I can't lie to her. That she'll just know.

Christ, I'm nervous. And I wish I could sober up a bit more. My head feels as though it's stuck in an eternal whirlpool.

'Not quite,' I mumble.

She smiles again and takes my hand, pushing away the cloth hanging over the door and the cave and pulling me again. It's pitch black inside and she immediately drops my hand. I feel a mild panic rising inside me. There is something about the deep, empty darkness of these caves that probably has bats and scorpions living in quiet corners that completely creeps me out at night. Double that with the fact that dead people were buried here and – I shiver, flailing around in the blackness, thick and heavy and hot as a winter blanket.

Seconds later, I hear the flare of a match before I see it, but then pockets of brightness as Chenoa moves silently around, a golden-haired ghost, lighting candles stuck into the ground and suspended from the roof like stalactites. There are two beds in the cave but on top of these tombs are only clothes, books and rucksacks. Nearer to the cave's mouth, two thin mattresses and pillows are on the floor, side by side. I look at them, then back at Chenoa who is smiling at me again, that lazy, aloof smile. What does she want me to do? Now that this moment is almost here, the moment that I've dreamed of for years and even more so in the past few days, since arriving in Matala, I wish desperately I'd listened more closely to the brags of George White, the boy from my class who's notorious for having slept with the most girls. Or so he *claims*. Pondering that thought for the first time, how far George White has *really* gone, Chenoa takes a couple of steps towards me.

'Undress me,' she says in a firm, bold voice.

Just hearing her say those words, I feel myself go hard. Shit. Whatever you do, I tell myself, don't get over-excited. Be cool, just like Charles says. Be cool. This girl wants me.

But for fuck's sake, don't get carried away too soon. I take a couple of swift steps towards her and begin to tug at the buttons on her blouse, fumbling as I do so.

'Not like that,' she says, taking both my hands away and holding them tightly between hers.

She looks at me hard, all trace of a smile gone.

'Slowly,' she says. 'Do it slowly.'

I nod and take a few deep breaths. Slowly. Right, slowly. All the encounters I've had with girls before, I've been the one in control, the one with more experience. They've all just been schoolgirls, looking for a bit of action on a Saturday night. But now, with Chenoa...well, this is something new altogether. I want it more than I've wanted anything in my life. But the truth is that I'm terrified. This panic that courses through me is so intense and real that I am relieved when I feel my erection subsiding. But then I am gripped with an even greater terror that I may not be able to get it back again at the right time.

'Jim,' Chenoa says, her face softening. 'Relax.'

Relax. Easier said than done. I take a few deep breaths and bring my hands up again to her shirt buttons. I know that she's staring at me but I can't quite bring myself to look her in the eye. Instead, I concentrate on the task at hand, repeating that word, *slowly,* like a mantra, again and again in my head. Once I've undone all the buttons, I push the blouse from her shoulders, revealing smooth brown skin and – again – those beautiful collarbones.

Her bra is more problematic. I fumble around behind her back for about ten seconds (I've successfully removed several bras in the past, so why is this one causing me so much difficulty?) before, wordlessly, Chenoa takes hold of my forearms and directs my hands to a small clasp in the front between the two cups. Well. This is a first. How long exactly was she planning to let me mess around at the back for? With one rapid ping, the bra opens like two curtains parting to reveal the most exquisite sight. Chenoa's breasts are the same colour as the rest of her, which means that she must have been sunbathing topless – how have I not seen this? I cannot take my eyes from them. They are somehow bigger, rounder, smoother than I imagined them to be. I bring my head down and bury it between them, sinking into their fullness and groaning softly as I place my hands on either side of her slim, firm waist.

Chenoa lets me keep my hands there for a few more moments before she brings my head up. She kisses me, two soft pillows cushioning my lips, a flicker of tongue and lingering taste of smoke and salt from the olives. This time, I pull away. Now. How to remove the bottom half? She is wearing a mini skirt and I really don't want to make the same mistake with the bra so I study it, looking for some clues. But there is nothing, at least nothing obvious. Whilst I am pondering this, Chenoa bends down to unstrap her sandals, slipping them off her feet which, I notice for the first time, are very small and, unlike the rest of her, not very smooth. Standing upright once again, Chenoa leans back against the cave wall, her head slightly on one side. She brings one knee up, the same way she did in the café, and as the candlelight throws dancing, dappled shadows across her body, I wish I had a camera. If I did, I would take a photograph of her in this exact position and nothing, *nothing* could possibly equal its beauty.

I'll have to get that mini skirt off one way or another.

Taking a deep breath, I slowly hook my forefingers into either side it, worn low on her waist and tug. To my great relief, it isn't tight and yields to my touch, coming down. It falls in a heap around her feet and Chenoa kicks it to the side, in the same direction as her shoes. I can barely bring myself to see what she is wearing beneath. Alright, I've seen her in a bikini. But this is different, of course. Because whatever she is wearing is mine to remove. And whatever is behind it…I feel my penis begin to throb violently. I can't bear this agony any longer, but she takes one of my hands and places it between her legs over her underwear.

I sense that I may have an element of control now and I increase the pressure of my fingers. She sighs and brings both her arms above her head as, all thoughts of slow stealth out the window, I hurriedly hook my fingers into either side of her underwear and whip them down. This time, I kiss her hard on the mouth, trying to move her towards the mattress with one hand as, with the other, I begin to undo the buttons on my jeans.

'Stop,' I hear her say, the first word spoken in a while, and the strength of her voice and the way it reverberates around the cave takes me by surprise. I pull away, my body aching in frustration as she pushes me so that I stand at an arm's length from her.

'Chenoa,' I say in a small voice that comes out almost like the whine of a child. '*Please.*'

She brings one finger up to my mouth to silence me and stands there naked before me as my whole body heaves with desire. It is so hot inside the cave and I can feel myself sweating profusely from beneath my armpits, behind my knees, down my temples.

'Patience,' Chenoa says firmly.

Patience? How much more patience do I need? I don't know how much more of this I can possibly take.

She takes a step towards me and kisses me again, as she does so lifting my t-shirt up from behind and instructing me with her hands for me to lift my arms above my head, our lips parting so she can remove it. She then begins on my jeans, firstly rubbing her fingers over the denim at the crotch as I moan. God, if it feels like this with jeans *on* then…

The buttons undone, Chenoa hooks her fingers into the waist of my jeans and pushes them down in one swift motion. I am so turned on I can barely find the momentum to even step out of them so stand there, rooted to the spot, jeans loose and crumpled round my ankles, frozen in an agony of lust combined with pure terror that I am going to come too soon. Chenoa wants to take this slowly, that much is clear, but I really don't want to, I *can't*, it is just all far too much.

As she begins to expertly rub her hands over my crotch – God, how many times has she done this before – I know that the only way I can make this work, the only way all this won't be a complete disaster – is if I think of something else. Something awful or disturbing or downright depressing. But as her mouth moves to my neck and then down my chest, slowly, slowly working her lips over my belly button, nothing at all comes to mind. All I can think of are her lips going lower and lower until – *Christ alive* – I flatten my back against the cave wall and close my eyes as she takes hold of my ankles and guides me to step out of the jeans. Pushing them to the side, I feel her mouth around my penis as I lean into the rough wall and squeeze my eyes tightly shut against the flickering light and sight of the top of her blonde head beneath me. I need to get it over with now. Do the deed, get inside her, before all this ends horribly, humiliatingly.

'Stop!' I hear myself yell, far louder than I intend, or is it the cave's acoustics? Her head jerks backwards and she looks up at me, eyes liquid in the candlelight.

'Not enjoying it?'

'No. Yes!' I hurriedly correct myself. A trickle of sweat runs in a straight line down the centre of my forehead and I bring one clammy hand up to wipe it away. 'Yes!' I repeat. 'It's...it's bloody amazing. But...' I peter off.

'But you want to make love to me now.'

Chenoa finishes my sentence. She stands up so that our faces are level once more. I realise that I am panting, partly because I am so damn hot and partly from pure longing. Over the top of her head, I can see our shadows flung on to the opposite cave wall, flickering in the candlelight. Right, enough is enough.

I grasp her tightly around the waist, hooking one of her smooth legs around mine so that I can move her round. Pushing her down on to the mattress, I feel her soften under my touch. She has been very much in control up until this point but now, this is more like it, she will let me do what I want. What I need.

I groan loudly as I lower myself on top of her and push her legs apart. She yields and, suddenly terrified that I might crush her beneath me with my weight, push my arms taut on either side of her. Oh Christ, Oh Jesus, thank you, God, I think as I feel myself go deeper and deeper inside her. My eyes are closed in pleasure and relief and when I open them slightly I look at Chenoa's face. I can't tell what she is experiencing – her face is quiet and impassive; she certainly doesn't look like she *isn't* enjoying it. As soon as I begin to move up and down above her, thinking that this is quite possibly the best moment of my life – no, not possibly, *definitely* the best moment of my life so far - I feel a release, as sudden and liberating as the sun appearing from behind the clouds. I hear myself let out a yelp and my stretched arms slacken, as I bury my face into her neck, breathing loudly into her ear.

'Oh, Christ,' I say, panting.

Chenoa doesn't say anything but remains motionless beneath me for several moments until, slowly, she begins to move, pushing lightly against my chest. I don't want this moment to be over. I want to stay like this forever; consign to my memory for evermore the shape of our entwined shadows on the opposite wall.

'You are amazing,' I say, looking at Chenoa's face, wanting to memorise that as well, beads of sweat framing her upper lip.

She half smiles as she continues to push my chest.

'Wait…wait,' I whisper as my penis continues to throb and empty inside her. I think I see something flash across her face – impatience? – and, with great effort and reluctance, I pull out of her and roll on to my back on the other mattress. Without saying a word, she stands up and walks to the heap of clothes. I watch her shadow lengthening across the cave and after I feel like I can just about breathe again properly, I prop myself up on my elbows and watch her as she steps into her cotton pants and pulls up her mini skirt. Rummaging around in a space at the back of the cave, she finds a new packet of cigarettes, extracts two and places them in her mouth as she leans into one of the candles to light them.

Chenoa walks back to the mattress, scooping up my jeans and tossing them over to me. She sits down, crossing her legs, and hands one of the cigarettes to me before inhaling deeply on hers. I suddenly feel very aware of my nakedness. My penis has finally stopped throbbing and self-consciously, I reach for my jeans and awkwardly pull them on. I'm glad to have a cigarette in my hand, an object to concentrate on, and I wonder if I'm expected to talk. What *do* you say to a girl after you've had sex with them? Are you meant to…well, compliment them or something like that?

Wait till I tell Charles about this. Play it cool, indeed. Clearly I've played it exactly right, otherwise I wouldn't be sitting here now beside a half-naked Chenoa in post-coital bliss. If the sex itself was amazing, liberating, then this is even better. Sitting here, with one of the most beautiful girls on the planet, in the knowledge that she has chosen me; that I have lost my virginity, *finally*, and this experience can never, ever be taken from me. As all these thoughts pass through my head, I feel bigger, stronger, more sure of myself once more. It's strange to be with a girl who clearly has a great deal more sexual experience than me. An element of this grates against the edges of my male pride. But at the same time, not in my wildest dreams could I have imagined my first complete sexual encounter would be with a girl like this.

As we sit in the silence, the cave darkening as two of the four candles Chenoa lit earlier burn out, I gracefully pull on my cigarette and practise blowing smoke rings.

'So,' Chenoa eventually says, her arms crossed over her breasts as she arches one eyebrow at me.

I smile at her, relieved at last to be feeling a little less hot and for the trickling sweat to have stopped. God, I think to myself and grin, of all the places to lose your virginity: in a cave. In a bloody *cave*. This is just brilliant.

'Something funny?' Chenoa asks, grinding her cigarette out in an ashtray beside the mattress.

'No,' I say quickly. 'Not funny. I was just...y'know. Thinking.'

Chenoa looks at me then stands from cross-legged, taking a few strides to the other side of the cave to pull on her top.

'Anyway,' she says in a quiet voice, pulling her arms through her pale blue shirt. 'How was it?'

I run my fingers through my hair, still slightly damp from my earlier dousing beneath the tap, but also stiff and sandy from lack of recent washing.

'Well, bloody hell,' I mumble. 'How was it? It was...Christ, it was bloody fantastic.'

I look at Chenoa at the other side of the cave. Her shirt sits on her crookedly, one side slipping over her smooth braless shoulder, exposing the top of one breast. She is surveying me with curiosity, one hand leaning against the cave wall and her feet crossed over.

'I've never had sex with a guy whose...well, whose first time it was. So, y'know. I'm interested.'

'Oh,' I say. I'm not sure I wanted to know that. She has no hint of mockery on her face though and I suppose there's no point feeling weird about it. 'Well,' I say, my voice small. 'It would be difficult really for it *not* to be amazing with you, Chenoa.'

'Oh yeah?' she asks, her voice a challenge. 'And why's

that?'

Another candle goes out and one side of her face falls into darkness. 'Why? Well, because...' I start to fiddle with the nail on my big toe before I look back at her. 'Well, because you're just so beautiful.'

Chenoa lets out a startlingly shrill laugh, the kind of laugh I never expected to come from her, given that her speaking voice is so deep and sensual. I want to see her face, to read something from her expression, but the limited candlelight has now thrown it into shadow.

'Oh, Jim,' she says.

'What?'

'Sex is not the same thing as beauty.'

I pause. Wait a minute, I've just paid her a compliment. And I meant it. Surely girls like to be called beautiful? I'm confused.

'I don't understand what you mean by that.'

'No,' Chenoa replies, walking slowly out of the shadows and standing at the foot of the mattress as she looks down at me. 'I don't suppose you do. But one day you may understand.'

I frown. Now it really does sound as though she is mocking me, or mocking my age and inexperience at least. But I really, really like this girl, for fuck's sake. I want to make love to her again, and again. I want her to teach me everything she knows but I sense I am losing her attention. Desperately, flailing around for words, I blurt out the first thing that comes to my head.

'And you? How was it for you?' The second the words have escaped from my lips, I regret them. But it's too late. I feign nonchalance as I stand up on the mattress and stretch, looking around for my jeans and t-shirt.

Chenoa says nothing for a moment, and then 'Well. You know.'

No, I don't know. Where the hell have my jeans got to? The cave is so dark now I can barely see anything at all.

'Y'know,' she repeats, 'bein' your first time and all.'

Right. What the hell is that supposed to mean? Perhaps it's better not to know. Stumbling upon my jeans, I pull them on whilst Chenoa bends down and seems to be inspecting the sheets on the mattress. I take a deep breath and walk up to her, waiting for her to stand up. As she does so, I gulp. Why do I feel so bloody nervous and tongue-tied?

'Chenoa,' I reach out and place a hand on her forearm, hoping that she'll make some gesture in return. When she doesn't, I press on. 'Chenoa. It was amazing. You're amazing. Thank you. I mean – '

'Jim,' she cuts in, her other arm rising as she lightly runs her fingers over my lips. 'Jim,' she repeats, before dropping her hand again. 'You're sweet.'

Chenoa continues busying herself with tidying up the cave as I am left standing there, turning that word over, again and again. Sweet. Strange choice of word. Sweet as in good? Or sweet as in bad? Young? Immature?

I pick up my t-shirt and look around the cave for my shoes before remembering that I left them at the café. At least, I think I must have done, for I clearly remember running across the beach barefooted. I feel far more sober than I was an hour ago. In a way I wish I were still drunk, because at the same time as feeling elated, I know that this elation is tinged with frustration and a desire that Chenoa be at least a little more enthusiastic about our encounter.

But, I rationalize, as I pull my t-shirt over my head, it's late, she's probably tired and there are many more nights in Matala ahead of me.

I make my way slowly to the mouth of the cave, arms reaching out into the darkness on either side of me as I go. I'll never get used to these dingy old caves, or like them for that matter. Although, I think to myself with a grin, the cave's interiors do now hold a certain significance for me that they never did before. Chenoa makes no move to follow me, she seems absorbed in her task of tidying up, though there really isn't much to tidy. At the entrance, I turn and look at her.

'See you tomorrow, then?' I try to keep the note of longing from my voice, but the words catch in my throat even as I speak them.

Chenoa looks up from what she's doing, her long hair hanging over one side of her face. She gives me a small, tight-lipped smile but then, her face softens as she sighs and walks towards me. She proffers her cheek which initially throws me but then, realising she expects me to kiss it, I lean forward and place my lips against it. I close my eyes for an instant, breathing in the smoke from her hair and feeling the smoothness of her skin against my mouth, and then she pulls away.

'Sure,' she says.

I hesitate. One of my hands is on the overhanging flap of material at the cave's entrance. I know I have to go now, that I have no other choice. But I can't quite bear to turn my back to her; somehow I feel that if I do, I will lose her forever. Why on earth do I feel like this when she has just willingly made love to me? I shake my head and try to dismiss these less than positive thoughts and smile at her warmly.

'Night, then,' I say in a cheerful voice. 'See you tomorrow.'

'Goodnight,' she replies, and before I've even left the cave, she's turned back to her task.

Chapter Nine

The following morning I wake up to a gruesome headache. I slept fitfully – it felt like the hottest night since we arrived. Or perhaps it was just the alcohol. But either way, as I pull myself into an upright position, I feel more like I've just turned eighty, not eighteen. I can't remember when I last brushed my teeth and my mouth tastes like a dried up old ashtray. Charles is still fast asleep – how the hell he manages to sleep so soundly in that rigid tomb, I'll never understand. I spot a half empty bottle of water on the ledge beside Charles and uneasily make my way over there and reach out for it.

Without opening his eyes, Charles swipes his hand out and swats me away.

'My water,' he croaks. 'Go and get your own.'

I ignore him, unscrewing the cap, drinking deeply and leaving about an inch in the bottom.

'Oh God,' I groan, stumbling back to the tomb and lying down again. 'I feel like shit.'

Charles swings an arm over his eyes to shield himself from the bright sunlight filtering through the cave opening.

'We need to hang something up there,' he mumbles. 'I

feel grim too.' He sits upright, rubbing his eyes, his hair sticking straight upwards as he takes one look at the almost empty water bottle and sighs before finishing it. 'Shall we go and swim?'

'I'll sink,' I reply, as I try to find a comfortable position.

'Even more reason,' says Charles, sounding more energetic now, 'to give it a go. Might help cure our hangovers.'

From my horizontal position, I look over at Charles and notice, with surprise, that in the flattering morning light, he appears to have a suntan. His chest isn't the same pasty white it was when we arrived and his face, despite the hangover, looks healthy and glowing. Even the stubble on his chin suits him.

Down on the beach, a few cave dwellers are eating bread and fruit, offering us some as we pass, whilst others continue to snore in their sleeping bags. The water is cool and refreshing and, ducking beneath the waves, I feel the intensity of my pounding head receding. Charles dives below the calm surface, coming up moments later with a fistful of sand that he lets run through his fingers. His dark eyelashes have formed into perfect triangles and his blue-green eyes glint in the sunlight. I push myself onto my back and form a star shape.

'So,' he calls out to me, 'had fun last night, did we?'

The memory of the previous night returns to me in a flash; I was feeling so awful when I woke up that it had slipped from my mind, though how that could be possible, I don't know. My arms and legs fall downwards beneath me as I come into an upright position and look across at Charles who is smiling at me openly. I can't wait to tell him. And yet. I also don't want to tell him, which is a surprise.

'Yeah,' I say slowly, winding the fingers of one hand round on the surface of the water so that it makes a little whirlpool. 'Thanks. And you?'

Charles is grinning at me 'Brilliant. What a place to spend your eighteenth birthday. Lucky bugger.'

I smile and push myself on to my back once again. I wonder if Chenoa is awake yet; what she's thinking; what her memory of the previous night is. My thoughts are interrupted by a loud 'Hey!' being called out at us from the beach. I swing my legs down and shield my eyes against the glare of the sun. Oh great, it's Ray. Precisely the person I really don't want to see right now. Ray bounds down to the water's edge, much like an over-excitable puppy dog, his large brown eyes shining in delight. He certainly doesn't look as though his head is about to explode like a light bulb thrown on the floor.

'Morning!' Charles calls back in a friendly voice.

Ray dips his big toe into the waves and then, deciding it's better to just take the plunge, shoots his arms above his head and dives into the water. As he comes up, just a yard or so from me, I find myself staring at his full beard again, admiring the way droplets of water glisten in its shaggy depths. I wonder once more what kind of a relationship Ray and Chenoa have. Non-exclusive, Chenoa said. But what the hell does that mean? Do they sleep with each other regularly and, if so, do they honestly not mind when the other sleeps with somebody else? In theory, I've always liked the idea of that; of free love and all that and sleeping with lots of different girls. Yet here I am, eighteen years and one day old, virginity successfully lost, but when I think of Chenoa, I feel a physical heave across my chest. I'm not sure I could ever share her.

'Good birthday, Jim?' Ray asks, without the slightest hint of insincerity in his voice.

'Yeah,' I reply. 'Good one.'

Ray is smiling warmly at me. At least, his beard and eyes seem to be smiling. I can barely see his lips. He looks expectantly at me, as though waiting for me to provide further information on why it was a good one, but when I remain silent, Charles, who's bobbing up and down on the waves, calls out from a few yards away. 'What are you up to today, Ray?'

'Run outa cash,' Ray calls back. 'Was thinking of walkin' to Timbaki to do some work at the olive oil cannery, but not sure I can face the long journey. So probably just goin' fig picking. You guys want to join?'

Charles swims over to us.

'That's a great idea. Jim and I have pretty much run out of money too, haven't we Jim?'

I'm silent for a moment, the sudden swell of a wave pushing up to the level of my chin. Charles is right, I really do need a bit of cash. For cigarettes and drink if for nothing else. But if Ray is going fig picking and Charles is going with him…

I lie back and let the waves push me gently up and down, a cut beneath my left thumbnail tingling from the salt.

'Chenoa going too?' I eventually ask, with as much nonchalance as I can muster.

I hear Ray laugh.

'She's still fast asleep. Don't think she's goin' anywhere today.'

I continue to sway with the waves, closing my eyes against the sunlight that is already very strong, the negative image of a huge golden globe forming against my closed eyelids.

'Jim?' Charles asks. Yes, yes, I know I should go. I know I've been smoking all of Charles's cigs and borrowing money off him. But I know that I won't go.

I ignore Charles for a little longer, pushing my arms and legs out to either side as the sun beats down upon me. Then, as though stifling a yawn, I reply;

'Think I'll stay here today. Got a killer headache, anyway.'

Charles doesn't direct any more of the conversation towards me and I hear muffled voices as Ray and Charles continue to make plans. As we do so, I feel my lips curling upwards. After these two fig-pickers have buggered off, I can go and wake Chenoa. Surprise her with some breakfast – I'm sure I must have some loose coins - and then we can spend the day together. Talking and making love. Making love and talking. Sounds like a plan.

The anticipation is fairly tortuous and I'm relieved when Ray and Charles finally stop nattering like a pair of old fish wives and go back up to the caves to get themselves ready, leaving me on the beach sunning myself. By now, the bodies wrapped up in the sleeping bags have stirred and I can see heads poking out over the top or, in a couple of instances, two heads and entangled limbs pushing their way through the undergrowth for sunlight

My back has stopped hurting from the sunburn and I'm satisfied that I have a great tan, though the lack of a mirror anywhere to confirm what my face looks like is slightly disconcerting. I love this place but Christ, does it make you lazy being here. I can easily imagine one day rolling into the next, no idea of time or date and even less idea of what is going on in the outside world. Not that I give a shit about that anyway, news is just depressing. I do, though, occasionally think of Ma and feel a small spasm of guilt. But I know that eventually she will understand my decision to get away for a while. As for father…*No!* I tell myself. *Do not even* go *there.*

I laze on the beach for another half hour or so and then, confident that Charles and Ray must have left, decide to head back to the cave to look for some money. On my way, I remember the sandals that I left at the café and, turning on my heels, make my way to the far end of the bay. Nobody has seen them though, they haven't been handed in and I realise, frowning, that I have no other shoes and certainly no money to buy any. Ah well, I sigh, I don't need them in Matala anyway.

Winding my way along the track to the cave, I spot Ardhendu sitting cross-legged on a ledge outside, in what looks like no more than a pair of underwear, eyes closed and meditating. His long hair is matted and I feel a wave of revulsion and irritation pass through me. There's something about this bloke and his sort in Matala that really gets my goat. *My guru in Benares…*I hear the nasal twang in my head. What a load of crap. I hurry on, pounding up the path just in case I get trapped with him again.

Back in the cave, there is no sign of Charles and I root around in his rucksack and trouser pockets for some loose change. I'll go fruit picking tomorrow so I can pay him back. But there's nothing. Frowning, I continue to look around. I know there must be some money somewhere, but where does he keep it? Suddenly, I have a brainwave and walk purposefully over to the sleeping bag Charles has rolled out over his bed. Lifting it up, I triumphantly retrieve a fifty drachma note and a few coins.

Full of energy now, I grab my toothbrush and trip back down the steep path towards Mama's Bakery. I can smell fresh, warm bread, perfect to wake Chenoa up with. Mama rattles away in incomprehensible Greek, leaning over the counter and pinching my cheek with surprising force. I have enough money left to also buy a few plums. I smile to myself as I leave the darkness of the small shop into the bright Cretan sunlight.

After stopping at the village tap to drink some water and brush my teeth, I take the long route back to Chenoa's cave, walking into a more fertile dip in the valley where a few straggled wildflowers grow, their spindly, parched stems straining their way up through patches of grass. I carefully pick several, take another stem of grass and tie them around the rather pathetic looking bunch. Ah well, it's the thought that counts.

I'm almost running now, feeling strong and happy and positive, my headache now just a distant throb. The coloured cloth is hanging over Chenoa's cave door and I take a deep breath and awkwardly pull it to one side, the bread and bag of plums tucked under one arm as I clutch the flowers with my other hand. It always takes me several moments to adjust to the dark and I squint into the dimness.

'Chenoa?' I call softly.

There is no answer and I lay the flowers and food down at the entrance and walk quietly to her bed. I can't help smiling as the memory of the previous night returns to me. What a brilliant, unique place to have sex for the first time.

I walk up to Chenoa's mattress and crouch down. But there is no sign of her. Crouching down, I place my hands on the sheets. They are still warm and the faint, sweet scent of her lingers.

'Chenoa?' I call again, hopelessly. I still want to believe that she's here, somewhere, tucked inside the cave yet I feel sick as I even think it, knowing that it's not the case.

'Fuck!' I shout out, my voice hard and aggressive and bouncing back at me from the cave walls, loud and mocking. I feel a balloon of red anger burst inside me and, without stopping to think about it, storm towards the cave entrance. I tear open the bag of plums and smash two of them hard against the outside so that they leave two large, purple stains. The plum stones drop uselessly to the ground and I kick them, stubbing my toe as I do so, cursing again. I walk to the ledge and look down to the beach, seeing if I have just missed her. But there's no sign of her, either on the sand or in the sea and I feel utterly dejected, furious and miserable. I am in no mood for rationalizing, that she may be back at any moment or that I will see her later in the day. I want her here now; *need* to see her so that I can still this swell of insecurity growing within me.

I pull at the stalk of grass that is keeping the bunch of wildflowers together and hurl them over the ledge. Immediately regretting it, I see a single flower that has fallen at my feet. Frowning, I stoop down and pick it up. I sigh deeply. Why am I feeling this? I can't put a finger on these emotions but I'm not used to them and don't like them. I am used to...well, to girls *liking* me. And yes, Chenoa must like me enough for the night before to have happened but somehow I still doubt her motives, her sincerity. I don't *want* to doubt her, but it's just this bloody aloofness I don't know how to deal with. Aren't girls meant to love it when you call them beautiful? Don't they enjoy being chased?

I shake my head. Despite the fact I've just turned eighteen I suddenly feel very, very young and inexperienced and I have enough self-understanding to realise that this greenness irritates me beyond belief. With a disconsolate grunt, I walk back into the cave and lay the single flower down on top of Chenoa's tangle of clothes. I see the pale blue top she wore the night before and raise it to my face, briefly breathing in her scent before dropping it again and walking back out. I pick up the warm bread and start to make my way towards my own cave, no idea what I can do today now. Ardhendu has finished meditating and is now in some kind of contortionist yoga pose.

'Greetings, Jim,' he calls out from an upside-down position.

I ignore him and continue making my way down the track. Almost at my cave, I think better of it and decide to go and see if Wolfgang and Susanne are around as I don't feel like being alone. Turning, I hurry back past Ardhendu who shouts after me, 'Greetings again, Jim', this time his voice tinged with a mocking edge.

I scowl and ignore him once more, reaching both hands up and taking a bite out of the bread. It tastes delicious, but as I chew it, my non-encounter with Chenoa and the presence of Ardhendu only serve to diminish its flavour.

Approaching Wolfgang and Susanne's cave, I find Susanne crouched down outside with a pile of clothes at her side, scrubbing a soapy clothes brush over a t-shirt on a hot, flat rock. Behind her, she has strung up a long length of string and various pieces of underwear and other garments are hanging in the warm sun drying. I briefly think of my own clothes and how badly they need washing. I wonder if she'd mind if I threw a few pairs of pants in?

When she sees me, she stops what she's doing. 'Jim!' she exclaims with genuine warmth.

'Morning.' I thrust my hands into my pockets and stand smiling at her.

'You had a good birthday?'

I shift from one foot to the other. I did. But I kind of wish people would stop asking me that now. I nod.

'Yeah. I've got some bread from Mama's. Still warm. Do you and Wolfgang want some?'

Susanne wrings out the t-shirt she is holding, pegs it up on the line and shakes her hands. 'Great. Wolfgang!' she yells into the gloomy cave. 'Jim's here.'

Moments later, Wolfgang emerges, blinking. He has an enormous reefer placed between his lips. I break a large hunk of bread off for him, then another piece for Susanne and the three of us sit in companionable silence outside the cave eating. I really like these two. They're straightforward. Uncomplicated. What you see is what you get. I lick my fingers to extract the salt sprinkled over the warm bread, relishing the thought that my father wouldn't be very happy to know I'm eating breakfast with two Germans.

After we've finished, Wolfgang lights the reefer and moves into the shade. I follow him whilst Susanne continues with the washing and the two of us sit in silence, appreciating the aroma and flavour of the grass we're smoking. Once our tongues have loosened, Wolfgang begins to ask me about life at home. I'm feeling stoned, but not too stoned to remember to omit and move around certain details so as not give my age away. I'm a student at art college, I tell him, just like one of those many students I came across on Eel Pie Island. When the conversation moves on to my parents, I'm eager to skirt around the subject, but that only makes Wolfgang press even further.

'Your parents are supportive of you being here, Jim?'

I flick the ash from the end of the diminishing reefer on to the ground. 'Supportive. No, I wouldn't say that exactly.'

'Do you think they are afraid?'

I raise an eyebrow. 'Of what?'

'Afraid of not seeing you. Not knowing where you are. Afraid of losing things again, like they did in the war.'

I straighten my back slightly and shift on the hard ground.

'Dunno.'

Susanne has finished with her washing and comes and sits beside us, reaching out for the reefer.

'Does your father ever talk about what he did in the war?'

'Yeah, right,' I mumble. I don't really want to talk about the war. 'Not a chance.'

'Ever asked him?' Wolfgang asks, finishing off the last small piece of bread.

I snort 'Asked him? My father is the grumpiest bastard on this planet. He's not going to tell me.'

'Yes,' Susanne says, large hazel eyes narrowing as she inhales on the joint, 'but you cannot know this if you do not ask.'

I really, truly do not want to start talking about my father. I want to smoke this joint and get stoned and be in peace. I decide to direct the question back at them.

'And yours? Your dad, before he...well, y'know, before he died. What was he doing in the war?'

'He was in the German airforce, dropping bombs on London,' Wolfgang replies.

Before I can stop myself, I burst out laughing so suddenly that I begin to choke. Through my spluttering, I take in the serious faces of Wolfgang and Susanne and try desperately to smother my laughing.

'You're kidding me?' I have an overwhelming urge to laugh, not because it's funny, but just because I don't know how else to respond to this.

'It's true,' Susanne replies, shrugging. 'He was dropping bombs on London, and other places in England. And eventually, his plane was blown up. It is shit,' she continues, running her fingers through her long hair, 'what these young men were made to do.'

I stare at her, then stare at Wolfgang. It's true. I have not the slightest idea what my father did in the war. And I don't care. I really bloody well don't. But clearly I am expected to, and I'm not sure which of these thoughts disturbs me more.

Wolfgang's face softens and breaks into a smile.

'Jim, man. You look so serious.'

'Well,' I mutter, pulling my knees into my chest. 'Heavy conversation. You know. War and all that.'

'Yes, but we are the blessed generation. The war screwed our parents up, but not us. All these Americans we see here? Most of them are running from their homeland so they don't have to be drafted into some hopeless war in Vietnam.'

'Like Edgar,' I say.

'Yes,' counters Susanne. 'Especially Edgar. He did six months in Vietnam, had some horrible experiences and decided enough. So he ran away from it all and left to go travelling.'

'He did?' I say.

'Yes,' Susanne replies. 'You should ask your dad what he did in the war.'

'Yeah. Right,' I scoff.

'You *should*,' Wolfgang urges. 'I asked my uncle once, the brother of my father. At first, he would not tell me. He became aggressive. But eventually, the stories, they came out and he cried. For hours, like a baby.'

The thought of my own father crying like a baby makes me feel physically queasy. I frown deeply. My headache has come back and I am tired, hungover, pissed off that Chenoa isn't around and now very, very stoned. This conversation is starting to annoy me, all this talk of war and discussions with fathers.

'Hey,' I say, wanting to lie down this very instant. 'Would you two mind if I had a little sleep in your cave? Not feeling too good.'

'Sure, sure,' Wolfgang says, jumping up. 'This stuff is strong. You need to go easy on it Jim, especially if you are not used to it. You are inhaling real deep.'

'Right,' I mumble, unsteadily pulling myself up. The last thing I remember before falling into one of the tombs, which now seems like the most comfortable thing in the world, is the sudden, sharp stench of sewage. And then, nothing.

When I wake, it takes me a long time to pull myself out of my deep sleep. My eyes keep opening and closing and it takes a great effort to pull myself upright. How long have I been sleeping, I wonder? I certainly feel better. My headache, which was clashing like two cymbals, has largely gone and, as soon as I have pushed my legs over the side and sat there for a few moments, I can tell my mood has also improved. I am just very, very thirsty. In fact, I think, I spend an awful lot of time here feeling very, very thirsty. Clearly I am not drinking enough water.

Walking out of Wolfgang and Susanne's cave, I realize I must have slept for ages because the sky has grown dark. Clouds have gathered, the first time I've even seen clouds on Crete and there is a heavy, purple-tinged leadenness in the air. Nevertheless, there is a large group of people sitting on the beach. I can hear their animated chatter and the sounds of a guitar straining into the shadowy sky. I feel good. It's the best sleep I've had since being in Matala. It's ironic that it wasn't even at nighttime, nor was it in my 'bed.' I try to spot Charles amongst the group on the beach, but don't think I can see him so decide to head back to the cave. I'll have a wash, feel a bit more human. And drink a gallon of water whilst I'm at it.

Perhaps I do need to play it a little cool with Chenoa. Let *her* do some of the chasing. Clearly, she likes me. She *must* like me, after last night. No, I won't go looking for her this evening. She can come looking for me. Having made this decision, my optimism surges and that, combined with the decent sleep, makes me scrabble at a quicker pace than normal up the path towards my cave, whistling as I go. I'm not really looking where I'm going and so I see the feet before anything else. Two pairs. One in leather sandals with nails painted violent red and the other in long, knee-high boots. Looking up, I see two impossibly young-looking girls (could it be that they are even younger than Charles and me?), with huge rucksacks hoisted onto their backs. The girls look like they may collapse beneath their weight at any second.

'Hi,' one of them says. 'We're new here.'

English, without doubt. You can't disguise that accent anywhere.

'Do you know if there are any spare caves?' asks the other.

This one, the knee-high boots girl, has auburn hair neatly styled into waves and, if you take away the rucksack, would look just like every other girl you'd encounter walking down Twickenham High Street. The other has adapted a little more to the Cretan climate and above her sandals is wearing a floaty kind of dress tied up in the middle with a belt. But even she, I think, looks as though she has just finished a boating excursion on the Thames.

Not wanting to let on that I've only recently arrived myself, I adopt a pose that I hope looks relaxed, yet authoritative at the same time, leaning slightly to one side with my hands on my hips. The truth is I haven't a clue. But all the same, I certainly haven't met all the Matala cave folk yet and people appear to be coming and going all the time.

'Well,' I reply slowly. 'There may be.'

'You're from England!' the auburn-haired girl enthuses.

I nod, faintly peeved that it is so obvious.

'Are there many English people here?'

'Not that I've met,' I reply truthfully.

The three of us stand in awkward silence, the girls evidently hoping their question about the caves may be answered. At that moment, Charles comes bounding up the path and I heave an inward sigh of relief.

'Jimmy boy!' he calls. 'I've been looking for you everywhere, where've you been? Oh...hallo.'

He stops when he sees the girls, immediately smiling and shaking their hands.

'You just arrived?'

'Yes,' the summer dress girl replies. 'We just arrived on the bus from Mires. We were asking your friend here if he knows which cave we can sleep in.'

'Well, yes!' Charles replies enthusiastically. 'You're in luck. Penny and Jurg left only yesterday. Their cave is lovely and spacious.'

I haven't the slightest idea who Penny and Jurg are. Trust Charles to know the ins and outs of Matala real estate.

The girl with the dress claps her hands together excitedly. 'What luck!'

'Would you like me to show you where it is?' Charles asks before both girls nod their ascent.

Amazing, but true, that in the few days we've been in Matala, Charles has changed. Not just physically, his skin tanning in a way I never imagined it would, particularly beneath the bottles of sun cream he lathers himself with. But also just *him*, his confidence, this new ease of manner, the way he speaks to people and the way people respond to him.

Charles starts to walk up the path with the two girls, chatting amicably to them as they go. Turning back to me, he calls;

'Are you heading back to the cave?'

I nod.

'See you there in a tic, then,' and I watch as the three of them round the corner.

I grin. A couple of nice young, impressionable English

girls. Perhaps Charles will get lucky after all? Alright, so I'm well aware that if I'd met them a few days ago, it probably would have been me pursuing them. Particularly as neither of them are bad looking. But now I have somebody else to think about. Somebody far, far superior. Although, I add another thought rapidly on top of this, I am going to play it very, very cool with her now. Make her want me.

I hear a crackle of thunder behind me. The sky looks ominous and I rush back to my cave to grab my towel and some soap so I can get a quick tap-wash in. By the time I arrive back up there, twenty minutes later, Charles is sitting outside the cave, absorbed in *The Agony and the Ecstasy,* frowning through his spectacles and bundled up in a thick jersey.

'Blimey,' Charles remarks, looking up at me. 'You look almost...clean.'

'*Efharisto,*' I reply, bowing.

Charles whistles. 'Wonders never cease. Learning some Greek now, are we?'

I sling my damp towel over the piece of horizontal string we erected outside the cave. 'Contrary to what you think of me, I am actually able to absorb a few foreign words here and there.'

'Evidently,' says Charles, pushing closed his book.

'How's the novel?'

Charles takes off his specs and blows hot clouds on to the lenses, rubbing them on his trousers. 'Fascinating. It's all about – '

'Charles,' I interrupt. 'Fascinating is enough. We're not at school now, I really don't need to know all the details.'

Charles grins. 'Have it your own way, Jimmy boy. But you're missing out.'

I extract my toothbrush and toothpaste from a tin mug placed outside the cave, spit on it and start to vigorously brush my teeth. 'How was fig picking?' I ask with a full mouth.

'Bloody hot,' Charles blows out, raising an eyebrow. 'Thank God Chenoa had brought enough water to keep us going all day.'

I stop brushing. 'Oh. Chenoa was there too.'

'Yeah. By the time Ray and I went back to their cave to get everything together, she was awake and wanted to come.'

I try to remain expressionless but can feel a frown creeping on to my face. I spit over the side and when I glance back at Charles I see that he is looking at me with a curious expression on his face.

'So what happened between you two last night?'

I pause. 'Did Chenoa say anything about me?'

Charles shakes his head. 'No.'

I wonder if he might not be telling the truth, but then again, Charles is the most honest person I know.

'Well?' He places his specs back on.

I hesitate. 'She didn't say anything about me at all? Ask anything about me?'

'No. She really didn't. But why? Why are you asking? Come on, Jim. Out with it. What did you two get up to?'

I bend down, placing the toothbrush and toothpaste back in the mug then sit down with my back against the cave wall. 'Well, I only bloody slept with her, didn't I?'

I've scarcely finished speaking when Charles expels a loud hoot, clapping his hands together.

'Be quiet, would you?' I frown.

'But that's bloody brilliant, old boy.' He walks over to

me and gives me a hearty thump on one of my shoulders. 'May I be the first to offer my congratulations. Popped your cherry in Matala, and on your eighteenth birthday no less!'

'Charles,' I hiss. 'Would you keep your voice down?'

'Why?' Charles replies, looking bewildered. 'Nobody's listening.'

'Yeah but…' I trail off. 'Even so.'

'You're not looking overjoyed about it, which seems…astonishing.'

I inspect my feet which, after my first full day ever without shoes, and despite the wash, still look rather dirty. I shrug and look back up at Charles. 'No. I *am* happy about it. Obviously. I just want her to like me, and I'm not convinced she does.'

'Don't be a tit, she had sex with you, didn't she? She must like you.'

I nod.

'Yes, that's what I keep telling myself. And it was bloody amazing. God, she is the most beautiful girl in the world. But, well, I was really hoping to see her today. But now I find she's buggered off with you two to pick figs.' I grimace.

Charles, to my irritation, simply laughs and starts to root around for some cigarettes.

'I know this has largely escaped your attention, Jim. But it's pretty much a hand to mouth existence here. A day of fruit picking means money for dinner and some wine and buying cigs.' Charles waves a new packet beneath my nose. 'Speaking of which, when the bloody hell was the last time *you* chipped in for these? You certainly smoke enough of them.'

Taken aback by the tone of Charles's voice, I glare at

him. 'Keep your hair on. I *will* do some fig or tomato picking or something like that soon, alright?'

Charles's face softens and he smiles at me good-naturedly.

'I'll hold you to that. But you know, if you'd come along today, then you could have earned some dough *and* spent the entire day with the gilded mermaid as a bonus.'

'Yeah, thanks for that,' I reply. I know I sound like a sulky child.

'Did she tell you about her degree?'

'Her what?'

'Her university degree. Turns out your lover girl's quite a brain.'

'Well…' I reach for a cigarette, Charles wearily nodding his ascent, 'We didn't do all that much talking last night, actually.'

'Hmm.' Charles passes me the matches. 'I can imagine. Anyway, she has a degree in Ancient Greek civilization and is currently working on a Masters in the female rituals of ancient Crete.'

I look at him blankly. It doesn't seem to fit at all with what I know of Chenoa so far. But again, why would Charles make that up, or why would *she* make it up? But she seems so…well, so anti-establishment. And getting a degree, and then another degree on top of it just seems so out of keeping with the persona she exudes.

'Really,' I say.

'Really.'

I inhale deeply on the cigarette, my first of the day. If you didn't include the killer pot I smoked earlier. 'What else did you find out about her?'

Charles leans back and crosses his arms. 'Ah. Well that kind of information is going to cost you.'

'Oh, yeah? Name your price.'

'Stop smoking my bloody cigarettes and nicking my money and get yourself out fruit picking. Wiping tables at the café. Whatever.'

'I haven't been nicking your money,' I retort defensively.

'You bloody well have, you tosser, and you know it. I know exactly how much I had and exactly where it was. Do you think I'm that stupid?'

I sheepishly avoid his gaze and flick ash from my cigarette. I feel a twinge of guilt and remain silent for a few moments.

'Alright then. I promise, tomorrow I will go fig picking. Scout's honour,' I grin, holding my fingers up.

Charles rolls his eyes then grins back. 'Actually, you're let off the hook tomorrow. It's Sunday and nothing happens in Crete on a Sunday. Even the donkeys get a break. But first thing Monday morning,' Charles waggles his finger in mock severity, 'I want you out on those fields.'

'Deal.' I grind out my cigarette. 'So, what's the plan for tonight?'

'Not sure. Fairly low key I imagine after last night. I think there are a fair few people around with sore heads.' Charles ducks into the cave and re-emerges a few moments later with a comb that he attempts to tug through his hair.

'I did see Thomas spearing a swordfish earlier himself, though Lord only knows how. He said something about cooking it up on the beach tonight and sharing it out.'

'*Who?*'

'Thomas. That Australian bloke. You know, the one with the enormous ears.'

'No, I don't know. Bloody hell, Charles, do you know everybody's name in Matala?'

'Erm...' Charles tugs at a knot in his hair. 'Don't know. Most people's.'

I shake my head. 'Do you think that Chenoa is going down to the beach tonight?'

'No idea.'

'Didn't you talk about it when you were picking figs? Y'know, discuss evening plans and all that?'

Charles sighs loudly then tosses the comb over to me.

'Your hair looks like it needs a go, too.'

'No ta, prefer the tousled look.' I throw it back and walk up to the ledge peering down at the beach, and then at the sky that is growing blacker and angrier with every passing minute.

'So, no. We didn't discuss evening plans. Bloody hell Jim, just lighten up a bit, would you?'

Something about the way that Charles says those words makes me flare with irritation. I turn on him, eyes narrowed.

'Lighten up? I'm perfectly light, thank you very much.'

'You're just coming across as a bit...well, I don't know. A bit desperate.'

I jump down from the ledge, my hands flying up to my hips. 'I'm not desperate. I'd care to remind you that I had bloody brilliant sex last night. Why the hell would I be desperate?' I know I'm sounding like a petulant schoolboy but that just makes me feel even more irritated.

'Alright!' Charles says, almost shouting.

A sudden shaft of dying sunlight appears through a break in the black clouds, shining directly down on to Charles and as he stands there in the spotlight, clothes scruffy, face furious, skin dark in the evening light, he looks like some kind of worked-up prophet.

'Just calm down.'

'*You* calm down,' I snap sulkily.

'Yep. Thanks, Jim. Listen, I'm just trying to give you my penny's worth of advice, if you'd bloody listen to it. All I'm saying is that Chenoa's an older girl. More mature. She's not like one of those schoolgirls you regularly grope on Eelpiland.'

I open my mouth to protest but Charles, voice raised, presses on.

'Well, she isn't. She's older, has seen more of the world than we have and done a great deal more and all I'm suggesting is that you tread a little differently with her. She likes you, clearly, though God only knows why.'

Charles's face softens a little. 'So just cool this needing her thing a bit, that's all.'

'Since when have you – '

'Yes, *yes*, I know what you're going to say as you do have a habit of repeating this *ad nauseum*. Since when have I been the authority on girls? Well, the answer, Jimmy boy, is that it's clear to anyone from the outside, authority or not, that a little restraint is called for here.'

I clap my hands together, feeling calmer.

'Bravo. Good speech, Charles. Anyway, I'm bloody starving. Shall we go and see if there's any of this Tommy bloke's swordfish left before the heavens open and we get completely pissed on?'

'Thomas,' Charles corrects me as he pulls on his sandals.

I start to hobble down the path, shoeless, towards the beach and shout back over my shoulder.

'Tommy. Thomas. Same bloody difference.'

The thunderstorm comes shortly after Charles and I get to the beach. Initially, most people put up with it, the guitars continuing and some even standing and dancing in the rain, reaching their fingertips and faces towards the elements. But as the downpour becomes harder, and whips of lightning flash across the sky, most people decide they've had enough and reluctantly make their way back to their caves or across the bay to the café.

In the chaos of the downpour, I don't know where Charles has got to. I think I can make him out scrambling on ahead - he's probably almost at the cave by now so, as I move up the path, I decide to chance it and duck off the track half way up, picking up speed as I make a dash for Chenoa's cave. I'm dripping wet and panting – I will never, *ever* get used to this steep ascent. Not wanting to stay out in the rain a second longer than I need to, I yell Chenoa's name from outside at the same time as pushing back the door hanging.

Inside, as my eyes adjust to the light I can make out Chenoa and Ray on one side and Ardhendu - bloody *marvellous* - and another girl whom I vaguely recognize, on the other. I'm not sure of her name though; Jilly? Jenny?

Several candles are burning and the air is thick with cigarette smoke. There is a bottle of wine open in the middle of them and all four of them are clutching glasses. Chenoa doesn't say anything, simply raises an eyebrow at me.

'Jim!' Ardhendu says. 'Jeez, look at the state of you! Did you fall into the sea?'

'No,' I reply coldly, 'It's raining outside.'

'Yeah?' Ray says. 'It's funny, but you know from inside

these caves sometimes you really can't hear the rain.'

Ardhendu laughs, but it doesn't sound like a friendly kind of laugh. It's more like a snigger.

There is a silence as all four of them look at me, their faces expectant. I flail around for words. I really don't want to say in front of them all that I'm looking for Chenoa, but neither do I want to just leave. I wait for Chenoa to say something but, when she doesn't, Ray speaks again.

'We were just having a little drink. Or tipple, isn't that what you Brits call it? A tipple?'

I feel a surge of admiration for Ray, for his easy manner and flowing patter of conversation, for his kind brown eyes and impressive beard. But at the same time I wish he wasn't here right now. Not him and not the others. Even though Ray has every right to be here, in his own cave, I feel horribly, irrationally angry with him.

'Want to join us?' he presses on, either oblivious to my discomfort or in spite of it.

The truth is that the last thing in the world I feel like doing is sitting down and chatting to these four. I take a deep breath and blurt out,

'No, but thanks anyway. Chenoa, can I have a word?'

Chenoa hasn't moved from her cross-legged position on the mattress. She is wearing the same denim mini skirt and pale blue shirt from last night and her hair hangs over her shoulder in a simple plait. From her fingers coils a thin twist of smoke, the perpetual cigarette. Chenoa looks like the kind of girl who was born smoking. 'Yeah, sure,' she replies, making no effort to move. *Christ*, do I have to spell it out to her?

I motion with my head to the cave's entrance. 'I mean…alone.'

'Outside the cave?'

Everybody's faces are turning from Chenoa's to mine, back and forth.

'Well, yes.'

'I thought you said it was raining?'

'Please.' I attempt to keep my voice low and level. I think I see a frown cross her face, but at the same time, she stands up from her cross-legged position, as gracefully as a ballerina, her long, bare legs unfolding beneath her. It is still raining hard outside and Chenoa winces against the lashing deluge, moving back inside so that only her face is outside. Now that I have her attention, I don't know what to say to her. I cross my arms, suddenly feeling cold for the first time since I've been in Matala. She looks at me questioningly.

'How are you?' I ask.

'Yeah. Good. Whacked though from picking figs.'

I nod and rub my hands together. 'I…' I falter and then begin again, 'I've been thinking about you today.'

Chenoa doesn't say anything, just squints up into the rain that lashes down in thick sheets. 'So I'm gettin' kinda wet out here. So are you. You sure you don't want to come in for a bit?'

I hesitate. Perhaps the others will clear off after a while. But then Ray…it's unlikely he will. I sigh and shake my head. 'No…but, how are you?'

Chenoa laughs, an easy, open laugh and as I watch her longingly, I want to kiss away the raindrops that are gathering on her face.

'You already asked me that.'

I smile awkwardly and bite my bottom lip. 'Are you busy tomorrow? It's Sunday.'

'Yeees,' Chenoa agrees slowly. 'It's Sunday.'

What I mean by this comment, of course, is that nothing happens in Crete on a Sunday and even the donkeys have a holiday and therefore she won't, of course, be doing anything.

'So would you like to do something together?'

'For example?' Chenoa reaches up and pats her dampening head.

'For example…' I can think of nothing. What would Charles do? What would Charles suggest now?

'Go for a walk? To see the Roman ruins?' I hazard. This is the kind of thing she's probably interested in, what with her degree and everything.

Chenoa takes her hands away from her head and smiles. That smile makes everything alright and restores my confidence. She *does* like me. But then she shrugs, that nonchalance of hers written into every curve and feature of her face and body.

'Sure. Maybe.'

Sure is good. Maybe, less so. But maybe will have to do for now and I catch that word like a butterfly in a net and hold on to it for dear life. I'm still feeling brave and lean in to kiss her on the lips. At the last second, she turns her cheek slightly so that I kiss the side of her mouth. She draws back, laughing lightly whilst, confused, I try again. But Chenoa begins to speak.

'Jim, I'll see you tomorrow.'

I clasp on to her one hand that is outside the cave. 'Promise?'

There is a moment's pause.

'Sure. Goodnight, Jim.' And with that, she has withdrawn

her hand and her head and is swallowed into the candlelit, smoky cave.

I stand there for about five more minutes, remembering the rain on her dark eyelashes and the feel of her hand, slippery silk in mine. I think of the contours of her collarbones and the shape of her lips, the bottom one slightly plumper than the top. Yes, I think, this must be what it feels like to be in love.

Chapter Ten

I wake late the next morning to the sound of Charles clipping his toenails. I groan and shift over in the tomb, pulling the cover over my ears.

'What?' Charles protests. 'It's late.'

I push the cover back down. 'How late?'

'Late. I've been up for ages. I've even been for a swim and to Mama's Bakery. Here,' he tosses some bread in a paper bag over to me.

'I thought you said nothing was open on a Sunday,' I mumble.

'Nothing *except* for Mama's. Somebody has to feed the hungry cave-dwellers, don't they?'

I hear the grin in Charles's voice and heave myself upright, rubbing my eyes as sunlight streams in through the cave door. All signs of the previous night's storm have vanished; with the sun still low in the sky, blinding sunshine pools onto the floor of the cave. Charles is whistling as he collects his toenail clippings into a neat pile and I can't help but smile to myself as I think of the day ahead of me: a day of sunshine, swimming and Chenoa.

'What's the plan today, Jimmy boy?' Charles asks, as

though reading my mind.

I open the paper bag, take a bite of bread then begin to pick through my clothes. Oh God, I really, really need to wash them. Or get them washed, though I can't begin to think of anyone who might be prepared to wash my smelly clothes. The image of the two new English girls I met the day before flickers through my mind, their open, enthusiastic faces and gushing voices. Hmm…I'll have to think about that one.

'I ought to give my clothes a wash,' I say with a sigh. 'But…it's just too tedious to think about.'

'If you had some money,' Charles scoffs, 'I'd say give me some, and I'll wash them for you. But you don't, so you're out of luck.'

'I have no idea how to wash clothes.'

'Jim,' Charles says as he pulls the sleeping sheet back over his bed. 'It's not rocket science.'

'I know.' I sniff under the armpits of a couple of t-shirts and grimace. 'But it's bloody boring. Anyway, I'm going to spend the day with Chenoa today.'

Charles lets out a low whistle. 'Are you indeed. Manage to get your hooks into her last night?'

I push all the clothes I need to wash into a little pile in the corner.

'Not exactly. But she did say she'd like to spend the day with me. I'm going to head down to her cave now.'

'Right. I'll come with you. Ray, I've discovered, is a first rate chess player. Almost, though not quite, as good as me.'

'Course not.' I say, pulling on my cut-off jeans. 'Come on, then.'

A light wind is blowing up from the sea so that its surface

shimmers like fragments of a diamond. I close my eyes for a moment. Matala. A place of eternal warm winds. A place of music and laughter. A place where I've fallen in love.

Reaching the cave, I find that Chenoa and Ray have just come back from a swim and their tanned, sinewy bodies are glistening in the sunshine. Chenoa is wearing her white bikini and looks much like I remember her from that first day. I stop before rounding the corner, simply staring and taking in the sight of her laying a towel out in the sunshine, until Charles pushes me from behind.

Ray looks up first and welcomes us, giving me a rather strange smile though, that I can't quite read.

'Hi Jim, hey Charles' Chenoa says from her reclining position on the towel.

'Hi,' we both reply at the same time.

'Storm's cleared all the clouds away,' she says.

Charles casually walks down to the cave and says something to Ray that I don't catch, before both of them duck inside. I hold back, wondering whether to ask Chenoa to come for a walk now or a little later. She looks very comfortable there sunbathing. And it's a pretty good sight for that matter, one that I'm also reluctant to relinquish.

I sidle up to Chenoa and sit down beside her, hugging my knees into my chest. Christ, it's hot already. I yank my t-shirt off and blow my fringe up.

'You good?' I ask.

'Yeah. Been for a swim already. Magic. You want some of this?'

From her horizontal position, Chenoa holds up a bottle of something. 'What is it?' I ask.

'Tanning oil,' she replies.

'Is that like suntan cream?' I ask dubiously.

'Not really. It makes you tan way darker.'

I eye her long, lithe, dark body from the corner of my eye and upend the bottle, liberally smearing the oil over my chest and face. It feels revolting. But nevermind, if it means I can get a tan like Chenoa's, that's fine. Charles and Ray appear once more from inside the cave with Ray's chess set and find themselves a shaded corner near the entrance, where they position themselves and start to set the board up. I peer over at them, handling the pieces as though they are nuggets of gold. I don't know how to play chess. Father offered to teach me once, long ago. Did I say no, or had I said yes but then it never happened? I really can't remember.

I look back down at Chenoa, white bikini against a red and yellow striped towel. She has put on an enormous pair of black sunglasses that I find disconcerting, as I can't tell if she's looking at me or has her eyes closed. I'm feeling brave so lie down beside her, though I have no towel and the rough ground scratches my back. But it's worth it if I can lie this close to her, a small patch of our shoulders just touching. Just as I am moving my hand across to catch her fingers, I hear Charles's voice.

'Jesus, who are these lot?'

Chenoa and I sit up at the same time, Chenoa pushing her huge sunglasses over her sweating forehead on to her hair. Ray and Charles have abandoned their chess game and have both jumped to their feet. Even from our sitting position, we can see the small but sturdy procession of people, dressed in dark, heavy clothes, making their way across the beach towards the caves.

'Oh *man*,' Ray says with a sigh, 'not again.'

'What? Who are they?' I ask.

'Tourists,' says Ray. 'Greek tourists. From Heraklion mainly, but some of them even come over from the mainland.'

'To visit Matala?' I ask blankly.

Chenoa leans back on her elbows. 'No. To see *us.* The people living in the caves.'

'You have to be joking,' Charles laughs.

'Nope,' Chenoa continues. 'Our fame has spread far and wide. You know even the school kids in Mires are forbidden to come and see us? Seriously. We're in famous.'

Ray jumps down from the ledge and walks towards Chenoa and me. 'What do you say, Chen? You want to head into the cave?'

'Nah,' Chenoa says in her lazy drawl. 'Let 'em take a few photographs, then they'll get bored and move on to the next lot.'

'Ok. Well if you're sure.'

'Yeah.'

Chenoa replaces her sunglasses and lies back down on her towel. I frown and get to my feet, just as Ray and Charles are settling back down to their game. There aren't many of them, but something about the darkness of the clothes they are wearing make them appear a formidable group. That is just weird, people coming to look at us and take photographs.

'You know,' Chenoa says from her reclining position, 'one time they even brought us cigarettes. And plums, wasn't it, Ray?'

'Yep. Plums.'

'Ok,' I state, feeling a little less antipathy towards the advancing party. Hopefully this bunch will have some cigs for us. I shake my head and go to lie back down beside Chenoa, closing my eyes against the glare of the sun. But moments later, I hear the murmur of voices and disgruntled, sit up again, shielding my eyes. There are five of them, dressed in heavy, stiff clothes, chattering away in Greek. They are all middle-aged and one has an Olympus camera slung around his neck, which I hear the click of, before I actually see. I glare at the group, the other three not paying them any attention. I attempt to do the same, but it's impossible. I can't. They are just standing there, yards away from us, babbling about us and pointing at us as though we're animals in a zoo rather than young people sunbathing and playing chess and minding our own business.

The least they could do, I think in irritation, is give us some bloody cigarettes if they're going to stand there and gawk at us like that. I look over at Ray and Charles, absorbed in their game.

'Ray!' I call over. Ray raises his hand in my direction but doesn't look up. 'Ray! Do you think they'll go soon?'

'Ignore them,' Ray says, his voice unperturbed.

'It's not very easy to ignore them when they're standing right in front of us,' I mutter so that only Chenoa can hear me.

'Just lie down, close your eyes and ignore them,' Chenoa says. 'Believe me, they'll go any minute.'

I continue to glare at them, the group oblivious to my irritation as they laugh and chatter. One of them, the oldest and fattest, is smoking a pipe and keeps pointing the end of it over in our direction between puffs. I take a deep breath and am about to lie down again when the man with the camera, a short, stout man with a shock of bushy black hair flecked with grey, moves forwards. As I am the only one paying them any attention, he begins to talk to me in Greek, pointing at the camera and then pointing at Chenoa. I have no idea what he's saying, but it's clear enough that the gist of it is that he wants to get closer to take photos of her. I shake my head vigorously, but he persists, smiling at me through nicotine-stained teeth and nodding.

Before I know what's happening, the man has stepped over the ledge and is standing in our little space. He moves closer to Chenoa and raises the camera up, filling his lens with her. That is it. I feel a hot rage tear through me. Which part about shaking my head and clearly saying no does this idiotic man not understand? I jump to my feet without giving it a second thought and with both hands, push the man's shoulders; not hard, but hard enough for him to stumble and for his face to crumple in surprise.

'Don't take photos of her!' I shout at him.

The contingent in the background raise their voices in protest, and both Ray and Charles stop their game, looking up and frowning. Chenoa sits upright on her towel.

'What's going on?' she asks in a low, level voice.

'This man,' I say accusingly, pointing at the man with the camera who has hurriedly re-joined the group, 'came really close up to you. He was ogling you so…I just told him to get lost.'

I wait, expecting her to thank me, but she continues to look ahead, pulling her knees into her chest. The group carry on talking in high, animated voices, shaking their heads and tutting and looking at me disapprovingly before they move back off down the path.

'For fuck's sake,' I say, forcing a laugh as I run my fingers through my hair and come to sit back down. I look over at Ray and Charles but both of them are staring at me, their faces devoid of humour.

'What?' I ask reproachfully. 'They won't bother us again now.'

Charles raises an eyebrow and looks at me questioningly whilst Ray's face remains expressionless. I turn to Chenoa, about to ask her if she is alright when I see, to my surprise, that she has stood sharply up and whipped the towel out from beneath her. Slinging it over her shoulder, and without saying a word, she turns her back to me and walks briskly into the cave. I stare after her, nose crinkling in confusion. I look back over to Ray and Charles to ask what the problem is, but they have both busied themselves with their chess game once again and neither looks like they are prepared to cast any light on the situation.

I stand up and walk towards the cave, pushing back the door hanging before stooping and walking in.

'Chenoa,' I call, before locating her in the far corner where the clothes are piled, pulling on a top. She doesn't reply and I move closer.

'Chenoa, are you ok?'

She turns her head towards me, amber green cat's eyes flashing.

'That was not cool, Jim. That was really not cool.'

'*What*?' I say, startled by the anger in her eyes. 'I don't understand.'

'No,' she says coolly, 'somehow that doesn't surprise me.'

Chenoa rummages around in the pile of clothes until she finds a pair of loose, cotton trousers that she pulls on over her bikini bottoms.

'What's that supposed to mean?' I frown.

'Jim,' she says in a hard tone as she squares up to me, hands on her hips. 'I said to ignore them. Ray said to ignore them. They come every Sunday, these people. It's not a big deal. But you couldn't leave it, could you?'

I open my mouth to say something, but she silences me.

'And then, even more importantly, this kind of...*ownership* of me. You think I can't look after myself, huh? I am *not* your girl, Jim.'

To hear her say that, in such plain, hostile words hurts so much that I can't think how to respond for several moments. I just stare, her nostrils flaring like a wild pony whilst I try to push away this feeling of intense hurt and disappointment. I would do anything for her, for this girl I've only just met but am certain I have fallen in love with. Yet she is throwing it back in my face, our night together, my feelings for her. Eventually, I try to laugh it off, but my laugh comes out as a snort.

'Christ, Chenoa, I was only trying to get them to bugger off.'

She stands there, delicate hands on her hips and she looks so angry and so beautiful that I have to physically restrain myself from walking up to her and kissing her hard on the mouth.

'Right,' she says, lips pursed in such a way that she clearly doesn't believe me.

'Chenoa,' I say, digging my heels firmly into the floor of the cave, steeling myself for her answer. 'The other night...well, what was it for? What did it mean to you? Or...' I pause, knowing that I shouldn't go on, but not able to help myself, 'Or...nothing? Did it mean nothing?'

Chenoa sighs loudly and drops her hands to her side before slapping them against her thighs in a gesture of irritation.

'Oh Jim, *c'mon.*'

'Come on, what? *You* come on. Just tell me what you want. What you don't want. I don't understand you. I'm trying to be...' I flail around for words, '*chivalrous*, but it's impossible to read you. You slept with me, so there must be something there, but I don't know what. So just do me a favour would you, and be straight with me.'

Chenoa raises an eyebrow, the anger on her face softening as she begins to root around for a cigarette. Finding none, she turns to me again and runs her fingers through her loose hair, which I'm momentarily distracted by. It is so fine and such an unearthly, golden colour.

'Jim,' she says in a gentle voice. 'Listen. You are really sweet – '

'But?' I cut in.

'But...God, you know this already. I'm not anyone's 'girl'. I'm just me. I don't commit to anyone, or anything. I live on my impulse.'

'Having sex with me was an impulse?'

Chenoa sighs again and leans against the cave wall, crossing her arms over defensively.

'You were clearly into me. And I wasn't averse to...seeing what it would be like.'

'Seeing what *it* would be like? You had sex with me out of curiosity?' I feel my fists clenching and unclenching.

'Your words.'

'But true.'

'Well, curiosity. In a way. Look, I've really had enough

of this conversation now.' Chenoa flicks her hair behind her back and starts to make towards the cave entrance.

I realise that this is it; that I am losing her and, in a final, desperate attempt to prevent her from going back outside, I take a step in front of her and grasp her by the wrists.

'Chenoa, OK. That's fine, if you only had sex with me out of curiosity. And I'm sorry I pissed you off out there, that wasn't my intention. But...well, what do you think about having sex with me again, out of curiosity? To see what it's like a second time?'

Chenoa begins to laugh, lightly shaking herself free.

'You're too much, you know that? Just relax, I'll see you around. We're neighbours, aren't we?'

She raises an eyebrow at me in that amused, lazy way of hers. I know I am being dismissed. Or rather, she is leaving the cave this very minute and I stare as her figure is swallowed into the bright sunshine outside. I've blown it, I *know* I've blown it and there is absolutely nothing I can say or do to change the situation.

I turn, in a fit of rage, and pound one fist against the cave wall, hurting my knuckle as I do so and cursing. They are probably all out there laughing at me right now, Charles included. Well, I don't need Chenoa. I don't need Charles either. I don't need any of them. He's been so fucking sanctimonious recently anyway. I storm towards the cave entrance, pulling back the cloth hanging so roughly that it comes down and I march through the three of them, hurrying down the path towards the cave. Fuck her, I think, just *fuck* her.

As always, the fury grips my body as blood pumps like a snare drum in my ears and my entire body tenses. I feel my shoulders shooting upwards and forwards, powerless to relax them. What must I look like, I think, as I half-walk, half-trip down the rocky path, sunlight beating down on my head.

When I reach our cave, I angrily tear back the curtain and fling myself onto my hard tomb, burying my face into the jumper that I use as a pillow. And then, to my horror, my eyes fill with tears and I wipe them furiously away, squeezing my eyes shut into the warm, scratchy material to prevent them from coming. *Stop* it, I tell myself, *just stop it.* But I can't, and the tears find a way out, dampening my jumper.

It's just a girl. I try to feed myself this line. *Just a girl, a bloody girl. There are plenty more of them.* But there aren't, not like Chenoa. Even if there were, that's not all that this is about and as I begin to cry openly into the jumper, all attempts at preventing the flow cast aside, I feel the confusion as I have done on so, *so* many previous occasions: that this feeling inside me is beyond my comprehension. It is deeper and stronger and all-consuming and although I am crying because Chenoa has rejected me, I'm also crying about something else. I just don't know what this something else *is* and that makes me feel sadder than ever.

Once the tears subside, I turn over onto my back and wipe my hand over my cheeks and beneath my eyes. I stare up at the craggy roof of the cave and wonder what I should do with the rest of this day. So, no romantic walk to the ancient baths. I didn't want to bloody go there again anyway. No. I am going to spend the day meeting other people and then tonight I am going to get completely obliterated. The lack of money crosses my mind but then I dismiss it quickly. I just need to be myself, I think, maybe turn the charm up a notch and people will buy me drinks. Girls will buy me drinks.

Except, my plans to socialise don't happen because the fact is, I really don't feel like talking to anyone. After an hour or so at the cave, kicking around and assuming that Charles will turn up, I head to the café with no clear plan in mind. Once there, I offer to wash up or help with the cooking. Fedor, the swarthy Cretan who owns the place, looks me over suspiciously then, without a word, hands me the scrubbing brush.

I stare into the bottomless well of dirty glasses, plates and bowls, everything covered with a film of thick oil. This is just shit. This is not what I want to be doing right now. I should be with Chenoa, being inducted into the fine art of lovemaking and instead, I sigh, as I dive my hands into the greasy tub, I am up to my elbows in other people's dirty plates. It takes me two hours to wash up and, once finished, Fedor asks me if I'd like to be paid in cash or wine. I hesitate – of course I ought to take the money. Buy a decent meal or save to go into Mires to get myself some new shoes. Thing is though, I know myself well enough to recognise that my will power just isn't strong enough for any of that, particularly given the way I'm feeling. That even if Fedor *does* give me money, it won't take long before I buy wine anyway.

I give into that logic and sit with a tumbler and the bottle at the table nearest to the crashing waves. The *retsina* appears to be corked, but I can't be bothered to argue about it. It doesn't affect the taste anyway, I think, as I sit and knock back glass after glass. A few of the cave dwellers come in for a drink or an omelette whilst I sit there. They nod their head in my direction and look as though they are going to approach me to strike up a conversation. But it must be something about my face that makes them stay away, and I'm not sure if that makes me feel more relieved or miserable.

By five o'clock in the afternoon, I've finished the bottle and the sun is beginning to lower over the sea. Charles appears at the door with a guitar under his arm and I feel a sharp twinge of hostility towards him. Why has it taken him all this time to come looking for me? He pads across the wooden floor of the café and pulls a chair out from the table so that he sits opposite me, taking in the empty bottle of *retsina*.

'What's up?' he asks, leaning the guitar up against a table leg and pulling his cigarettes out from his pocket and, without even waiting for me to ask, lights a second one for me.

I inhale gratefully and deeply. That was the only thing missing from my corked bottle of wine: several cigarettes to help wash it down with.

'What kind of a question is that?' I ask sulkily, noticing the slight slur in my voice. 'You know very well what's up.'

Charles leans back in his chair, cigarette drooping from his bottom lip, his blond hair stiff from sand and sun. He drums his fingers on the table and doesn't say anything.

'I don't understand it, Charles. I really like this girl. More than I've liked any girl before and that stupid incident this morning, I just don't get why she flew off the handle like that. Most girls would hate a complete stranger leering over them and taking photos. For fuck's sake, he'd come so close up. I was just trying to...get rid of him.'

Charles continues to be silent, blowing a couple of smoke rings with a pensive expression on his face.

'What do you think, Charlie boy?' I search his face and then hiccup slightly. 'Was I so in the wrong?'

Charles twirls his cigarette back and forth between his thumb and forefinger and frowns.

'Got nothing to do with me.' He pauses and then looks up at me. 'But for Christ's sake Jim, it's Chenoa this, Chenoa that…just forget about her. There are dozens more girls here who I'm sure would love to be seduced by you.'

I fiddle with the label on the wine bottle, peeling it off.

'I don't want to seduce any other girls,' I say miserably.

'*Jim*,' Charles presses on, 'Chenoa's not interested in relationships. Surely you must see that?'

'But she had sex with me!'

'So what? She's probably had sex with several other people here, besides her travelling companion, Ray.'

I try to keep the dismay from my face, but know I haven't succeeded. Charles sighs as he grinds out his cigarette in the ashtray. He picks up his guitar and begins to strum a few chords before he finds a sequence and starts to sing a song about how I should forget her and there are plenty more fish in the sea. I grin half-heartedly, but the smile doesn't last long before I begin to stare gloomily at my empty glass once again.

'There's a cook-up going on the beach at the moment,' Charles hazards. 'Fish stew. Wine. Why don't you come and join in?'

I pause. 'Is Chenoa there?'

'Yes.'

I shake my head glumly. 'Maybe I'll come later. I think I'll just stay here a little while longer.'

Charles pushes his chair back and stands up.

'Alright. But don't stay sad for too long. It doesn't suit you.'

As he is leaving the café, I call out to him. 'Charlie boy?'

Charles turns, his warm, open face now liberally dotted with freckles.

'You couldn't lend me a few drachma, could you? Just for another small glass of something.'

Charles rolls his eyes and, walking back to the table, empties his pocket of coins and lays them on the table before disappearing back out to the beach.

Chapter Eleven

The following morning, I have no recollection of getting to bed. I remember being in the café and ordering more wine. I remember Susanne and Wolfgang coming in and some kind of a conversation with them. And I remember, very vaguely, leaving the café and stumbling down the stairs. But that's it; beyond that is a large grey void edged with a few pictures slightly more in focus.

I have a wrenching headache and my mouth feels as dry as sand. Stretching my head over to the side, I see Charles's tomb is empty. I slowly, painfully pull myself up and unsteadily get to my feet. Outside, it is blindingly bright and hot and I find myself moving backwards and slumping down against the cave wall in a small, shaded part. I drop my head into my hands and groan. What happened last night? Why can't I remember the last part of it? Suddenly, I really, really don't want to be here anymore. Not in Matala, not in Crete. I'm loath to admit it to myself, but what I really want is to go home. For a while at least. Eat some of Ma's crispy bacon and scrambled eggs and sleep in my own bed. Of course my father is the last person on earth I want to see, but the way I'm feeling right now, I even think that I can put up with the grumpy familiarity of him for a bit too.

This realisation of homesickness comes as a shock. It never occurred to me that things could be less than perfect in Matala. Charles is so at home here. That is a surprise too, one that neither of us could have predicted before arriving. Matala is like a second skin to Charles and whilst he was the one full of cynicism for the pleasure-seeking, utopian-living travellers beforehand, it's now me who can't stand the sight of a fair few of them. They're all frauds, that's what they are. Alright, perhaps not all of them, but certainly a large proportion of the cave-dwellers. Chenoa included, I think bitterly. I don't fit in here, that much is certain, and I feel both relief and disappointment at this truth. But what next? The thought of hitchhiking home on my own makes me feel quite sick. I'm not sure if I can do it without Charles's flair for languages. Or his money for that matter.

I stick a foot out into the sun to see if it really is as hot as I'd first imagined when I came outside but the heat hits me like daggers of fire and I draw it back in sharply. Perhaps that's the answer, to talk to Charles and get him to come home, too. We could go back together, do our A Levels, and things will go back to normal at school and home. School, yes, even school with its narrow corridors and dusty blackboards, its uptight teachers and dull lessons seems strangely comforting this morning and the longer that I sit there thinking, the more I feel like going home. I count up on my fingers how long I've been here and am shocked to discover that it's only six days. It feels like far, far longer than that. *Weeks.*

So much has happened since Charles and I left Twickenham that misty morning. Some of it good. But a lot of it not. I wanted to love Matala. There is certainly very little about the landscape and the views and the enticing sea *not* to love about it. And this kind of beach paradise that has been created by a handful of young people from all around the world, well, that is all well and good in theory. But the fact is that it *isn't* a utopia. It is cliquey and fraudulent and people bang on about the same things again and again. No, I think, as I hunch my back against the cave wall. People here like the sound of their own voices far too much. *Peace and ban the bomb and anti-Vietnam and cold war and Afghanistan.* But they only like the *sounds* these words make; they enjoy trying to out-do each other with their tales and their theories. But it is all boring, just bloody boring.

Now Eel Pie Island, *that* is an interesting place. Great music, lots of pretty girls, dancing, cheap ale. I feel a pang for my homeland and my old turf, so real and immediate and violent that it makes my stomach hurt. I know that's hunger talking as well as I've barely eaten anything in the past twenty-four hours. I push all thoughts of food aside and turn my mind back to Eelpiland. The rickety bridge, the old lady with her headscarf taking the money, the moving dance floor, the fumbling on the grass. I smile just thinking about it. I'm sure I can entice Charles back home with the promise of further fabulous nights on the island. Speaking of Charles, where is he?

I force myself to stand up and limp over to the ledge rather pathetically. I must look a state. Heaving myself up on to it, I stand and survey the beach, shielding my eyes with one hand. Somebody has drawn an enormous ban the bomb sign in the sand with a stick and I purse my lips. I can see Ray sitting down, his tanned, hairy body stretched out in the sun. He appears to be calling something out to the sea and I move my face directly to the ocean where I first see Chenoa bobbing about amongst the waves and then Charles, practicing front crawl. At least, I think it's him, at this distance it's hard to be sure, but when he stops swimming to brush hair and water away from his face, laughing as he does so, I know for certain. I'd recognise that laugh anywhere, even from this distance.

Since when, I think sulkily, have those three become so tight? I really do not want to see Chenoa. Nor Ray for that matter. But I'm keen to talk to Charles, to discuss going home and so the only thing for it is to hang around the cave till he gets back. First though, I need some water. I find an empty bottle in the cave and pick my way down the path to the communal tap. My feet are becoming quite hard from lack of shoes but, even so, they still hurt when I'm walking over rocks and prickly grass and I wish again that they would turn up. It must have been one of these cave-dwellers who stole them. Probably that tosser, Ardhendu.

I fill my bottle twice, drinking deeply, before making my way back up to the cave. Half way up I stop to turn and look at the bumpy track that Charles and I arrived on. It feels like such a long time ago, though it was mere days. I know there is a bus that comes from Mires every so often, though it seems to be erratic. But we could always ask Mama and see if one is due this afternoon. It wouldn't take long to get all our stuff together and jump on the bus. The thought of leaving that very day gives me a burst of energy and I begin to run up the path. But then, the thought occurs to me again that I have no money. Not a single drachma. Charles will be very unhappy if I don't at least contribute to the cigarette fund and the thought of that long hitchhiking journey home without any cigarettes is more than I can bear. Sighing, I turn back and head in the direction of the café to see if there is any more washing up to be done. And this time, I think, I'll *force* myself to take the money and not that gut-rot wine.

Charles and I arrive back at the cave at the same time. My headache has started again after an unpleasant two hours of scraping food from plates and plunging my hands into greasy water. Charles, on the other hand, looks well-rested and relaxed, his skin glistening from the water. His spectacles are resting on the ledge and as I peer at him, I think how completely different he looks when he isn't wearing them. Almost like a different person. Charles has worn glasses for as long as I've known him.

'Ouch,' Charles comments when he sees me.

I look at him questioningly as he towel-dries his hair.

'You look like a bear with a sore head.'

'Yes, well, I feel like shit if that makes you feel any better.'

'Christ, you were in a sorry state last night. How much did you have to drink?'

I shrug moodily. 'No idea.' I reach up to scratch my nose and, as I do so, realise it is peeling quite badly. I don't want to talk about last night.

'I've just been washing up at the café.' I tell him.

Charles lets out a whistle. 'My God, you *must* be desperate for cigarettes or booze to subject yourself to hard labour like that.'

'Neither, actually,' I reply, coming over to sit in the shaded area.

There must be something about my tone of voice that makes Charles stop rubbing his hair. He places his specs back on his face and looks at me with interest.

'What, then?'

'Well, I'm going to go back.'

'Back where?' Charles asks blankly.

I roll my eyes. 'Back *where*? To Timbuktu. Back to London, you moron. To Twickenham. I've had enough. I want to go back.'

Charles is silent for some time and when I look at his face closely, he appears to be chewing the inside of his mouth. 'I see,' he says eventually.

'Anyway,' I continue, 'it can't be all that long before term starts. So we…well, you know. Ought to get back.'

At this, Charles bursts out laughing and picks his towel back up, rubbing his hair vigorously.

'Oh, *Lord*. Listen to you! Who would have thought it?'

I cross my arms. 'I don't know what you mean.'

'Course you do. *You* were the one desperate to come here. And now we're here, in this paradise, and you want to pack it all in and head back just because it didn't work out with Chenoa.'

I glare at Charles, biting my lip so that I don't yell at him. 'It's not just because of her,' I say quietly. 'It's other things, too.'

'For example?'

'I haven't had a bloody good night's sleep since we left England, for a start. And there's something fake, something *forced* about this place. Something strange about all these people living here in these ancient burial caves.'

Charles shrugs. 'I disagree.'

I ignore him. 'And another thing, I feel that I should make peace with my old man. It was a pretty bad blow-up we had. He's an idiot. But he's still my father.'

Again, Charles stops what he's doing and stares at me incredulously. '*Really*?'

'Really what?'

'I have never, ever heard you say a good word about your old man. Why now, suddenly?'

'I've just told you, haven't I?' I snap. 'We had a really bad argument. And I think I should go back and make it up with him. Or try, at least.'

Charles sits on the ledge opposite me in the sunshine. 'That's commendable, at least. I have to give you that, Jim.'

I shake my head and stare at my filthy feet. 'Your family…well, you just seem so harmonious all the time and…I dunno, *perfect*. I don't know what that's like.'

Charles sighs loudly. 'Oh, come *on* Jim, you really believe there's such a thing as a perfect family? That's just an illusion.'

'But you never disagree with your dad, do you?'

I look up at him, framed by a shock of blue sky, looking more than ever like he fits in here, like he belongs. 'Course I do.'

'About what then?'

'About…I don't know, not working hard enough. Bringing dirty shoes into the house. Swearing.'

I stand up and move over to the ledge. 'But that's just normal crap. You don't hate your dad, do you?'

'Well…' Charles pushes his specs further up his nose and frowns, 'course not.'

'I do,' I say quietly, staring down at the gleaming waves below. 'I fucking hate his guts. And he hates mine. And…' I pause.

'And what?'

'And I wish it didn't have to be that way.'

We are both silent for a few moments, a warm breeze playing with our hair and the sun tingling on our shoulders.

'Perhaps it needn't be,' Charles says solemnly and then turns to look at me. 'Yeah, maybe it's the right thing, to be going back. For you, anyway. But I'm not coming with you, I'm afraid.'

My head whips round as I stare at Charles. *'What?'*

'You heard. I'm not coming. I like it here. I feel…I dunno, *good* here.'

'But what about A Levels?'

Charles laughs again, pulling his cigarettes out of his pocket. He doesn't offer one to me.

'Look, I might come back for A Levels. Or…' he shrugs, pausing to light his cigarette. 'Or maybe I won't. I don't know yet.'

'Your parents will do their nut.'

'I can handle my parents.'

I feel a wave of panic, considering the very real prospect of having to travel back home alone. I remain silent, pulling my knees up into my chest and wrapping my arms around them.

'Are you serious?' I ask quietly.

Charles sighs and jumps down from the ledge, coming to stand in front of me and I look up at him, this best friend of mine who is feeling more and more like a stranger.

'Never been more serious. Jim, if you recall, *you* were the one who wanted to come here. Not me. You managed to talk me into it, and I'm grateful to you for that. But if you think I'm going to up-sticks and leave just because you've had enough, you're wrong, my friend.'

'But it's...but I'm...' I search around for words and, finding none, I pull my knees in closer to my chest and lay my head on them.

'What is it?'

'What?' I say, without looking up.

'What's *wrong* with you? I just don't get it. Look around, look where we are! This is the most magical place I've been to in my life. Surely it must be for you, too. But you've been...I don't know, just kind of uptight ever since we got here.'

'Uptight?' I raise my head from my knees and frown at Charles.

'Yes,' Charles replies simply. 'Uptight. Not joining in with things. Not making an effort to talk to people, get to know them. You've just been fixated on this one girl and – '

I groan and drop my head back down. '*Please* can we not start talking about Chenoa again,' I say, voice muffled.

The two of us remain like that for some time in silence, me sitting in that cramped knees-to-chest position and Charles standing, surveying me from above, hands on hips. Eventually, I speak.

'Have I really been uptight?'

'Truth?'

I lift my head up from my knees and nod.

'Yes. You have. Not the Jimmy boy I know.'

I shrug and wrinkle my nose. 'I don't feel like the Jimmy boy I know.'

Charles squats down onto his heels and looked solemnly at me. 'But *why*? When we're in Matala?'

'I don't know. Look, I've already told you that I'm not keen on a lot of the people here. They just...well, they get my goat. And then this whole thing with Chenoa…' I trail off. 'It's thrown me. Stupid, I know. She's just a girl. But she doesn't feel like just a girl.'

'Jim,' Charles says in a low tone, 'you made your own bed with that one. I mean, what the hell were you thinking yesterday morning pushing that man with a camera like you had sole custody over Chenoa. With Ray there and everything. If she was alright with it, you should have been too.'

I put a hand up. 'Forget it,' I say testily, 'just forget it. I don't want to talk about it anymore. Whatever I did, I can't bloody change it, can I? So do me a favour and don't rub it in anymore.'

Charles purses his lips and stands upright. Neither of us says anything for some time.

'When are you going to go?' he asks, eventually.

I look up again and run a hand through my stiff hair.

'Soon. I dunno. Tomorrow I reckon, if I can find someone to hitchhike with.' I look out across the horseshoe bay and sigh. Am I crazy, to leave all this after such a short time to return to a stifled house with emotionally repressed parents and all the grief I'll undoubtedly be at the receiving end of? 'Charlie boy,' I try again. 'Is there really nothing I can do to persuade you to come, too?'

Charles is silent for a few moments, scuffing the ground with his foot and my spirits rise, thinking that perhaps, just perhaps, he may change his mind.

'No,' Charles says quietly. 'Sorry, Jim. I'm not ready to leave yet.'

I grimace and nod. 'Righty-ho.' I force a smile and look down at my feet, tanned and dirty and scratched. 'Charles,' I say slowly. 'Did you bring a second pair of shoes with you?'

I spend a short while in the afternoon shoving all my belongings that are scattered around the cave into my rucksack. Charles vanishes shortly after our conversation for another swim, but he must have spoken to Wolfgang and Susanne because mid-way through packing they materialize at the mouth of the cave and poke their heads through.

'You're going,' Wolfgang says, joint dangling from his bottom lip.

I smile at him. These two are, really, the only truly decent people I've encountered in Matala.

'Yes,' I shrug, 'time to go home. Make peace with my old man. Get on with my life there.'

'You have been here such a short time, though,' Susanne says.

I look at her and grin. She always seems to be wearing an oversized man's shirt. But she's pretty. Not striking in the way Chenoa is, but her face is open and honest and uncomplicated. She looks you in the eye when she speaks to you and she has that lovely long, glossy hair.

'I know,' I tell her, 'I thought I'd stay longer. Truth is, though, I'm ready to go back now. But,' I stop packing and turn towards the two of them standing side by side, looking more than ever like brother and sister and I can't believe I hadn't noticed it before, 'are you ever in England? Because, y'know, it would be great to see you.'

Wolfgang slowly takes the spliff from his mouth and exhales, then holds it out to me.

'No,' he says with a smile in his eyes, 'we are never in England. Are you ever in Germany?'

I take the spliff from Wolfgang's extended hand and inhale deeply. The strength of it has an immediate impact on me and I feel my limbs loosening after the stresses of the day.

'No,' I burst out laughing, 'I'm never in Germany.'

Susanne and Wolfgang begin to laugh as well and a moment, suspended in space, descends upon the three of us as, involuntarily, we move inwards towards each other, arms winding around shoulders as the three of us hug, still laughing. This is how I want to remember Matala, I think with a broad smile on my face. This moment, in a warm, musty cave with my arms around the two most decent people here.

We spend a little longer talking, with promises of drinking wine and smoking under the stars that night, my last night. After I've packed up, I decide that I should go and say goodbye to Chenoa. Do I owe her an apology? I'm not so sure, and what's more, Ray is sure to be there if I do go. But nonetheless, I want to just say goodbye to her and leave on a good note. After all, I'll never see her again. And I did lose my virginity to this girl, for fuck's sake, not something I'll forget in a hurry. The gilded mermaid, I think with a wry smile. Charles's words. But a pretty good description.

I make my way down two levels, wondering who will be around on the beach this evening. Now that I know I'm leaving, my attitude towards Matala has softened; the people, even. I'm not happy about making my way home on my own but, at the same time, I know it's the right decision. I can almost smell Ma's bacon; hear the water of the Thames lapping against the shore beneath the bridge over to Eel Pie Island.

The cloth is hanging over the mouth of Ray and Chenoa's cave but it is still and quiet, save a swallow swooping low overhead. She must be down at the beach, I think in disappointment. Or picking fruit again. Outside the cave is an ashtray overflowing with the ends of cigarettes that I can smell from where I'm standing. I consider, for a moment, rooting around to see if there are any long enough to re-light before thinking better of it. I'd kill for a cigarette right now.

I really want to have a conversation with Chenoa before I go. I'm not entirely sure what I want to say to her, but now that I know I'm going, and feel calm about it, I just want to say goodbye. And thanks, maybe? Thanks for the memory? I was so bloody angry with her yesterday but now I just feel...I don't know, grateful for this experience. I've been here for less than a week but it feels as though so much has taken place and I know I won't forget these days in Matala in a hurry. And Chenoa is part of that – how can she not be?

I'm about to turn and head down to the beach, when a glint of something bright catches my eye. Beneath the door cloth, slightly to one side, lie a pair of glasses. I walk up to the door and stoop down, picking them up. I frown. They are Charles's specs, no doubt about it. No doubt whatsoever. What would they be doing here? Could it be that he's gone for a swim with Chenoa and Ray and left his specs here? Unlikely, I think, as he's blind as a bat without them and always puts them straight back on after doing anything. I walk over to the ledge and peer down to the beach. Although there's a group down there, I'm almost certain none of them is Charles.

Still holding the dark-rimmed glasses in my hands, I

move down from the ledge and back towards the cave. I push back the cloth and as my eyes grow accustomed to the dimness, I see them. Even holding Charles's spectacles in my hand; even *then*, it doesn't occur to me for an instant that my friend might be in there. They are just as shocked; looking towards me, they spring apart like opposing magnetic forces, their eyes flashing with guilt. No clothes have been shed; at least, not many. But it is unmistakable, that they have been together. They are together.

For several agonizing, protracted moments, Chenoa and Charles continue to stare at me, eyes wide and unblinking whilst I stare back, my head reeling. Charles. My best friend. With the girl I've fallen for. I feel blinded and numbed and muted and deafened by my inability to know how to deal with this situation. This is something that I never could have imagined even in my darkest moods. And because of this, because I have no idea what words or actions could possibly fill this chasm that yawns wide and ugly between us, I allow something else to take over. It's instinct, I decide later and, whilst I come to regret it, I have no idea how it could ever have been possible to alter the surge of anger that kicks in and consumes me so entirely. For I take three swift steps towards my best friend, pull back my arm and punch him in the face.

I have never punched anyone in my life. I've pushed people, kicked them, shoved them. Even bitten a boy at nursery school. But I have no idea how one should punch, and am even less prepared for the searing pain that tears like molten liquid through my right fist. It's an awkward punch, not terribly strong, but even so, the very act of it takes Charles by surprise. As he stumbles backwards, both hands flying up to his cheek whilst Chenoa gasps in horror, I shout 'fuck!' in shock and pain. I grab my right fist with my other hand but can't bear to be in there a second longer. Turning, I stumble towards the door, Charles calling my name behind me.

I lurch up the path, everything stinging: my fist, my eyes, my chest, my heart which feels as though it's rapidly dissolving like one of those Vitamin C tablets in a glass of water. As I flounder on, I pass somebody but don't even look up to see who it is, only pushing past them. Inside the cave, all I need to do is grab my rucksack with my good hand, awkwardly heaving it on to my back before rushing out and heading straight for the path. I'm sobbing now, crying in a way that I have no recollection of ever having done so before. I can hear the distant call of 'Jim! Wait!' but I'm not going to wait. Tears blur my vision and as I run along the track, I step on a thorn that splices into my heel.

'Jesus Christ!' I roar, hurling the load from my back as I turn my foot up and pull it out. I wince, picking up my backpack again.

Please, I think, please, please, *please* let there be a lift leaving this fucking place. Anything, I don't care what it is. I just need to get out of here. I pass the village tap, I pass Mama's Bakery, not stopping when she calls out from the dark interior and waves to me, I pass the tiny village church and I pass the point where Charles and I were dropped by the truck driver. I can see nothing, nobody on the road that leads away from Matala and I feel a surge of desperation welling up inside me.

I taste salt in my mouth and reach up. There is a thin trickle of snot dribbling down from my nose. Angrily, I wipe it away and scan the horizon, searching for anything that can take me away from here. My right knuckle has swelled up and turned a strange purple colour and, though the pain has lessened slightly, it still smarts and throbs and I keep rubbing my left hand over it. And then – almost as though by the strength of my desire sent out to the world – I hear the faint rumble of wheels before I see it. Rounding the corner from the village, I turn towards the noise and then there it is, the small open-backed pick-up truck, trundling along towards the main track. As it approaches, I can see and smell that the back is filled with fish in nets. But I don't waste a moment. Charging towards the truck like a man possessed, it comes to an abrupt stop, no doubt taken aback by the sight of this disheveled, sobbing boy.

'Mires?' I pant to the two fishermen sitting up front. They both stare at me from beneath the brims of their hats, their faces expressionless.

'Mires?' I say again, this time louder as I wipe more tears away. The man in the passenger seat points his thumb in the direction of the back of the truck and I nod at them gratefully before rushing round to the back, hurling my backpack in then clambering in after it. The truck takes off again with a start and I fall backwards against a net of fish, some of them still writhing around, half-alive. In disgust, I push away from the nets, trying to make space on the ground so I won't have to sit on or against the fish. But the back of the truck is so tightly packed that it's impossible.

Eventually, I give up and perch on top of a net, clinging on to my backpack as Matala recedes into the distance. I can see a figure waving his arms above his head and I hear the sound of my name being called again and again before it is swallowed by the wind and the waves. The final thing I see, before the truck lurches round the corner, is the curve of the bay and Charles jumping up and down against the deep lavender-tinged blue of the late afternoon sky whilst beside me, the silver scales of the still-living fish flap uselessly against their netted prison.

Chapter Twelve

I hope that one day the memory of my journey home from Matala might be erased from my memory. I also hope that, by some strange miracle, I might forget I ever had a best friend named Charles. A friend whom I played pranks with at school, whose room I sat in for hours on end talking about music and girls and weekend plans. A friend I went to Eel Pie Island with, and stood on the shoulders of, as the sprung floorboards of the dance hall lurched and bounced.

The journey back to Twickenham takes six days, but it feels to me like six years. I have no money, no shoes, and my right hand continues to throb and smart with pain and the memory of Charles's betrayal. There are times on that journey home that I hate Chenoa, but mostly it is Charles whom I inwardly rail against. What I want to know, and don't want to know at the same time, is when this romance between them started? Had it been just at that moment when I'd caught them together? Somehow I doubt it.

The anger and sadness play out in an endless cycle of waves as I travel northwards through Greece, Yugoslavia, Austria, Germany and the Netherlands. As always, these dual emotions are amplified so that I feel, at times, as though the strength of them might actually kill me. Can a person *die* from rage? Or from misery?

And then there is also the remorse I feel at not behaving differently with Chenoa, and the incredulity and bitterness that she should be attracted to my awkward, bookish best friend. Loneliness is not something I've had to contend with before, not *really,* but on that bumpy, uncomfortable journey home, it takes on a new form and I understand it on a visceral level.

My ripped jeans and t-shirt are hanging looser on me and know I look like a vagabond, particularly as I have no shoes, but I couldn't care less about that. One late afternoon in Vienna, so completely overcome by the pangs of hunger that gnaw at my insides with iron claws, I steal a sausage from a street vendor when he is looking the other way and hurriedly walk on, the scent of it wafting up to my nose as I hurriedly jog barefoot over the cobbles until I'm at a safe distance.

Emboldened by my success, I begin to steal more food, always from busy street vendors as most people in shops take one look at my shoeless feet and give me the kind of glare that means there's no chance I'll even be able to get into the shop, let alone steal from it. At night, I sleep in the trucks I hitch rides in or, on two nights, huddle in disused shop doorways wrapped in my one jumper. One morning in Frankfurt I even wake to find a few coins placed in front of me. I pull the coins out and hold them in the palm of my hand for some time, staring at them as though they are the most precious of gifts. I have no idea how much these strange coins are worth, but I immediately stand up and, ignoring my bare feet, keep walking until I find a bakery. There, I hand them over to a young girl with her hair pinned up beneath a cap and startlingly translucent skin and green eyes and point to the items on display, holding my hands up as I do so, hoping she will understand. Thankfully, she does and, taking one look at me, hurriedly picks up the tongs and drops two sugared buns into a paper bag. And then, looking around her shiftily, she quickly pops a couple more into the bag before thrusting it over the counter.

'Thank you,' I whisper and she inclines her head towards me in a short, sharp nod.

When I limp into Twickenham, a few days later, the cold has seeped into my bones, despite the weather being mild. I am hungry, bitterly exhausted, and I can't even bear to look at the sorry state of my feet. I walk along the Chertsey Road where my final lift drops me and, as I turn into London Road and begin to walk past familiar places, my spirits begin to rise. This is the off license where people congregate before a rugby match, clutching bottles of beer with scarves wound tightly around their necks against the wind and ruddy, laughing faces. This is the restaurant my parents brought me to after they forced me to get confirmed a few years ago. They'd sat there, smoking and sipping at the cheapest wine on the menu, whilst father regaled me about the virtues of being a churchgoer.

Here is Twickenham Railway Station. I stop and, from the opposite side of the road, stare at it. This is where my journey began with Charles, not so very long ago. Charles, I think again as a shaft of pain tears through me. I hate him for what he's done. But perhaps I shouldn't have left in such a hurry and at least let him have his say. And I shouldn't have hit him.

I sigh as I watch the commuters hurry to and fro. What's

the use of thinking about what I should or shouldn't have done? It's too late for all that. I have no idea of the time, day or date, but judging by the busy commuters it's a weekday, and still fairly early. A milk van trundles past, confirming that it's probably still before nine in the morning. Milk, I think. I haven't drunk any of that since leaving England. Strangely, I can't quite think what it tastes like. I keep walking, giving a cursory glance to The Cabbage Patch Pub where Charles and I first got served alcohol over the bar, age fifteen. I'd done all the talking – a friend of ours at school had offered the advice of making sure we had a scarf round our necks that covered our chins. Publicans could always tell if a punter was underage by their chins, he said. I'd been skeptical but tried it nonetheless. I was unconvinced that the publican believed we were old enough as there had been that telling pause as he peered at us, a scowl on his downturned lips. But then, as though he couldn't quite be bothered to turn us away, like magic, he served us. The two of us had scurried off to a dark corner table where we spent two hours over one pint of ale, crooning over our success.

As I get nearer and nearer to my house, the hunger I feel gnawing at the pit of my stomach is mingled with apprehension. Ma, I know, will be only too pleased to have me back. But Father? The fact that he hit me stings far less now, particularly as I can understand what it is to experience the kind of rage that leads a person to such an act. I don't care too much if he doesn't say sorry, I just want to wipe the slate clean and start again. Try and start again. I'm not quite sure how this will work, as I don't want to stop going to Eel Pie Island. But I'm clear that I *will* go back to school to do my A Levels and for the first time in my life, feel resolved to stop fighting with my father. Incredible really, I think wryly, that it should take a journey to a place that was against his wishes, to decide this.

Turning into my road, I pause. The row of terraced houses looks impossibly neat and twee with their flower-filled boxes on the windowsills and black painted iron gates. But inside one of these houses, I find myself thinking, upstairs in a bedroom on the right, sits a bed that is mine. With a mattress. And a soft pillow. Clean sheets and blankets. I'm not sure what I want more, to sink into the comfort of my bed or eat a decent meal. As I begin to walk, picking up my pace as I go, I correct myself. Talk, I think. I need to talk first to Ma and Father. Tell them I'm sorry for just buggering off like that. And then: toast, butter, marmalade (though Ma never lets me have both at the same time, but perhaps she will today) followed by sausages and scrambled eggs.

I reach number twenty-seven. Quietly opening the gate, I walk through and close it behind me with a chink. Walking straight round to the back, I take my backpack off and lay it by the door before padding to the small garden shed and fishing about for some old shoes. Ma will have a fit if she sees the state of my feet. There are none there, but thankfully I spot a pair of ancient woolly gardening socks. They have a big hole in one of the toes but they'll have to do. Pulling them on, I return to the back door and put my ear against it. I can hear the faint sound of the radio and then a number of blips before the news comes on. Eight? Nine o'clock? Either way, my parents must be up and about. Father has possibly even left for work which, I think, will be perfect as I can talk to them both separately. Taking a deep breath, I push down the handle.

The sight of the kitchen takes me by surprise because it is filled with smoke. Not that this is anything that extraordinary, because both my parents smoke in there sometimes. But there is something strange about it, layers upon layers that speak of *old* smoke, lingering for days and unaired rooms with closed windows. I sense immediately that something is wrong. Ma is impeccable about cleaning and airing the house out. Even when there are sub-zero temperatures outside, she always makes a point of opening the windows every day.

This sensation of unease is confirmed when, looking to the right of me, I see in the sink a large pile of unwashed plates and cups, several flies noisily buzzing above.

'Ma?' I call out. There is no reply. 'Father?'

I walk through to the living room. It is bathed in early morning sunlight that pours in through the windows but this room is the same: thick, stale smoke drifting lethargically through the air, pinpricked with dust motes. I am about to move upstairs when I see the slippers sticking out from the armchair that faces away from me, towards the bookcase. I rush forwards to the front of the chair. There is Ma, sitting motionless, an almost burned down cigarette in one hand. She looks awful. Never in my life have I seen her like this. Her unmade up face is bleached white and her eyes are red with deep, dark trenches beneath them. Her hair, which she normally takes so much pride in, is unbrushed and hangs in limp straggles across her face.

'Ma!' I cry as I fall to my knees in front of her.

The cigarette looks as though it will almost burn her fingers and I wrench it from her, looking around for an ashtray. Seeing none, I hurriedly march to the window, pull it open then hurl it outside before returning to her.

It takes a while for Ma to look at me. She continues to stare into the distance with a vague look upon her face.

'Ma!' I say again, this time more sharply as I shake her knee. She is still in her nightdress.

Eventually, Ma looks down at me, but her eyes keep flitting away from me. Her face and voice are expressionless.

'Jimmy,' she replies. 'Where've you been?'

'Ma, I've been in Crete. I told you, remember? I went with Charles.' I take one of her hands in mine. It is damp and clammy and a shiver of fear runs down my back.

'Where've you been Jimmy?' she repeats. 'I wrote to you. I wrote to you in Matala, but you didn't come – '

'*Wrote* to me? I didn't get it, I'm sorry, Ma. But why…what…'

For the first time, she looks me in the eye and holds my gaze. Her eyes are empty.

'Your father's in the hospital. The day after you left he had a stroke. They don't think he's going to pull through.'

I catch my breath. But he'd been well and lively and his cantankerous self just a couple of weeks ago. How could this have happened? Suddenly I become acutely aware of two things: of the thick smoke that crowds in on me and of the hunger that claws at my insides. Without looking at Ma, I stand up and walk around the room, flinging each window open. My right knuckle has almost healed but, even so, my actions are hurried, violent, and I wince with pain as I catch my hand on a latch. Then, without pausing, I move into the kitchen and pull open the bread bin, the cupboards, the fridge, looking for something, *anything* to eat. But all I can find is a limp head of lettuce, milk in a bottle that has clearly soured and biscuit crumbs scattered on the worktop surface. I persevere, yanking open cupboard after cupboard until eventually I find an unopened tin of kidney beans. I pull it down, find the tin opener and set to work, ignoring the pain in my fist as I methodically work it around the jagged edge.

Disbelief and rage and grief build up from the pit of my stomach and spill out from my eyes as, heaving and sobbing, I turn and bang my right fist again and again against the door of the empty cupboard. I squeeze my eyes tightly shut, trying to focus on my breath as I clutch the cold tin. After several moments of standing like this, I open my eyes and allow the last drops to spill down my cheeks.

There's no clean cutlery and, grabbing a spoon from the sink without even bothering to run it under a tap, I stand there and spoon mouthful after mouthful in. I barely even allow myself to swallow as I continue to stuff kidney beans into my mouth, half-chewing, half-choking. I can't think, I can't stop eating, Father can't be dying, it's not possible.

Once the tin is empty, I let it drop and watch as it rolls uselessly across the floor, a thin trickle of brown, salty liquid pooling out. I swallow painfully, rushing to the sink to retrieve a glass and filling it up from the tap, knocking it back in one.

Blindly, I grope my way back into the sitting room where Ma remains seated, impassively, in the armchair. She is not making a sound but two thin rivers of tears stream down her cheeks as she stares miserably ahead of her.

'Ma,' I choke. 'Ma.' I can think of no other word to say, and as I fall to my knees and cling to her, she softly turns her head to the side, lays it upon my shoulder and brings her hand up as she lifts her long, dry fingers to slowly stroke my hair.

I feel sick to my core as I walk down the long, echoing corridor towards the hospital room my father lies in. I don't want to see him. I *must* see him. It's my fault that he's here. I pushed him over the edge. What if I'm too late? What if he's died before I get a chance to tell him I'm sorry?

I break into a trot, pushing past a Sister in a starched white uniform and cap. She glares at me disapprovingly. *Room number sixty-one, room number sixty-one, where are you?* And then there it is, the black numbers stark against the white door. I take a deep breath and push it open.

My father looks as small as a child and as frail as a ninety year old. How is it possible for a person to age so much in such a short space of time? He is sunken, wizened, shrunk…asleep in the bed with his head lolling on one side and his mouth wide open, uneven snores escaping from him. The room is completely white: bright walls, blinding sunlight flooding through the closed, paneless windows. It is stiflingly oppressive in here and I march over to the windows and fling one open, just as I did at home earlier As I turn back, I realise I have woken him. One of Father's eyes is open and he is staring at me, half of his face motionless. Ma warned me the stroke has half-paralysed him and that his voice sounds strange. I stand rooted to the spot, but he opens his mouth and says something to me. I can't understand him. I edge closer, moving beside his bed.

Standing over him, staring at this wasted shadow of my father, I try to analyse how it makes me feel to see him like this. Pity? Revolt? Shame? Regret? The strange thing is that it is all these things and more. My instinct is to flee the room;

I would rather be anywhere else than here. And yet, I *must* be here. I have no choice, so I grab hold of the cold, metal railings beside his bedside to force myself not to run.

'James,' he slurs. I can hardly recognise his voice. I continue to clutch at the railing.

'Hello Father,' I gulp. 'I…are you…' I falter.

Really, I have no idea what to say to him, where to begin. Do I apologise for going off like that, for causing his stroke? I can hardly tell him about the lovely holiday I had; for a start, it *wasn't* lovely, and for seconds, it's the cause of his lying here now.

'Tea,' he says, 'get me some tea, James.'

I jump back from his bed, pleased to be given a job and duck out of the room, pacing back along the echoing corridor in search of some. When I can't find any, I ask a matron in white, who tells me she'll bring a couple of cups to the room for us. I nod and look at her in desperation, though I'm not sure why.

'You alright, love?' she asks kindly.

Am I? I don't think so, but I nod again and shuffle back off.

'A nurse is bringing it, Father.' I take a deep breath. I just need to say something. '*Listen-*'

'No, *you* listen,' he says in his strange, sideways new voice. 'I have to say something to you…to tell you something.'

I am taken by surprise. Apart from giving me complete hell, I really cannot imagine anything he wants to say to me. In fact, I know I shouldn't interrupt him, being as sick as he is, but I need to get this off my chest before I burst.

'Alright, then. But can I say something first?' Hardly

waiting for an answer, I plough on. 'The way I left like that to go to Crete, just – y'know – ran off, especially when you and Ma wanted to go on holiday...well, it was selfish and wrong of me and...' I falter. Why, in heaven's name, am I finding it so difficult to say this simple word?

'And I'm *sorry,*' I blurt out. 'I'm really sorry. I just wanted to go on holiday so much, *my* kind of holiday, not your kind of holiday.' I am horrified to discover that tears have formed in the corner of my eyes and are threatening to spill over.

Pull yourself together.

I plough on. 'I was angry with you...you weren't listening to me, and always speaking over Ma, and I think I wanted to punish you somehow. But I see now that it wasn't...well, it wasn't the right thing to do.'

And then a single tear does fall down my cheek. Impatiently I wipe it away with my sleeve and glance up at Father's face. He really does look peculiar. And yet, even with the partial paralysis in his face, somehow he looks less severe and certainly more vulnerable than I have ever seen him.

He waves a hand dismissively through the air. 'Never mind 'bout that now. Let me talk now, 'lright?'

I nod. His one good eye is bloodshot. It looks as though it is watering and I wonder if I should dab it. But no, I can't.

'It's 'bout what happened to me, long time ago,' he slurs, staring hard at me. 'I want to tell you 'bout it. Should've told you 'fore, but I didn't. Couldn't. Still find it painful to think about, let alone talk 'bout it. But I owe it t'you.'

I stand there, rooted to the spot. And at that moment, the door swings open and the nurse I spoke to earlier walks in carrying a tray with two cups of tea on saucers and a few biscuits. How on earth, I wonder, am I going to help Father with his cup of tea without scalding him?

'Can you manage, love?' she says, speaking to me.

I am about to ask her to help me when father gruffly answers for me.

'He can manage.'

She shoots me a sympathetic smile and, with that, she is gone. It is just father and I alone in this room with the story of whatever happened to him; with his secret. I look at the tea, and I look at his face. Then I locate a chair and pull it up beside his bed.

PART TWO

Chapter Thirteen

Crete, 1940

One minute, there's me at home. Sitting round all day, arse growing fat. The next, the call up comes. I move from the Isle of Dogs to Derby to Finsbury Park to Crete aboard the HMS Ajax in what feels like the blink of an eye. Lance Bombardier of the Royal Artillery in Suda Bay, to be precise. Helping to man a 3.7 inch Heavy Anti-Aircraft gun, a big old boy with a sixteen foot barrel and a crew of eight of us to manage it. We're stationed here to defend Suda and the British ships, so there are several sites on both the north and south sides of the bay. So we'll be ready if and when an attack *does* come. Which, right now, is hard to believe. Around me there's a sweep of bright blue bay. Crags brushing the edge of wide skies. A ruined castle on a tiny island out to sea. A graze of heather coating the rocks. Truth is, I'm happy. Just happy to be here. To be doing something, anything – *finally*. I know, I shouldn't admit this, but I'm a little disappointed it's so quiet here. There *is* no enemy aircraft — *nothing*. Must admit, I'm starting to wonder if they made a mistake in sending us to Suda.

Doesn't matter, though. At least I'm not twiddling my thumbs any longer, chomping at the bit to get away from home. Can't think of many things worse than feeling useless. First time abroad, this is. Furthest I've been before was to Brighton as a boy. Can hardly compare the two, can I? Damn hot here too, though it's November already. Shimmering heat and constant perspiring. But, as days become milder, I look round at all these men. Shirtsleeves rolled up, forearms changing colour in different shades between red and dark nut-brown. It almost feels as though we're here on a big jolly.

When do I really take note of Joseph for the first time? It's hard to remember but I think it's when I walk along the track into Sternes, the village above our position, for some exercise. I buy some paper to write letters home from a small shop and then walk towards the sea wall when I see him sitting in the village square. He's playing a game with a young lad. Something with pebbles. He doesn't see me, he's so absorbed. But I watch him for some time. Not with admiration, exactly. More surprise, because haven't seen any of our men interact with the locals in this way before. And he's in uniform, so he's clearly one of us.

There's a cigarette perched in the corner of his mouth, that he takes out every now and again with thumb and forefinger. Even from this distance, there's something about him – friendliness? Ease of manner? Well, whatever it is, it makes me want to hang about.

Can't say I'm lonely exactly. Not when I'm a bit of a loner myself, must admit. Suppose it's that I haven't met anyone yet I can say I've had a proper conversation with since I left England. A conversation about normal things.

Everyday things. Not just sniping about Hitler or the Jerries or Mussolini.

Anyway, I walk closer. Stand in front of him and the young lad. Hands on hips, just watching them. He looks up, green eyes flashing in the sunlight and a mop of black curls that partially cover one eye. He grins at me and then continues with the game. He could be a local with all that dark hair. And his skin's not pale like mine, liberally dotted with freckles.

They finish their game and both laugh. *Well done*, I say to the boy in Greek. *Looks like you beat him.*

Both the boy and the man look up at me in surprise.

'Good Greek!' the man says. 'Impressive.'

'I'm sure you speak some too,' I reply.

'Oh,' he shrugs, 'just a little schoolboy Greek. Not like that. What did you say anyway?' He looks up at me, shading his eyes from the glare of the sun.

From his few words, can tell he's not a toff. Perhaps that's why I haven't really connected with anyone. Can't deny it, but I've always felt skeptical about those sorts with their wealth and privilege and private school backgrounds. The accent's a dead giveaway. But no, not the slightest hint of toff in his voice.

'I congratulated him on winning the game.'

'Ha!' He stands up and stretches, then reaches down and rubs the boy affectionately on the shoulder. '*Efharisto.*' Turning to me, he thrusts out a hand and I shake it.

'Joseph.'

'I'm Alfred. But you can call me Alfie.'

'I've a cousin named Alfie. Fair bit older than you though, I'd say. How old *are* you?'

'Eighteen. You?'

'Nineteen,' he replies. Then, scratching his head, 'well, only since a few weeks ago.'

Joseph bids farewell to the boy. We walk towards the track that leads back to the base and he takes out his cigarettes and offers me one. He grins again, eyes glinting. Almost like a fire is lit inside them when he talks. And just like that, we are friends.

Strange, how we stick together like glue right from the start. Both of us still in our teens. Not the slightest idea, either of us, what war means. And here's the thing: we don't *need* to know what war means, these first months on Crete. Of course, it's just a matter of time before the *Luftwaffe* will turn their attention to here. But in the meantime, it all feels quite unreal and we're relatively free. Drills and patrols aside, we can take walks, get to know our fellow Bombardiers and practise our Greek on one another and with the locals.

I'm taken aback by these Cretans. Joseph less so. English reserve, that's what I'm accustomed to. All pleases and thank-yous, sturdy handshakes and how-do-you-do's. Well, it's *nothing* like that here. Wherever we go, we're given some bread and herbs, a few walnuts or even some fried potatoes. A little liver if we're lucky. Everybody seems so happy to see us, though I can't quite understand why. Don't think my fellow Brits would be quite so welcoming of foreigners on my own shores.

We don't have a single shared memory, Joseph and I. Can't reminisce about friends back home or stepping out with our sweethearts. Not family or shared experiences at school. None of that. But it doesn't matter at all, because we can talk about anything and everything: cricket, Noel Coward, gardening, clever card tricks. Doesn't take long to realise that he's the best chum I've never had. Never really needed one before, solitary sort that I am: only child, close to my mother, less so to my father who's always been distant, withdrawn. I just helped my father in the allotment at the weekends and got on with my schoolwork during the week. Did well, too. The first in my extended family to get into a grammar school. Not as though I didn't have friends there, I *did*. But was always quite content to rub along on my own. So never got invited to a great deal, or had much to converse about with the other chaps.

Then I meet Joseph. Funny, that we should get on so well. It's clear to anyone how different we are, me with my stiff reserve and him with that mischievous flicker in his eyes. Always seeking out fun; always finding it. But there's no saying why some people rub along well. I suppose that I understand, in a way I didn't before, it can be more about the words unspoken. Never hear him complain – not a single time. His Greek's terrible, but point is he *tries* to speak with the locals. Clearly his efforts are appreciated.

Joseph is the sort to burst into spontaneous song. To make up games effortlessly and encourage everyone to join in. To flummox everyone with his card tricks. He's as extrovert as I'm reserved. But the strange thing is, when we're together we somehow balance one another out. His gregarious style shifts down a notch and I feel more inclined to engage with others. To laugh at life. It's subtle, this. So much so that it takes a long time to even notice it. We never mention it though. There's really no need.

'I'm going to be a doctor after the war, Alfie,' he often tells me.

And I don't doubt it for an instant. He's got the drive and intelligence and has already spent all his school holidays working at his local hospital.

And me? What do I have to tell him in return? My ambitions are of a different sort. Haven't a clue what I want to be professionally. I've a brain and a good head on my shoulders, I know that much. Seem to have a flair for languages: French, Latin, Greek. I'm sure if I worked at it, I could get some more under my belt. Perhaps I could be a translator or interpreter, be employed by the Foreign Office even. But all I know for certain is that I want to be happy - find a nice girl and settle down, have a few children and a small plot to plant some runner beans.

The locals act as though we personally are going to liberate the mainland. Feels odd to me. I'm just a lad from Twickenham following orders. Joseph and I continue with the drills, but alongside that, the gentle pace of life continues. We go swimming in sea warmer than my bath water back home, even in October. We walk into Suda for haircuts, smoke cigarettes and drink *raki* in the town square.

Given how mild an autumn it is, winter falls like a hammer. The sea turns from translucent blue to murky grey-green. But still, nothing happens. It's quiet and the war feels a million miles away. So much so, I start imagining life back home once all this is over. The visits to Bristol I'll take to see Joseph. The girls we'll meet and dances we'll take them to. Perhaps I'll even convince him to move closer to London so we can see more of one another.

1940 passes quietly into 1941. We know that the inhabitants of the mainland are suffering; Athens in particular, ever since the Italians invaded last October. But it doesn't feel real to us here on peaceful Crete. Odd thing is, the longer we stay in this strange state of limbo, the more worried I feel. A curious sense of unease pits itself deep in my stomach. I don't believe the war can pass us by like this, not when there's so much hardship going on elsewhere, but I try my best to push these thoughts away. Concentrate on where we are now.

Joseph and I take our first swim of the year at the beginning of March. Just as winter releases its grip and we're enjoying the spring colours of the natural harbour and surrounding beaches.

'Where d'you learn to swim like that?' I call across to him as he runs out of the gentle waves.

'Bristol Lido,' he replies.

His hair is heavy and glistening with water and he shakes it back and forth, droplets spraying onto the sand.

'I good as spent all my time there when I was young. For six months of the year. Even more. I got used to swimming even when it was cold. So this – ' he thumbs back towards the sea, 'is just heaven.'

I smile and dig my fingers into the sand, warmed by the sun.

'D'you ever miss home?' Joseph asks as he comes and sits beside me, drying himself off with his shirt.

I shrug. 'Not really. Of course, I'd rather there was no war going on. But I like it here. I don't know. The war feels...like it's not really happening.'

'I know what you mean.'

I lie back. Head cushioned in the sand, eyes closed. 'S'pose we need to make the most of this whilst it lasts. Won't be forever.'

'The most of what?'

'*This.* The peace. Being able to come and swim in the sea. The freedom to walk into town and have a drink, chat to the locals; *all* of it.'

Joseph doesn't say anything for a few moments and I sink my fingers back into the sand; feel my arms tensing. And when he does finally speak, I hear a gravity in his voice that was not there before.

'Everything'll be alright, Alf. You do believe that, don't you?'

I shiver suddenly as the sun passes behind a cloud. I sit up, pull my shirt back over my head.

'Listen. What's going to happen's going to happen. Not an awful lot I can do to change it. I just – '

'You just what?'

I turn to my friend. He looks so impossibly optimistic. Sometimes I wish I could be more like him: worry less, be more open. But what he says next, takes me completely by surprise. Especially given the thoughts that had just been in my head.

'I wish I were more like you, Alfie,' he says.

His face falls serious as he fumbles in his trouser pocket then pulls out his pack of cigarettes.

'What?' Can't help but burst out laughing.

'Really,' he shrugs. He takes out a couple of cigarettes, hands one to me. 'You have this…what is it?' He scratches his head. 'A gravitas. Is that even a word?'

'Yes,' I nod. 'But – '

'People respect you. Look up to you. As for me, I'm just the joker. Sure, I may know how to tell a good gag and make people laugh. But really, where's that going to get me? Nowhere, that's where.'

He hands me one of the cigarettes, lights his own and then holds the flare of the match out towards me.

I am stunned. Truly stunned. For these words to be passing from the mouth of this man I'd always assumed was so full of self-confidence. But seems I'd been reading him wrong all this time. I lean forwards with my cigarette, but it's too late. The match has burnt out and I light another.

'That's nonsense. You know it is,' I say.

'What's nonsense?'

'That a sense of humour won't get you anywhere. Don't underestimate humour, Joseph. Now more than ever. People need it. The locals need it, we need it, *I* sure as hell need it. To help me lighten up a bit.'

He chuckles mirthlessly and shrugs. 'True. You are a bit of a miserable bastard.'

'Yes. You see?'

We grin. Look at one another with a new understanding. For beneath all his mirth and bravado, I realise Joseph is concealing a deep vulnerability. This is the first time I've seen it. But...people *look up* to me? It's not at all easy to believe, though coming from the mouth of my best friend, it seems almost plausible.

Two days later, it begins. The inevitable. There is a part of me that still wants to believe; has *always* wanted to believe, that all of this is a bad joke. That we can return to days of bay swimming and long evenings talking. Yet when it does come, it happens so quickly that I am jolted out of this place of comfort like a vicious slap across the face.

The alarm sounds early, sky still streaked with darkness of night.

'Airfield is under attack!'

These are the only words I hear, again and again. Blindly, I grope into my clothes and stumble outside with the rest of the men. Commands are confused at first. We simply hear tremendous noise, so we all rush to our anti-aircraft installations. Battery commander tells us to fire like hell.

So we do. I do.

Adrenalin surges in my ears like a snare drum as we put up a barrage, an endless staccato of bullets firing up to twenty rounds a minute, *takataktak,* into the bleak sky. But something isn't right. Staring upwards, I swivel my head this way and that to see what we're firing at. There's nothing there. We are firing at *nothing*. My hands freeze, immobilised.

'What are you *doing*, Nightingale?'

The battery commander behind me is yelling. Suddenly can't remember his name.

I turn. Stare at him.

'There's nothing there!'

'*What*?' He shouts over the barrage of shells fusing and exploding in the sky.

'I *said*,' I shout back, 'what the hell are we firing at?'

He frowns beneath his crooked grey helmet. 'Just keep firing, for *fuck's* sake. It's orders.'

Orders? To fire into a blank sky?

I close my eyes briefly. Take a deep breath. I am about to set up again to fire at – what? – when my head turns instinctively towards the sea that sparkles like cake icing. And that is when I realise, *this* is where the noise is coming from. Motorboats are entering the bay – one, two, three…*six* of them. They're heading towards HMS York, sitting quietly in the harbour. There is running, shouting, commands. Like dominoes we fall from the anti-aircraft buggies and run blindly.

We need to repel the boats, somehow. But we're trained against aircraft, not assaults from sea. We're completely unprepared. Everything is happening so quickly. We watch in horror as two of the motorboats charge into the bows and flames burst up in a pall of fiery smoke. This will result, I'm sure, in the first allied casualties on Crete. And then, the boats, packed with explosives, crash into a nearby tanker and another smaller ship.

If this is the start of it, I'm not sure it bodes well.

And yet, our GOC calls a meeting of all the Suda troops the following day.

'It's in the bag', he says, again and again, a confident smirk on his face.

We're told that intelligence has been filtering through and with our excellent Royal Navy support we've nothing to worry about and we're to start preparing for invasions.

But the motorboats packed with explosives crashing into HMS York replays in my mind. What about *that?* I glance across at Joseph. He is nodding knowingly. Leaning forwards in his chair. Not wanting to miss a single word.

Leaving the hall where we're assembled, Joseph claps me cheerfully on the back. 'This'll be a walkover, Alf,' he says, grinning at me. 'We may even be home for the start of next cricket season!'

I inhale sharply and a fleeting vision comes to me: Twickenham Green. The pick pock of cricket balls. The rough edge of my bat. Filtered sunlight and the sharp scent of summer grass.

The fear is still there. It has wriggled deeper. Is it the arrogance of the words we've just heard? This certainty of a morale-boosting victory on Crete against the Germans as if we're playing a friendly game of cricket. Doesn't feel right. Two seamen were lost in the York attack yesterday.

'Alf...Alfie!'

It takes a few moments to realise that Joseph is trying to get my attention as we file outside.

'Hmm?'

'You alright, Alfie?'

'Well...I...' I hesitate. How can I explain it to Joseph when I don't even know what's wrong? I frown and shake my head. 'Everyone just seems...a bit too sure of themselves. Or something.'

'What?' He laughs. 'It's going to be fine, Alf! We're in good hands, I really believe that – '

'Maybe,' I cut in. I even surprise myself at the terseness in my voice, 'But I don't think we can be complacent about anything.'

Joseph brushes his black hair out of his eyes and shrugs.

'You're right. But nobody's being complacent. It's just good to keep positive about what's to come.'

I nod slowly as we walk out into bright winter sunshine. All I can do is hope he's right.

General Freyberg, the Kiwi fellow who's leading this allied operation on the island, comes to visit the troops. Now I can't begin to quell this feeling in my gut. It has magnified tenfold from unease to all-out horror. All the chaps call him 'Tiny', though he's anything *but*. A great barrel-chested man who struts around like a peacock. He exudes arrogance and bravado like we're involved in a child's game of Cowboys and Indians. He seems to be stuck in the past, stuck in World War One and trench warfare.

'Just fix bayonets and go at them as hard as you can,' he says to us in his gravelly, rasping voice.

Fine, so he has a great deal more experience than me in such matters. But I don't have much confidence in him. There seem to be inconsistencies in his plan. For example, he's talking about paratroopers coming down, yet at the same time fixing our eyes on the sea, not the sky. The Royal Navy is strong… but what about airborne assaults?

Not far from here, to the West, the allies have a large airfield, Maleme. It's where a large number of New Zealander troops are stationed. Why is it I feel we ought to be there, not here, providing backup? I find myself constantly looking up at the sky, wondering what is coming. Feeling something far bigger in the air around me than I can comprehend.

Joseph reckons I'm over-thinking it. Keeps telling me this'll be an easy victory. That I ought to stay calm and preserve my energy for when we need it.

Turns out, that's the next day.

Chapter Fourteen

When we first see them, wave after wave of Junker 52s flying low over the Aegean like a flock of black crows, I know that this, somehow, is the beginning of the end. How else can I explain this dread that few others around me appear to feel?

It's still early, the calm sea glimmering in the early morning light. But we're up, out of bed at the crack of dawn. It's a clear day and even from that distance and height we can hear klaxons sounding from the planes. Joseph is standing beside me, smoking his first cigarette of the day. His face is turned towards the sky.

We hear it before we see it, the rumble of heavy engines. Followed by the sound of exploding bombs, presumably at the airstrip in Maleme. And then, the screech of a fighter plane. It sounds like the high-pitched screams of a woman.

'Jesus,' breathes Joseph, the cigarette dropping from his fingers. 'That's a Messerschmitt.'

'A *what*?'

'A Messerschmitt. My father has a book of military planes. I'd know one of these anywhere.'

I turn and study Joseph's face in profile. Jaw clenched. Brow furrowed. He's less sure about everything now, clearly.

A silence falls briefly. Heavy and ominous, like a thick blanket. But then through the sky, gliders skim and circle towards Maleme, moving downwards as if to land.

Though they are not close to us, we hear from the distance the tut-tut-tut of bullets being fired. A staccato sound much like firecrackers. I stand, frozen to the spot, despite the warmth of the May morning.

'They're landing,' Joseph calls, yanking my arm violently. 'Come on Alf, we need to get back to base.'

I turn to move. Shake myself out of my stupor. But no sooner do I start running, than I hear the unmistakable whir and heady throb of overhead engines. I look up, shielding my eyes against the glare of the sky. Junker 52s. We have been warned about these. First, there's the amount of weapon canisters that can be dropped through the bomb bay exits. And there's also the number of paratroopers that can exit from them.

Joseph continues to pull me as we hear the first explosions overhead. Gliders are bursting into flames mid-air. Within what feels like seconds, our tranquil strip of coast, the place that has borne witness to Joseph and me bathing, chatting, walking, smoking, laughing, is turned into a blackened battlefield.

Back at base, we're being ordered to get back out there and watch for when the paratroopers land.

'Aim at the Jerries' boots, men!' the GOC is shouting. 'They reach the ground quicker than you think, so you have more chance of striking that way. Go, GO!'

My hands are shaking as we run back out to the field where the anti-aircraft guns are positioned. Joseph vanishes from my side and I clamber up to my apportioned vehicle.

Two machine guns are already mounted and I am vaguely aware of the others I've been trained with, next to and behind me. Not far from us, we see patches of white as the paratroopers are descending. I feel sick. This is what I have been trained for. This is the sole reason why I am *here.*

'Christ's sake, Nightingale,' the man behind me is shouting. 'Don't just stand there. We need to fire, *now!*'

I nod mutely. Then shake my head. Then nod again and set into motion the muscle memory of my hands and arms as I prepare the weapons.

There are a few men coming down towards an olive grove on the other side of the field, more still caught on trees and trying to free their parachutes. But I focus, as I was told, on the feet. Take a deep breath. Fire.

Never imagined how I'd feel first time I killed someone. We're not taught how to feel in training. We're taught to fire. But I hit my target, steel helmet glinting in the sunlight. His body crumples to the ground, white canopy mushrooming around him. How can I possibly feel jubilant?

What is your name? I think, as I watch the life sucked from him. Quick as a breath of wind.

'Nightingale! *Nightingale!*' I am being shaken roughly on the shoulder. 'Over there, come on, man!'

We swing the vehicle anti-clockwise and fire towards a flash of black boots. The volley of shots miss, and he reaches the ground. Runs in desperation towards a green weapons canister. But the next shot hits him in mid-step. Violent spasms jerk through his body. Blood spews from his mouth before he falls, face-down, onto the earth. Second kill.

Where are you from?

Numbed, I am directed towards another target. This one, I am momentarily relieved to see, I have missed. But then he falls, harder, faster, a body slumping, dangling. Caught in a branch of an olive tree and *thud* – his neck cracking and hanging at an unnatural angle. Third kill.

How old are you? What are your dreams for the future?

No more. No more. Large clouds of grey dust settles against the blinding blue sky and around the corpses and their equipment. And then, everything goes still as other paratroopers come down too far away to fire. The air is still punctuated with the sound of distant gunfire. But Suda Bay, for now, is quiet.

'Jesus, what's *wrong* with you, Nightingale?' the burly fellow behind shouts. 'You still half asleep or what?' I turn around. Stare at him. He's shaking his head. Starts to mutter under his breath.

Later, after a brief breakfast of tinned bully beef that I cannot touch, we are told that when things don't go according to plan, the Germans go to pieces. Those words again that sicken me: *It's in the bag.*

I don't believe a word of it. Don't believe either that they understand what they're saying. Nor how stupid they sound. I hear men laughing. Triumphant. Comparing notes on how many they shot. *One was caught on the branches of an olive tree. Still alive! Managed to shoot the poor bugger before he could get out of his harness! Next time I'll get more, hopefully.*

Each word impales me. It's like they're talking about competing at a coconut shy. Do some people actually…*enjoy* this? Is it sport to them?

I push my tin of bully beef away from me. It is rapidly snatched up by an officer who instantly starts to hack it open with a bayonet.

I feel a presence beside me. Joseph. His eyes are downcast and he looks grim. 'Biscuit?' he asks quietly, offering his packet to me. I shake my head.

'So what happens next, Joe?'

He gives me a half-smile. Never called him Joe before. Do I feel more bound to him now than ever before with the shared blood on our hands? Maybe I do. I don't want to know about his experiences. I just want him to sit next to me. Drown out the sound of this interminable boasting.

He shrugs. Runs a hand roughly through his dark hair, knotted and unkempt.

'It's all kicking off over in Maleme and Galatas.' He gestures with his chin towards the west. 'Apparently, the locals are joining in out there.'

I look up. Take a swig of water from a tin mug. 'What d'you mean?'

'They're helping us shoot the paratroopers. There've been reports of women and boys at it. Priests even, the lot of them.'

I narrow my eyes. The little I know of the Cretans, they seem such a fierce, proud people, I'm not surprised.

By the time night falls, the Germans have not managed to take Maleme airfield. Nor the port of Canea. Nor the aerodromes of Retimo or Heraklion. Though a number of New Zealander allies have been lost and a great many more

Germans have been killed. My fellow officers are in celebratory mood. *Raki* is found from somewhere and they drink and sing, sing and drink. Smoke is still rising in thick, black columns from the bay from bombed ships, streaking the dark sky.

At night, I keep seeing the bodies of those men I helped to kill, dangling limply from their parachutes, whenever I close my eyes. I know that, come dawn, the Messerschmitts will be back again. I sleep fitfully, noises and voices and spits of gunfire crackling above my head.

Morning brings the terrible news I feared: Hill 107, the strategic position above Maleme Airfield, has been taken by the Germans during the night. Word filters through that it was left unguarded; that the troops had withdrawn due to poor communication. And now. What? We wait for a slaughter?

Sure enough, in the afternoon, the *Luftwaffe* begins strafing and bombing. We watch, helpless as all afternoon, paratroopers drop out of the sky like tiny black spiders towards the west. Hear the whine of engines, distant gunshots. Wonder at the fate of both the Jerries and our allies over near Maleme.

The mood is far more solemn now. Men are sitting around nursing headaches from the *raki* and the first real misgivings they've had about this campaign. When the afternoon brings a huge shroud of black smoke into the sky to the west, everything around us turns dark. Like the sudden descent of nightfall. Apocalyptic. A strange scent of olives and fragrant, burning wood reaches us. All we can assume is that the dropped bombs are ravaging through the olive groves.

The earlier confidence and bravado I saw in Joseph has left him, like blood being syringed from a vein. He is wan and pale beneath his tanned face. And tired. Perilously exhausted, like all of us, from lack of food or decent rest.

'I don't understand,' he says to me, 'why we're being told to keep our eyes on the sea. The threat is from the *air*, not the sea.'

'Will they counter-attack Maleme?'

'Not sure. I don't know, frankly, what the hell Freyberg is playing at.'

News reaches us of one disaster after another: a delayed counter-attack on Maleme and the airfield remaining under German control. Troops facing Stuka dive bombers. Air attacks on positions at Kastelli. The cruiser HMS Carlisle hit out at sea. Then HMS Warspite, Gloucester, Valiant. One by one they go down. It's like playing a game of Warships. Except this is real.

A troop of some 800 men, reinforcements, try to land at Suda Bay, but a violent storm lashes out at sea. They're forced to turn back. Couple of nights later, they're able to land. But we see they're not there to provide reinforcements, to ensure this battle is won, after all. They only carry a small number of machine guns and rifles for rearguard action. To buy enough time whilst the forces are all evacuated.

Evacuated. This island needs to be abandoned. Yes, Crete must be abandoned. The implication is explicit: we have no hope here any longer and must evacuate as soon as we can. *Sauve qui peut* – I hear these words again and again. Murmured like the tide. Every man for himself. Get out while you can. Otherwise, await your fate that is now overrun with the enemy.

Despite this, I feel almost sick with relief. I no longer care that the tide is turned firmly against us. I have not slept for days. Scarcely eaten more than crusts of bread and the odd biscuit. The heat is stifling. I fantasise about a cool spring day in an English meadow, mist and showers and scudding thunderclouds.

My relief is unfounded. The journey to the evacuation point on the south of the island is filled with hazards of its own. Knowing that Joseph is walking beside me fills me with something akin to intense gratitude. We barely talk. In fact, we have hardly spoken to one another these past several days. But that doesn't matter. Just having him here's more important than anything.

After rowing across Suda Bay, we must walk for forty miles. From the northern tip of Crete down to the south, where we're to be evacuated to Egypt. Yes, it's each man for himself now. But still, a strange companionship exists amongst us men as we retreat over this hostile terrain. There isn't a great deal of conversation. All too exhausted for that. But I learn names I didn't know before. See the goodness in other men I scarcely noticed as I was too consumed with Joseph. There's a fellow named Leonard, older than us. Mid twenties or thereabouts. I don't know where he's come from but he steps in with the two of us. He's a good sort. Unassuming. Not a toff, either.

By day we hear distant humming of reconnaissance planes. Sounds like the swarming of bees. Then it gets closer, louder as I hear somebody shouting with all their might:

'Aircraft! Take cover!'

We all dive to the ground. Joseph looks as though he is back in Bristol at the Lido pool. Executing a perfect dive into a nearby bush, arms outstretched. As for me, I stumble to the roadside, face pushing down into shrub and rock. The plane overhead fires a rapid burst of gunfire. It misses our assembled group by some twenty yards. Circles overhead then disappears back towards the sea.

I remain like that, my face cushioned and scratched by the undergrowth, even when I know the plane has gone. Could easily fall asleep like this, if only I had the chance. Can't remember the last time I had a decent amount of sleep. I turn my head to the side. Open my eyes. See the sun glinting on a white object among the shrubs. Slowly, I reach my hand out, brush my fingertips against it. Smooth. Perfectly oval. Joseph isn't far from me. He sees it at the same time. Our eyes lock, and then both move, magnetised, in the direction of the gleaming white object.

An egg. A simple, oval-shaped egg.

Who's to say how long it's been there? If it has rotted in the fierce afternoon heat or if it was just laid this morning.

Doesn't matter. Feels like a gift. Once we know the plane has moved away overhead, we haul ourselves wordlessly upright. I place the egg in the palm of my hand. Warm. Perfectly smooth. A memory of bacon and eggs for breakfast comes to my head, unbidden. My stomach lets out a ferocious growl.

Rations are low. Can a man survive on bully beef and biscuits? Suppose they can. Should think myself lucky for having anything to eat at all. Unlike some of these poor buggers we pass in the tiny mountain villages. Emaciated. Bodies that are alive but long-dead souls. The blank stares that come from eyes with the light already gone out of them.

So, an egg, rotten or not, feels like a gift of food fit for a prince. I find a nearby twig and tap it on the shell. It breaks easily. Without even smelling it, I tip half of it down my throat. Hand it to Joseph. Bitter. Pungent. Slimy. But immediately, I feel more energetic. Our eyes meet once again. Words aren't necessary to know what the other is thinking. That this is what it has come to.

Chapter Fifteen

On the second day of walking, we reach a mountain village. It is deserted, pockmarks scattered like marbles around whitewashed walls. An air of hasty abandonment: wooden doors swinging open on hinges and chairs left upturned. We shudder to think what happened here. The deserted *kafenion* has a few bottles of *retsina* and *raki* and men drink as though they are possessed. Upend the bottles and pour the strong liquid down their throats. Like they're drinking water. One man yanking the bottle from the hands to the next, a vile alcohol-fuelled game of Pass the Parcel. I see the frown in Joseph's eyes as he turns away, his face a mirror for my own feelings. It may numb the pain, but for how long?

More urgent in *our* minds is water. In the centre of the village lies a well, but one peer down it into its murky interior and it's clear the water is putrid. Some ignore this fact, so great is their desperation and thirst. Instead, Joseph, Leonard and I seek out the cold, fresh mountain springs, far less likely to make us sick. We silently douse ourselves. The backs of our necks and foreheads, then we cup our hands and pour the cool liquid down our throats. Till we're drunk and floppy on water.

Just off the square, we find an abandoned house, the front door wide open and the paintwork crumbling. We step inside slowly; doesn't feel right, being in somebody's home like this without being invited. A layer of dust covers everything and cobwebs hang liberally from the ceiling. But all we are interested in are the mattresses on the floor. Before falling into a dreamless sleep, I spare a brief thought for the owners of these bed. Where are they? Are they still alive? But I am too grateful for this unexpected comfort to ponder these questions for long. That night, I sleep better than I have done in a long time.

Next morning, at the crack of dawn, I creak upwards from my mattress. I feel eighty-one, not eighteen. Everything aches: Bones. Brain. Soul. Leonard's already awake, running a hand groggily through his fair hair, bleached pale by the sun. We both look at Joseph, lying on his front at an unnatural angle, mouth open, deeply asleep.

I gesture to Leonard, hand to my mouth. He nods and we exit the low, dark house to seek food of some kind. We decide to walk up above the village. Along a winding path, passing impossibly low doors and nothing but house after abandoned house. Save for the early morning bird song, it is completely quiet. All the other men must still be fast asleep, enjoying their night of comfort as I did.

I'm hoping that above the village there may be some kind of fruit tree or obvious wild herbs. *Anything.* Don't know what I'm looking for, neither one of us does. But there must be something around, or perhaps some old kitchen gardens.

And then: we hear it before we see it, the whir of an overhead engine. Out here in this meadow, we are horribly exposed.

'Quick!' I yell to Leonard. 'Get down! *Down*!'

We both fling ourselves into the long, prickly grass as the familiar sound of strafing echoes in our ears. Takes a few moments to realise something: what I think is the scream of the plane above, roaring off, is actually coming from Leonard. I turn to him. See his face contorted in agony. He's clutching his thigh with both hands. Blood is running liberally through his fingers. My first thought: relief, that he's only been hit in the leg and nowhere more serious. I jump to my feet and tear the arm from my shirt. Tie it tightly around his leg to stem the flow of blood.

'You're alright, Leonard,' I say as he sucks air in through his teeth, wincing in agony. 'You're alright.'

I scan the clear blue sky for a sign of the plane but it's completely vanished. Were it not for my injured friend right here, I may've doubted my own mind, as there's no trace of it at all.

'Joseph.' I squeeze Leonard's shoulder. 'I'll go and fetch him. Right away. He'll know what to do. I'll be back soon, *promise*.'

I sprint through the long grass and back down the winding, cobbled hill. I think that I must get water, and something to disinfect the wound with, and what else? I really don't know. Joseph will know. Joseph, Joseph, Joseph. I repeat his name again and again under my breath. Pick up speed tearing down the hill and burst through the door of the house we spent the night in.

He hasn't moved from that same position. I fall on him; shake him out of his deep sleep.

'Quick!' I cry, before he's even had a chance to wake up properly. 'It's Leonard! He's been shot.'

For the briefest of moments, Joseph looks confused as the information sinks in. But then, in a flash, jumps up.

'Where?'

'Up there, above the village.'

'No, no!' He waves his hand impatiently through the air. 'I mean *where*, where in his body?'

I shake my head. *Stupid*. 'His thigh.'

Joseph kicks into action. Efficient, driven. Just as I knew he would be. Already the doctor he will one day become.

'Are you wearing a belt?'

He doesn't wait for an answer.

'See if there are any old garments lying around here to use as cloths. And we'll need a splint of some kind.'

His eyes dart around the dim interior of the room before quickly grabbing a wooden board lying on the floor and then tearing outside into the sunlight.

'Show me where he is,' he says.

I lead the way, rapidly moving uphill along the narrow street. I feel like I'm dreaming. The sun has come up now, splashing across the cobbles and it's hot already. Too hot and my throat throbs, parched.

Within minutes we're there. Leonard is stretched out on his back, groaning, all the colour drained from his face. Blood is seeping through the shirtsleeve I tied around his thigh. I crouch down, place a hand on his shoulder and squeeze it.

'Alright there, Leonard. Joseph's here. You're going to be fine.'

Joseph is about to bend down to start looking at the wound when we hear the whine of the glider in the distance again. But it's getting rapidly nearer and louder, coming back this way.

'Christ!' shouts Joseph, a deep frown entrenching his smooth forehead.

We both scan around in desperation to find somewhere we can take cover. But this meadow is open, only scattered with the odd gnarled, ancient olive tree.

'Quick,' Joseph says as he runs around to Leonard's head. 'You take his legs. I'll grab his arms.'

'But we – '

'Alfie!' He shouts. 'We've got no choice. We have to move…now! Over there under the biggest of those olive trees.' He gestures with his chin.

The whine is closing in on us. I take a deep breath, reach down and try to pick up Leonard's legs gently. It's no use. Impossible to be gentle when you're trying to move with that speed across a meadow rutted with hillocks. The roar from Leonard's mouth melds with the screech from the glider. I briefly glance up at it: a grey, steel hulk splicing through the bright blue sky. It's flying perilously low. I'm praying for the first time in I don't know how long, that it'll crash into the hillside. Sweat is pouring down my forehead. I can hear my own heartbeat thumping wildly in my ears.

We are nearly at the olive tree. Almost there. Almost there…

And then, I hear it, but don't register what it is. Time moves slowly, spinning, roiling across the dry Cretan land. As I turn my head, move my vision back across the outstretched body of Leonard, I see Joseph's arms moving upwards and outwards, flailing like a windmill. Leonard's legs go limp in my arms as his head is dropped against the earth. The world is sucked of sound. I open my mouth and shout. But nothing comes out.

I lay Leonard down in the meadow grass. Hardly register his shouts of pain. And I move along his body to my friend as the glider whines up and away, moving back into the seamless sky.

I fall into the long grass beside Joseph, lift his upper body against mine. He leans against me, his blood soaking into my shirt and the russet earth.

I find my voice. Suddenly the sound has returned to my existence and I am screaming. At him. At anyone who will listen.

'Joseph, wait! *Wait*! You'll be fine, you're alright. I need to get someone. You'll be *fine*!'

But even as I shout, I know it's useless. It's already too late. One look at his face and I see that their target could not have been more precise: the bullet has pierced his eardrum. Penetrated deep into his brain. I stagger backwards beneath his weight and the sheer, hollow grief of what has happened. And I tilt my head backwards and howl a lament to the soft wisps of scudding clouds and endless sky.

Joseph.

Chapter Sixteen

When my best friend is killed, something inside me snaps. I blame myself, for what other way can I see it? I fetched him. If not for me, he would have stayed sound asleep in bed. Oblivious. Safe. Alive. And from this very moment, when I acknowledge he has gone, I begin to hate myself. It is an invasive loathing that worms its way into the core of my being. Pits me against myself so I almost can't bear to be alone with my thoughts. And yet I *must* be alone at the same time. For I don't want to stain others around me with this guilt and raw grief.

It should have been me. This is the mantra that turns round and round in my head. It personifies me and never for a moment does it occur to me to question its truth. That same morning, Joseph's body is hastily buried on the hillside where he was killed. I watch it all happening from a distance, but can't come close to be part of it. I sit under an old, gnarled olive tree and cry hot, choked tears of bitterness till no more will come. When it's all over, the men file back down the hill into the village. One or two of them reach out a hand and awkwardly touch my shoulder as they pass. I even hear a murmur of 'It's not your fault, Nightingale.' But it is, of course it is.

In the afternoon, we start moving again. Though my mind doesn't know what to do, my feet and body do, so I join the others. Leonard is in great pain, but he can move, slowly. I find I cannot even look at him. None of it is his fault, it's *mine.* I know it's not fair of me not to talk to Leonard. It's not just him, though. Can't talk to *anybody.*

After what feels like a thousand years of struggling on, we reach the mouth of a gorge. And there, like a mirage, is a deserted *taverna.* My feet carry me in there. I root around and, amidst the debris, find a half-gallon of dark amber wine in a cracked demijohn. I drink it back in two long swigs. To not have to think about what has happened. To see if it can help decrease the pain of Joseph's absence.

I feel better for a while. Walking through the gorge, I feel it bubbling up inside me, a need to laugh. So I do, listening to it echoing along the gully. I notice how the nameless, faceless men who were walking alongside me fall away from me like dominoes. I look backwards and read the wariness on their faces. Or is it hostility? They are probably thinking, *There's Nightingale, the man who led his friend to his death.* I wouldn't blame them if they thought that. Who are these people, anyway? I recognise all their faces, but right now cannot call up a single name between them. Just soldiers like me. Idiots. Pawns in this deadly game.

We finish our journey late one evening, as the sun drowns over the mountains. Three days after we began our journey south, we come out of the other side of the gorge and walk into a village on the coast, Chora Sfakion. If you can call it walking. There are men who can barely stand. Like Leonard, they are weakened by hunger and fatigue and injury. As for me, I suffer none of the above. I don't feel anything at all. Allied troops appear to be everywhere now, stationed along the gorge. They tell us that we'll spend the night on the beach, and then leave at dawn the next morning on the Ajax, the same ship I arrived on, bound for Alexandria.

I hear their words. Acknowledge them. Doze on the beach for a short while beneath a moonless, star-speckled sky. And then, at around two in the morning, stand up. I look at the sleeping men around me, exhausted, lying in contorted positions. Strewn across the beach like discarded apple seeds. Then I start walking.

It's not pre-meditated. My feet lead me and I'm in no position to stop them. Nor do I want to. I've no idea where I'm going. But this feels unimportant. Just keep moving, one foot in front of the other, walking back along the unmanned gorge beneath the stars. I wonder, briefly, if anyone will note my absence before that thought escapes me entirely.

As dawn approaches, I'm still walking. When you're this hungry, *this* tired, moving takes on a strange lightness. So much so, that when I see a shepherd standing on a rocky outcrop, I wonder if I'm dreaming. He's clothed in a white cloak. Appears as an apparition against the pale pink gleam of advancing daylight. But as I draw closer, he turns and looks at me, dark eyes boring into me. Gravely, he nods his head. Then he turns back to survey his grazing goats. I *must* be awake.

I'm about to walk past him when he draws his *sakouli*, the knapsack most Cretans carry, down from one shoulder. Without saying a single word, he unfolds some cheese and a crust of bread. Holds it towards me. He has a fine, dark, curled moustache and black eyes that burn like two pieces of charcoal, enhanced by the whiteness of his cloak.

Now I know that, actually, I *am* hungry. No, not hungry. Famished. Without saying a word, he hands me more. I try to refuse it but he pushes it back into my hands. The flavours of the cheese mingle – cream, thyme, salt – and the strength this food gives me means that I'm able to think a little clearer. I acknowledge, for the first time, that today I could be leaving Crete. But I don't want to. And I don't care to analyse the reasons for that too deeply. Just know that I can't.

When I finish eating the bread and cheese, the shepherd leads me to a nearby tree and points upwards. It's laden with plump, magenta-coloured cherries. He leaves me there as he walks off to tend to his flock. I look upwards, spindly branches of the tree pinioned against the sky. And then, without further thought, hoist myself up to the lowest branch and begin to pull off the fruit I can reach.

I don't know how many hours I sit there for, with the shepherd. I know it's an opportunity to practice my Greek and I do – a few words passed to exchange basic information. My voice sounds strange, particularly in a different language. Almost as though it's not my voice at all. I realise, with a start, that these are the first words I've spoken since Joseph died.

I learn he's called Yanni and lives in a village 'five cigarettes away.' I've been in Crete long enough to know that distances are measured not in kilometres. Such metrics are rendered useless with the impassable mountain slopes. Instead, they are marked by the time it takes to smoke a cigarette.

As the heat of the day intensifies, Yanni smokes beneath the cherry tree. He flicks the butt away from him and then turns his head slowly to me.

'Are you coming?' he asks.

I shake my head.

'I will go somewhere alone,' I speak slowly, wondering if I have said these words correctly.

Yanni half smiles, half laughs and shakes his head.

'You will die. You do not know these mountains.'

Would that really be so bad? I wonder. Who would miss me?

'Come,' he says again and begins to walk away from me.

The question is: am I ready to die? I have no expectations of life now and I am nothing to this shepherd. As he walks, he does not look back. And yet…he asked me to come, so the choice is mine. Something tugs at me, a thread of curiosity and the faint memory of being loved. And then: a voice that emerges from the depths of the fine spring air. Through the sound of the bells around the necks of the goats – is it the voice of Joseph? – telling me to go.

I squint my eyes as the white cloak of the shepherd contrasts starkly against the bright red poppies strewn around the fields. I take a deep breath. Then I jump down from the lower branches and follow him.

The village we walk into some time later appears, to me at least, lost in time. A taverna props up one side of the square. Scrawny dogs sit wheezing in the shade of a covered well and hens peck slowly around, taunting them.

He tells me to wait. Lumbers off with his long-strided

lope towards a house further up the hill. Minutes later, he's back with a middle-aged woman dressed in dark clothes, her face partially shaded by a grey-streaked black coif and long plaits pinned across her heavy brow. She walks straight up to me, hands on hips.

'*Anglika?*'

I nod.

She surveys me for a few moments longer and then her face breaks into a smile. It's full of so much warmth, yet so much sadness that it takes me by surprise. For the first time since Joseph died, it occurs to me that others are suffering too, and some far worse than me.

She gestures for me to follow her. We walk side by side through the square, past the well towards the gentle incline. Suddenly, I remember the shepherd and turn to look for him. But he's gone already. I see only the flick of the edge of his white cloak as he rounds a corner and vanishes.

What do they know of me, this white-cloaked shepherd and black-robed woman, with faces simultaneously cheerful and defeated? Nothing, save for the fact I'm English. And so, by default, one of them. But still, they share their cheese and bread with me and lead me to a tree laden with fruit, and then take me into their house. Would we do the same for foreign strangers back home? My parents? My neighbours?

When we enter her home, I see it consists of just a single room. It's dim and cool inside, a welcome respite from the cloying, midday heat. Beaten-earth floor and an archway above me, spanning from one end of the room to the other. It's blackened in patches from the hearth's smoke and supported by rough-hewn wooden beams. A cracked amphora, that looks as though it has seen better days, sits inside the hearth, presumably used as a chimney flue of sorts.

As my eyes become accustomed to the gloom, I see an old man sits in one corner of the room on an enormous, rush-bottomed chair beside a loom. He's dressed in patched boots and a torn black shirt above baggy trousers. I'm not sure if he's asleep or not, for only one eye appears to be slightly open.

'I am Natalia,' the woman tells me in Greek.

I look back to her. She has walked to the other side of the room and is pulling down an onion and tomato hanging on a string against the wall, before placing them on a wooden board topped by a few herbs and beans.

I nod. 'Alfred,' I say.

'Alf-*hred*,' she tests out in her mouth.

I nod and smile solemnly. Natalia screeches something over to the old man in rapid-fire Greek that I understand not a word of. His closed eye creaks open slowly and stares pointedly at me, before he grunts and closes it again. She begins to hack at the onion on the chopping board. Then she turns back to me and gestures to the corner of the room with her knife.

I hear Joseph's voice come to me. *Good Greek. Impressive.*

He always admired my command of Greek. Compared to him and the other men, it was fair. But now it feels pitifully inadequate. I ask Natalia to repeat what she has said. She smiles indulgently at me then continues to chatter incomprehensibly away. But now, her meaning is clear. For, in the corner, opposite the slumbering old man, a thin mat lies on the floor. And one word I *can* fathom from her steady tumble is *Sleep*.

I only need hear that word a single time. Without giving it any further thought, I'm lying prone on the hard floor. Heavy as a corpse, eyelids tugging down. Final thing I hear before I'm pulled into a deep sleep is the sound of another grunt from the old man in the corner.

When I wake, I think I might be dying. No idea how long I've been lying there for; whether it's day or night. All I know is that my entire body is on fire and my head thrums like the snare drum I played in the military band as a child. Try to sit upright but I'm pushed gently backwards against the mat. Vaguely aware of the sensation of something soft beneath my head that wasn't there before – perhaps a cushion of some sort.

'What's wrong with me?' I croak. But two pairs of eyes stare at me, uncomprehending. I dimly remember the hut, the kind lady, before a wave of nausea overcomes me. It is all I can do to muster the energy to turn to the side and spill out my insides onto the brown, earthen floor. I try to say sorry. But I'm hushed by the mouths that belong to the two pairs of eyes. A cool cloth is placed on my forehead and another damp one dabs at the corner of my mouth.

I close my eyes again. The effort of emptying my guts has exhausted me. I'm floating in a wordless, soundless plain as I am pulled back into a dusky oblivion.

Is it hours or days later that my fever subsides? I've no idea. All I'm aware of when I eventually manage to focus on my surroundings are the two pairs of eyes beside me. Without any awareness of how I might know this, I sense that the owners of these eyes have barely left my side all this time. However long this time may be.

My eyes settle on them. I see they are two young teenage girls, both with the same wide brow and slanted eyes of the kind lady. What was her name? Natalia. Yes, that was it. Seeing that I'm awake, one grins at me, her face cracking into a smile that reaches both ears. The other girl – the elder, I think, looks no less happy. But her smile is shy, her olive eyes doing most of the talking instead.

They whisper something to one another I don't catch. The younger girl jumps up from her kneeling position. She returns moments later with a plate and a torn white napkin. Before I know it, her sister has moved behind me. She's gently helping me to sit upright and the plate is set before me. Upon it, sit several small pies in a crescent-moon shape, flour dusting their surface.

I look from the plate back up at the two girls hesitantly. The truth is, though I've not eaten anything since the bread and cheese I shared with the shepherd – the memory of him returns in a flash – I'm not hungry. But the girls look so eager that I don't want to disappoint them. I pick up one of the fritter-like pies. It's warm to the touch and I lift it to my mouth. I feel self-conscious – both girls are staring fixedly at me.

I bite down and the pastry crumbles. From the broken folds of the small pie, the most heavenly smell emerges and my stomach lets out a noisy growl. The girls giggle behind their hands and I feel myself growing red. The pie is filled with soft, juicy white cheese and chopped mint. If I thought that the bread, cheese and cherries I ate with the shepherd were good, they were nothing in comparison with what I am now eating.

The younger girl raises her eyebrows expectantly.

I nod and smile at her. Better than good, I want to tell her. But I don't know how. If there was ever a reason to improve my Cretan dialect, here it is.

As I chew slowly, savouring the combination of flavours packed into warm pastry, I form the next sentence in Greek carefully in my head.

'What is it called?'

'Kalistounia,' she replies.

'Kalistounia,' I repeat. 'Very, very good. And your names?'

'I am Ida, and this is Lyra.' She thumbs in the direction of her older sister, who averts her gaze timidly.

I finish the pastry and look down at the plate that still holds several more. Ida follows my gaze.

'Eat,' she says. 'Eat another.'

It's impossible not to. As I chew, I look round the one-roomed house again. It's dark in here, impossible to ascertain the time. Suppose it's evening, judging by the oil dips that flicker in the shadows. I can hear soft pecking sounds. As I scan round the room, I make out two – no, three – hens moving around the earthen floor. Natalia is standing at the far corner of the room with her back to me. She's chopping something on a board and the old man in the baggy, black trousers has dozed off again in his chair. Where does everybody sleep, I wonder? There appears to only be one bed in the corner of the room, covered with a rough, home-spun blanket.

The older girl, Lyra, takes one of the pastries in her hand and walks up to the old man.

'Grandfather,' she shakes his shoulder gently. 'Grandfather, *kalistounia.*'

He awakes with a start. Wipes a trickle of spit that has escaped from below his bottom lip with his sleeve and clears his throat. I watch as the old man eats it hungrily and asks for another. Lyra dabs at the corners of his mouth with a napkin and then brings him a glass of water. His hands shake as he brings the glass to his mouth and Lyra helps him drink.

I wish I had something to give this family. But I left with only the clothes on my back and nothing more. I don't know what I'm doing here. Or how long I can conceivably stay. But it's the last thing I want to think about. Just need to rest a little and I'll decide what to do next.

As I bite into the third pastry, I think about Joseph's family. I know very little about them. Only that they live in Bristol somewhere. When he was buried, someone must have taken his identity disc to forward on to Records. But I've no idea whom. Perhaps one day a time will come when I feel like contacting them and explain what happened. Because all they'll get from Records will be the brief, standard letter. No emotion. No details. But then again, what would I begin to say to them? The bitter truth is, if it weren't for me, he'd still be alive.

The exertion of eating those pastries has exhausted me. I feel sleep tugging at my eyes, though I don't know how it can be possible when I've slept so much already. I wonder what was wrong with me? Though perhaps it was just sheer exhaustion, combined with a fever. I watch as Lyra helps her grandfather out of the chair. Like a compliant child, he reaches his arms unsteadily above his head as Lyra removes the black shirt. He's painfully thin beneath, ribs protruding like the strings of a harp. Is this age or hunger? Will I, one day, look like this?

Lyra removes a nightshirt from a wooden peg on the wall and tenderly lowers it over his bony shoulders and heaving ribs. Then she guides him to the bed. With a loud, weary sigh, he sits heavily down and moves his legs around. Natalia calls something out to her from where she is chopping vegetables and Lyra goes outside. She returns, a couple of minutes later, with a flat bedpan that she places beside the bed. But her grandfather's already snoring. As I rest my head against the wall, I feel the tug of sleep come to claim me once again.

When I wake early the following morning, I feel much better. My head is clear, I'm well rested and, for the first time, my initial waking thought is not one of crippling guilt. I roll over to my side beneath the homespun cloak that has been placed over me and see Natalia, the girls and their grandfather still sleeping. My questions are now answered, for they're all in one bed. The two girls with their dark heads closest to me and their mother and grandfather's heads at the opposite end. I wonder where their father is, Natalia's husband. I try to imagine how it would feel sleeping in the same bed as my mother and grandfather. Instantly, I banish the thought.

I feel full of energy. Don't want to stay in bed till the others are up, so I quietly push back the cloak and tiptoe out of the house. The contrast between the cool, dimness within and the fine white light that filters down outside through the surrounding trees dazzles me. I can hear a distant, indecipherable sound of thumping and another, softer layer of chiming goat bells from another valley.

I close my eyes, inhale the fresh, raw mountain air. Still dew-cool but with a gentle warmth filtering through the plane trees that surround the village.

'Yassas.'

I hear a voice behind me. It's so soft that it almost sounds part of the breeze. Turning, I see Lyra, the older girl, standing there. Her hair is loose around her shoulders, her olive-green eyes are still smudged with sleep.

'*Yassas,*' I return. I dig my hands into my pockets.

'I saw you get up,' she says quietly. 'Are you feeling better?'

I ask her to repeat her words. She does, instinctively slowing down her speech so I can understand her better. This time, I'm able to reply.

'Today I feel good,' I tell her.

She smiles, nodding. In the bright morning sunlight, I see Lyra's older than I'd thought. I'd put her at about fifteen and her sister a year or two younger. But now I realise she must be older than this, at least sixteen. If not more.

'Shall I show you around the village?' she asks.

I nod.

We begin to walk till we reach the centre, a large clearing shaded by a vast plane tree. I can hear trickling water. I follow the sound till I see a spring running by on the other side of the tree. Crouching down, I cup my hands to draw up some water and sip from it. It's icy cold and wonderfully invigorating. So I splash some of the water on to my face, running it round the back of my neck. When was the last time I had a proper wash? Instantly, I feel self-conscious.

Only hope I don't smell too bad. This evening, I resolve, I'll ask Natalia for a bucket of water and some soap.

When I first walked into the village with the shepherd, I'd not been aware that it was built into a slope, but I see now it sits on a ledge on the flank of a mountain. All around the village square, it drops precipitously off into steep olive groves and jagged, thorny canyons. Its location is unforgiving and hostile, though the people I've met so far have been nothing but welcoming.

We climb a narrow street. Not more than a path really to allow a donkey to pass. We come out at a chapel, a tiny, squat affair perching precariously on an outcrop.

'Come,' Lyra beckons to me.

She pushes against the wooden door that groans as it opens. Inside, the air's heavy with incense and dark as a tomb. Lyra crosses herself as I stand awkwardly by the door. I watch as she moves lightly across the stone floor. She lights a candle at the altar and places it with other lit candles, dripping wax into round, red puddles beneath them. She bows her head, closes her eyes, grasps the crucifix round her neck and whispers words beneath her breath.

I long to ask if she's praying for her father, or a brother she may have lost. This village feels strangely emptied of its younger and middle-aged men. But I oughtn't be presumptuous; who's to say a brother ever existed? And as for her father, well I can't very well make assumptions about him, either.

Don't know how to talk to girls. Never had a sister, and the school I went to was boys only. If he could speak their language, Joseph would have known what to say to Lyra and Ida. Not that I ever saw him speak to a girl. Just know he was that kind of fellow with his ease and naturalness.

Joseph. The realisation that I haven't yet thought of him today pummels against me. My lightness of mood deflates, lungs collapsing beneath my ribcage. Hadn't even realised I'd made a sound, but Lyra turns her head suddenly towards me, eyes wide with concern.

'Are you alright?' she asks.

'Yes.' I nod, biting my bottom lip. 'Fine.'

Instinctively, I shuffle forwards and light a candle, placing it next to Lyra's. She's looking expectantly at me. I feel self-conscious all over again. But I drop my head into my chest, close my eyes and say in my head, *Sorry, Joseph. Sorry.*

As I stand there, head bowed, an image of my parents flashes into my head. It's the very picture I remember when I walked down the path in front of our house early that morning to join up. Father stands rigid. Thin frame hunched in his overcoat. Those long clumps of grey strands covering his pate flapping about in the icy wind. Mother, grasping on to Father's arm for dear life, as though the very touch of him sustains her. She's wearing a bright red sweater. I remember that. And her nose glows almost the same colour in the early morning frost. There's a look of intense sadness and loss in her eyes. And this, before I've so much as rounded the corner.

I was so excited. Not a sliver of sadness or remorse to be leaving my home or parents or Twickenham. Didn't think for a moment about how *they* might be feeling to be saying goodbye to their only son. Well, you don't, do you? All those long, drawn-out months sitting in the kitchen huddled round the wireless, I wanted one thing only: to turn eighteen. Very same day I celebrated my birthday (if you can call it a celebration), I enlisted.

When I got back, I told Father. He nodded somberly. Didn't turn his face to look at me. Course, I know he had his own experiences in the first war. But I don't know where he went, what he did. Nothing. I know he lost two of his three brothers. Mother told me that, but I know nothing about them, not even their names.

Suppose Father was proud of me in his own way for enlisting so quickly, though of course he never said as much. Just before I walked down that path, my boots feeling a little too big and chafing against my big toes, he shook my hand squarely. I even thought I detected the glint of a teardrop in the corner of his eye. But when I looked again, I realised it was only a trick of the light. It was coming from the winter sun bursting over the row of terraced Victorian houses and London plane trees.

When I open my eyes and look up, Lyra's staring at me. I redden. How long have I been standing there for? She smiles gently. Without saying a word, she moves towards the chapel's entrance.

We walk slowly back to the house, enjoying the bird song and spring breeze. We pass a few people sitting outside their houses or carrying water in pitchers from the spring and greet them. Nobody looks surprised to see me, even in such a small village as this. I ask Lyra what the sound of thumping is. She tells me it's women washing clothes down by the stream. There's something comforting in the methodical beat of it. Don't know what kind of good fortune it was that led me here, first to the shepherd, and then to this family. But the thought suddenly comes to me that I won't be going anywhere for some time. And neither would they expect me to.

That night, we eat a simple dinner of bread with *khorta*, edible grasses. Afterwards, Ida takes my hand and draws me next to the fire. I find her Cretan far harder to grasp than her sister's. She speaks so quickly, bursting into youthful laughter after every couple of sentences. She's looking at me intently, her pretty, open face scanning mine for something, I am not entirely sure what.

After several more moments of this, Ida produces a cork from her apron pocket. Grins at me, just like a little imp. Then she places it onto the end of an iron toasting stick and thrusts it in the hearth flames. Leaves it there for a few moments then draws the fork out again, surveying the end of the cork. She prods it with the fingers of her other hand before returning it to the flames.

Lyra says something to her sister, a note of disapproval in her soft voice. She's speaking more rapidly than I've heard before; I suspect she doesn't want me to understand. But, next thing I know, Ida's leaning in closely to my face and rubbing the warm, fire-blackened cork slowly over my eyebrows. Ah, so *this* is her plan. To make me more like a Cretan. She may be able to change my eyebrows, but there's little she can do with the shade of my skin.

She leans back to survey her work. And from the corner of the room, grandfather begins to sing. His voice is soft, wavering at first. But as he continues, it increases in strength.

'This is a *mantinada,*' Lyra tells me. She's hovering behind her sister.

I nod. 'Beautiful.'

Grandfather sings a little then the girls join in with the

words *Ela! Ela! Ela!* – come - before the second half of the sentence is repeated. This pattern continues. It's comforting in its rhythm and it isn't long before I find myself singing along.

Once Ida's quite happy with her artwork, she darts off. Returns with a small, cracked mirror and holds it up so I can see myself. I look truly peculiar. She's blackened my light eyebrows to charcoal. Also, drawn her cork over the dusting of a moustache and beard that has grown. It's been so long since I shaved.

Turning my head this way and that, I survey myself from different angles. No matter which way I view myself, I look strange. It's confirmed by a flurry of giggles escaping Ida's mouth. Even Lyra claps her hand self-consciously over her mouth, olive green eyes gleaming mirthfully in the flickering firelight. Grandfather waves a wrinkled hand dismissively through the air. Then he takes up the melody again. I hand the mirror back to Ida, lean back in the chair. And smile.

Chapter Seventeen

As the summer temperatures climb, I remain in the village, not leaving a single time. I don't contact my parents. Nor the parents of Joseph. Nobody comes looking for me. Not that I'm surprised. There's a war going on. People have more important things to do than go searching for an irrelevant, young, soldier. Even so, I'm amazed how easy it was to just up and leave. To walk out of my life. Walk out of the war. There are few physical signs of it here, save the low number of men in the village. And that veil of sadness that, time and again, shrouds Natalia's cheerful features.

Every day, my Cretan improves. I attempt to teach Ida and Lyra a little English. I may be good at languages, but I'm a pitiable teacher. None of the family reads or writes. They tell me their education was poor, and brief. Lyra, in particular, seems ashamed of this. But it's clear she's bright; *both* girls are. They've simply not had the opportunity for schooling that I had, or Joseph, both of us grammar school boys.

Joseph. His death continues to hang over me like those thick, homespun cloaks the shepherds wear. Like an itch just beneath the skin that won't go away. Sometimes I replay the moment he fell during the darkness of night. I wake, thrashing about on the thin mattress, rivers of sweat pouring off my forehead. Often Lyra or Ida appear at my side with a cool cloth placed on my forehead, a glass of water, or a few soothing words.

None of them can say my name properly. With the exception, strangely, of Grandfather. So, I'm re-christened: Leonidas. Leo for short. As the days pass, I peel away the skin of Alfred. Adopt my new identity. As I settle into the language, my Britishness smooths away, sandpaper chafing against the edges.

They are my benefactors, these good, simple people. They've saved me from being crippled by grief and introspection. Helped me to keep living, here in the Cretan mountains, one slow day at a time. They've taken me into their home unquestioningly. Shared what little food they have with me. Not looked back since that day I walked into their lives.

Only way I know how to repay my gratitude is helping any way I can. I wash laundry with Natalia down at the spring. Help her to thump and rinse then spread it out to dry in the sun on large boulders. At first, she protests, but eventually I become a common sight amongst the village women. I carry large pitchers of water from the spring back to the house with Ida. She may be small, but she's at least my equal in strength. And I collect wild herbs and fruit with both of the girls, or sometimes just one of them.

On one such walk, Lyra and I have made our way through a dense cypress forest towards a copse of mulberry trees on the other side. It's late afternoon but the heat is still punishing. I think fleetingly of what it's like in June back in

Twickenham. Cricket on the green, the long evenings and the strolls along the Thames in the dusk.

As we reach the copse, Lyra places her basket down on the grass and walks towards a tree. Still with her back to me, she speaks.

'My father used to bring me here, when I was a little girl. We collected mulberries and made pies together from the fruit.'

I stop walking. Look up at the shafts of bright sunlight that stream through the canopied tapestry of spaces amongst the leaves.

'What happened to your father, Lyra?'

She turns her head to the side and I watch her carefully in profile. Her forehead's knotted. But there's a small, sad smile on her lips.

'He died, in Albania. At the start of the war.'

The Albanian occupation. I heard about this when I first arrived on Crete. How a large proportion of Cretan men of fighting age were emptied from the island. Sent to Italian-occupied Albania, into deplorable conditions and the harshest winter in living memory.

That is all she says and I know that even these few words have cost her dearly. There's something so vulnerable about Lyra, in a way quite dissimilar to her younger sister. Ida, I feel, can take care of herself. She has a fighting spirit. There is a mischievous glint in her eye and a steeliness I admire hugely. But Lyra…I imagine she was shy even before her father went to Albania. Even in that simple recall, it tells me enough to know she was close to him; that his death has drawn her even further into herself.

My feet move of their own accord. Over the fallen fruit

rotting like small red rubies against the orchard floor. Without thinking twice about it, and even taking myself by surprise, I stand beside her and catch her fingers between mine. They are long and cool and she does not move them.

'*Lipame poli,*' I whisper. Sorry.

She continues to stare at the tree. Her lips curl almost imperceptibly upwards, but her slanting olive eyes remain sad.

We stay in amongst the trees all morning, collecting fruit and trying to ignore the rumbling from our stomachs. Every so often, we break off from our harvesting and exchange a few words. Lyra doesn't talk much. Not like Ida. But it's as though each word that does come from her mouth has been carefully considered and weighed before it reaches her lips. She has a quiet wisdom about her. I think, as I've often done since being here, the extent to which she and Ida would've benefitted from an education.

We walk slowly back along the shady ravine, enjoying the dappled sunlight and the air, heavy with the scent of thyme and myrtle. For the first time in my life, I realise with a start, I feel truly content, secreted away in this anonymous village. I wonder if, conceivably, I can stay here forever. I feel at ease here. Not just in these surroundings, but with my new family. Of course, I sometimes think of my own parents back home. Father's pinched face and mother's bright red woolen sweater. I *must* try and get word to them. But how could a letter even reach them from somewhere as remote as this?

Lyra starts to hum something beneath her breath. I glance at her. I've become fond of her, I know. I've become fond of all of them, my adopted Cretan family. But as we approach the village, it's immediately apparent something's wrong. As soon as our ears tune into what we're hearing – the sound of high-pitched screaming – Lyra flings the full basket of mulberries to one side with uncharacteristic aggression. She hitches up her long black skirt and begins to run.

I stand, rooted to the spot. Stare at the scattered fruit fanning across the cobbles. I don't know what's happened, what's *happening*. But the gulf between my thoughts just moments ago, of making this village my permanent home, and now some unknown ordeal being inflicted upon this place I've come to love, gapes widely.

I can't move. Don't know why. Ever since the day Joseph died in my arms, I've numbed myself to further trauma. Perhaps refused to accept that any day, at any time, pain could knock again. Don't know how long I stand there for, but next thing I know, Lyra and Ida are sprinting towards me. Moving faster than I ever imagined possible. They grab my hands, one at either side. And they're pulling, pulling, yelling at me to hurry. As I pick up pace, I realise that the cries of the old lady, whoever she is, are continuing.

'The black cattle are among the vine shoots!' She is screaming it, again and again.

'What does she mean?' I call.

Ida flicks her head around. Her long black hair whips against the side of her face. 'The Germans!' she hisses. 'It's the alarm for the Germans!'

'But…'

'No questions,' cuts in Lyra. 'Just keep moving.'

We race through the village square, emptied of life. Up the steep slope we run, towards the house. Bursting through the door, Natalia's standing in the middle of the room holding a gun. It looks so ancient and rusted, I can hardly believe it works. She falls upon the three of us. Pulls us to her briefly, then pushes us away and crosses herself in rapid-fire motion. Grandfather remains seated in his chair beside the hearth. He's staring ahead of him with his glassy eyes, one gnarled hand slowly stroking his moustache. Not sure if he's even registered what's going on. I move towards him but Ida grabs my elbow.

'No time!' she cries. 'We have to get you hidden.'

Natalia's already pulling back a thick rug that covers the floor to reveal a trap door.

'Me? But what about all of you?'

'Yes, yes,' Natalia says. 'Also us. But especially you.'

No time to question any further, for we all hear gunshots in the distance. We freeze momentarily before one by one we make our way slowly into the black cellar. It is lit up by a match Lyra holds between her fingers. They insist on me going first. I feel panic rising like fire up my throat – this is *not* the way it should be. I need to ensure the safety of all of them first. But as I try to resist, Natalia grasps my wrist like an iron vice and squeezes. Her physical strength takes me by surprise and her coal black eyes burn into me. 'Down! Now!' she hisses.

I struggle into the blackness. A sense of claustrophobia threatens to knock the air from my lungs. Lyra reaches past me, arm brushing my neck. The darkness seems to go on and on, a never-ending snake coiling downwards. I wonder what on earth she's doing, when I hear a snap. I realise she's pulling up *another* trapdoor beneath this underground hiding place. Before I've a chance to question anything, or really understand what's going on, Lyra's pushing me into a smaller space and closing me in.

If I thought the sense of claustrophobia was bad in the higher level, it's nothing compared to what I feel now. Never in my life have I experienced anything like this. My breathing's ragged and my shoulders are hunched beneath the packed earth. I try to sit up but my forehead clunks against something. Raw panic rises in my chest.

Breathe, breathe, I tell myself. I stretch my arms outwards to understand the space around me. Then swivel round so I'm lying down, feet twisted at the end to accommodate my whole body. Eyes squeezed tightly shut. Only when I feel the panic lessening slightly am I able to tune into the muffled sounds going on above me. I imagine Grandfather's replaced the rug and returned to his chair. I hear shuffling and distant creaking. Then all is quiet and still.

My chest heaves up and down, eyes still closed. How long would it be possible to stay in this airless cavern before suffocating?

And then: a muffled bang. The low rumble of voices, speaking German. They are here. They are in the house. The voices crescendo and I wonder if grandfather is still sitting in his chair by the hearth, calmly stroking the curled ends of his moustache.

The reverberation of the voices continues for some time, then abruptly stops. Perhaps they're searching the room, or have already moved on. But then I hear a stamp directly above me; a swooshing noise. Instinctively, every muscle in my body contracts. I hold my breath. A whimper: Ida. The voices, closer to me. They've pulled back the rug and found the trap door.

Natalia cries out and a Jerry shouts back louder. I don't speak a great deal of German, but don't need to understand the language to hear aggression and anger. More shuffling, moving about above me as they're all pulled out of the hole. Then the sickening thud of the trap door banging shut.

The silence that follows is a silence of terror. Of black earth pressing in on me and contorted muscles. A suffocating inability to move. These people have transformed into my family these past weeks. As the wide ravine of not understanding one another has lessened, I've felt needed by them. Was I trying to take the place of their lost father, whom I know nothing of, not even a name?

The four of them have peopled my existence in this remote mountain village. And now, they march through my mind, one by one. Natalia: her stoicism and large swarthy, practical hands. She is so much stronger than me in every way - physically, emotionally. Grandfather: a man of so few words. But music pouring from him like butterflies released from a net. *Ela! Ela! Ela!* How is it possible that after all this time I've yet to know his name? Ida: the younger sister I always wished for growing up, but never had. Elfin smile, flashing eyes. The half-skip of her step as she hovers between girlhood and womanhood. I always hated being an only child. How lonely I often felt. How envious of other boys who went home from school to the company of siblings. And Lyra...

Here, my thoughts falter. I can readily define my relationship with the other three in my new family. But now I realise, perhaps for the first time, in that cloying underground darkness, that I don't know how I feel about her. Or rather, I become aware that, unlike Ida, she's not a little sister to me.

And so? I ask myself. Will I lie here beneath the ground whilst these people I've come to care for so deeply are extinguished like candle flames? Haven't you already failed the best friend of your life, Alfred?

Something like a roar escapes from me. Not only from my mouth, but my entire body vibrates with the fury and energy of this alien noise. I punch through the wooden board above me. Pull myself up into the hole where, till minutes ago, my friends lay. Now it's heavy with their emptiness and the petrified scent of their breath.

I blink into the darkness and haul myself up to the next level.

The first thing I see is Grandfather's walking stick lying on its side next to his chair. The door to the house is wide open. Angry white sunlight pours in and splashes on the earthen ground. I think of Natalia's gun, wondering if it was hidden on her or if she left it in the house. My feet kick into action. Like they're a separate entity. I move around purposefully, looking everywhere I can think of for a gun. I'm about to move outside when, on a hunch, I dart to the space where Natalia sleeps on the old, lumpy mattress.

And, sure enough, there beneath the mattress I feel something cold and hard. I pull it out and stare at it in the gloom. It's large and fairly rusted, just like the other one. I grab it, hurriedly open it to check it's loaded, then jump to my feet.

Outside, I hear distant shouting from the direction of the square. I run, head dipping to my chest. All thoughts of stealth escape me. My boots pound against the cobbles like gunshots and I force myself on to the balls of my feet. Bloody hell, what use am I to anyone if I get shot myself?

Near the square, I press myself against the sun-warmed wall. One hand creeps down to feel the gun. I peer around for just a moment to see all the villagers lined up in front of the well. Several soldiers are before them. There they are, Ida, Lyra and Natalia, staring straight ahead of them. Where is Grandfather? I snap my head back round. Hear my heart thumping dangerously against my ribcage and close my eyes.

'I will ask you again, where are the arms?' One of the Jerry's is shouting at them in thickly accented English.

Silence.

'And the wireless? The English? Where are they?'

Don't you know they don't speak a word of English? I want to shout at them. My fingers ball into fists.

He continues talking. This time his words are quieter and I strain to hear. 'Trouble…answers…not harmed.'

Have other English soldiers passed through this village? Nobody here has ever mentioned anyone else. They can't, surely, be looking for me? How could they possibly know I'm here? And if I give myself up, will this save the village?

Perhaps this is my opportunity to atone for what I did to Joseph. His life was sacrificed through my stupidity. And now, maybe, I can offer myself back.

'Where are the arms? Where *are* they? This is your final warning!'

A different voice shouts, more threatening. Sweat is running like a torrent down my forehead, streaming into my eyes. I wipe it away with the back of my wrist. With my other hand, I pull out the gun. Stare at it, hands shaking.

'Right, your chance is finished!' the German is shouting. 'Line up, all of you. Line up, here!'

I peer forwards, around the corner of the house. Watch

as he roughly shoves the villagers. He's grasping their shoulders, pushing them into some kind of order.

Now or never.

Don't fuck this up, Alfie, I tell myself. *Just aim, hope to God that this decrepit gun works, and fire.*

Trembling, I lift the gun but I have to wait until the Jerry has moved backwards; I cannot risk shooting the villagers. But right at that moment, I hear shots fired and high-pitched screaming. Was it me? Did I fire without even *realising*? The shots continue, volleying and echoing across the square and it's all such a tangle of arms and limbs, of falling and screaming that I don't understand what's going on.

Then I make out, high above the village, on the cliff edge, three boys emerging. They're holding guns aloft in the air. Squinting up at them in the distance, I recognise them: these are the Papadakis brothers. Just teenagers. Not much older than Ida and certainly not as old as Lyra. And one of them, I'm certain, has not even *reached* his teens yet.

My breath's coming out in short, ragged bursts. I drop the gun, a loud clank sounding against the cobbles. Somewhere from within the chaos of the square and the blood-sprayed ground, I see the three German soldiers lying. Unmoving. And it's as though the realisation of what has happened dawns on all of us at the same moment. A profound silence descends. Even the urgent peeps of the swallows darting overhead, disturbed by the noise, softens.

The Jerries are dead: the Papadakis brothers, mere children, have killed them.

I step out from behind the house, into the deadly stillness. And at once it's broken like ice splintering across a frozen lake. I'm running to the square and the boys are running down from their clifftop. We arrive there together and they survey their handiwork, kicking the side of one solider to check he is dead. One of them, the youngest, is already on his knees, rifling through the dead man's pockets.

I can think of only one thing: where is my family? Grandfather, Natalia, Ida, Lyra. I see Natalia first. In the commotion, she's been pushed to the side and has fallen against the hard ground. A cut splits her forehead. It streams blood into one eye and I rush to her, helping her to sit up. I pull my handkerchief from my pocket and press it into her head.

'It is nothing,' she growls, waving me away. '*Típota, típota.*'

But her hands are shaking uncontrollably. I press them both onto the handkerchief to stem the flow of blood.

Looking around, I see Ida. She's beside a fallen soldier, his blood soaking into her skirt. She's sobbing, fighting for breath as she takes great gulps of air, but only chokes as she exhales. I put my arms around her and pull her to her feet, away from the soldier. He's been shot in the chest and has fallen heavily on his back, his head lying at a strange angle and bloodshot eyes wide open, staring at us.

'It's alright,' I stroke her hair, hugging her to me. 'You're fine. You're fine. Where's Lyra? Your grandfather?'

But she can't talk. She only continues to shake her head and choke on her sobs. I disentangle myself from her and move through the stunned crowd. Some are sitting, some standing. The young brothers have come down from their cliff top and are rifling through the wreckage of the German soldiers' lives, flicking open wallets and scattering papers.

Lyra is nearby. She too is sitting on the ground. Her

knees are drawn into her body and her arms are wrapped around them. All the blood has drained from her face and she looks younger and more vulnerable than I've ever seen her. As I rush to her, to check she isn't hurt, she looks at me as though she's looking through me. As though she's never seen me before.

'Are they dead?' she whispers, not making eye contact with me.

'Yes, Lyra. They're dead.'

'We are all safe?'

'Everyone is fine. We are all safe.'

Recognition dawns upon her, of the enormity of what has just happened. That they have not died and that I'm now in front of her. She focuses on me finally, her olive eyes filling with tears. She stretches a hand out in front of her. Her fingertips brush my cheek.

'Leonidas. Leo.' She smiles through her tears. 'Alfred.'

My three names, rolled into one on the tip of Lyra's tongue. I almost don't feel like Alfred anymore. It's been so long since I've heard my name.

'Leonidas,' I reply.

'*Alfred*,' she repeats firmly.

She lets her hand fall. Then the tears spill from her eyes. The air is intermingled with the scent of blood and triumph and salt from Lyra's tears. This time, my fingers raise. I gently brush the tears away from her cheeks. She stares at me, smiling and crying at the same time. I didn't know that was possible.

And at the same time, we both hear a sound from beyond us. Turning round, we see grandfather. He's standing, stooped, in the middle of the square. His white hair is sticking up from his head and he's cackling triumphantly. One arm is raised in a fist that he punches unsteadily into the blood-scented air.

'*Ela! Ela! Ela!*' he cries.

Lyra gets to her feet. '*Ela!*' she joins him.

And then it's me. Standing up and stretching one hand into the arc of dazzling, cloudless sky. I close my eyes, shout it to the village. To my Cretan family and to these dead men who happened to be on the wrong side.

'*Ela!*'

Everything changes for me, that hot summer's day when my new family comes within a hair's breadth of death. I'm not talking only of my physical location, for after the death of the German soldiers, the entire village knows that the time has come to leave. Other soldiers will come searching for them. Finding them dead, they'll seek out the perpetrators.

First thing we do is to throw their limp bodies over the side of the ravine. Then they can't be easily traced. Boys and girls alike help. We scrub the cobblestones of every last trace of blood, till the air smells of soap and its main ingredient, olive oil. Nobody says a word. Everybody is in shock, moving soundlessly round the square, just doing what needs to be done. When the stones gleam like the slippery bodies of freshly caught fish, then everyone congregates beside the well. The villagers are mute, staring at one another.

It's Yanni, my shepherd-saviour, who finally speaks.

'We will leave at dusk,' he says slowly. 'Walk South West in the direction of the coast. I know of some caves there where we can hide.'

'What about the small children? The babies? Our old people who cannot walk?' asks one woman, swathed in black from head to toe.

'The children will be carried. And our elders must be helped. We stand no chance here. More soldiers will come, it is certain.'

'I'm not going anywhere,' Grandfather says, his thin mouth set into a stubborn line. I turn to him sharply.

'You *must* come!' cries Ida. '*All* of us.' She sweeps her arm around the gathered group of mostly women, children and elderly people. 'We will help each other and stay together!'

'Ay!' responds Grandfather, shaking his head and turning away. 'I will only slow you down. I cannot walk that far.'

'Nor me,' counters another old man. A few more murmur their agreement.

I turn to look at Lyra. Her features are contorted, jaw tensed tightly.

'We will come back,' Yanni continues. 'All of us, once the troubles are over. But for now, we must go somewhere safer.'

His words hang in the air, some nodding their assent and others shaking their heads.

'You are not the mayor!' says one voice. We all look to see who has spoken; it is the eldest of the Papadakis brothers.

'He is the eldest son of the mayor,' Ida whispers to me.

'No, I am not,' Yanni agrees. 'And in the absence of your father, decisions must be made.'

'My brothers and I will stay here and fight! We will protect our village,' he continues, sticking out his bottom lip.

Yanni shakes his head. 'You think you will be that lucky the second time around?'

The boy flares up with anger, his fists bunched up.

'Luck had nothing to do with it! You saw how we shot them, from so far! Did we injure a single villager? No!'

Yanni sighs and bends his fingers around his olive wood staff. He stares at it as though hoping for answers.

'You are right,' he says eventually. 'What you boys did was remarkable. And brave. But even so…' he breaks off. 'We cannot stay here. I won't force anyone to come. We meet at six in the square. Pack a *sakouli* with a change of clothes, food and water.'

And with that, he is gone. His white, ghostlike figure picks its way across the square towards home.

Grandfather has already started moving away from the crowd. He is limping over the cobbles, painfully slowly. I see that he is right: that he will not make the journey ahead of us. It will be grueling even for the able-bodied amongst us.

Wordlessly, we walk back to the house. Natalia is marching ahead, her chin high in the air.

'You stupid old man!' she flings at Grandfather as she passes him. 'I don't mind! We will leave you here to die!'

Ida catches up with her mother and grasps her arm tightly, leaving Lyra and I walking slowly.

And that's what I mean when I say everything changes for me from that point onwards. Walking behind Natalia, Ida and Grandfather, I finally admit something to myself. Though I regard Natalia as a surrogate mother, Grandfather as just that and Ida as a younger sister, I don't want to and *can't* think of Lyra in the same way.

I've never had feelings for a girl before. Didn't know how it felt. And though I imagined that *yes*, this must be what it's like for such feelings to be awoken, I wondered if I was confusing it for something else. I wondered whether it was the same protectiveness that I felt for Ida but thought, perhaps, it may be different just because Lyra was older.

But no, I think, as we walk beside one another to prepare for our departure. I can't ignore this anymore, and that's alright. And her feelings for me? How can I possibly know? Ida wears her heart on her sleeve, but Lyra binds her emotions tightly inside her. Not unlike the way I live my life, I suppose. And that's why I find something of my own needs reflected in her slanting, olive eyes. Both of us have lost someone we care for deeply. I sense neither of us has begun to repair our grief.

Like a mind reader, without looking at me, Lyra reaches out and clasps one of my hands. I gaze at her, see her face afresh. Her dark brown hair curves over her smooth cheekbone and the corner of a thick black eyebrow arches over the glimmer of an eye. Yes, she is beautiful.

I will her to turn and look at me. I want to tell her with my eyes that I'm here and that I won't leave her, but she continues walking. She's gathering speed with a new determination. In the evening breeze, she is a kite and I'm being pulled along behind her. That vulnerability I recognised in Lyra…I see now that I've misjudged her, for it's also her strength. A fleeting thought occurs to me as I pound the cobblestones in her wake: perhaps, if Lyra's grief can serve to empower her, the same can happen to me?

Chapter Eighteen

Grandfather doesn't come with us. Nor do the Papadakis brothers or several other elderly people who say they can't walk the distances required. The brothers tell us they'll stay and protect the remaining inhabitants of the village. Looking at their slight frames, but determined faces, leaning against the well, I think only how much I want them to succeed. Not only in defending this village but succeed in their lives. I've never encountered such courageous young boys in my life.

Grandfather isn't interested in emotional farewells. He bats us away as though we're irritating flies. There's a song on his breath as his fingers rise to the comfort of the curled ends of his thick moustache. Ida can't accept he isn't coming with us. She clings to his twisted frame, which reminds me of a gnarled olive tree, and sobs. Eventually, Natalia unclasps her fingers from around his waist and pulls her away.

There are fifty-eight of us in total. We trail down the path, *sakoulis* on our backs. The mountain air is heavy with the scent of thyme that grows in clumps along the track.

'Pote tha kamei xesteria,' sings the eldest of our company in a cracked voice.

He must be close to eighty. He walks with a tall, twisted stick and wears high black boots and torn breeches. *When will the sky be clear?* I've heard so many songs since arriving in the village. Music appears to run along the villagers' veins as readily as the swallows fly southwards when winter expels her first breath. But this is the first time I've heard this particular one.

As though reading my mind, Natalia turns to me.

'This is an old revolutionary song, against the Turks.'

I nod, enjoying the sound of the old man's voice. But, far more than that, I'm acutely aware of Lyra's presence beside me. I feel as though somehow she has always been walking beside me and I can't clearly remember a time when she wasn't in my life. Not a single word has been exchanged between us about our feelings, but it doesn't need to be. For now, it hangs in the air around us, as real and tangible as the flutter of poplars that skirt the track.

And so it is Lyra's presence that characterizes our journey. Not the fierce heat that enfolds us by day and the numbing cold of night. Nor the sound of trees filled with the melody of singing nightingales. Or the moment when Yanni shoots a hare and we cook it, sharing a mouthful each, cooked with oil and onions.

No, it's Lyra.

During those frozen nights, that take me so by surprise after the fierce heat of the day, wordlessly, she comes to me. We share a blanket as I draw her close and she nestles her head on my shoulder. I lie there trembling as I trace the outline of the waterfall of her shiny brown hair. I almost don't want to breathe for fear I may wake her. Beneath the sprinkling of stars that cluster the black sky like sprinkled salt, I read the frown that never leaves her, even in sleep, with my fingertips hovering an inch from her face. I don't want her to suffer, ever again. She's lost her father and most of the men and boys from her village and she's left her beloved grandfather behind in the house she was born in, to an unknown fate. She won't lose me now. She will *not.*

One night, she opens her eyes, sleepily, to see me watching her.

'Leo,' she whispers. 'Are you alright?'

I nod.

'Leo,' she whispers again. '*Alf-fred.*'

I love hearing her say my name. Clearly it's difficult for her to pronounce it properly. She reaches a finger out. Runs it lightly down my cheek and smiles.

'What is your other name?' she asks.

'Which other name?'

'Your family name.'

'Nightingale.'

'Nightingale? *Aidóni?*' Lyra's eyes widen. 'Like the bird?'

'Yes. Like the bird.'

She stifles a giggle beneath the blanket. 'It can't be true. Nobody is called nightingale.'

'Yes, they are.' I gently take her hand from my cheek. Brush her fingertips against my lips. '*I* am.'

The smile fades slowly from her face. We reach for one another under the cover of darkness and hold one another tightly. Fingers knotted in hair. The summer night heavy with the screech of cicadas and scent of heather, as we drink in the essence of one another.

Natalia and Ida see what's happening between Lyra and myself but they don't say a word. As for what they think about it, well, I can't say. It's only war that's allowing us to be this close. But it feels to me as though it's accepted, *expected* even. By day, Ida continues to be my little sister. She teaches me new songs as we walk. And chatters incessantly about nothing of consequence. It helps us all take our minds off the gravity of our situation: that we could be bombed from overhead at any moment. That as each day passes there are some in our group who grow frailer.

I love listening to Ida. Through her, my knowledge of the Cretan dialect is deepening. She teaches me the Cretan names for oleander and myrtle, for poppies and anemones. And Natalia continues to be my surrogate mother. She treats me wholeheartedly as a son, even as Lyra and I grow closer.

I haven't chosen this life. Crete has chosen me. Has everything that came before led me to this – walking over the mountains towards a hiding place with a family who've become more real to me than my own, with a girl who changes and strengthens me with each passing step? Was even Joseph's death part of this bigger picture, a necessary evil for bringing me to Lyra?

The pain of this thought stops me in my tracks. I'm shocked that this has even come into my head. Nothing, *nothing*, can provide a rationale for his death. Nothing, save my stupidity at calling him out that morning. But as I'm here, and he isn't, perhaps it's my calling to atone for his death through protecting Lyra?

I'd never thought of it that way before. I watch the sun slanting over the heather and stretch my hand out towards it. As I let my hand lightly brush over it, I'm shaken with the potency of this.

'Are you alright?' Lyra asks softly.

I look at her. I drink her in, every inch of her. How couldn't I have seen, the moment I met her, how beautiful she is? How could I have thought her only a girl when she is, in fact, just a year younger than me, a grown woman?

Lyra's long-sleeved blouse is rolled up to the sleeve. She has smooth, olive-skinned arms from the elbow down. I suspect the blouse was once white, many years ago. But now it has greyed from countless poundings against rocks down by the stream. One button is missing and another, near her neck, is open to prevent her from overheating. She has tucked her blouse into a long, shapeless black skirt that trails the rocks we walk over. Her long, dark hair is kept out of her face with a green, tasseled headscarf. One of the tassels has come loose and hangs above an eye that is more green than olive in this harsh sunlight. There's a tiny scar beneath her nose that I've not noticed before. And her lips, when she smiles, curve downwards slightly instead of up.

The sunlight is slanting up behind her. It causes a halo of light to fall softly around her body.

'Leo,' she repeats. 'Are you alright?'

I blink into the sun, bathing in the warmth of this moment. Nothing else matters right now. I nod and smile, not taking my eyes from her. Lyra blushes, colour flushing up her cheeks. She parts her lips to say something, then changes her mind. She closes her mouth resolutely and gestures with her head that we should continue walking. I follow in her wake, behind the rocky trail of laden mules and broken dreams.

That night it is colder than normal. Lyra shivers and I hug her to me beneath the blanket, stroking her hair. Her dark lashes fan out beneath her closed eyes and I think that she has fallen asleep. But suddenly, she pulls back, her eyes fixed on mine.

'*Efharisto,*' she whispers. Thank you.

'For what?' I murmur back.

'For finding us. For finding me.'

I never want to let her go. These days and nights walking over the mountain have been so filled with hardship for so many of our group, particularly the young and elderly. But the extreme hunger, the thirst, the heat of the day and cold of night have all been eclipsed for me by the nearness of Lyra. She's been my compass. A bright star guiding me over the mountains and through the ravines of this harsh, beautiful landscape.

I've not heard her complain, not a single time. I've watched the way she selflessly enquires after everyone around her and pushes more food in the direction of her younger sister. Hunger has hollowed out her cheeks over the past week and I, in turn, give more of my food to her. It's a wordless game we play as tiny morsels of meat and wild herbs and fruit dance from my plate to Lyra's to Ida's.

I have never told Lyra about Joseph. What's there to say? How can it help her to know, when she's suffered so much herself, losing her beloved father? After all, I knew Joseph for such a comparatively short time. I lie on the hard, blanket-covered ground, this beautiful girl in my arms. I scarcely want to blink, for fear I may miss something. And I acknowledge that it doesn't matter how long we know someone. We can go through our entire lives being in close proximity to another and yet still feel that vast, emotional gulf, skirting around truths, and anything of depth and substance. But then people like Joseph and Lyra can enter your life and almost before a word's been exchanged, the air around you changes. Yes, it settles with a certainty that this relationship, friendship, love, whatever it is, was written somewhere long ago.

I run a finger over Lyra's cheekbone. My heart fills with a longing for her. It's so powerful that I feel a flood building up inside me from a small, secret place. It wants to burst its dams in a torrent of passionate words. But I know nothing of spoken passion. Only simple words that speak of truth.

'I love you, Lyra,' I say in English.

Her lips curve into her beautiful, downwards-slanted smile.

'What does that mean?' she says.

'*S'agapó*' I say.

'Yes,' she says simply. 'And I love you, Leonidas. Leo. *Alf-fred.*'

Our fingers interlace behind her head. Simultaneously, our brows bend together, melding so that the top of our foreheads touch. Then, very slowly, like two pieces of a jigsaw finding communion with one another, we roll downwards. Between our brows, along the bridges of our nose, around the curving valley where the bottom of the nose drops off, until our mouths finally meet.

I've never kissed a girl before, nor have I been kissed. Of course, I was curious. Particularly when some of the fellows from school, whether truthfully or not, boasted about what it was like. But this curiosity never travelled beyond just that. I knew so few girls and had so little contact with them. And there was nobody whom I could envisage being on the receiving end of any possible interest I may have.

My first kiss is nothing like I could've ever imagined. Her lips are impossibly soft. When I was a small boy, we went to Wales one time to visit Great Aunt Lucinda. She lived near Snowdon and I'll never forget one spring morning when I ran in the fields outside her house. The sky was dotted with huge white fluffy clouds, those cumulus nimbus. We were so high in the mountain, higher than I'd ever been in my life. The clouds seemed so close and so solid, somehow. I remember running down the steep slope that hovered above one of the clouds and jumping with all my might. So that the clouds might catch me.

I landed hard on my backside and rolled down the hill. I snared my knee on a rock on the way down. As my mother cleaned it up in front of the fire back at Great Aunt Lucinda's, she asked me how it had happened.

'*Silly*,' she chided me, once I'd told her. 'You can't fall into clouds.'

But she was wrong. For here I am, experiencing my first kiss and doing just that. I'm falling into clouds with the softness of the kiss I share with Lyra. Our lips pillow against one another's, the final piece of the jigsaw fitting into place. As we search one another, I taste in her kiss her sorrows past, her dreams for the future and the contentment she feels in this moment.

At first it's only the softness of our lips finding one another. But as we continue to search one another in a language that goes beyond the ability to speak English or Cretan, I feel something else entering this new dialect Lyra and I share.

At first, it takes me by surprise. It feels so alien. Something probing, improbable, seeking. Something that hints of wild mint and longing. Of all these days, these weeks, spent in one another's company as our feelings for one another have developed. But only now, in this kiss, do these feelings take root and make perfect sense, forging a path forwards through our uncertain futures.

Coming out here, to Crete, it was to help fight a war for my country's freedom. But to lose a best friend? To fall in love? Never in a hundred years could I have imagined this would happen to me here. I've grown up. Grown out of my boyhood skin. I think of the boy who left Twickenham those months ago. We're not even nearly the same person.

Lyra pulls away gently and turns her head to the side and looks upwards. As though searching for something.

'What is it?' I whisper.

'That. Listen!'

The trees that surround us are filled with night birds. Beyond that, I can hear nothing, save the gentle inhalation and exhalation of Lyra's breath. The corners of her mouth creep downwards.

'What is it?'

'It's you!'

'*What*?'

'The birds singing. They're nightingales. The *aidóni*.'

I turn over to lie on my back, my head next to hers. Stare up into the faint outline of the darkened trees. Of course! I'd been so intent on Lyra's presence I hadn't noticed. But she's right.

After some time, I turn back and gaze at her. Her eyes are closed. Dark lashes fanning out against her cheeks. But that smile's still on her lips.

I move closer to her and kiss her again. This time, our

mouths remain locked for what feels like forever. We grow in confidence beneath that star-kissed sky, filled with the song of nightingales. I forget all about the chill of the night and the hunger that gnaws at my stomach in nauseating waves. This is all that matters now: Lyra and Leonidas, Leonidas and Lyra. Finally, when we gently pull away from one another, I place both hands on either side of her head. This is it, I think. This is how it is to be in love.

Chapter Nineteen

We keep walking. We keep placing one foot in front of the other. An endless procession through the blistering heat. We listen to the mountains echo with the sound of machine guns, the bursting of mortar-bombs and the distant rumble of what sounds like far-off thunder. But it is, we all know, the sound of villages being dynamited. We can only but wonder if our village has suffered the same fate. If the Germans' preferred method of methodically blowing up each house, one by one, has befallen our home.

The sounds that travel over the mountains to us aren't just noises of violence and destruction. They are also the steady, articulated echoes of the Cretan mountaineers, who call to one another over vast distances. At first I think it's the Jerries. But Natalia tells me that the people from the mountains have learnt how to pass messages to one another over vast networks of rivers, hills and valleys. Along with Lyra and Ida, the three of them stand in intense concentration, straining to pick up the odd word.

'I think they're saying to meet in a village on the other side of the valley,' says Ida.

'No.' Natalia shakes her head. 'They are not saying that. Listen again…'

And so ensues a heated discussion. Lyra smiles gently at me. She knows that to me, the distant words are indecipherable. These people will never stop amazing me.

By the time we reach the hills around the southern coast of Crete, we are all deeply exhausted. Not just that, but two of our party are suffering terribly, the two most elderly of our men. We slow the pace down to accommodate them, but we know it's no good. That night, it's particularly cold and one man, Dimitris, who sang as we left the village, simply does not wake up. He is not lying far from me, and I hear the quiet sobs of his daughter first thing in the morning. Propping myself up groggily on my elbows, I watch the most private and tender of scenes: a woman in the emerging dawn, bidding farewell to her beloved father.

We spend an hour burying his frail body, falcons wheeling in the sky above us. After prayers have been said for his soul, we begin to move again. But another elderly man who has been struggling, hangs back.

'I cannot,' says Costas, sitting heavily down on a rock.

It is painful to watch his grandchildren trying to convince him, for it is clear what is coming. I am surprised to see Lyra step in this time. Perhaps Costas reminds her of her own grandfather.

He takes Lyra's smooth hands in his own dark ones, covered in age spots.

'No child,' he says quietly. 'I am slowing everyone down.'

'You are *not*,' Lyra insists. 'It is not a problem to go slow – '

'*Child,*' he repeats. 'It cannot be. Now Dimitris has gone…I do not have the will to continue.'

I look at the proud features of this man, his face that I see would once have been handsome, beneath an old, tasseled kerchief that rests on his head, thick black eyebrows framing deep-set eyes, the colour of copper. His grandchildren, a girl and a boy of about fifteen, are now standing back. Perhaps they understand something that Lyra cannot. I feel suddenly choked with emotion and turn away. What world is it in which our elders are forced to lie down in fields to die? In which we are forced to kill one another, just because we were born in different countries?

'I would like,' I hear Costas say slowly behind me, 'nothing more than to die in the mountains. Let the birds of prey come and claim this old body of mine. I have had a good life, child.'

The loss of Dimitris and Costas is a blow to us all and none of us feel like talking much after that. Only on one day is the mood lightened, as we see British planes flying overhead. Ludicrously, at first I imagine that they're looking for me and instinctively duck for cover. Come now, when will you *realise*, I chide myself. This is not all about me.

Within seconds I hear whoops and shouts of joy from the villagers as the reality sets in: stores are being dropped to us. They fall way off mark. But if I believed none of us had any energy left, I was wrong. I remain hidden until the aircraft have passed far enough away and then I join the joyous throng of villagers running this way and that. We find clothes and medical supplies, tins of bully beef and sten guns. It's like Christmas, Easter and all our birthdays rolled into one jubilant event. And the supplies could not have come sooner, for I fear that more members of our party are not far from dying of hunger. I've lost count of the number of children I've carried on my back, their small bodies weak, and pitifully frail, from lack of food.

Once we've eaten our fill and re-armed and clothed ourselves, we continue with our journey southwards. As for me, I feel as though I'm existing now only for the stolen moments with Lyra, beneath the black cover of night: hushed whispers and secret kisses.

Or, perhaps, not so secret.

'Are you and Lyra going to get married?' Ida asks me one day. She's grinning back over her shoulder at me as we walk.

I stop in my tracks and look around for Lyra. I see that she is way ahead with her mother. I bite my bottom lip.

'I don't know, Ida.'

'Why don't you know?'

She has a mischievous gleam in her oval eyes. But there is also a seriousness in the haughty tilt of her chin.

'Because I don't know what will happen. I...I can't think of the future too much.'

'But you love her?' she demands, hands on hips.

It's her beloved sister we're talking about. I need to reply with the seriousness her question deserves.

A scent of the sea carried on the breeze comes to me and I drink in its fresh saltiness. I think about the fact that I was so sure, when I came to Crete, that I'd always be surrounded by water. I imagined it to be a tiny island. But the truth is that Crete isn't tiny at all. Its terrain is far more varied, filled with mountains, pastures, orchards and ocean bays, than I could ever have imagined.

'Yes,' I reply firmly. 'I love her.'

Ida's face softens. She nods briefly. 'Good.'

And then she sighs. It is a sigh that carves lines across her forehead and around her eyes. It makes her look far older than her fourteen years.

'I'm tired of walking,' she says quietly.

I can see she really is. She's undernourished and underslept, mauve trenches carved beneath her brown eyes.

'Sometimes I think the Papadakis boys were right and we should never have left the village. How could we know for sure the Germans would come?' She breaks off, sighs again. 'And even if they did, perhaps it would be better to die on your own land than this foreign place.'

'Ida!' I say sharply. 'Don't talk like that! Nobody's going to die.'

'But they already have,' she shrugs wearily. Sweeps her hands back in the direction we've come from. 'We've lost old Dimitris & Costas. We'll reach a hiding place that Yanni knows about, and then what? Just wait? Die of starvation? How long can we last?'

I rub the back of my neck. It's peeling from sunburn.

'The war can't last forever.'

Ida shrugs again. She looks once more like a child, a sulky child at that. She kicks at a large stone on the ground.

'Anyway,' she pouts. 'I'm happy that you and Lyra love each other. At least something good has come out of these days.'

I smile at her. Instinctively, I pull her towards me and envelop her in a hug. She lays her head on my shoulder. Then she sighs deeply again, her whole body leaning into me in exhaustion. This time, I feel the depth of her sigh taking root in the ground and weaving its way beneath the feet of the weary travellers.

Yanni is good as his word. How he knows about this place, I can't imagine. For it's impossible he'd ever have brought his herd of goats as far away from the village as this. But it doesn't matter. We're all just so relieved to have arrived somewhere. To be able to finally stop walking. The cave is vast, a couple of hundred yards back from the sea, dripping with stalactites and damp corners that branch into dim, smaller passages. Bats wheel and flitter around the cave's vault. And, from somewhere within its depth, there's a sound of running water. It feels like a deeply unhealthy environment.

And yet we have, at least, stopped moving. People can rest and sleep and refuel themselves from the supplies that we now have. Nobody wants to think about what we'll do when they run out. For I fear that here, closer to the coast, there's less wild food to be found.

I realise that this is the first time Lyra, Ida and Natalia have ever seen the ocean. No doubt it's the same for the rest of the villagers, as the reality of their wide-eyed gaze at the rolling waves becomes clear.

We continue to listen to the ominous rumbles from the distance. Sitting close to the mouth of the cave, we stare into the wide arc of blue sky above us. It's so bright it's almost painful to look at. We are all just waiting, waiting, for British planes to fly over. To shout out the victory that each and every one of us dream, but never speak of.

'Let's walk,' Lyra says to me, early one evening. 'I need to get out of here.'

She's right, the atmosphere is stifling, rotting as slowly

and surely as our souls beneath the humid sea mists. We breathe in the cave's dampness and breathe out bitterness. And I know it's only a matter of time before our numbers begin to dwindle again.

We walk along the ravine and up a hill to a cliff edge where we're afforded with wonderful, sweeping views of a pretty, curved bay. Lyra and I stand hand in hand on the edge of the cliff. Stare out to the gentle waves that glint in the fierce sunlight.

'It's so beautiful,' Lyra breathes as she looks down, unblinking. 'How big is it?'

'The sea?' I ask. 'Not entirely sure,' I reply. 'But it's huge. Vast. Water covers about two thirds of our planet.'

She nods somberly, impressed. 'And your country… England. Which direction is it?'

'Well…' I unclasp my fingers from hers. Turn slowly on my heels, pointing in a north-westerly direction. 'It's that way.'

'Is England anything like Crete?' Lyra asks earnestly. Her eyes light up in anticipation of learning something new.

I gaze at her beautiful, open face. I decide at that moment that if we marry, *when* we marry, I'll do everything in my power to support an education for Lyra. How can it possibly be right, be fair, that a girl as bright as this not have access to learning?

'No,' I reply. 'England is very different.'

'How?'

'Doesn't have mountains, at least not like you do, and the sea isn't this colour. The people speak differently, and look different. They even behave differently. We have large cities there and the climate is much cooler, even down at sea level. England is…' I falter. England's *what*? My homeland: my connection with my parents, my unremarkable past, and Joseph. And yet now, not a great deal else. After all, England is not where I'm bound to Joseph. It's here, on this Cretan soil. And it's not where I'm connected to this girl whom I now love with all my heart. And so it almost fades into insignificance for me.

'England is what?' she asks.

She takes a step closer to me. I can breathe the scent of the handmade soap she's been washing her clothes, hair and body with.

I put my arm round her shoulders and pull her close.

'It doesn't feel real to me anymore,' I say. And it doesn't. Even the language is losing its clarity. My dreams are in Cretan dialect and fragments of half-remembered English words.

'Do you think Grandfather is still alive?' she asks me suddenly. She takes my hand.

'Yes,' I reply truthfully. I squeeze her fingers gently. 'He is strong, your grandfather. So strong.'

She smiles at me gratefully. Strands of her dark hair flicker in front of her face and I smooth them away with my thumb.

Lyra. I still can't quite believe that I have the good fortune to be chosen by this girl. To be *loved* by this girl. The thought that if the war had never happened, we wouldn't have met somehow pains me. How can I possibly say that all this death and destruction had to take place in order for Lyra to enter my life? But how can I *not*? I curve my hand around hers. Then I bring her fingertips to my lips and kiss them. 'How I would love to swim.'

'Why don't you?' she laughs. Her olive eyes narrow into slits.

'Only if you come with me.'

Lyra smiles sadly. 'I don't know how to swim.'

'That's alright,' I squeeze her hand. 'You can stay in the shallows. And I'll go in quickly.'

She nods. 'Alright, then. Let's go down.'

We skirt around the cliff's edge, the sea beckoning us with every step. It is still and quiet as a breezeless day. There is nothing here. Nobody.

We walk slowly down the cliff. Over the fine, golden sand to the sea's edge. I pull my shirt over my head and turn round, grinning at her. The anticipation of the water is almost more than I can bear. I feel like a young boy.

'I won't be long,' I tell her.

She stands there in the shallows, long skirt bunched up in her hands. Gentle waves dance around her feet.

The touch, texture and temperature of the sea are perfect. I cry out in pure delight. Finally, I can resist no longer. I dive beneath the waves and swim out to sea, keeping my eyes open as they strain against the clear, salty green depths. When I pull up for breath, I turn round. Push my soaked hair out of my eyes.

She is standing at the water's edge and I take a snapshot of her in my mind. Feet in the water, hair flickering, framed against the glowing cliffs. This sight, I think, is something I must remember for the rest of my life. I've seen some beautiful landscapes in Crete, but nothing like this. The beach, the waves, the company…they've all conspired to bring me this moment. I'm more grateful for it than anything else in my life.

I'll ask her to marry me, I think. I don't know how, I don't know exactly when. But *today*, sometime, I'll ask her to be my wife. As a wave crashes over my head, I find that I'm laughing. Recklessly, happily, in a way that's been so beyond me for so many months. In fact, I think, when did I *ever* laugh like this? Even in England, when I lived in a time of peace? If I've learnt anything during war, it's to take each opportunity that comes your way. And take it quickly.

'Will you marry me?' I murmur to the sea, testing the words out in my mouth. The waves continue dancing, a steady flow. And each time they crest and break, I feel sure they bring with them words of affirmation.

I'm beginning to think that yes, just perhaps, I have a chance to keep moving, breathing, living. For so long I believed all of that would be forever beyond my reach after what happened to my friend. But watching her graceful figure moving out of the shallows and over the sand, the smile on my face is as wide as the skies and as real as her presence. She turns around. Waves at me, strands of dark hair blowing over her eyes. I raise a hand to wave back, and that is when I hear it.

I watch, helpless, as my beloved Lyra is catapulted high into the blinding blue sky. Her grey skirt billows out around her, forming an umbrella. She turns on to her side. Everything plays out in slow motion, the sound of the explosion elongated and amplified. I swear that, as she turns in a graceful arc against the cliff face that glows amber in the evening sunlight, I see a smile on her face. Is she looking directly at me, answering yes? Stretching her long, thin arms out towards me as she spirals like a ballerina?

Probably not.

But in all the times I've replayed this moment, this is how I've remembered it.

And then, a soft, sickening thud as her lovely body crumples beneath her, leaving the remnants of the landmine she has stepped on across the scattered, yellow sand. And my heart, broken wide open over her shattered body.

PART THREE

Chapter Twenty
Twickenham, 1967

How long have I been sitting here for? I feel as though I haven't moved, have barely breathed, as my dad has been speaking. The curtains have been pulled shut and the light pouring in through the open window has dimmed. I'm sure they were open before; someone must have come in whilst he was talking.

Now he sighs deeply and closes his eye, his one bloodshot eye screwing shut tighter than the other.

You are not going to Crete.

That was what he said to me, wasn't it, when I told him where I was going?

I blink, and the spell is broken. I was there, in Crete. With Dad and Joseph. With Dad and Lyra. With Alfred, Alfie, Leonidas, Leo. All this happened to him and I knew nothing, *nothing*. But to go through all this…and alone? Which leads me to my next thought.

'Dad…?'

I edge my chair even closer to his bedside.

'Dad?'

Has he fallen asleep? His jaw is hanging open slightly and he is taking deep, laboured breaths.

'Mmm?' he murmurs.

'Does Ma know everything you've just told me?'

He is silent for a few moments. 'More or less.'

I mull this over, wondering why on earth she never filled me in on any of it, when he mumbles '...but probably more. She knows, alright.'

I bite my bottom lip and then massage my forehead with the fingertips of both hands. I have a terrible headache. Never in my life have I listened to anyone for so long, or so intently. A memory of Wolfgang comes back to me, dirty blond hair, big brown eyes and a joint permanently burning down between his fingers.

Does your father ever talk about what he did in the war?

I'd balked at his question; I remember clearly that I couldn't think of anything I'd less rather talk about. But he'd pressed it... what was it I said in response? My elbows resting on my thighs, I drop my head into my hands and think hard. It was something along the lines of how my dad was the grumpiest bastard on the planet and he'd never talk about it.

How wrong could I have been?

'Your mother's been good to me,' he rasps, opening his bloodshot eye again. 'She's put up with a lot.'

'How did you meet her? How long after you got back from Crete?'

Are these words truly leaving my mouth? Are we really having this conversation *now,* when I am eighteen years of age? How have I never known the answer to this before, or never been interested?

'Jimmy,' he says, and I flinch. I have never heard him call

me Jimmy before. Jimmy boy, perhaps, when he's been angrily mocking me.

'I'm tired. I need to sleep.'

I nod. 'Of course.'

I get up and stretch my limbs. I feel as though I have aged fifty years since I've been sitting in that chair, travelling over mountains and experiencing extreme hunger, hardship and death. I have so many more questions I want to ask him, not only to do with Ma and his relationship with her, but also whether he kept in contact with Natalia and Ida? Whether he ever got in touch with Joseph's family? If Lyra's grandfather made it through the war? If he could point out on a map…?

I run a finger through my long, knotted hair, this hair that father has always urged me to cut. God, how I hated him. But now, as I stare at his shrunken figure in the bed, all I can feel is a deep sense of knowing him for the first time in the eighteen years of my life.

'Come back tomorrow, will you Jimmy?' he says quietly. 'We can talk more.'

I nod. 'I will, Dad. First thing.'

I am about to slip out of the room, when something makes me turn back abruptly. In three swift steps, I cross the room to his bedside. He opens both eyes and stares at me. His face is dry, red blotches and thin veins crisscrossing it like railway tracks. He looks twenty years older than before I left for Crete.

I stoop down and embrace the frail frame of my father lying in the metal hospital bed. It must take him just as much by surprise as me, for the minute I touch him, I feel him flinch beneath my touch. But moments later, his body relaxes from its rigidity and a hand comes up and pats me awkwardly on my back.

'Bye, Dad.'

'Night, son,' he murmurs. 'God Bless.'

Quietly, I leave the room. As I walk down the long, brightly lit corridor, I feel lighter than I have done in my entire life. I stretch my hands high above my head, increase my pace and push open the hospital door into the warm, late summer evening air that smells of blackberries and smoke.

Number twenty-seven Claremont Road sits empty. The removal van is outside and I stand idly watching, my back against the front door, smoking a cigarette. The two removal men heave and curse as they lift a heavy sofa into the back of the van. I see books and bookshelves disappear, a coat-stand, paintings wrapped up roughly in brown paper.

Pushing the front door open, I find Ma sitting on a box, staring at a framed photograph and running her hand over it. I move beside her and look at it: my parents on their wedding day, impossibly young. Knowing what I know now, I wonder if he thought of Lyra on this day? Ma looks so lovely. Through the sepia tones, her dark lipstick contrasts sharply with the whiteness of her veil and the posy of flowers she is clutching between her hands. There is so much hope in her beautiful face. Has her marriage been what she hoped for?

And Dad? As I crouch beside her, I stare into the face of my father on his wedding day, marrying not the woman he thought he would, but someone else. I think I can read that now in his eyes in this photograph. *But,* I think sighing, this picture has been sitting on a table in the living room my entire life. It is only with the benefit of hindsight that I can see anything at all, other than a happy young couple on their wedding day.

I never got to have another conversation with my dad. He died the same night that I went to visit him and heard his story. Did I know that would happen? I think a part of me did; that in some quiet and secret place, I was expecting it. And that was what made me turn back from the door of his hospital room and give him the first and last embrace of my life.

I turn to my mother and grasp her wrist gently.

'Ma,' I say. 'I'm going for a quick walk.'

'Don't be long, Jimmy,' she says quietly, continuing to look at the photograph. 'We'll leave in an hour or so.'

'I won't be long, promise.'

I stand up and stride towards the open door, the first sharp promise of autumn relieving me instantly. School went back last week, but not me. We are moving to Suffolk, to a village where Ma's sister lives, because there's no possibility of affording the mortgage payments in Twickenham any longer. I'll be starting a new school in a few days' time, to do my A Levels. It sounds a bit dire, in the middle of nowhere, but I suppose I'll get used to it.

With the old school going back, I thought Charles would have reappeared by now. My friend did, of course, succinctly express his feelings for Matala and the lifestyle. But I never seriously believed there was a chance he might not come back. I thought he may stay another week or so, but then return for his final school year. Charles is so clever; he has so many prospects. He could snap up any job he wants in an instant after school.

But he doesn't return. One late afternoon, about a week before Ma and I are due to leave, Charles's parents turn up at our house. Stiff, formal, they stand there in their Sunday best with their arms crossed as a stilted patter of words escape their lips. Ma nods her head mutely and I notice that Charles' mother doesn't take her eyes off me. Yes, they've come to say they're sorry about my father, but I know that Mrs. Adams is far more interested in talking about her son.

Once the formalities are over and Mr Adams has moved towards the front door, Ma following him, Mrs. Adams hangs back and looks at me expectantly from beneath her hat. I remain silent. I feel irrationally angry with her too for being the mother of a boy who could betray me so deeply and stare at her until she can no longer hold my gaze.

'Jimmy,' she says eventually, 'when is he coming back?'

I pick at my nails. 'I honestly couldn't tell you, Mrs. Adams.'

I glance up at her face, a picture of pure anguish. She is silent for a few moments, then asks;

'Why didn't the two of you come back together?'

I sigh. That's easy enough to answer.

'Because Charles wasn't ready to come back. And I was.'

Mrs. Adams looks at me incredulously. I know how strange it must sound and, before we went to Crete, I'm certain that should anyone have predicted such a situation, they would have placed the two of us in each other's shoes. She moves slightly closer to me and I notice a single tear escaping one eye, which she hastily brushes away.

'Are you telling me the truth, Jimmy?'

I stop picking at my nails and look her directly in the eye.

'Yes, I am.'

She nods her head slightly and drops her gaze. Opening her handbag, she fishes around for a piece of paper and pencil. Finding a Boot's Chemist receipt, she turns it over and hands it to me.

'Write your address in Suffolk, would you Jimmy. So I can give it to Charles when he gets back.'

I hesitate, sticking my thumbs into my trouser pockets and drumming my fingers against the side.

'I'll write to him,' I reply quietly. 'I know your address.'

She withdraws her hand, placing the receipt back and straightens her hat.

'Alright, Jimmy. I'll tell him you'll do that. And I'm dreadfully sorry about your father.'

It's just a short walk from my house to Eel Pie Island. Regardless of that, I haven't even been down to the river since being back. This river, that's been part of my soul, the narrow strip of water between my normal life and the mythical land where I once danced to the forbidden beats of Eelpiland. Now the river only serves to make me acutely aware of the absence of Charles and how much I need him at this moment. But now, in this last hour in Twickenham, I dig my hands into my pockets and cross Heath Road. I keep my head down because I don't want to see anybody I know and have to answer more questions about my father or Charles.

The Thames appears ahead of me and the bridge; that bridge that appears so less dramatic or compelling by daytime. I take a sharp intake of breath as I look at the Eel Pie Hotel rising out from the island's wild, green foliage. I feel, at this moment, that if I were to be granted one wish, any wish in the world, it would be to go back to that evening I swam over to the island. Perhaps, then, I never would have met those two older boys – what were their names? – and Charles and I never would have gone to Matala. But then, I think, shaking my head and digging my hands further into my trouser pockets, if it weren't for my absence over the summer, Father would never have opened up to me in the way that he did. I would have stayed here in Twickenham, working in his office. He probably would not have had his stroke. And we would have kept grating on each other, fighting, day in, day out.

I step on to the bridge as gulls fly overhead and a cool wind buffets my face. Walking slowly, not like the other times I've been over here when I could barely contain my excitement to get onto the island, I reach the end of the bridge. No old dear with her crooked headscarf and high-buttoned coat taking my threepenny bit now. Just a free reign of the island.

It feels eerily quiet and I notice things I've never seen before, probably because I've never been here during daylight hours. I notice, for example, how overgrown everything is: a tangle of weeds and creepers and rhododendrons. I notice the paint peeling from the old walls of the Eel Pie Hotel and its unkempt lawns rolling down to a crumbling wall bordering the Thames. I allow myself a small, wry smile as I remember heaving myself over that wall, dripping wet, only six weeks ago. That fateful night. It's incredible how I can feel so completely different in such a short time. Looking back now, I see a boy: young, naïve, hopeful, arrogant. Whereas just weeks later I have changed beyond recognition. I've travelled, lost my virginity, my best friend and my father. But, more importantly than any of this, I've heard Dad's story.

I stand at the bottom of the garden, looking back on to the mainland and pull my collar up around my ears as I feel a surprisingly cool wind whistle around me. Turning round, I walk slowly up to the hotel; that great hulk of a creaking building that is achingly familiar to me. I'm not quite sure why I'm here; what I want to see because, of course, nothing will be happening at the club at this time of day. But this place is important to me. There is a before and after to my life. Eelpiland represents the very best of *before.*

I know that I'll always think of it as the place I grew up; more so than home, or school and more so than Matala. Eelpiland has been a constant. Years before I was even old enough to come here, I dreamt of it. Charles and I would talk about it endlessly, sitting on the bed in his room, as Charles dreamt of music and I dreamt of girls. And then, that first time that we actually made the crossing from the mainland to the island: though separated only by a narrow channel of water, it was like a crossing to another world. It was as close to a magical land as I would ever travel.

I walk to the front door, absent of jostling crowds and first see the white rectangular piece of paper nailed down, and then two thin wooden planks crisscrossed over the door. I catch my breath and walk closer to the sign.

'Eel Pie Club closed until further notice. Arthur Chisnall charged for using the premises for public dancing, in breach of his license and fined the sum of ten pounds. Case currently under appeal.'

I catch my breath. I read the notice again, and then a

third time. A date is printed in small letters beneath, it is 4th September, just five days before. Surely the club can't be closed, not really, not permanently? Too many people come here. Too many people love it and use its services, not just the dancing and music, of course, but the meetings, the advice and talks that Arthur Chisnall gives for all the young people.

I blink, steeling myself, waiting for the anger to come. I close my eyes and flex the fingers of both my hands in preparation for it. Tears escape my closed lids, flowing as free and easy as the Thames that moves several feet beneath me. But they are not tears of rage or of sorrow. They are tears of acceptance, of saying goodbye to this part of my life and stepping forward into my future.

Ivy Cottage
Windy Lane
Lavenham
Suffolk
1st August 1969

Dear Mr. and Mrs. Redmond,

This letter may come as quite a surprise to you. You don't know me, but my name is Jim Nightingale. I'm the son of Alfred Nightingale who died last year. I don't really know how to write this – I've never been much good at letter writing – so I'm just going to come right out and say it.

Before he died, my father told me about his friendship with your son in Crete during the War.

First, in Suda Bay, and then later as they tried to make their way southwards across the island. I have no idea how much you know about the details surrounding the death of your son – probably not much. Serving together, Dad and Joseph became very close. My dad described him to me as 'the best friend I ever had.'

I'm sorry Dad never contacted you himself. The thing is, he always blamed himself for Joseph's death and I'm not sure he could bring himself to write to you. So I'm doing it for him.

A man they both knew had been wounded early one morning in May 1941. Knowing that Joseph was planning to be a doctor, Dad went to get him. But as soon as he got there and started trying to fix him up, a sniper shot him through the ear and he died in Dad's arms. He was killed instantly and didn't suffer. Dad never got over it.

I'm sorry to have to tell you all this, but I'm sure you'd want to know.

Yours sincerely,

Jim Nightingale

I read the letter through twice more and seal the envelope. I walk into the sitting room where Ma is reading the paper and turn the envelope round to face her. She smiles at me and leans forwards, her warm fingers stroking my cheek.

'Well done, love.'

I smile and walk outside into the sharp August sunlight

in the direction of the village post office.

I hear the tinny sound of music playing and pause on the pavement. An ice cream van creaks up to the kerb and two little boys on bicycles tear wildly towards it, virtually flinging their bikes down in their eagerness. They hand over their shilling to the man inside and ask for a funny face ice cream, their words tumbling out. As their treats are handed over, the two boys glance at one another, just fleetingly, but long enough for me to recognise the expression of sheer glee on their faces. But, even more than that: their friendship.

Perhaps the next letter I write will be to Charles. Or perhaps it won't. *God,* I miss him. I turn the envelope round in my hands, this letter bound for the family of my dad's best mate. I hope it doesn't make them feel too sad. There's been enough sadness.

Suddenly, I feel strangely light. Because I know that it will *help* them. And I also know that one day, when the right time comes, I'll see Charles again. He's too good a friend to lose forever. There's no way I'm ready yet. But it will happen. It just has to.

I dig into my pockets, find some change, and buy myself a funny face too. As I walk towards the village post office, I lick off the eyes. Then the nose and the mouth. And I ruffle up my hair, grinning into the hot, august sunshine.

Chapter Twenty-One

Ipswich, 2011

All those years ago, when I spoke to Charles's mother and told her I had no idea when her son would be back from Matala, I was telling the truth. At the time I had every intention of sending him a letter but, it turned out that I never could bring myself to write to my old friend. If I'd learnt anything from that final conversation with my father, it was to move on and not hold grudges; that life was too precious to waste time. I digested that truth on a visceral, as well as an emotional level, rendering it stranger still that I felt unable to pick up a pen and write to him. And as each year passed, it became harder and harder to take that step. So I didn't.

Instead, I got on with my life; survived without Charles in a way I never thought possible. Without my right-hand man to distract me at school, and without the lure of Eel Pie Island, I didn't do badly in my A Levels. It turned out that I had an eye for design, something I'd never realised before, so I went on to train as an architect. I grew up, fell in and out of love many times before I could recognise lust for what it really was. And then I met Leila.

It was 1978, a hot day in June. She had a tumble of rich auburn curls and wide hazel eyes and was wearing a black denim jacket over a long, summer dress and not a scrap of makeup. We were on the B28 that took us careering round the ring road to the south west of Ipswich. I always used to joke about Ipswich bus drivers, that they must spend the hour or two before their driving shift in the pub, but this one had us all hanging on for dear life to the straps above us and the seated passengers clutching at their padded seats till their knuckles gleamed white.

Something made me want to get off at the same stop as her and I travelled three stops past my own and edged past the people in front, just so I could walk down the steps behind her. I had no plan. I just wanted to talk to her, somehow. But then I needn't have worried, because fate – or whatever you want to call it – transpired to help me out. She was carrying a folder under one arm and a single sheet of paper slipped out of it and floated along the pavement.

We noticed it at the same time. I hurried up behind her and bent down to retrieve it. But so did she, and as I pulled away, in our confusion our heads clunked, hard.

We both slapped a hand to our foreheads in pain, staggering backwards a little.

'Sorry,' we said, at the same time.

Still with her hand to her head, she straightened up. 'Are you alright? Thanks for helping.'

'Well, I wasn't very helpful in the end. Are *you* alright?'

She rubbed her head again then dropped her hand. I noticed the fine sheen of sweat above her top lip. 'Fine. I'm fine.'

'OK. Well...' She paused, pushing her curls back over her shoulder. 'Bye.'

I watched her turn and walk along the pavement and I frowned. Taking a deep breath, I jogged after her.

''scuse me.'

She turned, her curls flying out of place again, eyebrows arched in surprise.

'Would you...can you...' I cleared my throat, told myself to get a grip. 'Maybe we can go for a drink sometime?'

She laughed then, not in a mocking way, but more with surprise. Her front teeth had the slightest gap in them.

'Thank you. The thing is...well...' She looked around her, as though expecting to see someone she knew; bit her bottom lip. 'I'm actually seeing someone right now, so...' She trailed off.

Dammit. I put my hand up apologetically. 'Understood. That's fine.'

But neither of us moved. We continued to stand there, outside a bookies with an old man on a zimmer clattering out of, the metallic frame flashing in the sunlight.

She broke the silence, gesturing towards my forehead. 'I think you'll need to put some cream or something on that.'

I smiled. 'Think you will, too.'

She took my phone number; wouldn't give me hers. Said she'd phone me, maybe, sometime. But I didn't hold out much hope. I thought she was just trying to politely get rid of me.

So when she called, a week later, I was almost speechless with happiness. I sat on the floor with my back against the door, fiddling with the telephone cord.

'What about the bloke...the one you're seeing?'

There was a pause and I could hear the sound of a glass chinking against the phone and her taking a sip of water. 'Actually, he was a bit of a loser.'

I burst out laughing, joy pounding against my ribcage.

I took her to The Three Bells, the most salubrious, I hoped, of the pubs I went to. We sat by the river, ducks waddling up to peck at our shoes. She was even more beautiful than I remembered and, above her right eye, sat a perfect, purple, egg-shaped bruise.

'Matching bumps,' she grinned, pointing to mine, and we both started to laugh. I was smitten. Leila. The woman who finally stilled the tempestuous seas of my heart.

As for Charles, I sometimes wondered about him; where he was and what he was doing. And as time went by, I thought less of what had happened in Matala and more of those years in Twickenham, particularly Eel Pie Island and all the fun we'd had there, back in a time when everything, I thought nostalgically, felt far more simple.

I heard, back in 1971, that the Eel Pie Hotel had burnt down in a fire. I thought of Charles more than ever that year. I started to write a letter to him several times but I could never find the right words. Each time ended with me scrunching the paper up and hurling it into the bin.

Once, a couple of years after the fire, I had a training session not far from Twickenham. It was an icy, December day and I'd pulled off the busy A316, once known as the Chertsey Road, the beginning and end point of my hitchhiking journey all those years ago. In the car, I pulled on my woolen gloves, scarf and hat and stood on the riverbank as the seagulls screeched overhead. The last time I was here was the day I found out that the club was closing and then left the only home I'd known and along with it, my childhood. This time, I made my way slowly over the bridge, hardly bearing to bring myself to look up and see the space where the Eel Pie Hotel had once stood.

When I eventually did, there was no smoldering mass for, of course, the fire had taken place an entire two years previously. There was nothing to see at all. Just grass pushing up through the frozen earth; life continuing despite everything. I stood on the bridge, gloved hands pushed down into my duffel coat, and I smiled.

So it turns out that I'm not the centre of the universe after all, I said to my eighteen-year old self. *I never have been.*

I stared at the empty patch of land on Eel Pie Island, feeling strangely peaceful, then turned and walked back to my car.

Yet, even with that experience, benign and positive as it was, I'd failed to convince myself to contact Charles. I could even have stopped in at my friend's old house off the Twickenham High Street to see if he still lived there. But I didn't.

It wasn't until almost fifty years later that I stopped considering contacting him as something abstract and implausible. I was living in Ipswich and was walking through the city centre. It was one of those days when spring was starting to reveal itself, pushing warmer rays through the leaden clouds and spurts of new growth strained through the delicate clumps of lesser celandine beneath trees and through cracks in the pavements. I was on my way to a meeting, but was early and wanted to linger and enjoy this feeling of freshness that enveloped me. I paused outside a bookshop and browsed the new titles, then I continued walking and stopped outside Ipswich Travel. It had been quite some time since Leila and I had taken a proper holiday together. I knew how much she loved Italy...perhaps I could find a week away for us both?

The shop window was emblazoned with posters advertising villas in the south of France, cultural tours of Morocco and palaces in far-flung places such as India, surrounded by palm trees, the sky around them an unnatural, cerulean blue. I had already started to move away when something drew me back; an invisible string reeling me in. I wasn't sure why, or even where I should be looking, but my eyes flickered around the large windows until they settled upon a small, A4 sized poster with a brightly coloured and patterned guitar taking up one half of it, surrounded by flowers and scattered ban the bomb signs.

On the right side of the page I read the following words:

The Myth of Matala is Alive.

A reunion of the youth, who were staying in the caves in the sixties and seventies, will be held from June 11-13 in Matala.

I took a sharp intake of breath. Matala.

It had been so long since my mind had wandered to the sun-baked earth of that place. Before I could check my emotions, mirth bubbled and fizzed within me until I burst into laughter. An elderly lady was walking past me; she stopped, eyed me suspiciously and then moved on. I frowned; I felt strangely nervous, delirious even. *Peace and Love* the poster advertised. It looked like a teenager had designed it. It was so...garish. And yet, it made me feel something. But what? After all these years, I still felt something for the place. Or was I confusing these feelings for a lost time, a time never to return? My vanished , interrupted youth?

I ran a hand roughly over my face, pausing on my chin as I scratched it. I really needed a shave. I allowed my reflection to come into focus in the shop window and I stared at myself, trying to remember exactly what I looked like when I went to Matala. Dark, floppy hair, brown eyes. Fairly good-looking and yet, most definitely, an over-inflated estimation of my charms. Was that teenage boy still in there, somewhere? As this image blurred, I gazed at my current reflection. For years, I'd dyed my hair dark but couldn't be bothered now; I was too old for all that. I always kept my hair short these days and, on the odd occasion, a rogue brown strand would fight its way through the grey to remind me of that hair from the past I was once so proud of. My face was fairly lined – well, Charles *did* always tell me to wear suncream when we were in Matala, but I never listened to him back then, and nor to anyone else for years after that. I took in the checked shirt beneath my sensible black rain jacket, a swathe of t-shirt revealed at the neck. The shirt was tucked into my Levi's around my comfortable waist and, on sudden impulse, I pulled the shirt out.

I continued to stand outside the travel agent, reading the poster again and again, before looking at the flyers next to it advertising hotels and apartments in Matala. It must be completely different now from how I remembered it.

And then, as though my feet had taken on a life of their own, I turned abruptly and walked as fast as I could to the nearest café. Poking my head round the door, I asked a waitress if there was wi-fi. She nodded and I hurried in, ordered an espresso, slung my jacket over a chair and pulled my laptop out of my bag. I'd never used Facebook before and I stumbled around for a little while, creating an account. Once that was done, I went to the search box and typed Charles Adams. I held my breath as the results came up. Oh God, there were dozens of them.

I skimmed through those that couldn't possibly be him: the teenagers and college students, those with different coloured skin. There were only a couple who appeared to be older men, around my age. One of them had a lined face but black, clearly dyed hair. Charles would never dye his hair that colour. Would he? I clicked through to the other one and found myself leaning up close to the computer screen. Nearly everything was private so I couldn't look at photos or any of his timeline information. I sat there for some time, one hand covering my mouth and the fingers of the other hand drumming on the tabletop. I was interrupted by the waitress coming to ask me if I wanted another drink.

'Sure, another espresso, please' I replied.

I looked back at the photo. Right age, more or less. But not a hint in that picture, not even the slightest inkling, of that face, so indelibly marked in my memory. This man was standing on a hilltop, in walking boots and a raincoat, smiling openly into the camera. Grey hair poking out from under a beanie. Lines splayed out liberally from the corners of his eyes. But no. *No*. I would recognise him.

It couldn't be him.

I closed the laptop and sighed loudly. And then, on reflex, re-opened it and typed a message to the last Charles Adams.

'Hello Charles. This is Jim Nightingale here. Please send

me a message back if I have the right Charles.'

I read it again, then scrubbed out the last sentence and wrote instead, in capital letters 'HOW ARE YOU?' I found myself smirking slightly and shook my head before replacing the laptop lid. I continued to sit at the table, not moving, just summoning up the image of Charles from years ago as memories of him surfaced like bubbles rising to the top of a glass: at school, winding up the teachers; in his terraced Victorian house, nose in a book in his musty living room; on Eel Pie Island, all blond hair sticking up from his head, freckles, skinny frame and black-rimmed glasses.

I didn't even notice when the espresso was placed in front of me. That poster in the travel agent window was bringing it all back. At first, the memories of Matala reemerged only in shades of grey and black: the place where I had my heart broken. The place where I lost my best friend. The place where phony hippies convened, searching for sun, seclusion and a path away from the guilt generation. By the time I had stared into space for over ten minutes, my espresso grown cold and people filtering in and out of the café, the lens had widened. I also remembered, in hazy fragments, the following details: the warm smile of Mama, in her bakery, when she handed bread over the counter; the distinct golden blue of the waves; the exhausting journey up to the first top cave but then the reward of turning to see the curve of the bay spread out before me; the taste of the wine, dry as the Cretan earth; the glisten of sunlight and seawater on Charles's skin as he threw back his blond head and roared with laughter.

And not only that, but the lens into the past encompassed a more realistic filter: my heart was not *really* broken, as much as it may have felt like it at the time. And I didn't *lose* my best friend. I was the one who moved away and never got in touch with him. As for the phony hippies…well, weren't they just a group of young people trying to get away from it all? If anything, *I* was the one who could never be honest with myself. I had such a lack of confidence and self-awareness back then, whilst also believing myself to be the centre of the universe. It was never going to be an easy combination.

A screaming child in a pushchair jolted me back to the present time. I glanced at my watch, took a sip of my espresso, grimaced at its temperature, emptied some coins onto the table and hurried out of the café for my meeting.

I couldn't stop thinking about Charles Adams. *Charles.* Our friendship…it was so…so what? Satisfying. Close. Fun. We had laughed a lot. Of course, I'd built friendships since then, but none of them had come close to what I had with Charles, I was certain of that. Would he even want to know me now? People changed as they grew older, didn't they?

I pushed the Facebook message to the back of my mind. But then, three days later I logged on to my account, and there it was, the small, red number one on the envelope icon, signaling a message. I tapped my fingers on the tabletop and frowned at the screen. Could it be him? Or would it be a different Charles Adams saying I'd got the wrong person? My fingers hovered over the keys and then jabbed at them. I held my breath.

Five words:

My God, is it really you?

I leant back in my chair, closed my eyes and felt

something welling up inside me: the fragments of a friendship that had once been more satisfying to me than anything else. My father lost his best friend in the most tragic of circumstances. But now, I had the chance, right there in front of me, to resurrect that relationship from the past. I opened my eyes, turned my face to where the light shone through the window, smiled deeply, then returned my gaze to the laptop screen and began to type.

Chapter Twenty-Two

We met, for the first time, in a pub in Chiswick, close to where he lived.

I walked into the pub and stood for several moments in a shadow close to the doorway, watching a man who had to be Charles sitting at a table by the window. A thin shaft of sunlight spilled through the window on to his hands and those were what I found myself focusing on. Never mind about his face, I thought, his *hands*...they had grown old. Somehow that surprised me more than anything else. He started fiddling with the narrow vase on the table filled with giant daisies and, as he did so, he turned his head and I stepped out of the shadow.

Charles's hands fell away from the vase and he leant back and stared at me. I'm not sure how long we remained in that frozen tableaux for; probably just a few seconds, yet it felt like hours. What was he noticing about me? Who's to know, but this is what I noticed about him: the two-day old grey stubble grazing his chin; his nose, thinner and sharper than I remembered it; the two deep grooves that ran between his eyebrows like parallel ski tracks; that he wore his age well and had become something close to handsome – no, not close, he *was* handsome – and that he still wore black-rimmed glasses.

I'm not sure if it was Charles or I who broke the stillness, but as he stood up from his seat, I took four long strides across the wooden-slatted floor, flung my arms around him and closed my eyes.

It's a strange thing, missing a person for almost half a century without truly knowing you miss them. Because what happened was that after the pain had receded all those years ago and I embarked on my new life in Suffolk – away from Twickenham, away from Eel Pie Island, and away from Charles – I'd never really allowed myself to dwell on my old friend for too long. If I ever had a twinge of missing the Charles-shaped space in my life, I learnt to busy myself with something else.

But now, standing there with my arms wrapped around his comforting form, it was as though all those emotions I'd kept at bay, year after year, caught up with me.

Tears were stinging my eyes, but I didn't care because I was no longer, thank God, that painfully self-conscious eighteen-year old. Eventually, we pulled back and just stood there, grinning idiotically at each other.

'I'm pretty sure, Mr Adams,' I said slowly, 'that I owe you a drink.'

I drank rum and coke, Charles a pint of bitter. The news spilled out of us in non-chronological bursts as a tumble of grandchildren, jobs, children, homes and holidays took form in shifting shapes between us before bursting like balloons in their haste to be replaced by the next missed event from our pasts.

There was still one important question though, that

hung unspoken between us, and it wasn't until the third drink that I was brave enough to go there.

I opened the pack of ready salted crisps, offered it to Charles then popped one into my mouth.

'Chenoa,' I said, chewing slowly. 'Whatever happened to her?'

'Yes,' said Charles. 'Chenoa. I did wonder when we'd get on to her.' He brushed the salt from his mouth with his grown-old-fingers, leant back and flung his arm across to the next seat. He looked at me thoughtfully. 'Let me show you something.'

He shifted in his seat as he rummaged in his back pocket, pulled out his wallet and extracted two small photographs. The first was one of those passport type photos taken in a booth that you rarely find these days. Charles looked a few years older than when we'd parted, and next to him, squeezed into the booth, was Chenoa. Hair longer, smile wider and wilder than I remembered it and a necklace of tiny seashells strung around her neck.

'*Jesus*,' I said. 'You stayed together.'

Charles nodded.

'Was this taken in…England?'

He nodded again. 'Twickenham.'

'She came back to – '

'That's right.'

'O-*kay*,' I breathed. 'And then…'

But he was already handing me the next photograph; laying it down beside the first little black and white one on the wooden table. This picture was in colour.

'This was taken a few years ago,' said Charles.

An attractive older woman with grey-blonde hair stood next to him in front of a houseboat.

'Hang on.' I picked the photo up carefully and scrutinized it. 'You mean...'

I looked from the photo, to Charles's face, back to the photo.

'Yes,' he replied simply.

'You mean, she's your...'

'Wife.'

'And you're still...'

'Together. Yes.'

'Jesus *Christ*.'

A sharp-edged corner of a tiny piece of crisp chafed against my throat and I began to cough so violently that it took several thwacks on my back from Charles to help me stop spluttering.

Eventually, I recovered and knocked back the last finger of my rum and coke. Then I turned to look Charles squarely in the eye. Our eyes, I thought, the last part of our bodies that change. His were blue, running into green on the outside edge of his iris. They still had that flash of intelligence in them, that warmth.

We began to laugh, initially a nervous chitter that made our legs jiggle up and down and gradually evolving into a full-bellied rumble, tears streaming down our cheeks. An elderly couple – well, I say elderly, but they were probably no older than us – eating dinner at the table beside us, frowned at us disapprovingly, which only made us laugh even harder.

Charles and Chenoa. Chenoa and Charles. So they'd fallen deeply, passionately in love that summer of 1967 and the gilded mermaid had decided she did not want to be unattached forever after all. She just didn't want to be attached to that big, hairy bloke, Ray, and *certainly* not to me.

We eventually got kicked out of the pub after last orders. I couldn't remember the last time I'd been that drunk. I said goodbye to Charles and made my way towards the station, hopping in zigzags from one puddle of light to the next spooling across the pavement from the streetlamps. I had a song on my lips, and a bounce in my step and I sent, there and then, a silent prayer of gratitude up into the dark London sky to the inventor of Facebook.

Starting up a friendship again, after an interlude of nearly half a century, it's like nothing else I've experienced. I couldn't get enough of Charles, drinking in the sight and sound of him, the events and stories that we never shared but, even so, felt part of one another.

The first few times, it was just the two of us, meeting at a pub or a bar. We even went to see what had become of L'Auberge in Richmond. It was long gone, of course. In its place sat a Nando's chicken joint, teenagers spilling noisily out of the front. Where would they be going now, I wondered? Not to Eel Pie Island, that much was sure. We decided not to stick around, but instead strolled companionably down the towpath that hugged the Thames, towards Twickenham, as we had done so many times, filling one another in on all those missing years.

'You still play the guitar?'

I had to ask the question; to know if that talent, that amazed and pissed me off in equal measure, had stood the test of time.

'Only to my grandchildren,' Charles replied, grinning.

'But you were so good.'

'I wasn't bad,' he said as he shrugged, pulling his hands out of his pockets. 'But it was never going to pay the bills, was it? Anyway, I'm always surrounded by music in my work, so I don't mind that much.'

I cast a glance across at Charles, taking in his outfit, so different from mine. Of course, his clothes were different from those we wore back in the Sixties, and yet, unlike me, he could have belonged to a different era. He looked effortlessly rakish and debonair in his slim-fitting black jeans, with what looked like a silk scarf tied around his neck and a black trilby-type hat resting on his grey hair. How *did* he pull that look off? He should have looked like a twat, particularly with that scarf. But he didn't, at all.

'But music production *does* pay the bills?'

'More or less. And it's fun, I get to meet lots of different musicians. Some of them are just fantastic and others are pains in the arse. Complete primadonnas. Think they're God's gift to the world…not so unlike you back in the day.' He stopped on the towpath and chuckled, before turning and gazing out over the river that lapped gently up against the banks. Then, looking back, we caught one another's eye. I still couldn't quite believe it; that this was Charles Adams standing solidly in front of me after all these years. Not a memory of him, not an idea of him, but really *him*. I felt a flood of gratitude and joy and looked him directly in the eyes.

'I really missed you, you know.'

We were momentarily distracted by a wooden boat rowing past us, crashing into the banks as the young couple within it shrieked with laughter.

Then Charles looked back at me, eyes crinkling with happiness.

'I missed you too, Jim. A ridiculous amount.'

We stood for a few moments more, basking in the warmth of the summer day and one another's company.

'How about a pint?' Charles asked. 'There's a pub called The Barmy Arms near the Eel Pie bridge. It doesn't do a bad local ale.'

I smiled widely. 'You're on.'

I felt nervous about seeing Chenoa again but Leila hadn't even met Charles yet and she was longing to, so one Sunday we caught the train down to London, took the over-ground to Chiswick and walked along the towpath. I had half expected him to live in a fusty old house somewhere, filled with ancient books and guitars, not a houseboat. But of course, this was just the Charles mixed from my memory and imagination, not the real Charles.

Walking alongside the river, I peered at the names of all the houseboats we passed until we stopped outside *Matala Mayflower*. It was painted immaculately in dark, bottle green and there was a quaint little patio at the front of the boat with geraniums and pansies gushing from cracked flowerpots and a wrought iron table and chairs. Never in a hundred years would I have imagined Charles living somewhere like this.

Leila reached out and touched my arm.

'You alright?'

I turned to face her and nodded.

'Yes.' I took her hand and kissed it. Leila. The most

beautiful woman in the world.

Thankfully, any of the awkwardness I thought I'd feel around Chenoa vanished instantly as she and Leila hit it off right away. Charles and I stared after them in surprise as they vanished into the houseboat to get a corkscrew and some nibbles, chatting away like old friends. Chenoa's Canadian lilt was largely gone as she'd moved straight back to England with Charles. She'd spent her life in academia, teaching at universities and writing books on Female Ritual and Femininity in Ancient Greece.

I think I'd forgotten the details of what she looked like all those years ago. All I remembered was that astounding beauty. She was *still* lovely to look at: with her hazel green eyes and lustrous hair, but her beauty no longer overwhelmed me. The first person you make love to in your life – do they remain, irredeemably, a part of you? No, I don't believe they do and I'd be sentimental to say otherwise. Besides, I had Leila next to me. There was a moment, however, when Chenoa handed me a glass of wine. As I reached out and took it, her eyes were laughing. Not in a mocking way, but she just looked so...I don't know, so *happy*. What was it Charles used to call her? The gilded mermaid. Well, I'd never known this mermaid at all, gilded or otherwise, not even a tiny bit. I'd only lusted after her. I grinned back. Perhaps now, after all these years, I'd actually get to know her as the mere mortal that she was.

Down below deck in their houseboat, I scanned the few bookshelves, less dusty tomes that I remembered from Charles's house in Twickenham, and more shiny copies of Chenoa's books mixed with modern literature. There were photographs of their children and grandchildren on the wall that I couldn't drag my eyes from. I wanted to know everything about him; not to miss another thing in his life. As he measured out gin and tonics in the small kitchen area behind me, I turned to watch him in silence. His hair may have changed colour, but it still stuck up. His concave teenage boy's belly may have filled out, but he still had skinny legs and knees.

After several drinks that evening, up on deck, Leila came and sat on my knee, squeezing my thigh. I pulled her into me, closed my eyes and breathed in her scent of star anise, a spice she cooked with above all others, as Charles tuned up his guitar and Chenoa tinkered around inside. And as the sun sighed into the Thames, I was happier than I ever imagined possible to discover that my old friend could still play a mean blues.

Chapter Twenty-Three

Ironically, our renewed friendship solidified through loss. After the initial excitement of finding one another had worn off, almost like the first flushes of love, we settled into an easy camaraderie but didn't see each other a great deal. That was, until the day I admitted to myself that my mother's increasing levels of distress signalled something, other than ageing, was wrong.

She was already eighty-three by the time Charles and I renewed contact, so it didn't come as a surprise that her health was starting to fail. But I think it makes no difference what age a parent is when their light starts to fade. She began using the same sentences, over and over again, her voice tight, overwrought, mechanical. And she had fixations: on whether there was enough oil in the car or if I had put the right amount of sugar in her tea. She began to lose things, more often than normal. She would forget where she was, or even *who* she was. I put it down to age; pretended to myself this was normal for as long as I possibly could.

But then, one day, I was called by a stranger from Costa Coffee in Ipswich. I'd insisted that Ma carry my phone number in her bag on a laminated strip of cardboard at all times in case she got lost or forgot where she was. But we'd never had to use it, until then.

'Hello, Ma,' I'd said as I answered my phone.

There was a short silence, and then I heard a man clearing his throat.

'Good Afternoon. My name's Alexander. I'm with your…mother?'

'Yes. Is she alright?'

'She's fine. We're in Costa Coffee. But I found her wandering around on Queen Street looking very confused. She was a little distressed so I bought her here and she's having a cup of hot chocolate.'

'That's very kind of you. Could I talk to her, please?'

'Hallo, Jimmy!' Ma's voice came on the line, breathless and gushy and I knew, heart sinking, that she really didn't know what was going on.

'Are you alright, Ma?'

'Oh yes, never been better! This very kind boy has brought me a cup of hot chocolate. It's delicious! I've put extra cream on top.'

'Yes, but are you feeling alright? He said you were distressed.'

'Distressed?' She paused and I could hear her breathing heavily down the line. 'I'm not sure why he said that. It's a lovely day out and I was just taking a little walk.'

'Alright, Ma. Just stay there and I'll – '

'Jimmy?'

'Yes?'

'Who is this boy?'

I frowned and massaged my fingertips into my temples. I knew the time had come when I had to take my head out of the sand, shake it off and confront the future.

My younger son Teddy named his first daughter after my beautiful Ma, Nancy. And as the young Nancy grew and blossomed, her soft dark waves of hair and achingly beautiful face, indisputably inherited from her namesake, the edges of her great-grandmother's character faded and blurred. And yet, each time my granddaughter was placed in her arms, Ma's face came alive, that bright fire rekindled in her eyes. Whether she knew the identity of this child was doubtful. But it didn't matter, she loved her tenderly and unreservedly.

Charles had lost his father to dementia and, when I watched my own mother go through the same thing, I'm not sure I could have managed without him. He understood, to a certain extent, what to expect and the signs to look for. Coping strategies, emotional support. Just the odd word here and there, it helped me more than I knew how to express. He became, again, the brother I never had and it wasn't long before those many years we'd spent apart felt inconceivable, an unbroken line of low clouds in a winter sky. Leila aside – and my relationship with her was different – nobody had ever come close to replacing my friendship with Charles.

It was slow and painful, watching Ma decline. Some days she was fine and I couldn't have questioned her level of self-awareness. I even remember one evening that I was visiting her when she suddenly came out with it:

'I'm not the same, am I, Jimmy? The same as I used to be?'

I took her hand that trembled like a leaf in mine and squeezed it.

'It's alright, Ma. You're doing fine. You're doing brilliantly.'

Her lips curled upwards, a small, rueful smile as she gazed out of the window, away from me.

'No.' She shook her head. 'I'm not the same. Things are changing. We both know that, you and I. It's alright, you know.'

She looked back at me and smiled bravely. My mother. My ally.

Weeks before she died, she began to talk to me in the third person, telling me all about her son Jimmy.

I sat by her bed and listened as she spoke about her troubled teenage son who was more like her husband than he would ever care to admit.

'I try to help them get along,' she sighed heavily, 'but they can't. *Won't.* Just too stubborn, too pig-headed, the pair of them. He's inherited so much from his father, but at least he doesn't have those nightmares.'

'Which nightmares, Nancy?'

'*Those.* You know, the ones that keep him awake, night after night, sweating and screaming.'

She tutted, laying her head back against the bolstered pillow and closing her eyes. 'Poor Alfred.'

It had been so many years since I had thought about those sounds that came from my parents' room, but as soon as she mentioned it, it came flooding back....the shouts and groans that, as a teenager, I had always assumed, sickened, resulted from my father pinioning my mother to the bed; of forcing her against her will. All that time, it had been my father lost in the terror of a place so dark that even sleep gave him no peace. Even all these years later, I was still coming to a new understanding of the depth of his suffering.

Everything dropped away in the face of her death, leaving only what really mattered. In her care home, Ma became bed-bound and silent. She chose to stop eating and took just a few sips of juice each day. Her body became light and she curled herself up into a foetal position. Her hands crossed at her thin wrists, which, more often than not, started to cover her face, blocking out the world. Her spotted, brown skin fell away from her bones as her skeleton made its way into the foreground.

I would edge one hand inside hers, and the other I placed on the back of her neck. I spoke into her ear:

Hello Ma, it's Jimmy. How are you feeling today?

On the odd occasion, she would still nod, a crooked smile playing on her lips to acknowledge my presence and, even less often, with what seemed like a huge effort, she turned her head on the pillow and opened her eyes to look directly at me.

Those times were almost shocking; her eyes were still a clear, vivid blue and bored into me with a disarming perception.

I was told at the care home that it was just weeks to go, perhaps even days. Did this lessen the grief? I don't think it ever does. With the end so close, memories returned that had lain just beyond reach for decades: the precise, sharp smell of crisp bacon frying; the tiny crescent of mascara perpetually smudged beneath her beautiful eyes; the slant of early autumn light falling on the clustered leaves that crunched beneath our feet as we took the first of many walks together, through the Suffolk village we moved to.

Those noises I'd heard for all those years in the dark of night, filtering across from my parents' bedroom, took on a different texture. I'd always imagined Ma was bullied by Dad. Perhaps, in a way, she was. Yet he was troubled, so troubled. And I saw her role differently now. I envisaged her soothing him; running cool fingers across his brow and whispering words of comfort, trying to chase away those ghosts that haunted him at night. After all these years, she had ceased being a victim to me. She hadn't just helped him through the pain of his past and cared for him. No, Ma had saved him.

Chapter Twenty-Four

July 2013

The year following my mother's death, Charles and I decided to go on holiday together and take our older grandchildren with us. We considered Portugal, Sardinia and the south of France. But really, it could only ever be one place.

After we'd unpacked our bags at the hotel, we all walked straight down to the beach. I still had to pinch myself that this was Charles, walking beside me with his long-legged, easy gait, unchanged after all these years.

But Matala, unsurprisingly, wasn't unchanged. The beach was strewn with sunbeds and the bay liberally dotted with tavernas, cafés and shops, selling bright, floaty sarongs, olive oil and miniature VW Beetles. I thought, though, about some of the beach resorts I'd been to in the past, examples of coastal development gone horribly wrong, and couldn't deny that Matala retained a low-key charm. High-rise developments were few and far between and the locals were sensitive to the colonies of nesting turtles that waddled down to the beach, following the light of the moon.

On a wall in the exact spot of the café where I once sat and drank myself into oblivion, having rubbed my knuckles raw scrubbing oil from greasy plates, someone had taken cans of brightly-coloured paint and emblazoned large flowers across the wall and these words:

Welcome to Matala. Today is Life. Tomorrow Never Comes.

And yet, despite all the changes, as we stood with our feet planted into the warm, golden sand, Charles and I turned to face the caves. Now these, *these* remained unchanged, had done for centuries in fact. As our grandchildren flitted around us like colourful butterflies, I squinted my eyes slightly, and time fell away, layer upon layer as the years peeled back. The people moving slowly around up on the cliff side were no longer tourists, but cave dwellers, trails of smoke rising from cooking pots and cigarettes.

I turned to look at Charles, his eyes creased and his lips curled into a smile. He was, no doubt, lost in his own memories of his time here. After several moments, he turned to me and grinned, pushing his silvery hair back out of his eyes.

'Would you look at that, Jimmy boy? Our caves.'

I chuckled. 'Our caves.' I turned back to the sandstone cliffs that were beginning to glow amber in the late afternoon light. 'Shall we?'

Tourists had to pay to visit the caves now. A man, Stavros, with salt and pepper stubble, sat in a small hut at the bottom of the cliffs, doling out tickets so people could see where cave dwellers once lived.

'We were here in 1967,' Charles said to Stavros as he handed over his money.

'Wait…*you? Here?'* He flicked his shades up, brown eyes opened wide in disbelief.

'Yes,' smiled Charles. 'And him,' he thumbed towards me.

Stavros stood up from his seat, walked out of the booth and clapped us both on the back, roaring with laughter. 'So these caves are yours! You are the original hippies!'

I laughed along with him. It was all rather hilarious. I stayed here for what…a week? And for me, at least, the word 'hippy' conjured up images of flower power and tie-dyed clothes and anti-war protests and everything, really, that I never was. I was just a boy filled with testosterone who wanted to get laid, desperately running from his father. But none of this seemed to matter now.

'How can I possibly charge you,' Stavros continued, pressing the coins back into Charles's hand, 'when these caves belong to you?' He shook his head, continuing to laugh. Some Greek tourists walked past and Stavros shouted out something to them, pointing in our direction.

Before we knew it, we had a throng of people around us, shaking our hands, their eyes gleaming with respect, much to the amusement of our grandchildren.

The four kids ran up the steep path ahead of us, whilst Charles and I huffed and puffed behind them.

'*Christ,*' said Charles, 'it was never this knackering getting up here before, was it?'

'Probably not,' I stopped, pulled my cap off my head and fanned myself with it, 'but we were just a tad younger and fitter back then.'

Charles turned to look at me. 'You absolutely refused to wear a hat. Do you remember how sunburnt you got?'

'Sunburnt!' I scoffed. 'That was a deep, dark tan, my friend.'

We smirked at one another and kept walking.

'Oh my God, I think this is where those German twins stayed.' I stopped, panting, and peered into the gloom.

'Which German twins?'

'I can't remember their names. Tall, blond, friendly.'

Sophie, Charles's eldest granddaughter, squealed, prostrate, from the tomb.

'Don't tell me you *slept* in this, Grandpa?'

'Well, not in this cave. But yes, I did. It was actually pretty comfortable.'

I snorted. 'It was not.'

'I can sleep anywhere. Always have been able to.'

'You snored the cave down as well,' I said.

Sophie giggled. 'Will you show us your cave now?'

'We slept in two different caves, didn't we Jim?'

'That's right. One was really high up and cramped and the other somewhere near here. Far more spacious.'

'You remember where they are?' Sophie asked, her pretty, earnest face looking up at me. She was fourteen and came from a generation, I mused, that would probably never hitchhike; that wouldn't leave the house without a phone; that most certainly wouldn't be able to travel away for weeks on end without regular contact home.

I smiled at her. 'How could I forget?'

That evening, we walked through the town on the far side of the bay, looking for somewhere to eat. We stepped over murals in ornate patterns carved into the paved walkway, a small town square clustered with café's, and through a reggae pub, blaring Bob Marley.

Charles and I didn't need to even mention it to one another, but we both knew that we wanted to go as high as we could, for a good view of the caves. As we made our way slowly - but with far greater ease – up the path, we walked past vendors selling hand-crafted jewellery and leather goods, a few small houses with geraniums spilling out of flower pots in the windowsills and wooden fishing boats bobbing in the water below us.

Our grandchildren found it first, a place called Sunset Taverna that couldn't have been more perfect. Perched at the highest point of the bay with sweeping views of the caves in one direction and the sun bleeding into the gentle sea in the other. As the children clambered over the rocks in front of the restaurant, Charles and I ordered a Mythos beer and sat at a table.

We were in no hurry to order food; the kids were happy and we both felt it: the deep contentment of being here with one another. After the second beer, the names came back to me that I'd been trying to remember.

'Susanne! Susanne and...Wolfgang! That's it!'

Charles raised an eyebrow at my outburst. 'That's what?'

'Those twins, the German twins from the caves. They were called Susanne and Wolfgang.'

Charles squinted, scratching his cheek. 'I don't remember them.'

'You were friends with *everyone*. The most sociable bloke of Matala.'

He smiled, a little ruefully and turned to look at our grandchildren. Then he looked back at me, gazing at me squarely in the eye.

'I'm sorry I hurt you so much. I wasn't thinking straight. I behaved badly.'

I paused. 'I'm sorry I punched you.'

'Oh, it wasn't really a punch,' Charles drawled as he lifted his beer glass to his lips, 'more like a little tap.'

He laughed lightly and I grinned, before my face fell serious again.

'And I'm sorry I never wrote to you. I was so angry with you and...well, grieving my dad too. It feels like an awful waste, doesn't it, to have spent all those years apart.'

Charles placed his beer on the table and looked towards the rocks at our grandchildren.

'Yes,' he agreed, 'although...I don't know, maybe it makes the reunion after all these years that bit more significant and satisfying. I'm glad that you made it up with your old man before he died as well.'

I leant back in my chair and smiled. 'Yes. Me too.'

'Will you tell me about it one day? You know, you mentioned how he told you all about his time in Crete.'

I paused and glanced over at my grandson, Luke. Perhaps it was something to do with the light, or the angle he was standing at – or maybe it was just because we were talking about him – but for the first time, I noticed the resemblance between him and my father.

'Of course,' I said, looking back at my friend. 'It's an amazing story.'

'He was a dark horse, your dad, wasn't he?'

'He certainly was.' I smiled slowly and nodded, then took a deep breath. 'Did...did I ever tell you about when we were young and I used to get those strong emotions flood through my body that I couldn't control?'

Charles shook his head. 'No. But I knew.'

I stared at him in surprise. 'What do you mean? How did you know?'

'Well…it happened so many times and it was clear that something powerful was going on for you. But it wasn't something I knew how to ask you about at the time. I remember once in particular, when we were at school, one of the teachers had pissed you off. I can't remember how, or why. But you stood there with your fists clenched and your face went completely purple. I thought you were going to punch him.'

I nodded somberly. I couldn't remember the incident, but I could recall the feeling perfectly.

'And then suddenly,' Charles continued, 'your whole body went limp, like all the fight had been sucked out of you and your eyes filled with tears and it looked as though you were going to burst into tears. It was weird. It seemed so out of keeping with you, with your *character*. That was one of the first times I saw you like that. But then it happened a lot. I stopped thinking anything about it at all. It was just…well…*you*.'

I rubbed my thumb over the icy numbness of the beer label, which was starting to peel from the bottle, and nodded.

'Yes,' I said. 'I haven't told anybody about this apart from Leila but…' I hesitated. It wasn't an easy thing to put into words. Even with Leila, I'd struggled to find a logical explanation for it; it was just something I felt… no, I *knew* was real.

'What is it, Jim?'

'Well, the thing is, that once my father had told me all

about what had happened to him, I never got that feeling again.'

'Never?'

'Not once. Not a single time. The emotions were so intense, I would have known if it had come back again, but it really didn't.'

Charles popped a black olive into his mouth and chewed on it thoughtfully.

'That doesn't surprise me, you know.'

'Why? It sure as hell surprised me.'

'You inherited it, I'm sure, from your father.'

'Inherited what?'

'The trauma he went through. I bet he never resolved it, right? I bet he never spoke to anybody about what happened to him. Not properly, anyway. I watched this programme on television once, a few years ago, about how unresolved trauma can be passed from one generation to the next and manifest itself in all kinds of different ways...'

'Yes, but this was a *physical* as well as an emotional thing for me.'

'I know, but the trauma can manifest physically. I'm serious, Jim. Look it up. There's bound to be stuff about it on the web.'

'Jesus.' I fell silent for several moments. 'You don't really believe that can happen, do you?'

'Of course I do! You're living proof of it, aren't you? I can't believe it's a coincidence that you made up with your Dad and those sensations suddenly vanished.'

I paused and took a long sip of beer.

'I don't really understand that.'

'Think about it,' Charles said patiently. 'I know you

haven't told me what it was your old man went through, but I'm guessing it wasn't much fun for him. He was probably deeply disturbed by his experiences. Nowadays there's counseling and therapy and Lord knows what else, *Christ,* even on the NHS. Back in post-war Britain? Not a chance!'

He popped another olive into his mouth.

'So what did your father do? He internalized everything. Completely repressed all his trauma. And what happens if a person represses trauma? Well...' he shrugged, 'not only are they going to suffer, but chances are someone in their family will as well.'

I leant back in my chair and rubbed my neck beneath my hairline, still warm from the day's sun.

'I never thought about it like that.'

'Course you didn't. That's why you need *me.*'

Charles grinned warmly at me and I took in anew my friend's shock of grey hair and his unchanged style of glasses. The years dropped away and, as I smiled back, I felt an overwhelming flood of affection for him. I still wasn't sure I understood it, or believed it for that matter. Inherited trauma...it seemed too intangible for my brain to process.

But it no longer mattered. For I had made peace with my father when I still had the chance, and now I had found the boy from my past, who was like a brother to me. As the sun slowly settled into the sea and flung shafts of golden light onto the caves, the laughter from the ghosts of our past selves mingled with that of our grandchildren. And I knew there was nowhere, right then, I'd rather be.

Matala, 1968
The author's mother, Elizabeth, is standing at the top in the spotted bikini. Her sister, Susie, is seated in the middle with the cropped hair and their friend, Pam is seated on the end with her hair in bunches.

Matala, 2016
The author's mother, Elizabeth, is wearing the hat. Her sister, Susie, is in the middle and their friend, Pam, is at the end.

LETTER FROM REBECCA

Dear Readers,

Thank you so much for choosing to read *The Secret Life of Alfred Nightingale.* I do hope that you enjoyed sharing the journeys of Jimmy and Alfred. I would love to know what you thought of this story – please do leave a review on Amazon, even if it is just a few words, reviews are incredibly helpful and it would mean a great deal to me.

You can keep up to date with my writing projects through my blog, via my Facebook page, through my Twitter account and by signing up to my newsletter (see below.)

If you enjoyed *The Secret Life of Alfred Nightingale,* you might like to read my other novels. *The Poet's Wife* is set in Granada during the Spanish Civil War and Franco's dictatorship and is told through the eyes of three generations of women from one family. *The Girl and the Sunbird* is set in colonial British East Africa and Mau Mau Insurgency in Kenya and tells the story of the devastating choices one brave woman is faced with.

With my very best wishes and thanks once again for reading my book,

Rebecca

@bexstonehill

RebeccaStonehillBooks

www.rebeccastonehill.com

Also by Rebecca Stonehill:

The Poet's Wife
The Girl and the Sunbird

Please do sign up for my mailing list. This will keep you updated with my writing projects! I promise to never share your email with anyone else.

rebeccastonehill.com/signup

ACKNOWLEDGEMENTS

I am indebted to the following:

Andy, Maya, Lily and Benji, for their boundless faith in me, and putting up with me during those times I am with them in body but not mind.

Elizabeth Jacques, for her youthful wanderlust, for visiting Matala in the first place and sewing that initial seed, inspiring me through her photo albums and tales to write this story.

Nick Thripp, for providing me with the true, trouser-hiding anecdote that opened my story, and his friends John Marks AKA "The Ape" and Roger Kohn for mining their memories to become my official 1960's fact-checkers.

The late Major Paddy Deacon, who courageously shared with me his story of how he lost his best friend in Greece in WW2, providing the inspiration for Alfie and Joseph's friendship.

Debbie Rix, Sharon Maas and Renita D'Silva, my wonderful long-distance writing support network, whom I could not have done without.

Holly Martin and Sharon Riley Sant, for taking the time to talk to me about their self-publishing experiences and generously sharing their wisdom.

Tilda Bowden, an invaluable support closer to home, with a shared love of words and all things literary.

Susie Bidwell, Philippa Infanti, Pam Bailey and Elizabeth Jacques, my partners in crime in Matala in September 2016 during my research trip. Raki, Red Beach, dancing, colourful locals and stuck fish-bones, we had it all!

Louise Stanion, who generously allowed me to use her words to describe a family member's decline into dementia. I was so moved by her description and all credit goes to Louise for her poignant depiction of this condition.

Eleni Georgopoulou, for smoothing out my Greek phrases – *efcharistó*!

Viktor 'Lefteris' Kakavos, for chatting to me about the youth culture of the 1960's and what it was that drew travellers to Matala.

Maria Matthaiaki and Catarina Georgilaki, for their memories and insights into 1960's Matala, plus the coffee and best baklava on the planet!

Peter Gumley, whose photographs and reminiscences of his time in the caves as a young man helped me to paint a fuller picture of the setting and mood.

Arn Stohmeyer, for writing the invaluable *Myth of Matala*, packed to bursting with fascinating insights, and for the extra information provided.

Louise Coquio, for her insightful, discerning and sensitive editing and for being so enthusiastic about this story.

Betsy Braden and Bavara Hush, for providing me with their Matala memories and, in particular, Betsy's diary entries.

Mark Swan from Kid Ethic for his artistic talent, creating my incredible cover that surpassed my wildest dreams.

Jason and Marina Anderson from Polgarus Studio, for their fantastic and patient formatting service.

Iain Lowe, for his invaluable fact checking of Crete during WW2.

Shirley Read-Jahn, for being a stickler for detail, her fantastic skills as beta-reader and her open-hearted wit and wisdom.

Printed in Great Britain
by Amazon

60278469R00231